Praise for *A Family A*

'This story had me wrapped around its finger. What a warm reading experience. The authenticity of the characters are what endeared me the most to this tale. A gem!'
– PHEMELO MOTENE, broadcaster

'Think of an African Jane Austen (the clue is in the novel's first sentence) writing a sexed-up depiction of the state of our modern relationships. We're taken by hand through the causeways of our manners, mores and traditions; the origins and misuses of our cultural practices; the sometimes misguided appeal to myths, custom and religion to perpetuate things such as gender violence and the caste system; the lure of money and material wealth as weapons of predatory sexuality and toxic masculinity; the stubborn spirit of religious millennialism as the background of so much tragic African thinking, superstition and all. In short, *A Family Affair* is a modern soapie with a southern African zeitgeist.'
– MPHUTHUMI NTABENI, author of *Broken River Tent*

'A contemporary African saga that serves up all the ingredients: rags and riches, contested patriarchal legacies, hero women, sacred cross-border alliances, history, sex, the megachurch. Tradition and modernity have been told so well. The Greenleafs have nothing on the Mafus. This is the Zim that betrays her suffering and otherness imposed by those who are not intimate with her. The trio of the Mafu sisters makes the perfect set of jewels of a grand tale. What an epic story. Rich in the tradition of Virginia Andrews with hard-hitting depictions of social facts. And romance – so much romance!'
– KARABO K. KGOLENG, writer, broadcaster, public speaker

Also by Sue Nyathi

The GoldDiggers (2018)

'This book is a page-turning tale of struggle and triumph.'
– Sunday World

'Nyathi's book is rich in detail and never dull. There is inspiration from
her characters for South Africans hoping to rise from humble beginnings
to success against all odds.'
– Business Day

'Nyathi has woven a work of fiction which is vividly authentic …
in a lyrical and beautiful way.'
– Destiny magazine

'If there was ever an author who could do a book like *The GoldDiggers*
justice, it would be none other than Sue Nyathi.'
– Drum magazine

A FAMILY AFFAIR

A Novel

SUE NYATHI

MACMILLAN

First published in 2020
by Pan Macmillan South Africa
Private Bag X19
Northlands
2116
Johannesburg
South Africa

www.panmacmillan.co.za

ISBN 978-1-77010-667-3

e-ISBN 978-1-77010-668-0

This is a work of fiction. Any resemblance to actual events, places or persons, living or dead, is purely coincidental.

Editing by Jane Bowman
Proofreading by Katlego Tapala
Design and typesetting by Nyx Design
Cover design by Ayanda Phasha
Author photograph by Mogau Ramaila of 3rd Eye Visuals
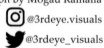 @3rdeye.visuals
@3rdeye_visuals

Printed and bound by Bidvest Data, Cape Town

To my siblings,
Nduna, Kwanele, Nozipho
With love

Family
Like branches on a tree we all grow in different directions
but our strong roots keep us all together.

BIRTH

HOLY MATRIMONY

It is a truth universally acknowledged that a single woman of childbearing age must be in want of a husband. A truth that has been supplanted in the minds of many a woman and a truth that Zandile wrestles with that fine summer morning in December. She finds refuge in the bathroom, far from the madding crowd, and wrings her hands nervously over the full, tulle skirt of her wedding dress spilling around her. She wonders whether it might not be too late to make a run for it. She's heard of weddings that carry on without the bride and groom. The guests could still salvage the occasion and make a party of it and they could go straight to their honeymoon; a perfect escape from the craziness around her.

She wants to get married but she's not so sure she wants *this*. Her family has been at war with one another since this whole wedding thing had begun. Every detail had been a bone of contention, from the venue to the guest list to the menu.

As a young girl, she had dreamt about her wedding day. She had spent countless evenings with her sisters fantasising about the kind of weddings they would all have. None of them included any noisy politics. Their fantasies had been fanciful and fairytale-like.

She looks up at the small window but as slender as she is, there is no way she will be able to squeeze her body through it. She's stuck and she feels like she's suffocating. There is no way she can tear off her dress and make a run for it. Not now. Not at the final hour. A whole church awaits her arrival and an even bigger reception, with fancy place cards and printed napkins.

Suddenly there is a loud knock on the door which snaps her out

3

of her daze. Her mother's voice sounds through the door.

'Zandile, are you *still* in there?'

'I'm coming, Mama.'

'Zandile, everyone is waiting!'

She can sense the irritation in her mother's voice and it fuels her anxiety.

'I'm coming!' she says, more abruptly this time.

Zandile flushes the toilet, trying to keep up the pretense of actually needing to go to the bathroom. She stands up, gathers her skirt, and her wits too, and stares at herself in the mirror and smiles uneasily.

You are going to be fine, she reassures herself.

She *is* going to be okay.

She is going to get through this.

She walks through the house and towards the front door and is greeted by the brilliant promise that often accompanies a new day. It isn't even midday and the sun is beating down with an intensity that typically precedes an afternoon downpour. The rain is welcomed in the drought-stricken city of Bulawayo but most agree it would be better if the heavens would hold back on their showery blessing today. As she steps outside onto the patio, she is confronted by the jubilant singing and loud ululating of middle-aged, matronly women. They form a tunnel from the front doorstep of the Mafu household, down to the winding driveway, where a cavalcade of cars waits expectantly. Grass-woven mats with elaborate Ndebele artwork line the path that she walks on. They are her grandmother's contribution to her special day, woven with patience and love, her fingers wrinkled with age. The mats are protecting Zandile's snow-white dress from getting soiled, with its sweeping train, held by her sister, Yandisa. But this is not the primary reason for them; it's an age-old tradition that a bride's feet must never touch the ground, lest an enemy steals her footsteps.

Everyone agrees that Zandile looks like a princess in her Vera Wang wedding dress with its tight-fitting, diamanté-encrusted bodice accentuating her tiny waist. The dress flares into a full skirt of lace, tulle and organza. Those who are close enough to see, marvel at the elaborate beadwork and motifs. The women whisper amongst themselves how much the dress must have cost, especially imported from New York. Like every bride on her wedding day, Zandile looks exquisite. Her hair is swept up into a chignon, a pearl and diamond tiara resting on her head. Her flawless make-up expertly applied by a dedicated team at Clinique Caress, the local beauty salon. No expense had been spared and much time was expended to achieve her effortlessly beautiful look. An older woman from the crowd steps forward and pulls Zandile's veil down, covering her fine features. An indication that she is a virgin. Untouched. Unspoilt. In her hands Zandile clutches a simple bouquet of white orchids sprayed with green vines. All eyes are transfixed on her as she makes her way to the Mercedes Benz that is waiting to ferry her to the church. The exuberant singing accompanies her and the matronly women clap rhythmically, their buttocks bouncing in unison, swathes of material swirling around them.

'*Woza lay' umakoti!*'

This line is repeated over and over again, their voices rising to a feverish crescendo. Weddings are celebrated as something of a spectacle and filled with much ceremony and it is a day every woman is groomed for throughout her life.

Primed, primped and plucked for the day when she is ripe for matrimony. On this day, she will leave her father's home and unite with her husband in holy matrimony. They will start a family and the process will repeat itself. From one generation to the next. Same script, different cast.

THE OTHER HALF

'W oza lay'umakoti!'

The joyful voices follow Zandile as she gets into the car, the flowing train of her dress occupying its own space on the seat next to her. Yandisa goes back into the house and reappears armed with a vanity case in one hand and a bottle of champagne and long-stemmed glasses concealed in a gift bag in the other hand, away from the hawkish eyes of the matronly lot. Their oldest sister, Xoliswa, has already settled herself in the driver's seat and Yandisa sits in the passenger seat next to her. Zandile is comfortably reclined in the backseat, relieved to be out of the limelight. Through the open window she spots their mother. Even though her face is shielded by a huge peach hat adorned with a big bow and dramatic feathers, she can see a lone tear streaming down her fat cheek but it still doesn't obliterate the smile that fills her face and extends all the way to her gold-adorned ears.

'Mom is so happy!' says Zandile.

'Of course she is. At least *one* of her daughters made it down the aisle,' replies Yandisa flippantly.

'Because marriage is *such* an achievement!' pipes up Xoliswa, in a tone slightly shaded by sarcasm.

The weight of her remark is lost on Zandile whose face is lit up with a radiant smile. She is happy to be surrounded by her siblings on this auspicious day; it has been years since they have been all together, in one place, at the same time. She is appreciative that her wedding day has brought them all together. X, Y and Z. She is the last born of the daughters and arrived during the fruitful years when the family fortune had been secured. Her sisters were born in the barren years in the turbulent 1970s when their father was still trying to establish himself. Xoliswa made her debut into the world in 1972 and at that time their parents occupied a humble abode in the township of Makokoba. Yandisa had followed three years later and Zandile was born in 1978. Many agreed that the name Zandile was befitting because the absence of a male heir was conspicuous in the all-girls Mafu household. The expectation had always been that their mother would try for the proverbial male child but she never did. She was emphatic that nothing came after 'z' in the alphabet.

'How are you feeling?' asks Yandisa, taking her sister's hand.

'To be honest, I'm petrified!' says Zandile.

She laughs nervously and feels her gut coil and unwind in slow motion. She has felt like this since she woke up that morning, nervous and happy all at the same time. Yandisa responds by pouring her some champagne in one of the long-stemmed glasses she brought in the gift bag. Zandile accepts the drink and gulps it down greedily.

'I'll have one too!' says Yandisa.

'You are on bridesmaid duty,' scolds Xoliswa. 'No drinking on the job!'

Yandisa sticks out her tongue and reaches for a glass anyway. Behind her back, they call Xoliswa 'Deputy Mother' because she's always trying to whip them into line with her remonstrations.

The engine purrs to life and the car lurches forward as they begin the journey to the church. The ceremony is taking place at the Roman Catholic cathedral in the middle of town and not at their father's church. Zandile is pleased and loves the historical cathedral building with its high ceilings and stained-glass windows and biblical images. Catholic churches have so much character, unlike the hall her father built for his congregation. Her admiration of buildings led her to pursue a degree in architectural studies. She still has to complete her professional exams before she can call herself an architect but the pursuit of a professional qualification has been put on hold for the qualification of marriage.

'Zandi, how did you know Ndaba was *the* one? I mean everyone says you just know but how did *you* know?' asks Xoliswa, looking at her sister through the rear-view mirror.

In all the chaos and planning for the wedding, she had hardly had a chance to chat to her sisters. She had flown in from the British Virgin Islands five days earlier to find the house crawling with relatives who constantly needed to be fed. They were all on full board; bed and breakfast, lunch and supper, with all the frills in-between. There hadn't been a quiet moment, or a dull one for that matter and it had been a constant rush doing last-minute things. Unbeknownst to her, someone had forgotten to take the candles to the church and the décor people had been calling non-stop to say the flowers hadn't arrived at the venue. But her sisters made sure she was none the wiser when it came to those details.

Zandile lets Xoliswa's question linger in the air before responding and thinks back to the day she met Ndaba. Ndabenhle Khumalo came into the Bulawayo City Council, where she works in the building permits department, to get building approval for a home he wanted to build in Burnside. She took one look at his plans and had redrawn them for him, knowing her talent would eventually get her a job in the planning department. At thirty-five, he was much older than her and had an air of sophistication about him which she later learned was because he had lived overseas for a while. She was only twenty-two when they started dating and her mother had always been concerned that he had a wife.

'What has he been doing all these years?' she would ask Zandile.

'Establishing himself,' she would answer vaguely.

Zandile is in complete awe of Ndaba and her tummy still feels like it is doing flick-flacks when he looks at her. When he touches her, she feels a hotness spreading to her loins and she blushes unabashedly. Her sisters don't believe her when she says they haven't done the deed yet but theirs has been a whirlwind romance. They only dated for six months before he proposed to her on her 23rd birthday. The last six months have been spent planning their wedding. It is also the time their relationship has really been tested the most.

I love Ndaba. I love him a lot. He is smart, he is funny and he makes me laugh. I can talk to him about anything and everything. He is my best friend. He is very generous and considerate. There is nothing in this world that he wouldn't do for me. He adores me, he spoils me. He pays for everything, even if I have my own money. I have his bank card and I can spend his money on whatever I want. He is protective over me but he is also very jealous. I see it when I talk to another guy. He won't say anything but I see how he clenches his jaw or his brow furrows. When we fight he doesn't scream at the top of his lungs. If anything, I am the one who starts shouting. I know sometimes I test his patience a lot. He is patient. Very patient. He can get mad at me at times but he doesn't stay mad for long. This is good because I sulk. He isn't too fussy about a lot of things. He is hardworking. He is very ambitious. He will be able to provide well for me. He will be able to give me a good life. He will take care of me. I feel secure with him and that is a good feeling. I cannot imagine being without him. I cannot imagine him not being there to share the ups and downs of life with me. I don't know if that makes him the one but he is the one for me.

'I guess you just know,' answers Zandile, with a lazy smile, 'and I prayed about it. I prayed hard.'

'Please don't come at me with that heaven-sent crap,' says Xoliswa glibly.

'Ndaba wasn't sent from heaven!' responds Zandile. 'I don't believe God picks a partner for you. He will send people in your direction but you need to pray for discernment. Not everyone who comes your way is good for you.'

Yandisa reaches out and squeezes her sister's hand tightly. She had been there to witness their relationship from the time the first seed was planted. She watched the flourishing of the first flowers of love until it bloomed and blossomed. Everyone else might have had their doubts about Ndaba but she was convinced of his infinite goodness.

Xoliswa eyes her sister circumspectly through the rear-view mirror.

'I still think you are making a mistake with this guy. You barely know him!'

'You could be with someone for nine years and still not know them!' says Zandile.

'Exactly. You've been dating Thulani for over a decade, what's stopping you from marrying him?' counters Yandisa.

'Maybe I know too much,' replies Xoliswa flippantly.

They all erupt into laughter. The mood in the car is cheerful again, diffusing what could have become a tense argument. Yandisa turns up the volume on the radio and Celine Dion's voice fills the air. The sisters start singing along to 'Because You Loved Me'.

All the cars are festooned with balloons and drive in an entourage to the church. Blaring hooters sound for miles, alerting people of the impending wedding. The congregation hears the bridal party long before the cars start pulling into the car park. They have been anxiously anticipating the bride's arrival for the past hour. The groom is standing anxiously at the altar, his groomsmen trying to allay his nerves. Even the pianist can't distract the congregation any more. All eyes are fixed on the door, waiting for the bride's grand entrance.

TWO BECOME ONE

Xoliswa walks in first, leading the bridal procession in her capacity as matron of honour. She is a tall, statuesque and imposing beauty and everyone agrees that she looks like her father and has emulated him in so many ways. Like the son he never had but deserved. She has Abraham's dazzling, dark complexion and is as beautiful as he is handsome. Her hair is swept up in a bun with a sweeping extension cascading down her back. She is wearing an off-shoulder, dazzling sapphire gown that sweeps the floor. When Xoliswa walks into a room, she commands attention. As she walks into the church, everyone immediately rises to their feet. 'Such an accomplished girl,' people murmur as she glides down the aisle but they then quickly lament her delay in getting married.

'Our brother made a mistake by letting the youngest daughter get married before the older ones,' complains Sis Ntombi.

'But how long was he supposed to wait? You wanted him to close the door on Zandile's good fortune?' replies Sis Lungile.

'*Kanti*, what is the story with Thulani? It's been years. What is he saying?'

'I don't know. You *know* I haven't spoken to Xolie. We haven't had a moment together since she arrived.'

'Well, *I* would speak to her,' says Sis Ntombi with the authority of an older sister, 'but you know how she gets around me.'

Sis Lungile nods and turns her attention to the bridal procession. The two flower girls are in white frocks of lace and tulle and matching ballet pumps and are endearing. They are accompanied by two pageboys dressed in blue sailor suits. As they have rehearsed a

11

thousand times over, the children scatter rose petals on the red carpet down the aisle. They look to each other, as if seeking reassurance from one another that they are doing the right thing. Then, one by one, the older bridesmaids drift into the church swathed in floor length, thin-strapped, silky sheath dresses. Zandile's best friend from university, Nonhle, follows suit, trailed by Khethiwe, Sis Ntombi's daughter. They aren't that close but Sis Ntombi had insisted that Khethiwe be part of the bridal party. Zandile had wanted her other friend Kirsten to be a bridesmaid but Sis Ntombi had threatened to boycott the wedding if her daughter was not included. Yandisa completes the line-up of bridesmaids. Of all the girls, Yandisa is the only one who resembles her mother. Her complexion is that of creamy cappuccino, just like Phumla's. Her aunts agree that she isn't beautiful and had it not been for her colouring, she would be very ordinary. She isn't tall and svelte like her sisters but short and curvaceous in her stature. Her breasts are almost spilling out of her dress which clings to her wide hips and shapes her ample derrière. Her aunts both agree that Yandisa's buttocks are bordering on being offensive.

'And she sticks it out deliberately,' mumbles Sis Ntombi, not hiding her disapproval.

She can see how the men in the congregation are unashamedly ogling her niece. Sis Lungile giggles and shakes her head.

'She needs to lose weight,' continues Sis Ntombi.

'She got the worst of her mother,' comments Sis Lungile. 'Phumla looks like a pig and between her and Abraham they are both cruising for a heart attack.'

'It's those tithes. Have you noticed how they've ballooned since opening that church?!'

The two sisters both suppress their giggles.

There is a protracted pause before the pianist launches into 'Here Comes the Bride'. The groom looks anxious standing at the altar trying to maintain his composure but he is wringing his hands anxiously. His brow is knotted with anxiety that dissolves away when he catches sight of Zandile standing at the door of the church. He smiles and from behind her veil he can make out her lips curving into a smile. Her heart skips with joy at that moment and she wants to run down the aisle into his arms but is constrained by her father, whose arm is intertwined with hers. She knows she has to contain her joy as she takes measured steps towards her husband-to-be.

Abraham Mafu is a tall, hefty man whose black suit with coat-tails is billowing around him. Most know him as Pastor Mafu, the man with the miraculous healing hand but before that he was known as Mandla Mafu, an enterprising businessman with a thriving construction business. That was years before he decided to establish his Kingdom of God ministry and before he received his anointment as a pastor. But today he is merely a proud father, handing his daughter over to his future son-in-law. All eyes are on father and daughter as they make their way to the altar. Ndabenhle walks towards them, keen to claim his bride. The congregation watch admiringly as Abraham hands Zandile to Ndabenhle, knowing it is a ceremonial gesture. The real exchange took place six months earlier when Ndabenhle presented ten sturdy heifers to the Mafu homestead in Filabusi. Zandile's virginity had been top of the list as the two families heckled over the bride price.

The priest steps forward and asks the congregation to take their seats. He welcomes everyone and goes on to reiterate how it is a monumental day to be engraved in their hearts forever. Xoliswa is invited to the altar to do the readings; a task she executes with elegance and grace. Their father is then asked to give the sermon. Abraham preaches for an hour and a half until the resident Catholics are yawning in disapproval. Afterwards, he steps down from the podium and is met with wild applause from the members of his own congregation. The priest happily reclaims the reins of his church and continues with the ceremony.

'Before I unite these two in front of the Lord, is there anyone in this congregation who feels that they should not be joined in holy matrimony?'

There are none. Everyone is in agreement that they are well matched and that the union of the Mafus and the Khumalos is a good one. The moment passes and the ceremony proceeds without further interruption. The bride and groom turn to each other, starry-eyed with love and optimism and recite their wedding vows. Zandile promises to love and respect him and he in turn promises to love and honour her. They both vow to be true and faithful to each other. They stand in front of the congregation and proclaim that they are in it for the long haul, through wealth and poverty, in sickness and in health. They declare that they will only be separated in death. Tears are streaming down their faces by the time they finish exchanging their vows. Some guests are weeping quietly in support. Couples who have not held hands for a while find themselves reaching for each other, moved by the exhibition of love. The swapping of rings ensues, sealed by a long leisurely kiss to which the crowd applauds jubilantly. Minutes later they emerge from the church as Mr and Mrs Khumalo. There is much ululating and confetti throwing and the well-wishers descend upon the couple, showering them with congratulatory hugs and kisses.

Two have now become one.

OUR PERFECT WEDDING

The reception is held at the iconic Nesbitt Castle set amidst well-groomed gardens and acres of sprawling, manicured lawns. The Gothic-looking castle immediately evokes images of a damsel in distress imprisoned by a ruthless Lord waiting to be rescued by her knight in shining armour. It is an ethereal setting which forms the perfect backdrop for a garden wedding. Even the weather has complied and no dark clouds have formed, admonishing any likelihood of a downpour. Uniformed waiters circle the garden serving drinks and pretty hors d'oeuvres which cause people to complain that there is no 'real food'. A violinist plays music in the background, serenading the guests, while the bridal party are taken to a sequestered spot in the grounds of the venue, to capture the iconic moments on camera.

Nesbitt Castle is a prestigious venue and Zandile had fought hard to secure it because her father had wanted to host the wedding at his church so he could invite the entire congregation. He didn't care too much about the ambience or the photos, he just wanted the flock of his congregation to witness the momentous occasion. In the end, Zandile won the battle and they had whittled the invites down to the elders in the church and those who tithed generously. She couldn't have allowed her father to steal her teenage dream. Many nights when they were growing up, Yandisa and her sisters had lain awake at night, planning and plotting their weddings. Yandisa was the one who always spoke about having a big wedding with a thousand guests but Zandile had always wanted a small, intimate one.

Her ideal wedding would have been a hundred guests but it ended up at three hundred because her father had threatened to not attend the wedding if he couldn't have *all* 'his people' there. Her mother had also wanted a whole lot of people bussed in from the Eastern Cape and she had gone on about how 'her people' were always being excluded. Zandile's people only occupied one table at the wedding. In contrast to her family, the Khumalos were more laid-back and generally complied with most of her father's demands, with a few exceptions here and there. They had been adamant that they were Roman Catholic and that their son would be married in the Roman Catholic church. Ndabenhle's mother had been insistent they were not about the 'happy-clappy' life, as she played with the glass-beaded rosary around her neck. The Mafus had also been Roman Catholics once upon a time before their father established the Kingdom.

After the photographs, the Master of Ceremonies, Silandula, a friend of Ndaba's, welcomes everyone with much fanfare and aplomb. Introductions are made, starting with the bride's family and then the groom's. There is a distinct hierarchy to be followed and the parents are made to stand up first, followed by the grandparents. And then the great-grandparents, if they are still alive, in this case there are none from either side. Next come the aunts and uncles. Such generic terms in English yet in Ndebele, the language is able to explicitly enunciate the difference between an aunt from a mother's side and an aunt from a father's side. Very important differences. Very important terminology. Very important people too and if they weren't considered so, they always had a way of overstating their importance in the family hierarchy. After they are seated, nieces and nephews are introduced. Then it's the cousins' turn. It doesn't matter whether it is a first cousin or a third cousin or a cousin twice removed, as is so often heard in English royal family circles, 'cousin' is an all-encompassing word. Even a close friend of many years could be considered a cousin even though, after careful inspection of the family tree, there is no family relationship whatsoever. Such is the fabric of extended family. It covers even those who might not be 'officially' in the fold. Then come the friends, the neighbours and the work colleagues.

As she sits on the dais next to her husband, Zandile reflects on the fact that she doesn't know half of the guests present. There is uncle so-and-so who she last saw in 19-voetsek. Then there is Auntie Phatiswa who has come from as far afield as Umtata and who is tottering around in her high heels like a newborn calf because she is already inebriated. All the guests have complied with the dress code of 'Sapphire with a touch of gold. Smart casual attire. Strictly no jeans' but even though the invitation explicitly stated 'No children allowed' there is an auntie walking around with a child strapped to her back. Guests were asked to RSVP before the 30th of September 2001 but only a few people complied. The rest have just showed up and even though an invitation was extended to Mr and Mrs Moyo, they have arrived with Mr Moyo's brother who was in town for the weekend. Two extra tables have to be set up to accommodate the overflow of guests, much to Zandile's annoyance. Her husband puts his hand over hers.

'It's going to be fine,' he assures her. 'It's not the end of the world. I'll pay for the extra tables, let's just enjoy our day.'

His calm voice placates Zandile and he leans over and kisses her on the forehead, flattening the lines of worry that have formed on her brow. After the introductions, the MC announces that starters will be served. The programme is already running two hours behind schedule because of Abraham's fevered sermon in the church that had gone on far too long and that no one had been brave enough to stop. During the meal, a local traditional dance outfit entertains the crowd with their choreographed dance moves. The rousing drumbeat and the unrestrained ululating from the elderly women fill the air. Every now and then a few gogos join the dancers in a robust attempt to demonstrate their rhythm and ability to keep up, despite their age.

Only when the last plate is cleared does the MC declare it is time for the speeches. He keeps glancing at his watch emphasising that brevity is required by all speakers. Abraham is the first to take to the podium. Like a typically proud father, he harps on about how happy he is to have his daughter married off and that clearly the curse on his family has been broken. This is followed by loud screams of 'Hallelujah. Amen. Praise Gawd'. He narrates to the guests the joy he felt the moment Zandile was born and that he always knew in his heart she was a special child. He talks about her exploits as a toddler and the guests laugh enthusiastically. He goes on to give a blow-by-blow account of Zandile's achievements from the day she was in grade one till the day she graduated from university. He boasts that the Khumalos are lucky to have Zandile as part of their family.

'Dad should have just made a film,' mumbles Yandisa.

'God forbid. You know what Dad is like, it would have been a feature film,' giggles Xoliswa.

Yandisa laughs and reaches for her big glass of brandy and Coke while Xoliswa sips champagne from a long-stemmed glass. She has lost count of the number of glasses she's had but the bubbles are making her feel light-headed. Their mother has already admonished them about drinking and gave them a long lecture about how there are church people present and that they need to behave. Both girls promptly ignored her and continued to drink without any restraint. There is an open bar stocked with everything from short, stout bottles of beer to slim, elegant bottles of wine. The serving of alcohol has been a contentious issue surrounding the wedding. Abraham had insisted there should be no alcohol, while the Khumalos insisted that there could be no wedding without alcohol. When Abraham extolled the sins of alcohol, Ndabenhle's mother had challenged him about how Jesus turned water into wine at the wedding in Cana. It was probably the only verse she knew but that day it was the verse that counted because it meant the wedding wasn't going to be a dry and sober affair.

'Thank God for the Khumalos. If we aren't careful Dad will turn this into a prayer meeting!' says Yandisa sarcastically.

'You know, I don't remember this side of Dad,' remarks Xoliswa.

She had left home before his reformation had really taken hold. She had been twenty-three at the time, a newly qualified chartered accountant getting accustomed to life in New York, where she was on secondment with an accounting firm. In all the time since she left, she had never been home. Not because she didn't have the money, she had plenty of it but because for the last six years she had been playing 'house' with Thulani, the supposed love of her life. Thulani and her were the ones who should have been getting married today. It wasn't fair. How is it that Zandile can meet a man and get married a year later and here she is six years later struggling to get Thulani to propose?

'Xolie, are you okay?'

It's Yandisa's voice that brings her back to the present.

'I'm fine,' says Xoliswa, 'Just great!'

But she is miles away from feeling 'great', an exaggeration of her current state of mind. Fine is probably much closer to the truth. She was *just* fine.

When Abraham finishes his speech, the guests erupt into loud applause. Only a few actually listened to what he had said, the rest are just relieved that he's going to sit down. Since Ndabenhle's father is late, Butho, the oldest son in the family, stands in his place to speak. He gives a short speech about how he raised the groom after his father had died and expresses his utmost pride in seeing Ndaba finally married, because they thought he was over the hill. This is met with rapturous laughter.

'Yes, we were getting worried whether everything was okay down there. I mean in all these years we never even heard of a girl saying she had been impregnated by Ndaba!'

More raucous laughter follows. Zandile doesn't laugh, feeling the jibe is uncalled for as it has been a subject of much untold pain for her husband. Even unmarried men are stigmatised.

'*Siyabonga Zandile. Uyenz' uNdaba indod' emadodeni.* You have made Ndaba a man amongst men.'

There is thunderous applause. Zandile squeezes Ndaba's hand and is glad when Khumalo Snr stumbles back to his seat. A few more speeches are made before the main meal is served.

Food can make or break a wedding. It's often said that the more the guests eat, the more generous they will be at the gifting part of the ceremony. There is a foot-long buffet table with an assortment of meats ranging from a leg of lamb with garlic and rosemary, succulent herb-crusted roast beef, grilled lemon and herb chicken breasts and Cajun hake fillets. At the salad bar, guests can help themselves to cooked pasta salads and salads with butter lettuce tossed with blue cheese or goat's cheese. Most of the names are unfamiliar to the guests; Waldorf, Caesar and arugula but everyone flirts with the unfamiliar and eats to their heart's content. The starch dishes are equally interesting: oven-roasted herbed potatoes, wild rice pilaf, coriander mashed potato and pasta in a tomato and basil sauce. The dessert table is the most popular with an assortment of tarts from apple to lemon, milk and peppermint, delicate phyllo pastry filled with berries and delectable chocolate brownies and ice cream.

While the guests eat, they are entertained by the famous Rusike Brothers who belt out all their famous hits, taking people back to their youth. Zandile then has the obligatory dance with her father before Ndabenhle whisks her away. The MC opens the dance floor and everyone dances around the newlyweds; Yandisa getting into the thick of things with her provocative dancing. Her aunts are mortified and when the song ends, Sis Lungile and Sis Ntombi drag her aside and ask her to dance appropriately.

'Yandisa, please tone it down,' implores Sis Ntombi. 'What will the Khumalos think of us?'

'I honestly don't give a fuck,' Yandisa splutters. 'I am going to enjoy my sister's wedding. You two need to sit your tight asses down.'

Sis Ntombi frowns in horror and Sis Lungile has to bite down an irrepressible urge to laugh.

'Be respectful!' chastens Sis Ntombi. '*Sibadala.* Respect your elders.'

Yandisa storms away and soon returns to the dance floor and joins the circle that has formed. She steals the limelight with her zealous dancing and guests stand up at their tables to applaud her flamboyant moves. Sis Ntombi marches up to the DJ and demands that he turn the music off as it is time to proceed with the rest of the programme. However, much to her horror, the next item on the programme is the groom removing the garter from the bride's thigh. Ndabenhle's father-in-law is mortified when the groom seems to take his time. Zandile then throws her bouquet into an expectant group of single ladies and Yandisa emerges victorious. Xoliswa watches the commotion from the sidelines, preferring to sit it out and throw back another glass of Moët Nectar Imperial. There is more spirited dancing before the cutting of the cake and Ndabenhle teases and taunts his bride before putting a morsel of cake in her mouth and licking the cream off her lips. This elicits much whistling and catcalling. The bride and groom take to the dance floor for a final waltz while the guests enjoy watching the dreamy couple. As the reception draws to an end, the bride and groom thank everyone for coming and leave together, ready to start their new life of wedded bliss.

'Ngiyakuthanda. Uyezwa? I love you. Do you hear me?' Ndaba says to his new wife.

These words bring a sunny smile to Zandile's face, making her eyes sparkle like the two-carat diamond ring on her finger.

'I love you too,' she replies, looking deeply into his eyes.

She adores her new husband and can't wait to show him just how much she loves him. Theirs has been the fairytale wedding she always wanted and they are going to live happily ever after, until the clutches of death prise them apart.

MIND YOUR MAN

In the movies, there is always that iconic scene where the bride and groom drive off into the sunset, tin cans attached to the bumper of their car, with the 'Just Married' sign. In Ndebele tradition, when the sun sets, the bride is driven to her new husband's home for an initiation ceremony, aunties in tow. Sis Ntombi and Sis Lungile had already volunteered themselves for the task at hand and had tried, unsuccessfully, to negotiate with the Khumalos to bring Zandile the morning after the wedding. But the Khumalos had been resolute, insisting they wanted to receive their *makoti* that night. The aunties recruited Xoliswa and Yandisa to be part of the delegation as the bride wasn't allowed to arrive at the house alone and had to be accompanied by her sisters or other close female relatives. Their mother had insisted that Maria, a poor relative of theirs who worked hard, be part of the delegation too. Poorer relatives were often enlisted to accompany the bride to their new family's home to help with all the tasks.

Phumla was well aware of the rigours of the initiation into a groom's family, as she herself had discovered when she married into the Mafu family thirty years earlier. Her husbands' sisters had been militant, making her fetch water from miles away and cooking over an open fire, even though there was a wood-fired stove at the homestead. They thought they would break her down but having grown up in the rural Transkei, Phumla had completed all the tasks effortlessly. But she vowed never to raise her daughters that way and saw no need for it, especially when they could rather get an education and outsource menial tasks. Maids had flitted in and out of the Mafu's home over the years, cooking, cleaning up after them, washing and ironing piles of laundry and carrying out all the domestic duties. Her husband's sisters had always disapproved of Phumla having help, saying that her daughters were spoilt but Phumla ignored them. For years they used this against her, claiming it was the reason her daughters were unmarried and telling her she had raised them badly.

But today Phumla can walk around with an air of smugness because today one of her daughters is married. She inspects Zandile, who has changed into a demure, floral dress with a lilac jacket and is sitting on the bed having her make-up touched up.

'You will be fine, *mntanami*,' says Phumla, taking Zandile's hand in hers.

Zandile nods, fighting back the tears and her mother stands up, kisses her on the forehead before walking out of the room. Her presence is no longer needed and the aunties will take over.

Zandile looks around her bedroom. When Xoliswa had moved out of home, Zandile had inherited her bedroom because she had always shared a room with Yandisa. To have her own space was liberating and it had felt like she had inherited a piece of land; no more fighting over territory with Yandisa. She loved that room and always looked forward to being back there when she returned home for university holidays. Thinking of all the memories, she feels sad to be leaving but is excited at the thought of sharing a house and a room with her new husband.

'*Kanti*, where is Yandisa?' Sis Ntombi asks Xoliswa, interrupting Zandile's thoughts.

'I have no idea,' Xoliswa replies, sitting at the dresser, fighting back rising nausea as the room starts spinning around her.

'Xolie, please find her. We have to leave in a few minutes so call all the gogos so that we can start,' Sis Ntombi instructs her. Xoliswa steps out of the room gingerly, regretting her decision to drink so much that day. She ventures into the garden, where the after party is in full swing, and weaves her way through the crowds but there is no sign of Yandisa.

She suddenly feels the bile rise up in her throat and quickly runs back into the house. She makes it to the guest toilet just in time and brings everything up. When she feels like she can't bring anything more up, she rinses her mouth with water and feels a lot better and a whole lot more sober. She goes back to the bedroom which is filled with women seated all over the floor. Sis Ntombi shouts at her straight away for taking so long and not returning with Yandisa.

'I looked everywhere,' says an equally annoyed Xoliswa, as she collapses next to Zandile, who has been relegated to the floor.

'Well, it's getting late, we'll just have to go without Yandisa,' says Sis Lungile.

'Not that she would be any help anyway,' snaps Sis Ntombi, 'but it would have been nice if you had presented a united front.'

Sis Ntombi then puts on her solemn face and switches on her sombre tone of voice. The one she reserves for funerals and occasions just like this. Her eyes scan the entire room before she begins her address to Zandile.

'*Sokumele silay'umntwana,*' she implores, making eye contact with the older women in the room almost as if to get their buy-in.

'*Ukulaya*' involves imparting advice to the bride on how to conduct herself in marriage. The task is carried out by the more experienced married women in the family, whose marital CVs span two decades or more. Sis Ntombi always steps up because she considers herself a veteran in the marital field. Sis Lungile was also married once upon a time but her husband died a decade ago, leaving her to raise two boys single-handedly. Xoliswa has heard her mother whisper in hushed tones that Uncle Silas had committed suicide but it was something that was rarely spoken about. Sis Lungile never remarried but it was rumoured that she still kept the company of men.

'Marriage is tough, my dear. *Tough!*' intones Sis Ntombi. 'I have been married for twenty-five years. It hasn't been easy but *uyabekezela.* You have to persevere!'

'*Uyanyamezela!*' reiterates another auntie from their mother's side.

'*Uyancengancenga!*' adds Sis Lungile, reinforcing her sister's words.

Xoliswa rolls her eyes. She has sat through so many of these sessions with various friends and cousins, the only difference being the delivery based on how seasoned the orator is. The blueprint is always the same. Remain steadfast. Marriage is a house you have to build brick by brick, cementing it with patience and forgiveness. Where there are cracks in the marriage you would have to mend them with love.

'Marriage is hard,' reiterates Sis Ntombi, just in case no one heard her the first time. 'To survive it you will learn to have a forgiving heart. If you want to last long in marriage you will also need to learn to forget past wrongs. You will only truly understand the meaning of forgive and forget once you are married.'

There are soft murmurs of agreement. The toughness of marriage lines many faces in the room. Eyes hollowed out because of the many tears shed over the years and half-spirited smiles defeated by the rigours of marriage. Weathered souls eroded by repeated exposure to the abrasive winds of abuse.

'This ring comes with challenges. Many of them. But never forget that *he* chose you. Out of all of the women *he* chose you.' Sis Ntombi raises her left hand for everyone to see her diamond ring that has long since lost its shine. There is wild applause and vehement nods of approval. This seems to stir Sis Ntombi further and she becomes more spirited in her address.

'Many women want marriage but can't get it! You are lucky, my child. You are very lucky! Many women will be jealous of you. Even your so-called friends. Stay away from women who are not married. You are in a different league now and your unmarried friends will only give you bad advice. They will destroy your home.'

Xoliswa shifts uncomfortably on the floor. She wants to raise her hand and ask whether this advice also extends to unmarried sisters but restrains herself.

'From this day forth your husband is your best friend. Whatever happens in your home, stays in your home. We must never know what happens behind closed doors. In a marriage there is only room for three people: you, him and God. When you have problems pray, *mntanami*. Pray hard. You were raised in a Christian home so you know how to pray. Don't ever stop praying! My knees are bruised from all the praying I have done over the years.'

Sis Ntombi lifts her skirt to reveal her dry kneecaps. She is in her element, her zone, and as Xoliswa watches her, she thinks how her dad is not the only orator in the family. Clearly theirs is a family of charismatic speakers. She chuckles at how animated her aunt has become, using her hands to emphasise her point. Sis Ntombi nudges Zandile on the floor, who bites her lip to stop herself from laughing.

'Your Uncle Ben has kept me on my knees. Many times he brought me to my knees when he wouldn't come home at night. One day you will know the pain of finding lipstick on your husband's shirt. Or the smell of another woman on him. I used to think it would never happen to me. Not *my* man I used to say!'

Then she claps her hands together animatedly, 'Whuuuu *amadoda* … it happens to all of us!'

Then, as if on cue, the women break into a loud chorus.

> *Amadoda ayafana.*
> *Amadoda yizinjazabantu.*
> *Amadoda yidoti zabantu.*
> *Indoda ijikamayilele.*

> All men are the same.
> Men are dogs.
> Men are trash.
> A man turns when he sleeps.
> Then he turns on you.

The women recite the sayings like a war cry. Like they are preparing for battle. Sis Ntombi is the general stirring them up for the fight and the morale in the room is high as the women echo her sentiments in unison. Armed with confidence, Sis Ntombi continues with her feverish address.

'Don't be deterred by the cheating. Remember, all those who are not married want to get in. They want to destroy your home. You must fight for it, Zandile. Fight. Till death do you part, Zandile. You fight till death!'

Punches are thrown into the air. Fists shaken at invisible aggressors. These women are seasoned fighters. They have battled with the known and unknowns and emerged victorious.

'For twenty-five years I have fought for my home, Zandile,' Sis Ntombi carries on. 'I've protected it. *Amawulemanengi ngaphandle.* There are many whores out there looking for a home. You fight for yours, Zandile. You fought to get here and you must fight to stay.'

A long pause follows. Xoliswa wonders if it is to give her words a chance to have more of an impact.

'You must also remember you are not just marrying uNdaba. I know you young people, you think it's just him and me against the world. You are marrying the whole Khumalo clan. All of them. Even that evil gogo of his that you don't like.'

There is more laughter around the room.

'Love his relatives like your own, Zandile. His people are your people. His mother is your mother. If you buy your mom a dress, buy his mom one too. Treat them equally. Give his mother the respect she deserves. She birthed him, she raised this man for you. You wouldn't be getting married if it weren't for her. Choose your battles wisely. Don't pick unnecessary fights with your *mamazala*. There are some fights you will *never* win.'

There are murmurs of agreement all around.

'You must never forget your place, Zandile. Your husband is the head of the home. You are beneath him and you are there to serve him.

You must always be subservient to him. Remember, you are the neck and he is the head. The head doesn't turn without the neck.'

Xoliswa feels nausea threaten to rise again but she knows it's not because of the alcohol this time but the vitriol her aunt is spewing.

'Every morning make sure you wake up before your husband. Make sure you bath and get dressed before he does. It is important that you look presentable. The same way you are now must be maintained throughout marriage. Your husband must never see you looking like a hot mess. Watch your weight. Take care of yourself. Take care of your husband too. Make sure his clothes are washed and ironed. I still put out clothes for your Uncle Ben …'

'I always wondered why he was so badly dressed,' Xoliswa whispers to Zandile, who suppresses yet another giggle.

'Cook for your man, Zandile!' Sis Ntombi instructs. 'Food is the way to a man's heart. Make sure you learn the type of foods he likes and cook them well. Always pamper your husband. When he comes home from work, serve him tea and cake or tea and scones. Always cook supper for your husband, don't leave it to the maid. Many of you have come crying to us because your husband is sleeping with the maid. That's because you allowed her to take over your home. Draw boundaries. Your maid doesn't clean your bedroom, Zandile. Do you *hear* me?'

Zandile nods in affirmation.

'No maid washes your husband's underwear or your sheets? *Uyezwa?*'

Zandile nods with the solemnity required of an occasion such as this. Sis Ntombi exhales deeply. Her passionate speech has taken a lot out of her so her sister steps forward, taking over the reins.

'And make sure you bath every night before you go to bed,' beseeches Sis Lungile. 'Hygiene is extremely important. When you wash down there make sure to use cold water. It keeps the vagina tight.'

There are animated chuckles around the room.

'It's no laughing matter,' says Sis Lungile gravely. 'Sex is what keeps the marriage intact. Men thrive on good sex. Never deny a man his conjugal rights. Whenever he wants sex make sure you give it to him. It doesn't matter if you are cooking or cleaning, stop what you are doing and attend to your husband's needs. His needs come first. Even if you fight you must never deny him sex. *Never!*'

Xoliswa fights the outrage threatening to spill out of her. What about *her* needs? What if she didn't feel like having sex that night? Why is it always about the men and his pleasure? Surely sex was made for mutual pleasure? There are times when she isn't in the mood and says no to sex. Or when her and Thulani have fought there is definitely no sex on the menu that night.

'If you don't satisfy your man, someone else will,' says Sis Lungile, cutting into Xoliswa's thoughts. 'There are many women out there who will give your man what you won't, so make sure you perform. Don't lie on your back and expect things to happen!'

'But be warned,' cautions Sis Lungile, 'men will cheat. It's in their nature but what you need to learn is that it doesn't mean anything. They need variety. Chicken one day, beef stew the next. You'd also get bored if you ate oxtail every day of your life. Trust me, there will be many women who will come in and out of your husband's life but don't take it to heart. You are his wife. You are the one with the ring on your finger. Chapter 37. You are a one-life stand not a one-night stand.'

This is met with thunderous clapping and cheering. It has been clearly articulated: marriage is a prize. The ring is a trophy and something that must be protected at all costs.

THE UNHOLY TRINITY

Walking into Genesis nightclub, you are immediately enveloped by the thick and smoky air. The blaring music greets you long before you even set foot inside the club. The music is the draw card and it never fails to whip the crowd into a mad frenzy of dancing. Laughter is floating in the air and voices rise above the loud music in a cacophony like hens in a chicken coop. Genesis is always crowded, always with the same faces. Some beautiful faces and some not so beautiful but everyone dressed in beautiful clothes. A myriad of colours flash across the heaving room, pulsating with the vibrancy and energy of the people inside the club. There are the twenty-something-olds on the come-up wanting to make their mark in life. The established thirty-something movers and shakers who have made their mark or if they haven't, are faking it. Then, of course, the forty-something-olds cruising through midlife, trying to reclaim their youth on the dance floor. Not far from them are the teenage wannabes, the young impressionable girls who want to fit in and be in the 'in crowd'. They grow up way too fast in the dark corners where the lighting is dim, casting shadows of doubt. So illusive and so seductive.

Yandisa is a regular patron at Genesis and the host always reserves a table in the VIP section for Ladies Night on Wednesday, Happy Hour on Thursday and Friday nights, because that's when everyone goes clubbing, and on Saturday nights, and tonight is no different. Her boyfriend, Wesley, picked her up from the house after the wedding after insisting she go out with him, even though she initially didn't plan to go out. He arrived in his BMW G-string which was painted a brilliant yellow and had tinted windows. It was the only one like it in Bulawayo and everyone knew it was Wesley's car and because she was always seen in his car, she was referred to as Wesley's chick. Wesley was accompanied by his two mates, JB and Charles. JB made room for Yandisa in the front seat and migrated to the back.

'Aren't you going to come inside at least and greet my sisters?' asks Yandisa as she settles into the front seat.

Wesley shakes his head dismissively, he doesn't want to tell her that he knows Xoliswa. 'We don't do *masalad* parties,' he says, using the derogatory term to refer to the kids of affluent black families who live in the low-density suburbs of Bulawayo and were educated at the city's private schools. And who are deemed to be cultural outcasts who've adopted the so-called 'Western' way of life and frown upon their own cultural traditions.

'Look, I can't just leave my sister's wedding, Wesley. We are going to the groom's place in a few minutes.'

'I am not leaving you here, Yandisa,' says Wesley. 'And stop acting like it's *your* wedding.'

'Wesley, my sister needs me.'

'*I* need you more,' he says, looking at her imploringly.

Yandisa needs no further prompting and Wesley drives away, one hand on the wheel and the other on her fleshy thigh. No one tries to make small talk because he turns the radio on full blast and the sounds of Mdu fill the interior of the car. Yandisa taps her feet to the repetitive beat. Wesley had introduced her to the world of kwaito music, a popular brand of township music imported from South Africa. Prior to that she had been a strictly rap and R&B fan, lost in the world of The Notorious B.I.G., Missy Elliott and SWV. Before she met Wesley, she had only clubbed at more upmarket places like Talk of the Town and Visions but now she frequents places that are considered seedy like Mzilikazi Gardens, Top Ten and shebeens out in the locations, with him. But that night he suggested they go to Genesis, the chic nightclub on the outskirts of the CBD and so that was how she found herself sitting in the VIP section of the club, tapping her foot to Foxy Brown and nursing a glass of brandy.

Wesley and his friends are embroiled in a heated debate about the controversial OJ Simpson case. All the men are in fervent agreement that OJ Simpson had been justified in killing the bitch and her lover. Yandisa has nothing of substance to contribute to the conversation so she turns her attention to her Nokia 3210. She has a slew of missed calls from her mother from earlier in the evening which she had ignored and there are several text messages from her sisters asking her where she was but she ignored those too. She texts her friend from work, Sunette, and asks if she's coming to the club. Sunette responds that she is 'like 50 kilometres out of town' but promises that her and her boyfriend will come past later.

'Are you okay?' asks Wesley, draping his strong masculine arm around her, peering to see who she's chatting to on the phone.

'I think I am,' replies Yandisa.

She doesn't want to offend Wesley but she would like it if he paid more attention to her than his friends but perhaps she should stop being selfish. After all, she always has his full attention when they are alone.

'Don't you want to dance?' she asks him.

'I'm not in the mood,' he says dismissively. 'I had training today. I'm exhausted.'

She likes the song that's playing because it's the song that was playing the night her and Wesley met. She had been out with her girlfriends, celebrating a birthday when he had picked up their tab and then called her to sit at his table. She had gone willingly, proud to have been singled out by him. Not only did Wesley play rugby for the Zimbabwean national team, he was considered one of the hottest guys in Bulawayo. His reputation as a bad boy preceded him and that was what Yandisa found the most alluring about him. Plus his muscled torso and broody eyes.

'I *want* to dance,' she says to him, pouting her lips.

Wesley isn't moved, 'I'm not in the mood,' he responds with finality.

So Yandisa stands up, excuses herself on the pretext of going to the bathroom but only goes as far as the dance floor. She squeezes in amongst the bodies that are moving rhythmically to the beat. Soon, a nice-looking guy sidles up next to her. He is agile on his feet and before long, him and Yandisa have picked up a steady rhythm together. They dance in sync, almost as if their movements have been carefully choreographed. Soon, people are making a circle around them and Wesley bamboozles his way into the circle and quickly whisks Yandisa away.

'Wesley, leave me alone!' she hisses.

'You are making a spectacle of yourself,' he says to her through gritted teeth.

He smiles as they walk past some fans on the dance floor. It's a tight smile that disappears as quickly as it appears.

'Yandisa, I don't want you making a show of yourself! You are *my* woman for fuck's sake!'

'Wesley, I was *just* dancing. Do you have to be so uptight?'

'I won't have *my* woman dancing like that,' says Wesley.

He grips her arm roughly and pulls her towards the door. He motions to his friends to alert them of their sudden departure. Yandisa is flushed with embarrassment as he drags her out of the club and tries to shrug him off but he tightens his grip, squeezing her so hard that she grimaces in pain. He loosens his grip when they are in the parking lot.

'I was just having some fun! I didn't do anything wrong!' she shouts.

'You're behaving like a whore!'

'Don't call me a whore! How *dare* you call me a whore!' she yells at him.

'Shut up, Yandisa. You're drunk!'

'No, *you* shut up!' she retaliates.

She feels a stinging slap across her cheek. It is so unexpected that she looks at him, stunned. He has never hit her before. She rubs her inflamed cheek almost like she's making sure that just happened.

'Get in the car!' he shouts at her.

She doesn't argue and slinks into the passenger seat like a frightened animal. She hopes he is going to take her straight home but instead he careers in the direction of his flat. When they get to his flat, he parks the car and demands she go upstairs with him.

'I'm not getting out of the car,' she says, folding her hands across her chest. 'How do you get to slap me across the face? Even my own father doesn't hit me!'

'Maybe he should. You are out of order, Yandisa!'

'No, Wesley. No. You have no right to hit me!' she argues.

'Okay, I'm sorry,' he says. 'Now get out of the car.'

'I'm not getting out of this car,' says Yandisa stubbornly.

He pulls her out of the car, puts her over his shoulder and carries her up the stairs to his flat on the third floor. All the while she is kicking and screaming but he carries her with ease. Wesley disregards her protests and instead smothers her cries with kisses as he throws her onto his unmade bed. He pins her down to the bed. Yandisa eventually succumbs to him, tearing her nails into his back while she fights back her own tears.

RITES OF INITIATION

It's that time of the morning when lovers are usually spooning in a loose and naked embrace. His arm casually looped around her waist, not in a possessive way but rather to reassure her. Their heads nestled together on a single pillow, as if seeking a connection in their dreams. They would have developed a steady breathing rhythm, both overcome by exhaustion from their rigorous lovemaking. This, however, is not the picture that emerges that Sunday morning when Zandile wakes up in a narrow single bed, her spine backed up against the wall. The only body pressing up against hers is Xoliswa's, who is cushioned between her and the space where Sis Ntombi slept. Maria had opted to sleep on the hard parquet floor. This is far from the wedded bliss Zandile envisioned for her first day of marriage. She is supposed to be waking up in a deluxe hotel suite wrapped in the arms of her husband. Instead, she has slept fitfully and when her aunt shrugs her and Xoliswa awake, she is shocked to see that it's morning. Her eyes are still heavy with sleep and her joints ache from the discomfort of the bed.

Zandile and her family arrived at the Khumalos home in Sunninghill at 9 pm the previous evening, where an even bigger wedding reception awaited them. They had had to stand outside the gate when they first arrived because Sis Ntombi insisted they would not go inside until more money was paid to the bride. Zandile is covered, as per the dictates of tradition, and the Khumalos have to pay to unveil her. This was another ritual and procedure that had to be followed to the T.

The Khumalos ignore their requests for a while and eventually emerge an hour later with money. Sis Ntombi insists it isn't enough and threatens to take her niece home. The Khumalos are reluctant to part with more money but Sis Ntombi is unwavering in her position. Zandile is panicking as she doesn't understand the need for the Khumalos to have to pay more money. Finally, the Khumalos capitulate and more money is handed over to Sis Ntombi. It is all a game and Sis Ntombi calls it the 'spoils of war'. The women who accompanied the bride will share in the takings given to Sis Ntombi.

They finally enter the Khumalo home and Zandile remains covered and can hear the singing around her. The older women ululate and dance around them. They are ushered into a living room where several women are huddled on the floor. The men are either standing or sitting on the sofas. Before they can sit down, more money is demanded. On the final payment, Zandile is unveiled and there is more ululating and loud applause. She is introduced to the family using her clan names.

'OMafu, oNkonjeni, oMathayi, kaNgizanyani, oKhokhozela okwenqina lisiya eDlomoDlomo.'

A man in the room recites the clan names for the Khumalo clan: 'OMntungwa, oMangethe, sphahla sendlunkulu, oDlangamandla.'

This heralds loud applause and ululation. After the recital is over, Nandi, Ndaba's sister, leads Zandile around the room and introduces her to everyone, observing the family hierarchy. She greets everyone with a slight curtsey and the wives of two of Ndaba's brothers, Edna and Zodwa, who were also *makotis*, are present to welcome her into the family. They embrace her warmly and all the women ululate excitedly.

Zandile has been told over and over again that Ndaba's mother is now her mother and should be treated as such. Zandile has met Ndabenhle's mother on two previous occasions. Selina is a thin, hawkish woman with beady eyes. She is dark in complexion, her body weathered with age. For a woman in her seventies she is very alert and in good health.

'Come and sit with me, MaNkonjeni,' says Selina, patting the vacant space beside her.

Addressing Zandile by her totem is a sign of respect and it is what she will continue to be called in her marriage. Even though she is now 'Mrs Khumalo' she will never lose her identity.

'Yebo, Mama,' acquiesces Zandile, casting her eyes downwards, like she has rehearsed so many times with her aunts. Looking her directly in the eye would be seen as a sign of utmost disrespect.

'Welcome to the family, my child,' Selina continues in a dry, brittle voice. 'Feel free, you are one of us now.'

'Thank you,' replies Zandile reverently.

Drinks are served and, intriguingly, her mother-in-law opts for a glass of sweet, red wine. Zandile is tempted to join her but Sis Ntombi throws her a scathing look and so she opts for a Fanta Orange instead. Food is served and plates are piled high with samp, beef stew and coleslaw. Sis Lungile insists they eat everything they are offered because it would be bad manners not to. The merrymaking continues well into the night and even after they profess exhaustion and go to bed, the party continues.

'I didn't sleep well,' complains Zandile.

'Neither did I,' says Sis Ntombi. 'Who could sleep with all that noise?'

Even though they had all elected to go to sleep, the wedding after-party had continued till the early hours of the morning.

'I didn't even hear the music,' says Xoliswa, who had passed out the minute her head hit the pillow.

Sis Lungile had left the night before deferring all the duties to her older sister and so Sis Ntombi had elected to stay, saying that Uncle Ben could survive one night without her.

'Come on girls, get up, bath and get dressed. We have work to do,' Sis Ntombi says to them bossily.

Sis Ntombi had woken up an hour earlier and was already dressed in an African print dress with a matching doek. Zandile, Xoliswa and Maria trudge off to the bathroom leaving her to make the beds with army-like precision. When they return, she hands them each a broom and issues them all with instructions. Zandile is grateful that Xoliswa and Maria are with her but cusses Yandisa for not being there to help too.

'Right!' she begins, assuming her position as sergeant of her small regiment. 'We'll start by sweeping the yard and we won't do anything else until we have been paid for our work.'

Much to her surprise, Zandile sees they already have an audience when they start sweeping outside. A few elderly women are already seated out on the patio absorbing the early morning heat. The women are using grass brooms, not the conventional brooms found in supermarkets and they are bent over double, much to the amusement of their audience. They pile the dirt into heaps and money is dropped on each heap. More money is paid for Zandile to enter the kitchen. Only after they have been paid for the labour do they proceed with other chores like cooking breakfast.

Even though it is only the closest family present it appears there are so many mouths to feed. Small mouths and big mouths and every demographic cohort is represented. From tiny babies to geriatrics who have lived through eight decades. Young or old, they all have one common objective, and that is to eat.

As always, it is important to observe protocol even when serving food and so the men eat first, followed by the women and children. It is the first time Zandile has laid eyes on her husband and she kneels before him as she has been told to do. They can't kiss but he holds onto her hands longer than necessary when she hands him a cup of tea. She can see the yearning in his eyes and quickly looks away and continues to serve the other men in the family. Her husband's relatives really give new meaning to the word 'extended' family and the Khumalo home is like a refugee camp. A marquee has been set up in the garden to accommodate the spillover of guests.

They slice what must be sixteen loaves of bread, butter the crumbly slices and then smear them with dollops of bright red Sun jam. Huge urns of milky white tea are set out and just like the alcohol was rapidly consumed the night before, the tea is consumed with the same fervour. Toothless, old women ask for more bread and tea, much to Zandile's annoyance but she smiles good-naturedly as she kneels down to serve them. They remark how beautiful she is and reiterate that Ndabenhle is lucky to have found a wife like her.

After breakfast, the sink is piled high with dirty teacups, saucers and plates awaiting them and Zandile is ready to collapse with exhaustion. Xoliswa is smoking a cigarette out on the doorstep and Sis Ntombi loses her temper when she sees her.

'What is this? Huh? You think this is the fancy British Virgin Islands?'

Zandile and Xoliswa laugh at their aunt's angry outburst as they soldier on to reduce the pile of dirty crockery. When they hear the midday news blaring on the radio, they are shocked at how much time has flown by. Xoliswa had been hoping to catch a midday nap but Sis Ntombi tells her they have to start on lunch. A white goat is then presented to Zandile and her aunt. Sis Ntombi nods that it is favourable and explains that it is the goat that will be used *ukucola*. Ideally, this rite would have been done post-lobola but Abraham had been against it saying he didn't believe in it because it did not align with his Christian beliefs. He said they could do whatever they liked once Zandile was under their roof. Ndaba and his brothers leave to slaughter the goat.

Nandi comes through to the kitchen with instructions on what has to be served for lunch: chicken stew and *isitshwala*. Sis Ntombi volunteers to cook the *isitshwala* with finely ground millet which they have brought with them. They have already put out the large, black, three-legged pots usually reserved for weddings and funerals.

'I can do the chicken,' volunteers Xoliswa.

'They don't even have chicken,' says Zandile, rifling through the fridge.

She looks in the chest freezer which barely closes because of the humongous carcass jutting out but doesn't find any. She goes outside to tell Nandi that she can't find the chickens and Nandi laughs till the tears run down her cheeks. The joke is lost on Zandile.

'The chickens are there,' Nandi says, pointing to a chicken run at the back of the house. Zandile feels her blood curdle. She has never slaughtered a chicken before and returns to the kitchen to relay the enormity of the task ahead.

'Maria, go start the fire,' commands Sis Ntombi. 'Xolie, you stay here and start chopping vegetables.'

'Auntie, I can't kill a chicken,' confesses Zandile.

Sis Ntombi starts to laugh; a high-pitched, raucous laugh and says, 'Aren't you the one who wanted to get married? You thought it was a joke?'

'This is not what marriage is about!' howls Zandile in protest. 'I didn't sign up for this!'

'Well, you are going to have to learn fast, my dear!' she says to her niece.

Sis Ntombi frogmarches Zandile to the chicken run and the hens cluck with hysteria as they enter it and Zandile immediately cowers into a corner.

'You are going to have to catch one!' insists Sis Ntombi.

Zandile squeals and shrieks as the chicken she tries to catch, clucks and screeches and furiously circles the hatch. Sis Ntombi watches the chaos, her hands resting firmly on her hips. Some members of the Khumalo family are drawn to the unfolding drama and laugh at their *makoti*. To avert the attention away from Zandile, Sis Ntombi catches a chicken and secures it in her arms. She holds it down with her feet and with one sweeping motion chops its head off. The blood sprays on Zandile, who shrieks in repulsion but Sis Ntombi ignores her and slaughters another bird quickly and efficiently, showing no remorse.

Zandile runs and throws up. Sis Ntombi tells her to clean herself up because her and Maria have been tasked with dressing the chickens. Xoliswa manages to keep a safe distance from the chaos, not wanting to ruin her manicure.

When Zandile returns, she is called to where an audience is gathering. The goat has been slaughtered and Butho takes the bile from the gall bladder and anoints Zandile with it. On the top of her head, the back of the neck and on her wrists. The ceremony of *ukucola* is to incorporate the bride into the Khumalo family and they call on the ancestors to welcome Zandile. She is given the bladder to wear as a bracelet to symbolise that the rite has been performed. Zandile can't wait to get rid of it.

Sis Ntombi and Xoliswa will be given half of the goat to take home with them and the rest of the goat is cooked for the day's celebration. Sis Ntombi wrestles with the three-legged pot of *isitshwala* and Zandile tries to be helpful but her eyes can't get accustomed to the smoke. She coughs persistently, tears streaming down her cheeks and feeling thoroughly annoyed, her aunt chases her back inside the house.

'Go cut onions or something!' Sis Ntombi shouts. 'Good God, my brother's kids are useless!' she grumbles to herself.

Xoliswa and Zandile chop vegetables together and laugh about 'the chicken fiasco'. Lunch becomes an early supper as it is served two hours late but nevertheless everyone agrees that it was an excellent meal. It is rude to leave immediately after eating so Sis Ntombi waits an hour before she announces their departure. She says her husband needs her but Zandile knows she is lying. Xoliswa jumps onto the bandwagon and says she needs to start packing as she is returning to the British Virgin Islands in a few days time. Zandile feels like she is being deserted.

'Maria will stay with you,' says Sis Ntombi, seeing the bewilderment in her niece's eyes. 'You'll be fine. You are with family now.'

Zandile shudders at the thought. So this is what it was all about, for better or for worse, she thinks. She bids her aunt and sister goodbye and even though she is surrounded by people, she feels desolate and alone. She holds back her tears as they back out of the driveway.

Later that night she collapses into bed exhausted and finally lies down beside her new husband.

'Come on now,' says Ndabenhle, putting his arm around her, 'by this time tomorrow we will be on our honeymoon.'

'I can't wait,' says Zandile, snuggling closer to him.

Ndabenhle holds her in his arms lovingly and kisses her over and over again.

'You did well today. I was proud of you,' he says to her.

'Don't lie. I am so useless. I couldn't even kill a chicken!'

He laughs, 'I didn't marry you to kill chickens.'

He stares at her intently, stroking her cheek and the lust is apparent in his eyes, while the hesitation is palpable in hers. Her heart pounds in her chest and he says, 'Don't worry. I can wait one more night.'

She sighs with relief. She is far too exhausted to do anything and Ndaba understands and kisses her forehead lovingly.

'We are going to do everything right. Just the way you wanted. Candles and rose petals,' he adds.

She leans into him and kisses him passionately. This is what marriage is about, she thinks to herself. This is the part I signed up for. The Khumalos can keep their chickens, she has found the real prize.

Her prince.

OF MOTHERS AND DAUGHTERS

Their father had always been strict about curfews when they were growing up. They used to have to be home by 6 pm in summer and 5 pm in winter and he was inflexible about it. You couldn't be a quarter past or half past late and any deviation from the time would elicit the wrath of Abraham. Yandisa broke all her father's rules and the ones she hadn't actually broken, she bended or manoeuvred around deftly.

That morning is no different as she scales the six-foot wrought iron gate. It is 5 am and the sun is illuminating the driveway as she runs up to the house. She lets herself in through the back door with the duplicate key, that she makes sure is always handy for times just like these. Before she had a key, she used to have to rely on Zandile to let her in the house. She has been sneaking out of the house for years and had once even drugged her parents after she was denied their permission to attend a party. She had popped sedatives in their 9 pm tea which they demanded was made for them every night.

Walking into the house that morning, there is the muted silence of sleeping souls. She tiptoes through the kitchen and nearly jumps out of her skin when she sees her father's bulky frame leaning against the kitchen counter. Yandisa holds her hand to her chest, as if to still her beating heart.

'Yandisa, where are you coming from at this hour?' Abraham says sternly.

Yandisa doesn't respond. She knows from experience that such questions don't necessarily warrant a response but her silence only serves to further infuriate her father. He mistakes it for insolence.

'Yandisa! Where the hell are you coming from?'

43

'I was at a friend's place,' replies Yandisa, folding her hands over her chest.

'Don't lie to me!' roars Abraham.

'I'm not lying!' says Yandisa, looking him squarely in the eyes.

'I won't accept this nonsense in my house. Just pack your bags and get out!'

It is at that point her mother comes drifting into the kitchen, wearing a blue kimono, with the sash loosely tied around her waist.

'Yandisa,' says her mother in a grave tone of voice, 'what kind of behaviour is this?'

Yandisa stifles a yawn. She is exhausted and wishes her mother would save the lecture for later.

'You left here on Saturday without telling any of us where you were going. Did you forget that you were supposed to accompany your sister to her in-laws' home?' her mother asks.

'I have had enough of this, Yandisa,' interjects her father. 'I want you to pack your stuff and get out,' he repeats.

Yandisa has heard it all before. This is the part where she has to hang her head in shame. She searches for the words 'I'm sorry' which sound so clichéd after saying them so many times over the years, rarely with any sincerity. As she apologises, she knows it will happen again. A pattern that repeats itself over and over again like a record playing on repeat.

'Yandisa, if you want to behave like a whore you will do it outside my house,' berates her father. 'This isn't a whore house and I won't have you treat it as such.'

Behind him, her mother is nodding furiously in firm agreement.

Yandisa apologies again, this time more forcefully. 'I said I'm sorry!'

'No, Yandisa. You never are!' screams her mother.

'I want you out of my house, Yandisa. When I get home tonight I don't want to find you here. I am tired of being disrespected in my own home!' Abraham says as he shuffles out of the kitchen, leaving his wife to have the last word.

'Do you honestly think these men you jump over fences for will marry you, Yandisa? Do you really?' her mother says sternly and trudges back to bed. Yandisa follows suit. She can already feel the stirrings of a headache.

She is roused from her deep slumber an hour later.

'Yandisa, wake up!' presses Babalwa.

'Babs, what is it?' mumbles Yandisa, her eyes still firmly closed.

'You need to take me to school! Zandile isn't here, remember!'

'What time is it?' says Yandisa groggily, pulling the blanket up around her neck.

'It's time to go! I don't want to be late!' screeches Babalwa.

Yandisa has forgotten that she has to be at work by 8 am. Mondays are always manic, more so when you have a terrible hangover. She feels like the devil's foot soldiers are doing cartwheels in her head.

'Alright,' says Yandisa, forcing her eyes wide open.

The soft morning light streams through the windows, causing her to blink furiously. She rubs her eyes, trying to erase the need for sleep. She clambers out of bed, puts on her tatty, old dressing gown and then forces herself to shower. She screams when cold water hits her body and goose pimples erupt all over her skin. Two minutes later she gets out the shower and dries her body quickly and trudges back to her bedroom to get dressed.

The beauty of working in a bank is that she doesn't have to worry about what to wear every day because they have a standard uniform, making her life so much easier every morning.

All the while, Babalwa is trailing behind her, shouting vociferously that she is going to be late for school. It is 7.20 am when Yandisa finally backs out of the driveway in her red VW Beetle, giving her exactly ten minutes to get Babalwa to school.

'Yandisa, now that Zandile is gone you will have to take me to school every day, you know, Babalwa says. 'You know Mama doesn't wake up before ten.'

Yandisa exhales deeply, the enormity of that statement finally dawning on her. She doesn't want the responsibility of ferrying Babalwa to school; it had always been Zandile's duty every morning and their mother always picked her up in the afternoon. From the time Babalwa entered the world nine years ago, various members of the family were active in parenting her, while Yandisa watched from a distance, only participating when she *had* to.

Yandisa was shy of sixteen when she gave birth to Babalwa. After being in labour for twenty-four gruelling hours, she had finally expelled Babalwa into the world. Unlike a lot of mothers, she didn't feel overwhelmed with love and if anything, the experience depleted her both physically and emotionally. She had been relieved to rid her body of the protruding encumbrance. It had felt like she walked around for nine months displaying her shame and finally she was purged of it.

When her baby was first handed to her, Yandisa felt no excitement. Her mother and Zandile had cooed and crooned over the little girl's cherubic face and marvelled at what long hair she had. Breastfeeding had been a challenge and she gave up after her first bout of cracked nipples. Babalwa was promptly put on formula and Yandisa felt relieved as she could reclaim her breasts as her own. Babalwa no longer needed her for sustenance and anyone in the family could feed her.

Her mother literally took over mothering the newborn. She was the one who put Babalwa to sleep at night and the one who woke up at 3 am to feed her. She was the one who took her to the clinic for all her mandatory inoculations. And as the baby grew, so did the detachment between mother and child.

When Babalwa cried, she ran to her grandmother and when she said 'Mama' for the first time, it was to her grandmother.

Whereas some mothers might have felt resentment, Yandisa felt relief. She always felt motherhood had been thrust upon her and had never forgiven Babalwa's father for the imposition he caused in her life.

'Yandisa, when are *you* going to get married?' asks Babalwa that morning in the car on the way to school.

Yandisa sighs, 'What's with the questions, Babs?'

'All big people get married. Mama is married to Papa. Zandile is married to Ndaba. Aren't you ever going to get married?'

Yandisa shrugs her shoulders, 'I don't know. I've never thought about it.'

'I wonder if my mommy was married to my daddy. Mama says I was left when I was a baby.'

Yandisa swerves, almost hitting another car. She doesn't like the direction the conversation is going and wants to steer it to a safer ground but her daughter is undeterred.

'I sometimes wonder who my real daddy is,' Babs continues.

'You shouldn't worry about your daddy. You have parents who love you very much,' Yandisa says, desperately trying to cut the conversation short.

'I know, I know! But I'm just curious. Don't you get curious about things, Yandisa?'

Yandisa wants to tell her that her daddy's name is Marshall. Marshall Munyoro. But this isn't the right time and she wonders if there will there ever be a right time. Yandisa feels exasperated and can't understand where the onslaught of questions from Babalwa is coming from. She shifts in her seat uncomfortably and turns on the radio, hoping to drown out any further questions. She is relieved when they arrive at school and she pulls into a vacant spot in the parking lot. The conversation about Marshall has been unsettling and her daughter has taken her to a place in her past where she prefers not to return to. Babalwa jumps out of the car and waves Yandisa goodbye.

Other mothers are walking back from the classrooms and it makes Yandisa wonder whether she should have offered to walk Babs to hers but she shoves the thought to the back of her mind. She has never been a mom to Babalwa and she isn't going to start now.

Just then 'Make That Move' by Shalamar fills the interior of the car, the song that was playing the day she met Marshall all those years ago.

WHO'S YOUR DADDY?

Yandisa thinks back to the day she met Marshall almost ten years before, standing in the sweltering heat, her thumb sticking out trying to flag down a car. She can feel sweat under her armpits and running down her thighs. August has brought with it merciless, dry and scorching heat. Another taxi zooms past her, bodies packed inside, black faces pasted against the windows. These 'Emergency Taxis' or 'ETs' are the old, beat-up Peugeot 504 wagons, easily recognisable in traffic. Yandisa can't understand where the 'emergency' part comes into it as they are unreliable and never available when you need them.

She contemplates flagging down a car but her mother has warned her repeatedly about the dangers of hitchhiking and told her gory stories about women losing their private parts after hitching a ride with a seemingly likeable stranger. She puts these stories to the back of her mind as an emerald green Jetta slows to a screeching halt next to her. The driver's window rolls down and a man's face comes into view. He is shockingly handsome and Yandisa finds herself at a loss for words.

'Hi,' she says eventually, clearing her throat. 'How far are you going?'

'I'm going wherever you are going,' he says to her smoothly.

She eyes him curiously before responding. 'Well, I'm going to Hillside.'

'Then let's go.'

Yandisa hops into the empty passenger seat and the air conditioning in the car is a welcome relief from the blazing heat outside. She settles into the seat and fastens the seatbelt. The car lurches forward and speeds northwards.

'So, what's in Hillside?' the man casually asks her.

'That's where home is,' she replies.

'Well, I'm Yemurai Marshall Munyoro. What's yours?'

Normally she would lie but for some unknown reason she feels she can trust this stranger. He's too good-looking to want to run away with her private parts.

'Yandisa Mafu,' she says.

'Ahh,' he grunts. 'We have the same initials. It must be a sign.'

He goes on to quiz her about how old she is and she tells him she is in her third year of high school. He seems genuinely surprised and says to her, 'You look much older.'

'It's because I am fat,' she says matter-of-factly.

He chuckles, 'You're not fat at all!'

Yandisa is used to being teased about her weight. She was an early bloomer and started wearing a bra when she was ten years old and menstruating when she was eleven, so she's often made fun of. The teachers at school tell her to wear tights under her gym skirt because her big bum makes her skirt lift up at the back.

'So, what do you want to do when you leave high school?' Marshall continues.

Yandisa shrugs her shoulders, 'I have no idea.'

She is pretty average when it comes to school and isn't particularly good at anything or bad at anything either. There's no subject she particularly likes either. Actually, she hates school. She hates the rules.

'You're still young, you'll figure something out,' he tells her.

'What do you do?' she asks, throwing the question back at him.

He tells her he is a businessman and runs his own logistics company. She doesn't know what that is but tells him that it sounds exciting. She notices they have turned into Hillside Road so she gives him directions to her house. A right turn there. A left turn there. He pulls up outside and she thanks him profusely for the lift.

'It's a pleasure,' he says. 'Can I call you? I like chatting to you,' he says suavely.

Yandisa recites her home number and he scribbles it on the back of his business card and promises to call her. She doesn't have to wait long as he calls her that same evening and asks if he can pick her up from school the following day. She agrees and puts down the phone, feeling excited.

He doesn't disappoint her and shows up the next day in the car park, where Towanda and Dumile are waiting with her. He takes her out for lunch at Bulldogs Pub and she orders a Fanta Orange and a burger and chips. He just orders a pilsner and watches her as she talks animatedly about her day at school and about her friends. He sits back in his seat but isn't really listening to her as her full lips open and close, wondering how it would feel to have those lips closing on his manhood. It's her laughter that brings him back to the present. She has an infectious laugh and he finds himself laughing with her.

'Something tells me we are going to get along very well,' he says to her.

'Oh, really?' she says, cocking her head to one side.

'Oh, yeessss,' he says slowly, the words drawn out, soft and sensual. He carries on looking at her and it feels like his eyes remain on her for what seems forever. The moment is theirs. She'll never forget the way he looked at her in that moment. She looks away first and glances down at her napkin. She feels shy, strangely so. The waiter arrives with her food and Yandisa welcomes the interruption. Between bites of her burger and chips, the conversation flows and is as sweet and syrupy as the dessert that he orders for her. Marshall compliments her profusely, constantly making her blush. The hours fly by and it's only much later that Yandisa realises it's almost five o'clock and says she has to be home. He is reminded of her age at the mention of a curfew.

When he drops her off at home she thanks him for lunch and he thanks her for spending time with him. He then leans over and kisses her, deeply and slowly, before pulling away. Yandisa steps out of the car feeling mesmerised and is in a daze as she watches him drive away. He has cast a spell on her and now occupies a space in her heart previously reserved for Donell Jones and New Edition.

Marshall soon starts picking Yandisa up from school every day and she makes sure she is prepared for their afternoons together and carries a change of clothes in her satchel. That particular day he arrives to fetch her and she has changed into a lacy bodysuit and denim wrap skirt. They have lunch at Grass Hut, a dimly lit restaurant which gives the illusion of darkness outside but when you leave you are confronted by glaring sunlight.

During lunch, Marshall encourages Yandisa to have a drink and try some alcohol. A waiter hands over a long list of exotic cocktails and she tries one sweet drink after another. The fancy drinks, with their fruit and fancy umbrellas, are as alluring as Marshall. They leave the restaurant a little after 4 pm and Yandisa is anxious to get home before her parents do but Marshall suggests they make a quick detour to his house. He says it is time she knows where he lives.

The interior of his house is well furnished with dark teak and leather furniture and surprisingly well kept for a bachelor.

'You have such a beautiful home,' Yandisa says, plonking herself down on the black, leather sofa.

'Thanks,' says Marshall. 'Can I pour you another drink?'

'No more drinks,' she replies quickly, holding up her hands in resignation.

The room is starting to spin slowly around her like a Ferris wheel and Marshall sits down next to her and pulls her onto his lap. He kisses her tenderly, his tongue gently prying her lips apart, tantalising and teasing her. Yandisa moves closer to him, responding to the sweet caress of his probing tongue. They fall back onto the cushions, their mouths locked together and she feels him touch her breasts.

'I just want to look at your breasts,' he says, after breaking away from the kiss. 'I swear I won't do anything to you.'

With a sweeping motion, he pulls her bodysuit down her shoulders, followed by her bra which he unclasps with adept hands. His breath is coming in short, ragged gasps, in tandem with his rising excitement. He holds her breasts in his hands, the soft globes of flesh and hardened nipples beckoning to him. Yandisa knows she should tell him to stop but when he starts sucking on one of her nipples, her protest sticks in her throat. Instead, she strokes his smooth, shaven head, running her hands gently down his back. His hands are soon all over her body and she feels them tugging at the waistband of her skirt.

'Don't!' she says, her eyes fluttering open.

'I just want to look at you,' he says seductively.

He cups her face in his hands. 'We don't have to do anything you don't want to do. Trust me, baby. I won't do anything you don't want me to do.'

He melts away any further anxiety with the dreamy look on his face and so Yandisa allows him to undress her. As he pulls her skirt down, together with her white, cotton panties she feels the last vestige of her resolve slip away. She is naked and feels extremely vulnerable but his touch is reassuring, as are his words.

'You are so beautiful,' he tells her over and over again. 'I have never seen such beauty in my life.'

Yandisa glows in his praise as his eyes devour her hungrily before his lips follow.

'Don't you want to see me naked too?' he asks her.

Yandisa acquiesces. It should be alright, she thinks to herself, especially because she is stark naked. With trembling hands, she helps him undress and they lie down on the carpeted floor, naked beside each other. She loves the feel of him next to her and thinks how nice it would be if they could be like this forever.

'Yandisa, I want you,' he says, moving a lone braid from her face.

'No, Marshall!' she replies, sounding panicked. 'I don't want to have sex with you.'

'Yandisa, what are you afraid of? I know you *want* it!'

'Marshall, I'm just not ready,' she says, sitting up. The cloudiness in her head is slowly starting to dissipate and she reaches for the closest item of her clothing. She feels Marshall's arms around her waist and he pulls her back down, kissing her neck, her earlobes and her mouth, silencing any protestations she has. He kisses the length of her body, leaving a trail of warm, wet kisses to her belly button. Then, without warning, he lowers his head between her legs and she feels his tongue lapping at her. His slow measured strokes leave her panting. As he kisses and caresses her private place, Yandisa feels herself overtaken by feelings she didn't even know existed. She is lost in a whirlwind of sensations sweeping through her body as Marshall's tongue arouses her to a feverish pitch. She feels like shooting stars are exploding in her head and she is writhing with pleasure, groaning with ecstasy. But the groans turn into screams as he starts to force himself inside her.

'Marshall! No! No!' she shouts.

Marshall covers her mouth with his hand and pushes all the way inside her.

'It's going to hurt for a little while then it will be okay,' he whispers in her ear.

He continues to thrust into her, forging his way past any resistance. She writhes beneath him, struggling to get free but his huge, muscled body pinions her to the floor. She is prisoned by his passion to fulfil his desire which abates after he has thrust himself into a frenzied orgasm. Physically spent, he collapses onto her limp body.

'Aaaggh baby,' he sighs, 'that was beautiful.'

He kisses her on the lips but she is non-responsive. His smile is immediately extinguished by the staid expression on her face.

'Come on now, sweetie. Tell me you enjoyed it too,' he urges her.

'Get off me,' she says brusquely. 'Just get off.'

'Hey baby, come on now.'

'I said get off me. Get your bloody body off me!'

She is almost hysterical and he's worried she might start

screaming. The last thing he needs is the neighbours descending on them and so he complies with her request and they get dressed in silence. Then he drives her home, in silence. It's only when they are parked outside the gate that she speaks. Her eyes are wet with tears, filled with sadness.

'Oh God. Tell me this didn't just happen,' she whimpers.

He doesn't say anything in response. She knows the answer to her half-hearted attempt at a question and is enveloped with a feeling of loss.

'How could you, Marshall? You raped me!' she shouts.

He stares at her and realises she is teetering on the verge of hysteria again. What has he got himself into? What if she goes to the police and cries rape?

'I didn't rape you,' he replies calmly. 'You wanted this!'

'No, I didn't. I told you to stop. I said no,' she tells him calmly.

'Yandisa, I didn't rape you. We had sex and you wanted it as much as I did. You came to my house. You took off your clothes. If you go to the police and tell them it was rape who do you think they will believe?'

He lets the question linger in the air.

'You raped me,' she croaks.

'No, baby girl. I made love to you. We made love. The first cut is the deepest.'

Yandisa stares at him with deep loathing. She wants to scratch his face and leave deep welts in his cheeks.

'Forget about the police. Just forget this whole thing happened,' he tells her.

Yandisa climbs out of his car and slams the door so hard the windows vibrate. She will never be able to forget this. Never. She has sobered up to the reality of a very painful situation.

Sleep is elusive that night. Every time she closes her eyes, images of what happened in Marshall's house play over and over and she tries to reorganise the scene so that it has a different outcome. She always knew she would lose her virginity one day but this isn't how she imagined it. She was supposed to feel cosseted and loved, not disrespected and violated. She eventually succumbs to a fitful sleep but is roused by her mother's persistent screaming.

'Wake up, Yandisa. You'll be late for church,' she shouts.

'I don't want to go to church,' Yandisa shouts back through her closed bedroom door.

'You *are* going to church,' her mother says insistently.

Reluctantly, Yandisa clambers out of bed and heads to the bathroom. When she removes her bloodstained panties, she is assailed with the trauma of the previous day. She sits in the bath, soaping her body over and over, almost as if she is trying to wash away any evidence of Marshall. Loud, gut-wrenching sobs reverberate through her entire being. She doesn't know how long she stays like that but when she hears her mother call out she knows it's time to get out, dry herself and gather herself. She downs several painkillers with her orange juice when she goes downstairs.

Yandisa finds herself starting to doze off in church but her father's sermon about fornicators and adulterers keeps jolting her awake. In an impassioned voice, he implores each congregant to treat their body like a temple for the Lord and not a playground for the Devil. The Kingdom's congregation is still small but everyone stands and gives Abraham a rapturous applause.

'My closing words today are to forget the lust of the flesh and give yourself fully unto the Lord or the fires of hell and damnation will consume you.' He shuts the Bible and leads everyone in prayer.

Yandisa feels like she has gone to hell and back and goes to bed every night feeling miserable and wakes up with misery beside her. Every time she thinks of Marshall, fresh tears form and wet her face once again. What fuels her anguish even more is that he never calls her. It's not that she wants to talk to him, she wants him to call and apologise. To express some shame about his actions but she has been discarded like a piece of rubbish. His silence communicates so much and the days drag interminably, stretching out her pain. In class, she is often distracted and can't concentrate on the tasks at hand. She desperately wants to confide in Dumile and Towanda when they ask about Marshall but she can't bring herself to. Her depression mounts and she feels like she is going through life in a daze.

'Yandisa, are you alright?' her mother asks her one day, a few weeks later.

'No, I'm not alright,' says Yandisa.

'What's wrong?' asks Phumla, realising that whatever Yandisa is about to tell her is more important than peeling the potatoes for dinner.

'Come sweetie, you can tell me. If you can't tell your own mother, who can you tell?' Phumla pulls Yandisa into her arms and she starts to thaw in her mother's warm embrace. Her mother hasn't held her like this for years and she starts to cry. She wants to tell her mother the truth but she can't find the right words. They are stuck in her throat and as her mother squeezes her tighter, the harder she cries.

'It's okay, my baby,' says Phumla, soothingly.

She feels bad for not taking time to sit down with Yandisa. They are constantly fighting about boyfriends and her prolonged absences from home and when she is home, she spends the time locked in her room, playing loud music.

'I am sorry I haven't been there for you,' her mother says gently.

'It's not that,' says Yandisa, lifting up her face and looking at her mother. She has to pull herself together. 'I just haven't been feeling well.'

That night Yandisa sleeps in her mother's bed since Abraham is away on a business trip and Phumla had decided not to accompany him. Yandisa still can't bring herself to confide in her mother and Phumla doesn't push her. But for those few hours, Yandisa feels safe lying close to her mother. She wants to lie there forever and dreams about herself as a little girl playing with carefree abandon, of running to mommy to kiss and make everything better.

When the dawn of a new day is upon her, Yandisa realises the innocence of her childhood is gone forever and in its place is the bittersweet taste of adulthood. She has to face the trials and tribulations that await.

THE LAST SUPPER

The last supper is going to be small and intimate. After the mêlée of the wedding, things in the Mafu household have quietened down considerably. Xoliswa is the last of the wedding guests still in the house. Strangely enough, she does feel like a guest in her own home maybe because she hasn't lived there for years. Nonetheless, she doesn't get to enjoy guest privileges because every morning she oversees things at her father's construction business. He owns commercial space on Fife Street, some of which has been converted into the company offices while the rest has been let out for retail use. Although she has only spent a week in the office, Xoliswa can see the books are in a mess, what with her father trying to juggle the church and the business as best he can. Abraham has started holding three services a day, one in the morning, one in the afternoon and one in the evenings and calls it the 'balanced spiritual diet'. During the day, Phumla visits sick people in hospital and offers prayers or counselling to members of the church who are having a tough time or need some spiritual guidance. But without Abraham's daily guidance and involvement, the business is starting to flounder. The small team of staff, made up of a bookkeeper, quantity surveyor, project manager and receptionist, are all slacking off in his absence. They need the direction of Abraham, who is never there most of the time.

The company isn't really canvassing for new business yet they are maintaining the same overheads. Xoliswa finds herself mulling over things that can be done to take the company's vision further and increase turnover. She never gets a chance to discuss any of it with her father though because she hardly ever sees him. Church business often runs into the night so she hopes that the last family supper might give her a chance to deliberate the business with him. But deep down she knows her father is becoming more and more disinterested and the business is taking the backseat to his newfound love affair with the church.

That day she had gone into the office for the last time to say her goodbyes. The staff were visibly miffed that she is leaving and bought her a bunch of flowers to show their appreciation. She also feels sad to be leaving because she enjoyed being in the driver's seat.

The future of the company remains at the forefront of her mind that evening as she cooks all her traditional favourites for dinner that night. It will be a long time before her palate tastes creamed pumpkin leaves, road-runner chicken, stewed tripe, pork trotters and *isitshwala samabele* again.

Sis Ntombi and Uncle Ben are the first to arrive and before he is even offered a seat, Uncle Ben asks for a whisky and soda. Sis Ntombi gives him a withering look of disapproval but he ignores her. Xoliswa serves him out on the patio, where he is sitting cross-legged waiting for the rest of the family to arrive. Sis Ntombi follows the food aromas into the kitchen, confirming that Xoliswa is definitely ready for marriage.

'Is there anything I can help you with?' asks Sis Ntombi, peering into the pots.

'I have everything under control,' replies Xoliswa smoothly.

She has been cooking since she got home from the office and has enlisted the help of Sis May to chop vegetables and wash dishes. She is a seasoned cook, having finessed the art preparing meals for Thulani over the years. Without prompting, Sis Ntombi pulls out a chair and sits down. Xoliswa pours her a glass of Mazoe Orange juice adding ice cubes, just as she likes it. Sis Ntombi sits down next to the fan and complains about how hot it is.

'Why don't you join uncle outside on the patio? It's much cooler there,' suggests Xoliswa.

'Oh no,' replies Sis Ntombi. 'I *really* want to talk to you. We didn't get a chance with all the drama of the wedding and you have been so busy at the office.'

Xoliswa's busy-ness has been deliberate and intentional; she had wanted to steer clear of her aunt.

'How is Thulani? I thought he was going to come down for the wedding,' her aunt asks.

'He had work assignments that he couldn't get out of,' Xoliswa replies, sounding vague.

'*Uthini*? What is he saying about you two? It's been years.'

'He is not saying anything, Auntie,' says Xoliswa curtly.

'Well, aren't you worried?' Sis Ntombi shoots back.

Xoliswa stops stirring the pot of trotters and looks at her aunt.

'Well, what would you have me do, Auntie? Propose marriage?'

'Well, yes. You make it seem like a bad idea. I mean after all these years are you saying you haven't even raised the issue? What are you waiting for?'

The doorbell rings and Xoliswa excuses herself, pleased to have a reason to cut the conversation short with Sis Ntombi. Sis Lungile has arrived and the aunt and niece hug and kiss one another hello. Sis Lungile joins Xoliswa and Sis Ntombi in the kitchen and unlike her sister who steers clear of alcohol, Sis Lungile pours herself a glass of Shiraz and joins in the conversation that Sis Ntombi continues with Xoliswa.

'Fall pregnant if he is not proposing,' suggests Aunt Lungile. 'It works like a charm.'

Sis Ntombi eyes her circumspectly, 'You mean the way it worked with Yandisa?'

'*That* was different,' says Sis Lungile, not quite sure how her sister can draw parallels between the two situations.

'Please. We don't want the embarrassment,' says Sis Ntombi acidly.

Sis Ntombi hasn't forgotten the humiliation the family had to endure when Yandisa had fallen pregnant and vividly remembers the day they all found out. Abraham had been delirious with rage and his sisters had tried, albeit unsuccessfully, to try calm him down, assuring him that everything would work out for the best. He had recently started his ministry when Yandisa announced her pregnancy with a great sense of apathy and disinterest.

'We'll marry her off and it will be okay,' says Sis Ntombi reassuringly.

'Marry her off? She is fifteen, for fuck's sake!' Abraham roared at his sister.

'Well, what other choice do we have?' counters Sis Lungile.

'How could this have happened? How?' Abraham raged.

All eyes on the room fall on Phumla and she jumps to her feet.

'How is this *my* fault?' she responds to the unspoken implication of blame.

'You are too lax with those girls!' screeches Sis Ntombi. 'They do whatever they want, when they want. Are you surprised this has happened?'

'*Uyaxoka*, sisi!' says Phumla, switching to Xhosa which she often did when she's angry, the English language incapable of truly conveying her ire.

Sis Ntombi wags a finger at her, 'You're a bad mother. This happened under your watch!'

Like two bulls in a kraal, they stand facing each other, their bountiful bosoms heaving with anger.

'That's enough,' says Abraham coming between them, acting like a spray of water to douse the flames of their burning antagonism.

'Yandisa is our child. We are all responsible and let's handle this matter like adults,' he says calmly.

An agreement is then reached that Sis Ntombi and Sis Lungile will escort Yandisa to the home of the man who is responsible for impregnating her. The next day when they pull up at the driveway of the house in Khumalo, Sis Ntombi is visibly impressed.

'At least he has money. I would have been mortified if you had wasted yourself on a nobody,' she says to Yandisa.

Sis Lungile buzzes the intercom and the gates part to let them in. They park the car next to a Polo and a Mercedes Benz that are already parked in the driveway. A coloured woman with curly tousled hair comes out to greet them. She is gracious in her manner and invites them into the house. They are ushered into the living room, where they are settled in gold-gilded and tapestry-upholstered armchairs. Sis Ntombi's eyes dart around the room, taking note of the décor, seeing what she could possibly replicate in her own home.

'What did you say he does for a living?' Sis Ntombi asks Yandisa.

'He's a businessman,' replies Yandisa disinterestedly.

'Whatever business he is in, it's a good one,' Sis Lungile adds.

At that moment the woman who greeted them when they arrived returns with a jug of Malawian shandy which she distributes between the glasses that have been placed on the table. Sis Ntombi complains that the juice is too sweet and asks for plain old Mazoe Orange juice. Marshall suddenly appears in the doorway, settles himself into an armchair and the lady excuses herself, giving them privacy.

'How can I help you ladies?' he says to them all.

'My name is Mrs Ntombi Ntini,' Sis Ntombi begins. 'I am here with my niece, Yandisa. I'll cut to the chase. She is pregnant and she says you fathered her child. And we believe you are responsible. Do you have any carnal knowledge of her?'

For the first time since they arrived, Yandisa lifts her head and looks Marshall in the eyes. As her big brown eyes fall upon him, Marshall casts his eyes aside. He feels nothing but awkwardness in that moment. Yandisa is really a sweet girl. Soft and pliable, she was always eager to please him. He had taken advantage of her easy trusting nature and the only thing she is guilty of is being naïve. She was a pawn in a game that she was too young to understand. He exhales noisily.

'I know Yandisa. I gave her a lift home once but I don't know what she's talking about with this child thing.'

Yandisa's face falls, as does her dignity. Sis Ntombi and Sis Lungile can't mask their horror at his response.

'Marshall! You raped me!' screams Yandisa.

'I did no such thing,' he replies calmly, 'Listen ladies, I have a beautiful wife and we are expecting our first child. Why would I go around raping young girls?'

'Why would she lie?' counters Sis Lungile.

Marshall shrugs his shoulders, 'She's your niece. Ask her.'

'Let's go,' says Sis Ntombi, hoping to avoid further embarrassment. 'Apologies for wasting your time,' she says to Marshall.

Sis Ntombi cusses Yandisa all the way to the car and tries to catch her breath between each insult. Yandisa is crying uncontrollably and Sis Lungile desperately tries to placate her but fails miserably.

'Do you even know who the father is?' shouts Sis Ntombi.

'Stop that, sisi. That's enough,' chastens Sis Lungile. 'We don't need to traumatise her any further.'

'How is she traumatised? She is the one who opened her legs!'

'She is a child! That man took advantage of her!' responds Sis Lungile.

'You believe that nonsense? She is loose! Yandisa is loose, just like her mother!'

Sis Ntombi revs the car, drowning out Yandisa's uncontrollable sobbing. They have an unclaimed pregnancy on their hands which they have to explain to Abraham.

'She should just abort the baby,' says Sis Ntombi to her sister, ignoring Yandisa. 'I know a doctor who can take care of it.'

'You think Phumla will agree to that?' counters Sis Lungile.

'Who cares what Phumla thinks? Abraham has just opened a church, he doesn't need this embarrassment.'

When Abraham's sisters tell him what happened, his blood boils with rage until his blood pressure reaches an unprecedented high and he has to briefly be taken to the hospital. He is insistent the man be arrested because Yandisa is underage. Sis Ntombi also insists that the scandal will not do the family any good, especially at a time like this. She suggests an abortion which Phumla vehemently refuses.

'We are church people!' she says with righteous indignation.

'You've been church people for two minutes!' spits Sis Ntombi. 'Let her abort and start her life with a clean slate!'

'No,' hisses Phumla. 'I will raise the child as mine if I have to. Yandisa can go and stay with Sis Lungile in Harare until the child is born. When she comes back after giving birth it will be like nothing ever happened.'

It was not uncommon for children to be 'adopted' by other members of the family. If anyone were to ask, they would simply say Yandisa had transferred to another school in Harare. That she simply was not enjoying the school she had been attending.

'I'm fine with that,' says Sis Lungile siding with Phumla, much to her sister's disdain.

And so the fate of the unborn child was sealed that day and a scandal is averted. None were any wiser when Phumla entered church a few months later cradling an infant in her arms. 'Our miracle baby,' her and Abraham had declared to their congregation, raising the little girl up in the baptismal service. They had adopted a child who had been abandoned by its mother, was the story they peddled around. Like Moses, who had sailed into the arms of the Egyptians, baby Babalwa Bianca Mafu had sailed into their arms. And just like her name, they considered her a blessing.

Sis Ntombi is brought back from her thoughts when Sis Lungile says to her, 'This is completely different, 'Xoliswa is *almost* thirty. She can have a child of her own if she wants.'

Sis Ntombi exhales deeply, 'Best before thirty. If you don't get married now, Xoliswa, I'm afraid you've missed the boat. Give Thulani an ultimatum or, like your aunt suggests, fall pregnant. You might be able to fast-track your way into marriage that way.'

The temperature in the kitchen is raised and Xoliswa feels hot and clammy.

'I need to shower before everyone else gets here!' she says to her aunts.

She feels refreshed after her shower and when she walks out the bathroom, she hears her mother and Yandisa having a noisy confrontation in Yandisa's bedroom. The door is open so she can hear the entire conversation and can see her sister and her mother sitting next to each other on the bed.

'So you are going to leave just like that?' Phumla says to Yandisa, less as a question and more of a statement.

'You heard Dad! You were standing by his side when he kicked me out of his house!'

'Yandisa, I've tried. I try to stand by you but you always let yourself down! You're a disaster waiting to happen! Why can't you be more like your sisters? *Why*?'

Xoliswa can imagine her mother throwing her hands up in the air in resignation and Yandisa rolling her eyes at her. They have entered the familiar territory where Yandisa is forever compared to Xoliswa and Zandile. They are the blueprint for perfect daughtership while Yandisa is the delinquent in the family.

'Mom, why can't you accept me for who I am? I will never be like Xoliswa or Zandile!' Yandisa shouts.

Phumla responds brusquely, 'Because this is not who you are. You are better than this, Yandisa. You could be so much more but instead you choose to waste what you have and what you could be!'

'In your eyes, I will *never* be good enough!' Yandisa responds.

'You could be if you tried, Yandisa but you don't even try. Every day I look at you and wonder where your father and I went wrong. We have given you everything but you have thrown it all in our faces.'

'Mama, I am not going to listen to this any more.'

Yandisa continues throwing things haphazardly into her suitcase which is wide open on the bed. Phumla stares at her for a long time, shaking her head and finally walks out of the room, almost colliding into Xoliswa who is standing in the doorway.

'Talk to your sister. Maybe you might be able to knock some sense into her head,' Phumla says offhandedly.

Tentatively, Xoliswa enters the room as if she is walking on eggshells; she doesn't want to cause any further upset. She tightens her gown around her waist before settling on Yandisa's rumpled bed. Her younger sister doesn't acknowledge her presence but walks around her and pulls some dresses out of the cupboard and throws them into her suitcase.

'I really wish you wouldn't leave like this,' says Xoliswa.

'What other choice do I have? I am tired of being treated like a fourth-class citizen!' exclaims Yandisa.

'Yandisa, how about you behave responsibly and maybe then *uBaba* will treat you with more respect?' scolds Xoliswa.

Yandisa side-eyes her, 'What would you know, Xolie? You've been gone for six years!'

Xoliswa takes a deep breath and decides to approach the conversation from a different angle.

'So have you found a place to stay?' she asks, sounding concerned.

'I'll be staying with Wesley. Not that it's any of your business,' Yandisa responds aggressively.

Xoliswa exhales loudly, 'Do you think that's a good idea? Moving in with Wesley? Don't you think you should wait until things are a bit more serious between the two of you?'

Yandisa stops packing and turns to face her sister.

'That's rich coming from you. *Konje!* How many years have you and Thulani been living in sin?'

'That's different and you know it,' says Xoliswa.

'How is it different, Xolie? Why don't you get off your high horse for a second! What am I doing that is any different from what you are doing?'

'Yandisa, I *know* Wesley. He has been womanising since I was in high school. How long have you been together? Two months or is it four? Do you even think this thing is going to last?'

'It's six months but anyway … *asikho lapho*,' says Yandisa flippantly.

Xoliswa stands up, wringing her hands.

'And Babalwa?' she adds.

'What about her?' snaps Yandisa.

'Yandisa, don't you feel any sense of responsibility towards her? She is *your* daughter!'

Yandisa stares at her sister long and hard as if she is evaluating her for the first time.

'Don't judge me, Xolie. Don't you dare sit there and judge me!'

Xoliswa lifts her hands in resignation; 'Okay Yandisa. It's your life. You know best.'

'Yes, it is and stay the fuck out of it,' Yandisa says in response.

Xoliswa exits the room much faster than how she entered and goes to her room, gets dressed and presents herself to the rest of the family outside on the patio. Phumla is comfortably ensconced in a rocking chair and Babalwa is sitting on her lap. Her father is seated beside Uncle Ben.

'There you are!' says her father as she walks outside, his face beaming with untold pride. 'We were wondering what was holding you up! Is dinner ready yet? I'm starving.'

'Sorry, Daddy. I had no idea you were home yet.'

'Well, I told everyone at church that I had to rush home because it is my daughter's last night. Everyone understood,' explains Abraham.

'Well, everything is ready,' Xoliswa says, inviting everyone to the dining room.

The regal ten-seater table is set with fancy napkins, gold cutlery and a candelabra as the centrepiece. The chair for Yandisa remains unoccupied.

'Isn't she joining us?' asks Sis Ntombi, indicating the space at the table.

'No, I'm not,' says Yandisa, standing in the archway, two suitcases at her feet.

Sis Ntombi looks to Sis Lungile; both are puzzled.

'I'm leaving,' states Yandisa.

'Yandisa, why don't you stay for dinner,' says Xoliswa, trying to placate her. 'I've already cooked.'

She pats the empty chair beside her, indicating that there is space for Yandisa at the table. That there is still space for her in the family.

A hooter suddenly sounds outside and blares for what is a lot longer than necessary. Yandisa waves goodbye before wheeling the suitcases out the door and the heavy oak front door closes behind her. An uncomfortable silence hangs over the table and Abraham's low baritone voice eventually breaks it.

'Let's put our hands together and say grace.'

They hold hands and Abraham prays for the gift of family. He thanks the Lord for Xoliswa and her presence these past few days and asks the Lord to watch over Yandisa. He says that she is a lost sheep and that all lost sheep eventually find their way home. He concludes the prayer with an 'Amen' and the rest of the table repeat it in unison.

A FOOL'S PARADISE

The journey to what Xoliswa now considers home has been a long and arduous one. Such is the conflict of being a transnational, of having to navigate between your motherland and step-motherland. In the British Virgin Islands there are distinct divisions between the belongers and non-belongers yet, despite not having her citizenship, she still feels some sense of belonging, having lived there for the past six years. The islanders are warm and friendly and you can hear the cheer in people's voices when they greet one another. There is also that familiarity that comes with living in a country with a small population of less than thirty thousand people where it feels like everybody knows everyone. It feels the same in Bulawayo where it feels intimate and almost incestuous at times.

As she drives to the dingy Bulawayo airport, Xoliswa is very aware of all the shortcomings in her hometown. She is frustrated by the lack of development and it feels like she is taking a step back in time. Aside from the new Bulawayo Centre shopping mall on Fort Street, everything is exactly the same, just as she had left it six years ago. She couldn't understand Yandisa's excitement about the mall when they had gone to lunch at Walkers Pub and she found the prices astronomical and the service appalling. Comparing it to other malls she had shopped at all over the world, it is underwhelming but for Bulawayo it is a major feat. Everyone wants to meet there, eat there and be seen there and she's sure if she hadn't been exposed to anything else she would also be awestruck by it all. But there is something comfortable and familiar about Bulawayo, in all its backwardness. Something she can't put her finger on, yet it tugs at her heartstrings with a quiet persistence and makes her deeply sad about leaving.

The whole family congregated at the airport to say goodbye. Phumla cried uncontrollably, teetering on the verge of hysteria while Abraham managed to contain his own tears and focused on comforting his wife instead. Xoliswa hadn't been unable to hold back her tears. Babalwa cried because it seemed like the appropriate thing to do but she felt very little attachment to her Aunt Xoliswa.

Their faces were a hazy blur as they parted at the immigration gate. They gathered on the flight deck to watch her board and frantically waved and called her name as she walked towards the plane. The Air Zimbabwe aeroplanes all displayed a gold 'Great Zimbabwe bird' at the centre of its black tail fin and yellow, red and green triple stripes on its stern. Xoliswa remembers her social studies teacher at school going to great lengths to teach them what the colours represented.

Black symbolises the majority of the people in the country, even though it always seemed as if white people outnumbered them. Red is to commemorate the blood that was shed during the liberation struggle, with many of the war veterans holding high-ranking positions in the government or army. Yellow symbolises the country's mineral wealth which was being exploited by multinationals such as Anglo American. Green is symbolic of the land and the vegetation; an agrarian country that is known as the 'breadbasket of Africa'. The land issue dominated the headlines at the time as war veterans were demanding to be compensated for their role in liberating the country. Finally, the white is for hope and peace and the mantle worn by most Zimbabweans with pride, as a peace-loving nation.

As Xoliswa steps onto the plane, she reflects how proud she is of her country and how proud she is to say that she is Zimbabwean, no matter where she is in the world. Even though most people aren't familiar with the landlocked entity in Southern Africa. As the plane taxies down the runway, so do the tears rolling down her cheeks. The plane soars into the air leaving Bulawayo behind and soon her trip home will be just another memory.

The flight from Bulawayo to Harare is short and uneventful and forty minutes later they land at the Harare International Airport. Xoliswa checks in to catch her connecting flight to South Africa's cosmopolitan capital, Johannesburg, where she has arranged to spend a night catching up with her old high school friends Natasha and Mpho, who now both reside there. Rutendo, the fourth friend of their group lives in the United Kingdom. They had been a formidable foursome since high school but are now separated by geography. Over tall, elegant, pink cocktails they appraise each other about the highlights of their lives, trying to illuminate stories they've shared over email or on the phone.

'So, I hear your sister is dating Wesley,' says Natasha, as they peruse the menu.

Xoliswa shakes her head, 'I know! Shocking, right? I don't think it'll last.'

Mpho exhales deeply, 'I can't believe after all these years Wesley is *still* in Bulawayo, whoring.'

'Where else would he go?' says Natasha flippantly, fingering a gigantic diamond on her finger that dazzles in the light.

'Well, I'm so glad you met Busang and I'm so happy you have moved on from the whole Wesley thing,' says Xoliswa.

'It took me long enough,' laughs Natasha, 'but it was only after Wesley that I learned to appreciate the love of a good man.'

'And you, *mngane*? Any progress with Thulani?' asks Mpho, changing the subject.

Thulani and her met after high school when they were both serving their articles at the same auditing firm. Their attraction was instant-aneous, even though she played hard to get and only agreed to go out with him a year after they met. Xoliswa lost her virginity in the second year of their relationship at the time they were auditing a firm in Hwange. By then, Thulani had moved out of home and shared a flat in town with two of his mates. Xoliswa had been a regular visitor, often concocting lies to her parents about working out of town so she could spend the night in Thulani's arms making hot, passionate love. When they both qualified, they agreed that going overseas was the logical next step in their careers and so moving in together seemed like the logical step in their relationship. They relocated to the British Virgin Islands but of course no one back home knew about their living arrangements. Cohabitation might have been acceptable in other cultures but in theirs it was unpalatable and terms such as 'ukutshayamapoto' were used to describe couples who lived together without the marriage certificate. As much as their culture frowned up on it, so too did their religion with the term 'living in sin' used to label couples. They shoved all those undesirable phrases aside because they were in agreement that they were in a serious relationship which would one day culminate in marriage.

There had been little time to travel home and their hectic careers meant that whatever time they had, they used to travel the world together. They had been to countless countries and cities including London, Rome, Paris, Moscow, Sydney, Kuala Lumpur and Singapore. Xoliswa's only contact with home had been photographs and lengthy one-hour phone calls. Calls that so-and-so died or so-and-so had had a baby. Photographs of Babalwa's first day at school. Babalwa losing her first teeth. Babalwa's birthday parties.

Life at home carried on while she was cocooned in a bubble of love on a remote island. Her and Thulani's was an idyllic love story that played out to the backdrop of tropical sunsets but that love seemed so remote and so removed from everything right now.

'I'm expecting him to pop the question any minute now!' Xoliswa says in response to Mpho's question.

Her answer is met with excited giggles and clapping of hands. Mpho is the only one in their clique who is married. She met her husband, Clive, at Rhodes University and they got married straight after graduation and have two children.

'How is Clive?' asks Xoliswa.

'He's great,' replies Mpho. 'My prayer is that you will all meet great men who will love and appreciate you,' she says to the group.

They clink their glasses together, toasting to a bright future. After dinner they go to a club and dance the night away. The following morning Xoliswa wakes up with a blistering hangover that she tries to nurse with a greasy breakfast. She avoids visiting any of her mom's relatives in Johannesburg as she had her fill of them at the wedding. Instead, she indulges her passion and goes shopping, buying Thulani a few T-shirts and a pair of shoes for herself. The dollar gives her more buying power against the rand so she marvels at how 'cheap' things are. Like Bulawayo, the British Virgin Islands don't have large shopping malls and to get a similar kind of shopping experience she would need to fly to the US mainland, so she makes most of the experience before heading back to the airport. Fifteen hours later she lands at JFK in New York and has to catch another connecting flight to Puerto Rico, adding an additional four hours to her journey. She managed to sleep on the plane to New York, even though travelling economy class doesn't offer much in the way of comfort. Travelling home has almost bankrupted her, what with the cost of the flights and all the other financial contributions she made towards the wedding in addition to her parents' upkeep. She could never have just arrived home and said, 'Folks, I'm home.'

She is going to spend the next three months paying off her credit card which she maxed out but despite this it had been so good to go home. As short-lived as her time there had been. She doesn't know when she'll be able to go again but she had loved being there for Zandile's wedding.

The last leg of her journey is a quick flight from San Juan to Tortola, the sleepy island that she calls home. Unlike the airbuses she has been on for the greater part of the journey, the smaller aircraft offers no cushion from the turbulence as they fly over the ocean. Not one to pray very often she recites 'Our Father who art in heaven' before they take off. No matter how many times she has caught a flight back to the island on a small plane, she never gets used to it and always feels like they are going to fall out of the sky. She is glad when they disembark less than an hour later, aircraft intact.

Stepping out of the air-conditioned airport she is greeted by the uncompromising duo of heat and humidity. But it can't rival the heat of Thulani's embrace as he draws her into his arms. Even after all these years he can send her heart catapulting and give her butterflies. She inhales the familiar scent of his cologne, a combination of bergamot, citrus. She really missed him and even though she has only been gone nine days it felt like nine months.

They leave the airport in the sporty jeep that they drive around the island, ideal to navigate the steep roads. The one thing she had missed was driving along the coastline with an unrestrained view of the ocean and because it's Sunday morning, she's just in time for their ritual of Sunday brunch and curling up in Thulani's arms afterwards. He takes her to the Tamarind Club, one of their favourite hangouts and a mixture of locals and tourists alike and the live performances always give the place a nice Sunday vibe. Xoliswa orders a concho stew steaming with shrimp and crabs. With seafood such a rarity in Bulawayo, her palate had missed the flavours. Thulani is having a chicken quesadilla and complaining about how much he missed her home cooking.

'Navigating the kitchen was a nightmare so I mostly ate out and Susie and Jim invited me for supper so that was great,' he tells her.

Susie and Jim are part of the expat community on the island, as are most of their friends. There are other Zimbabweans living on the island too and many nights have been spent together feeling nostalgic about 'home'.

'It feels good to be back,' says Xoliswa.

'How was home? How is your family?' asks Thulani.

She tells him that her parents are fine and then fills him in on all the family drama that transpired and culminated with Yandisa moving out.

'Can you believe she is moving in with Wesley?!'

Thulani's jaw drops, 'You're kidding me!'

'I kid you not,' she replies with a grin on her face.

She regales him with stories about the wedding and then casually informs him that she had briefly visited his mom and siblings and that they seemed fine.

'Mom did call me after you visited and she wanted to know when I am coming home so I think I'm going to go next month.'

Xoliswa's heart sinks, 'Oh baby, I won't be able to come with you.'

He looks away, 'I think I need to do this trip alone, Xolie. It will be good to reconnect with my family, especially because I haven't seen any of them since Dad died.'

She reaches out and squeezes his hand. He hadn't made the trip to Bulawayo to bury his dad, he hadn't even gone home for the unveiling and that had been two years ago. His brother had sent the video which until today Thulani has never watched. There had been other funerals they hadn't attended, weddings they had missed. Videos that had been sent of such occasions. Such is the life of living abroad. They are exactly twenty-eight hours away from home and two thousand dollars away from getting there.

Thulani motions to the waiter and pays the bill. She can't wait to get home and had missed their three-bedroom apartment overlooking Road Harbour. She missed waking up to the sea breezes and Caribbean sunsets, the humming sound of ship horns and the green, leafy vistas and hilly terrain.

She'd even missed the sticky humidity, a welcome reprieve from the dry heat in Bulawayo. She had missed frolicking on the beach and the charmed life that comes with living on a tropical island but most of all she had missed Thulani.

The minute they walk through the door of their apartment, he closes it and pushes her against it. Then they are kissing with a searing passion that makes Xoliswa gasp. With one sweeping motion he pulls her dress over her head and throws it one side. He tenderly sucks her breasts while pulling down her G-string. Then he is kissing her all over, gently biting her, making her shriek with delight. In-between lip-smacking kisses and sensual touches his shirt and shorts come off with an eagerness that surprises them both. Buttons break. A bra snaps. He takes her on the floor, hard and fast, like an incensed warrior. She curls her legs around his buttocks, pulling him into her most intimate embrace, her nails clawing into his back with a need that overwhelms her. He pummels into her with wild abandon, driving into her familiar warmth. Her cries of pleasure fill his ears, igniting his passion even further. She is transported from the room into another realm beyond their heaving bodies, past the reality of the moment and her body explodes into a magical orgasm which tingles from her head to her toes. Afterwards, they lie panting, their hot, sticky bodies wedged together. They make love again before collapsing with exhaustion and succumbing to sleep.

The next morning Xoliswa wakes up, her hand feeling for Thulani's body that has already vacated the bed. She sits up with a start, the sun illuminating the room with a brilliant glow. She slides out of bed and puts on a silk gown which she fastens around her waist. Thulani is having his first cup of coffee out on the balcony overlooking the sea. That is how they begin each day. She slides her arms around him, hugging him from behind, the strong scent of arabica coffee infused with the spicy, peppery notes of his cologne.

'Did you sleep well?' he asks, turning in the circle of her arms.

'I slept like a log,' she responds.

They kiss briefly before he withdraws from her arms. Rather too quickly she thinks to herself but dismisses the feeling. She is being overly sensitive. She settles in the chair across from him and he returns to the kitchen to get her a cup of coffee and get a refill. He tells her

SUE NYATHI

he's going to leave for work in the next thirty minutes to avoid the morning congestion on the few large roads that carry the traffic on the island. She has taken an extra day off so as to ease herself back into the working week and give her body time to recuperate from the journey.

'You know, I've been thinking about us,' says Thulani, as he sits down.

Xoliswa's stomach rolls with apprehension. That is not how she imagined his marriage proposal would start. Nor did she imagine she'd have dishevelled hair, unbrushed teeth and be in her gown. But at least the sun shining down on the ocean behind them is a picturesque backdrop.

His brow is furrowed with anxiety and he again says, 'I've been thinking about us a lot. Me. You. I just can't do this any more.'

Xoliswa doesn't realise she has dropped her coffee mug until it hits the ground and shatters into smithereens. She then realises the hot coffee splashed her thighs and she gasps. Thulani lurches forward, looking concerned.

'Are you okay?' he asks her earnestly.

'No, I am not okay, Thulani. How could I be okay?' she shouts, much louder than she intended.

He runs into the house and returns with a paper towel and tries to blot her stained gown and wipe the floor.

'Leave it,' she says dismissively. 'I'll clean up the mess later.'

They stare at each other and there is an awkward silence. Xoliswa is hoping he is going to burst out laughing and say it is all a joke. That he's teasing her. But seconds pass which become minutes and the silence is unbearable.

'Fuck, this is hard,' he says, finally breaking the silence. 'I know you want to get married but I can't give you that. I don't even know if I want marriage and kids Xoliswa.'

He never calls her Xoliswa unless he is angry or very serious. Or about to break her heart. She is always Baby. Sweety. Lovey. Xolie. Never Xoliswa.

78

'I don't know how else to tell you this but I can't carry on like this. I can't,' he says.

Xoliswa clutches her head in her hands as if to calm the throbbing headache that has already developed. She holds back the tears that threaten to burst. She's not going to cry in front of him. He might be breaking her apart but she isn't going to break down in front of him. Her lower lip quivers, threatening to break her resolve.

'Xolie, I don't know how else to do this. To make it less painful. It's hard for me too you know.'

Unsure what to make of her silence he retreats into the house. She can hear him gathering his things but she's too dazed to move. Paralysed by the shock of his revelation. She hears the front door slam, giving her a start and stands up, her feet standing on the broken mug. Shards pierce her flesh and the tears come. She sobs loudly, without any restraint. How could this have happened? How could she have not sensed that there was going to be trouble in paradise?

WOUNDED SOULS

The smell of decaying food assails his nostrils and he wrinkles his nose in disgust at the dirty dishes piled high in the sink. He flings open the fridge door and is dismayed to see a lone slice of cheese, furry around the edges and, save for the reeking carton of milk, long surpassed its best before date, there is no sign of anything edible. He slams the door in frustration and as he marches out of the kitchen he notices the dirt-stained tile floor that hasn't seen a mop for weeks.

People have often accused him of living like a pig but Yandisa has truly turned his home into a pigsty since she moved in a month ago. Initially, he was excited at the prospect of having her sharing his space, having access to her twenty-four hours a day, seven days a week but living with her has exposed him to aspects of her personality he now wishes he never knew.

'Yandisa!' he shouts, as he frogmarches down the short passage to their bedroom.

He finds Yandisa outstretched on the unmade bed, fast asleep. He can't recall the last time he has seen the bed made and she doesn't even bother to change the sheets which are encrusted with sperm and other bodily fluids they've exchanged.

'Yandisa!' he shouts again, slapping her buttocks which wobble under his palm.

Perhaps if he was in a better frame of mind he might be turned on but he is highly irritated and notices for the first time she has put on a considerable amount of weight.

'Yandisa! It's way past seven. Aren't we eating? When was the last time you cooked or even bothered to clean this place?'

He is tired of eating thick Russian sausages accompanied by oily chips that coat your face and fingers as you eat and yearns for a steaming hot plate of *isitshwala*, fried chomolia and a juicy steak to go with it.

'Wesley, I'm sure there's some bread in the fridge. Fix yourself a sandwich. I'm tired.'

Wesley feels a wave of aggravation rise like bile and he slams his clenched fist into Yandisa's face. She yelps like a wounded dog.

'Get up! Get the fuck out of my bed and cook something!'

'Why did you hit me?' she cries out, cowering at the corner of the bed, rubbing her cheek.

'I asked you to do something and I want it done now, Yandisa.'

'You have no fucking right to hit me, Wesley!' she shouts back at him.

Wesley scrambles onto the bed like an enraged bulldog and rains down another blow on Yandisa's face.

'This is my house. If you don't like it here then you can get out. I won't stand for this bullshit!' he says, almost in a frenzy.

She doesn't respond and continues rubbing the throbbing pain now on both sides of her face. Wesley reaches into his pockets and throws a wad of money at her and orders her to go and buy some food.

'Can I have the car keys?' she asks in a small voice.

'You can walk, Yandisa. You need the exercise.'

Yandisa hurriedly pulls on a dress and walks briskly to the 7-Eleven that is two blocks away. It is a cool and balmy night and the streets of Bulawayo are almost deserted, most people having vacated to their homes in the suburbs. As she walks, she can't contain her tears. Her sobs rouse a few beggars lying on the pavement but she doesn't care. By the time she arrives at the tiny supermarket, her eyes are red and swollen from crying. She throws random things into a trolley she thinks she might need: a 750-millilitre bottle of Olivine cooking oil, a 5-kilogram packet of Pearlenta MaizeMeal, a few packets of Royco soup, a pack of boerewors and a pre-packed steak. She buys some tomatoes and vegetables from vendors who are sitting outside the shop.

By the time she returns to the flat she is dry-eyed but her face is stinging and throbbing with pain. She catches sight of herself in the mirror in the lift and her cheek is swollen and red like an overripe tomato. Her head is pounding and she curses herself for not thinking to buy painkillers. Sour-faced and not uttering a word, she puts a meal together for Wesley while he lies on the worn-out suede couch, watching reruns of the Zimbabwe versus Egypt soccer match.

She hates cooking. Growing up she was able to get away with not cooking at all because Xoliswa or Zandile would prepare the meals, if the maid was not around. On the very rare occasions she was forced to cook, her family always complained about the mediocrity of her food anyway. She hated domestic duties in general and always found ways of dodging mundane household chores.

As she prepares the meal for Wesley, it is with very little confidence or interest in what she is doing but she does her best, fearing any reprisal from Wesley.

She finally serves the meal after the 8.30 pm news, taking the tray to him on the couch.

'Aren't you eating?' he asks, as he takes the plate from her.

'No,' she says and purses her lips.

'Why? What did you put in the food?'

Yandisa sighs, feeling exasperated: 'I'm not hungry, Wesley.'

'Come sit next to me,' he implores, patting the space next to him.

She is reluctant at first but then obliges him. He puts his arm around her.

'I'm sorry about hitting you. I lost my temper,' he says tenderly.

He kisses her on the cheek but she is unresponsive. He eats in silence and after a few mouthfuls, tells her the food is pretty good. She doesn't believe him. Especially after struggling to flatten the lumps in the *isitshwala*.

'Yandisa, it would be nice if you took care of this place. Clean up a bit, do the laundry,' he says, as he puts down his knife and fork.

'I'm not your maid, Wesley,' she retaliates.

'You know you are so fucking spoilt, Yandisa. So spoilt.'

'No, I'm not!' she protests. 'I just didn't grow up doing these things and there are people who are paid to do them!'

'My mother was a maid, Yandisa. You know that woman in your house who cleans up after you and washes your underwear? Well, that was my mother.'

Yandisa cringes with embarrassment and wishes she could take back her words but what has been said cannot be unsaid.

'Unlike you, Yandisa, I never had much. You grew up in a big house in the suburbs.'

Yandisa is confused. Wesley once drove her down Burnside Road and pointed out a double-storey home where he said he had lived most of his life. She can't recall if he ever explained why him and his family ended up moving out.

'I lived in the servant's quarters with my mother. On weekends when she was off, we went home to the location. Have you ever been to the locations, Yandisa?'

Yandisa shrugs her shoulders nonchalantly, 'No.'

She knows they have relatives from her father's side who live in the locations but she can't recall ever visiting them. They are the ones who always make the pilgrimage to their home and as far as she is concerned, they live in a different realm, far removed from hers. A world she prefers not to step into.

Wesley carries on. 'My mother wasn't always a maid. She used to be at home and look after me and my sisters, just the way all mothers should. I remember playing with Evelyn and Primrose and she would be there, watching over us. We lived in a small house, even smaller than this room.'

The tiny three-roomed matchbox house was where his earliest childhood memories were formed. There was a lounge and kitchen, equipped only with a stove, fridge and cabinet and two bedrooms.

83

The parents occupied one bedroom and random relatives occupied the other. The children, including cousins, all slept together in the lounge. Since they all lived in such close proximity to one another, Wesley was not spared from hearing his parents' sexual coupling or boisterous fighting when their father came home drunk. They would hear him singing, even before he entered the house, and knew he was going to beat them. No one was spared. When his father died, the noise died with him but they were stuck in a financial quagmire.

'You have no idea what it's like to be stuck, Yandisa. You have no idea what it feels like to wake up and suddenly have nothing. All your life you've had it easy and everything handed to you on a silver platter.'

Yandisa is quiet, waiting for him to continue but instead Wesley bursts out laughing. It is a deep, raucous laugh that comes from a painful place deep inside his soul. The laughter dies as quickly as it erupted. She wants to speak but he puts his hand over her mouth, silencing her.

'You see, my mother couldn't read or write. Her father didn't have the money to send her to school. Plus, because she was a woman, she would get married anyway so there was no use in her going to school. When my father died she had no way of holding the family together. He left a tiny pension which she used to pay off debts she never knew he had and the people from the court came and took everything until we were left with an empty shell of a house.'

Wesley is quiet for a long time, with a faraway look in his eyes. Yandisa reaches for his hand and squeezes it and the gesture prompts him to continue narrating the story of his impoverished past.

'Have you ever been to bed without anything to eat, Yandisa?'

'No,' Yandisa says solemnly.

'Well, I have. So many times. I would cry myself to sleep because I was so hungry and there was nothing my mother could do about it. In the beginning, we lived on handouts but those soon dried up.

I remember at one point we were so desperate we were eating mice. We would have eaten each other if it had carried on much longer. My mother eventually reached a point where she couldn't take it any longer and she strapped me on her back and went job-hunting.'

There is another pained silence.

'We walked because we couldn't afford to catch the bus. Sometimes we slept under trees and sometimes we slept outside petrol stations but day after day she knocked on people's doors, begging for work. And everywhere we went, we were chased away like dogs.'

He pauses to regain his composure, his cracking voice giving voice to the cracks in his soul. Yandisa extends her hand out to him. She wants to pull him into her embrace and comfort him but he shrugs her hand away.

'Don't pity me. I don't need your pity, Yandisa!'

'I'm not,' she wails.

'You think I'm dirt, don't you?'

'No, Wesley. I don't think that at all!'

His voice is devoid of any of the emotion he displayed a few minutes ago and instead he starts laughing derisively.

'Yandisa, I'm not one of those pretty, rich, little suburban boys you're used to. I am ghetto through and through!'

'I don't care what you are, Wesley. That's not why I am here!'

'Then why are you here?'

'Because I love you, Wesley.'

'You're just saying that, Yandisa. You're in love with the image. I've managed to fool a lot of people, I even had you fooled. I speak well, I act like one of you. Hey, I even play rugby. Do you know how I managed to fake these things? Do you know why?'

Yandisa shakes her head.

'Because some white old bastard decided to give my mother a job. He saw us and felt pity for us and that's how we came to live in the suburbs. Because old Granger felt sorry for us.'

He falls quiet again and looks visibly troubled, not sure whether he should continue.

'What happened to Granger?' asks Yandisa.

'The fucker is dead now,' replies Wesley acidly.

Yandisa is shocked. Surely he shouldn't be talking like that about someone who probably gave his family a new lease on life?

'Granger is dead and I'm glad,' Wesley continues. 'I learned some tough lessons from that man. He taught me nothing is *mahala* in this world. You see when Granger took us in, he made my mother work so hard for every cent he paid her. She was grateful for the work and glad to earn money to put food on the table and send my sisters to school. Then Granger took a liking to me. I was the good little black boy and he didn't have kids, you see. He was just this white pig living on his own. Granger sent me to school, he paid for my uniforms and everything else that goes with a private school education and for a while I couldn't believe my good fortune.'

Wesley's eyes sparkle as he speaks, radiating the hope and optimism he must have felt at the time.

'Here was this man doing everything for me. He was giving me the chance that my sisters were denied and I was determined not to screw it up so I worked hard. I wanted to prove to this man that I was worthy. He showed me a life that I never had and gave me a glimpse into the life that I hoped to have. He became the father I never had and there was even a time when I started resenting having to go back to the location. I hated being in that house, I hated the poverty. I wanted to splash around in Granger's pool and read books in his library. I was a good boy. Very good. At school I was top of my class and I played every sport I could. If there was a team, I was on it. That man gave me hope. Then just like that, he took it all away.'

There is another protracted silence as Wesley gathers his thoughts, re-arranging them in his head.

'One day while practising backstroke, Granger comes outside and stands at the edge of the pool and watches me. He encourages me. Then afterwards when I was changing in the pool house he came up behind me. Started touching me …'

His voice falters.

He doesn't finish the sentence.

He doesn't need to.

Yandisa instinctively puts her arms around him but he pushes her away.

'I made sure he never tried anything like that with me again. I beat him so hard that the blood vessels in his eyes burst and they had to take him away in an ambulance. I was lucky he didn't press charges but my mother lost her job and we were on the move again. This time we both went looking for jobs and I landed some apprentice job as a trainee mechanic. They showed me the ropes while on the job but of course I had to quit school. Couldn't afford it. My old coach encouraged me to continue playing and so I did. So yeah, I guess things have turned out okay.'

She puts her arms around him. This time he doesn't push her away and leans into her lovingly.

Strange as it seems, she feels closer to Wesley now than she ever has. She kisses him softly while her hands slide underneath his T-shirt and stroke his nipples. She comforts him the best way she knows how.

THE HONEYMOON

Walking into their hotel room, Zandile immediately sees the rose petals on the floor, leading from the doorway to the huge four-poster bed in the middle of the room. The staff have created a swan with the fluffy white towels and filled it with decadent chocolates and a complimentary bottle of champagne. Ndaba lays her down on the bed and pours the champagne down her breasts till it forms a path down the flat plane of her stomach and collects in her belly button. His lips follow the trail and he kisses her all over, his mouth lingering at her pelvic bone. She is breathing heavily, already on the verge of losing control.

'Can I taste you?' he asks, tugging at her G-string with his teeth.

'Ooooh yes,' she groans.

Ndaba laps at the honey between her legs and the tone is set for their honeymoon.

They spend an idyllic week in a private villa in Camps Bay overlooking the Atlantic Ocean. They enjoy long walks on the golden beaches that line the ocean. On one particular walk, they wade into the water, splashing each other like children. Zandile shrieks when she feels the cold water and Ndaba catches her in a passionate embrace to 'warm her up'. His eyes never leave hers while his fingers probe between her legs.

'How do you feel when I touch you like this?' asks Ndaba, huskily. 'I want you to tell me.'

Zandile steadies her breathing and closes her eyes, trying to find the words to articulate the sensations coursing through her body.

'You make me feel like I'm being poured with hot liquid and my whole body is being set on fire, slowly. It spreads through me … *aaggh* … right down to my *ummm* … toes and then I feel a rush and I go crazy because it feels soooo … *aaagggh* … good and I don't know what to do with myself because … *ummmm* … I'm so mad with wanting *ooooh* …'

Zandile doesn't manage to finish her sentence as her words are swept away in an orgasmic tide. Ndaba cups her buttocks and lifts her up until her legs are tight around his strong waist and her hands are around his neck. He shifts his manhood so he can ease himself into her and Zandile arches her back but looks around, feeling uneasy.

'No one will see us,' he reassures her, as he slides into her, the fiery warmth of her body in contrast to the coolness of the water. No one will see what is transpiring in the water but Zandile's face, suffused with joy and ecstasy gives it all away and he kisses her to muffle her cries of pleasure.

The nights are spent having dinner at quaint seaside restaurants and making love well into the night. They do the touristy things like go on a ferry and visit Robben Island, on a wine tasting in Franschhoek and catch the cable car up Table Mountain but the rest of the time they spend lying on the pool deck, soaking up the sun and relishing each other's company.

Even after they return home, they continue to behave like they are still on honeymoon and can't keep their hands off each other. The difference is that they no longer wake up to an ocean breeze or have the luxury of sleeping well into the day.

As per her aunt's strict instructions on her wedding day, Zandile gets up first every morning, reluctantly extricating herself from Ndaba's warm embrace and totters to the bathroom and gets in the shower. That particular morning she hears Ndaba come into the bathroom after her and he squeezes into the cubicle and stands behind her.

'Thanks for waking me up,' he teases.

'I didn't want to disturb you,' she says, smiling.

He reaches for the shower gel and squeezes some onto a sponge and lathers it onto her body. It foams to a creamy lather and he massages it on her neck, her breasts and her stomach and his hands stray between her thighs. She can feel his fingers stroking her and he knows he is pleasing her when he hears her purring with pleasure. Zandile is soaking wet and it was not just from the water alone. She can feel Ndaba's hard rod prodding into her buttocks and when she can't take it any more, she turns in the circle of his arms and kisses him. Their kiss deepens in its urgency and she wants to devour him. He lifts her up and she wraps her legs around him. He takes her in the shower, water spray all over their heaving bodies, a hazy image in the steaming shower.

When they emerge from the bathroom, they are both wearing smiles and the undeniable glow that only comes from glorious morning sex. Zandile sits at her dressing table and applies her make-up with proficient ease. She rubs a layer of Revlon Colorstay foundation into her skin and applies shimmer powder to her cheeks. With a steady hand, she applies eyeliner around the rims of her big brown eyes and eye shadow to her lids. All this adds to the undeniable glow that has formed an imaginary halo around her.

'I don't know why you wear all that make-up,' Ndaba remarks. 'You are already beautiful as you are.'

Zandile flashes him a radiant smile, 'I'm just enhancing what I have!'

'I prefer you without the make-up.'

'I'm not doing it for you. It's for me!' she protests.

He smothers her objections with a long, lingering kiss.

'Ndaba, we're going to be late for work!' chides Zandile as she feels her towel fall from around her breasts.

'You are just so irresistible!' he says. 'God, I love you!'

'I love you too,' she responds, staring at his reflection in the mirror.

He kisses her again before going to get dressed. She has already laid out his clothes on the bed: a pinstriped blue shirt and brown chinos but he complains that he doesn't like the tie she has chosen for him and goes to the wardrobe to pick out another one. Zandile meanwhile puts the last touches to her make-up and then puts on a blue silk blouse and a matching skirt.

While Ndaba is shining his shoes, she quickly rushes to the kitchen to make her husband breakfast. She never has much of an appetite early in the morning and it usually only shows up at around midday but Ndaba has a raging appetite when he wakes up, one that needs to be satisfied. She serves him fried chicken livers on toast and he gobbles it down with zest while she packs his lunch box with leftovers from the previous night's supper of lamb curry, rice and sambals. She doesn't pack herself a *skaftin* because she is meeting Yandisa for lunch. Ndaba and her drive to work together, chatting animatedly about inconsequential things. This is in sharp contrast to some couples in the traffic who are wearing morose faces and not talking or the ones arguing volubly, oblivious to anyone around them. Zandile hopes they never end up like that.

Ndaba drops her off, gives her a long, leisurely kiss and she wishes him a good day and he tells her he'll call her later. And he does. Three times before she leaves for lunch.

At lunchtime, she walks across the road to the Sisters restaurant at Haddon & Sly and when she arrives, Yandisa is already seated having a glass of rosé. They hug each other warmly before Zandile admonishes her sister about drinking in the afternoon.

'It's just one glass, Zandile. You act like I have committed murder,' says Yandisa cheekily. 'So what did you bring me from your honeymoon?'

Zandile immediately hands over a gift bag and Yandisa examines the contents excitedly, like a child opening presents on Christmas morning. She squeals delightedly when she sees the dresses that the gift bag contains and Zandile has to restrain her from rushing to the restaurant bathroom to try them on.

'I thought that with your active social life you might need

something nice to wear!' says Zandile with a naughty wink.

Yandisa hugs her sister with unrestrained gratitude and then settles back into her seat and starts to quiz her sister about the honeymoon.

'So, how's the sex life?' asks Yandisa knowingly.

'It's ama-zing!' replies Zandile. 'Damn, if I'd known sex was this good, I wouldn't have waited so long!' and insists she got more honey than she bargained for. They give each other a high-five across the table before exploding into laughter. This is cut short when a man, looking very prim and proper in his uniform, comes to their table to take their lunch orders.

'Lunch is on me, by the way, I have Ndaba's chequebook!' declares Zandile.

'Oh yes!' pronounces Yandisa. 'We must eat our brother's money!'

Yandisa quickly pages through the menu looking for the most expensive thing she can order while Zandile settles on a chicken salad which Yandisa declares is 'boring'. She orders a rack of ribs and specifically asks for an extra-large portion of chips to take home for Wesley.

'Are you going to eat all that?' asks Zandile, raising her eyebrows.

'Yes,' replies Yandisa unflinchingly.

Zandile fingers her two-carat diamond ring and contemplates telling Yandisa to consider cutting down her portions because she is spilling out of her blouse and ballooning out of shape, the skirt she is wearing is really tight around the waist and she is forming a small kangaroo pouch. In hindsight, Zandile wishes she had bought the dresses a size bigger but in the end she doesn't say anything because she doesn't want to offend her sister.

'So, how's married life?' asks Yandisa, after a brief silence between them.

'Besides the mess, I think I can live with it!' replies Zandile. 'Ndaba is so untidy and leaves his clothes all over the place!'

'He sounds like me!' laughs Yandisa. 'Wesley is always complaining that I'm so untidy so I got this lady to come and do the cleaning. I just can't.'

'Maybe we can share her,' suggests Zandile. 'This business of me doing all the housework is just not on. The one good thing is at least Ndaba washes his own shirts so I just have to iron them.'

'At least he wears shirts! Wesley wears greasy overalls!'

Both sisters roar with laughter and agree that domestic chores do not translate into domestic bliss.

'I want to hear all about the honeymoon,' says Yandisa, giving Zandile a wink.

'We had a fabulous time!' gushes Zandile.

As she tells Yandisa all the details, her eyes sparkle and Yandisa wishes Wesley could be romantic like Ndaba. Plus, she's also wishing she could have chosen how she wanted to lose her virginity, and if she could, she would want to do it the way Zandile did. Losing her virginity is something she tries hard not to think about but hearing Zandile speak about her experience has triggered her.

'Yandisa, are you okay? You haven't even touched your food?' observes Zandile.

'I'm not that hungry,' replies Yandisa, signalling for the waiter to bring her another glass of wine.

Zandile gives her a disapproving look.

'Now that you've lost your virginity, maybe you should lose your sobriety too, Zandile!' snaps Yandisa.

Zandile ignores her and carries on eating.

'I spoke to Xoliswa yesterday,' she says, changing the subject. 'Deputy Mother is coming home.'

'What?' gasps Yandisa.

'Yes. She said she is serving her notice at her job and will be home in a few weeks.'

'Oh wow. So they've finally decided to come back to Zim,' says Yandisa.

'No. She is coming home, Thulani is staying there.'

Yandisa's brow furrows in confusion and Zandile shrugs her shoulders, equally surprised at the news.

'She says she is coming to help Dad with the family business because apparently Dad says he's not coping.'

Yandisa scratches her head and wonders why Xoliswa is leaving her tropical paradise. What wind has blown to force her to return? Over dessert, Zandile and Yandisa commiserate as to why Xoliswa is returning to Zimbabwe without Thulani but conclude that they will find out soon enough.

THE PRODIGAL DAUGHTER

They watch Xoliswa as she descends the flight of stairs of the Boeing 707. A thick bob frames her face and she walks gracefully, sylphlike and elegant in sweat pants and a loose-fitting hoodie. The whole family eagerly wait for her to walk through the arrivals gate. Up until that moment, Xoliswa's return is something they had all just talked about but it is now a reality. The minute she steps through the doors, she is embraced with hugs that threaten to squeeze the life out of her. Phumla is the first to remark how much weight she has lost. They can all feel Xoliswa's emaciated frame underneath her hoodie and sweatpants.

'With my cooking, I will fatten you up in no time!' says her mother.

'Look at me. I am testimony to that cooking!' says Abraham, patting his protruding belly.

'How did you get so thin?' asks Phumla, looking concerned.

Xoliswa wants to tell her mother that she can't eat. That she has hardly eaten since that fateful morning when Thulani broke up with her. That the food gets lodged in her throat and she can't force it down, leaving her feeling even more hollow and empty inside. She has survived on milkshakes during the week and alcohol on weekends and serving her two-month notice period had felt like two years. It had been the longest period of her life and every day she had been forced to face Thulani in the office. He had moved out of their apartment which they had put up for sale and they agreed they would share the proceeds of the sale. Xoliswa used her share of the money to pay off her credit card and the rest she'll probably use to purchase a

95

property in Bulawayo.

'We've redone your old room,' her mother says as they walk to the car park.

'Your mother worked so hard to do it up for you,' emphasises Abraham.

She is sandwiched between her parents and a few steps behind them, Zandile and her husband follow with her luggage in tow. Yandisa is visibly absent.

'I'm just happy to have you back for good. God answered my prayers!' proclaims Phumla.

'I am happy to be home too,' says Xoliswa.

She hasn't felt this happy in a long time and they are all in high spirits as they climb into Abraham's sleek, new Mercedes Benz that he says was a gift from the congregation. On the journey home, they chat excitedly, catching up on the past two months. On arrival at the Mafu household, there is a large crowd gathered and a marquee has been set up in the garden, festooned with balloons. Xoliswa can't contain her tears. It's like she is receiving a war hero's welcome and is every bit the wounded soldier, yet none of her scars are visible. With a sunny smile, she greets every relative who has shown up to welcome her home. By the time she acknowledges the fiftieth relative though, her smile is starting to fade. A peaceful first night surrounded by her immediate family would have been preferable at this point. She feels like she is being passed like a ball from one relative to another and forced to endure painful comments and intrusive questions.

How was Britain? Cold?
No, actually I was in the British Virgin Islands. It's hot there.

You've grown so thin. Is there no food on the islands?
There is plenty of food, I've just been trying to lose weight.

*You've grown so thin. Are you sure you don't have a
disease?*
*Like AIDS? No, I'm fine. At least I was the last time I
tested.*

*You've gone lighter. The weather overseas certainly agrees
with you.*
I actually love my dark complexion.

When are you getting married?
Not anytime soon but thanks for asking.

It is the marriage question that her Aunt Ntombi decides to hang onto
when they are alone in a corner. Xoliswa isn't ready to confide in her
aunt that Thulani broke up with her. She's not ready for the 'I told
you so' and the truth is that she is still nursing a hope that they will
reconcile.

She soon found out about the other woman once her and Thulani
broke up. The island was a small place and word got around fast.
Apparently Thulani had been fucking a younger woman who had
been at the firm on secondment. Ntando was her name. But she was
gone now and so was Xoliswa and now Thulani had no one. Maybe
being alone would give him time to evaluate his choices and consider
what is important. She's hopeful that he'll come to his senses and
realise that what they had was more important than some flimsy
fling with some floozie. The ten years they spent together counted for
something, didn't they? Surely he couldn't just throw it all away?

'I think it's good that you are back home,' says Sis Ntombi, interrupting
her thoughts. 'I think Thulani was taking you for granted. Now that

97

you aren't there, he'll see how much he needs you.'

Xoliswa agrees with her aunt and responds, 'If the distance doesn't get him to marry me then nothing will.'

'Your problem is that you were too available, Xolie. Don't ever be too available to a man. *Uyazitshiphisa*. You cheapen yourself. Nobody buys the cow when the milk is free. Nobody.'

Sis Ntombi's words sting and Xoliswa can't ignore the welts they leave on her psyche. She politely excuses herself, pretending she needs the loo. She doesn't return to the party and Phumla apologises on her behalf, telling everyone she was tired which was not entirely untrue.

When she wakes up the next day, it is to a deserted house. Phumla has left her a message on the fridge, 'Gone to church. See you later' squiggled with hearts which makes Xoliswa smile. She's hungry, something she hasn't felt for months and peruses the fridge, helping herself to leftovers from the party. She eats until she can't eat any more and then goes back to bed. It is four in the afternoon when she stirs again and is surprised to find that she is still home alone so she busies herself and starts cooking supper. Her efforts are much appreciated when her parents arrive home looking exhausted.

'It was a long day,' says Abraham. 'We had the usual two services and then there was the couples service in the afternoon plus the children's ministry.'

'I sang at the ministry!' declares Babalwa, beaming with pride.

'You should hear her sing, Xolie, she has the voice of an angel. I feel anointed every time I hear it!' boasts Phumla.

'To think that anointing came out of Yandisa,' mutters Abraham under his breath.

Phumla shoves him in the rib, 'Pastor!' she chides gently.

The meaning is lost on Babalwa who is setting the table at Xoliswa's instructions. She is still the family's best-kept secret.

'You should come to church next week,' says Phumla to Xoliswa.

'I don't church, Mama,' replies Xoliswa dismissively.

They grew up Catholic but had not been particularly devout and

Xoliswa is still unable to understand the root of her father's newfound evangelism.

'You need God in your life,' says Abraham, seeing an opportunity to preach the gospel.

'I believe in God, I just don't need to go to church' replies Xoliswa.

'Yes, but you need to be born again in the spirit,' says Phumla.

'Hallelujah! Amen!' sings Babalwa.

Xoliswa decides she will definitely need to ramp up her house-hunting as there is no way she can survive the religious rhetoric of the house. They sit down to dinner and hold hands as Abraham says grace, all of them ending the prayer with 'Amen'. Xoliswa is delighted to have rediscovered her appetite and wolfs everything down, including the dessert of leftover cake from the party, smothered with custard.

'This was so good,' says Abraham, rubbing his belly. 'Now I can start on my weekly devotions.'

'Before you go Dad, can I have a word with you about the business?' asks Xoliswa.

Abraham expels a deep breath, 'What is it, Xolie?'

'While I was away, I started working on some ideas to transform the business and I've drawn up some plans that I want to share with you. I'm excited as I think there are so many ways we can build the business.'

Abraham cuts her off, 'Listen, child, that business is yours. I don't want anything to do with it.'

Xoliswa is taken aback. 'Dad, are you serious?'

'Very. I want to serve the ministry full-time and that business is an albatross around my neck. I'd be happy for you take it over completely. I'll attend the annual board meeting to see how you are progressing.'

Xoliswa's eyes widen with disbelief, 'You're giving me carte blanche?'

Abraham nods gravely, 'Yes, I am. I'll get my lawyers to formalise things this week. You'll be managing director and I will simply be chairman of the board.'

Xoliswa stands up and throws her arms around her father.

'Thank you, Dad. Thank you for trusting me with this. I won't let you down!'

'Just remember,' responds Abraham, 'this is the family legacy. You won't just be letting me down, you'll be letting the whole family down.'

Xoliswa nods, acknowledging the responsibility she's been given. She knows it is going to be a huge task but she's ready for it. She can't sleep that night, her head buzzing with excitement. She shoves her broken heart and broken dreams to the back of her mind and concentrates on building another dream she can pour her heart and soul into.

WINNERS AND LOSERS

Yandisa missed out on the festivities of Xoliswa's welcome home party but it hadn't been deliberate on her part. Of course, some members of the family were telling anyone who cared to listen that she didn't attend out of sheer spite.

She was at work when she received Sis Ntombi's phone call at her cubicle the day of the party. Her position as a bank teller means she isn't allowed to receive calls during work hours but Sis Ntombi is insistent that she needs to talk to her. Working as a bank teller isn't the career Yandisa would have chosen for herself, it was merely a case of her father knowing somebody who knew somebody. With no qualifications to speak of, she really is relying on her father's goodwill. Abraham's name still carries a lot of weight in town.

'I'm at the house, why aren't you here to help with the cooking?' asks Sis Ntombi sternly.

It is typical of Sis Ntombi to launch into a conversation without so much as a 'Hello Yandisa. How are you? It's been a while, are you keeping well?'

'I'm at work,' replies Yandisa calmly. 'You know I work on a Saturday. Besides when have you ever seen me cook?'

Sis Ntombi's *mxcim* that follows is loud and drawn out, the sound slithering from her lips like a hissing snake.

'Make sure you are here after you knock off work. We are expecting you,' she instructs her niece.

'Wesley has an important game today so I'll see you later,' replies Yandisa.

'More important than your sister's arrival?' replies Sis Ntombi.

101

'Yes,' says Yandisa glibly.

'Ku shap, sisi. We'll see how far you get with that man of yours. *Kuzophela!'*

Sis Ntombi abruptly hangs up and Yandisa stares at the phone incredulously. She takes a deep breath and decides to let her irritation slide as she replaces the phone on the handset. She won't let her aunt ruin her day. It isn't her fault Xoliswa's welcome-home parade clashes with a national rugby fixture. Yandisa plans to see Xoliswa after the game and besides, she's back for good so there'll be plenty of time to see her.

The minute the bank closes its doors that afternoon, Yandisa starts to balance her books and finishes first, much to her manager's surprise. She quickly changes out of her uniform into a rugby shirt and a pair of tiny, frayed bum-bum shorts. Standing outside the bank, waiting for Dumile and Towanda to pick her up, men wolf-whistle at her, mesmerised by the butterfly tattoo on her thighs.

They make it to the stadium a few minutes before the 3 pm kick-off time and settle down in the VIP section, next to the other wives and girlfriends. The stadium is packed, everyone eagerly anticipating the start of the game. The beefy players from the Namibian team run onto the field first and their entrance elicits a few cheers. The Zimbabwean team run onto the field to much applause and fanfare, having the home-base support. The players stand in their regimented formation on the field and the atmosphere in the stadium is electric. Spectators are on their feet listening to the elevated voices of the players taking their turns singing their national anthems. 'The ceremony before the bloodshed', as Yandisa likes to call it. The stage is set for what will hopefully be a spectacular game. The referee blows his whistle signalling the start of the game which begins with a kick-off from the centre of the field. This sets in motion a muscled frenzy of testosterone-fuelled males running and darting towards the ball. A player catches it and the other players charge towards him. Soon, there is a contestation for the ball and Wesley, in his striped green, yellow and white shirt emerges, clutching the ball possessively. The stadium rise to their feet as he runs across the field, dodging his muscled opponents with agility.

'Come on baby! Come on, Wesley!' screams Yandisa.

In her hands, she is holding up a huge banner with I LOVE WESLEY written on it in big, bold black letters. She's wearing a number 10 striped rugby jersey with Wesley's name written on the back.

Everyone knows Wesley is the most tactical fly half that has played for the national team and when he reaches the touchline, the crowd goes wild. Yandisa jumps up and down in delight and momentarily drops the banner to hug her friends. The commentator compliments Wesley Bhunu saying he has opened the game with an impressive touchdown. The scoreboard immediately reflects five points and there is a lull in the stadium as Wesley takes the conversion. He kicks the ball and sends it flying over the crossbar, scoring the Zimbabwean team another two points. The singing, ululating and chanting that follows drowns out the commentator, who is still commending Wesley's performance. The game continues, back and forth, brawling and tussling, as the players try to possess the ball and score points. The crowds are kept on their feet with the scintillating ball play, intermittently interrupted by the referee when the rules are broken. Forty minutes later, the referee blows the whistle to signal half-time. For Yandisa and her friends it is a signal to stock up on more drinks. The mood in the stadium is buoyant with Zimbabwe firmly in the lead with a score of 14 to 7.

However, the lead they established is quickly eroded in the second half and the Namibians came back stronger and fiercer. The spectators try not to lose heart when the opponents touch down and score one try after another. The stadium rings with fervent cries of encouragement for the Zimbabwean team. Wesley manages to score another try but it isn't enough to rescue the team, who are trailing behind by ten points. Yandisa feels like she is on an emotional rollercoaster with all the tension of the game and continues to scream and cheer until her throat is hoarse and dry. Her companions have given up and are instead focusing their efforts on drinking as much alcohol as possible before the end of the game.

The mood in the stadium vacillates between joy and despair when the opponents go on to score two more tries before the referee calls the match to an end with the blow of a whistle. Despite the crushing loss, everyone is in agreement that the boys played well and Yandisa is about to make her way to the field to congratulate Wesley when a white man with greying hair approaches her.

'Hello,' he says, offering his hand out to Yandisa. 'Could I please have a quick word with you?'

Yandisa eyes him warily. She's keen to get to the field before a swarm of fans descend on Wesley and start buzzing around him like bees.

'It's really important,' says the man, sensing her hesitation.

'What is it about?' she asks.

'I saw you on the podium cheering for Wesley Bhunu. Is he your husband?'

'He's my boyfriend,' replies Yandisa proudly.

'Oh, that's nice. And your name is?'

'Yandisa,' she replies.

'Yandisa. That's an unusual name. What does it mean?'

'To multiply, to increase,' she replies. 'It's a Xhosa name. My mother is Xhosa.'

'You look like you have the power to multiply.'

Yandisa sighs in exasperation, wishing the man would get to the point. She shifts her hands on her hips, beginning to think he's just some idiot peddling cheap come-on lines.

'Anyway,' he continues, 'I don't know if you might be able to help me but I've been trying, unsuccessfully, to recruit your boyfriend. I'm a talent scout for the Manchester rugby club and we really want to sign Wesley up.'

'Well, why don't you just talk directly to Wesley then?'

'I've tried but he won't listen to me so I thought maybe if I appealed to a brother or sister, or even his girlfriend, I might be able to get through to him.'

He hands Yandisa a big brown envelope and a business card.

'This is completely legit, you can have it checked out by a lawyer if you like. But please talk to Wesley, he has a bright future ahead of him.'

Yandisa's eyes perk up. If Wesley's future lies in that envelope, then so does hers.

'Sorry I forgot to introduce myself. My name is Gill Hornsby.'

'What's in it for him if he joins your club?' asks Yandisa, not really interested in his name.

'Well, for starters he'll get exposure, international exposure. If he turns professional so many doors will open for him. What is he making now? Probably horse shit. Once he starts earning pounds imagine how comfortable your life will be.'

Yandisa looks at the business card and is certain that Gill Hornsby is going to become a very important man in their lives.

'Everything he needs to know is in that contract. He can get his lawyers to go through it and send it back to me if he is happy. Please get him to give me a call.'

'I'll do that.'

'Thanks so much, Yandisa.'

Gill takes her hand and shakes it firmly. After he walks away, Yandisa holds the envelope to her chest. She can understand why Wesley probably wouldn't have taken the man's offer seriously. After what happened with Granger, he has an inbred suspicion of white men. Well, she'll talk to him and convince him that this is a lucrative offer. If he goes to England, in fact if they both go to England, God knows what doors will open for them.

Most of the players, including Wesley, have deserted the field by the time she gets there so Yandisa heads to the change rooms to find him. She waits outside for more than half an hour and Wesley is the last of the players to emerge. She runs and throws her arms around him but he is stiff in her embrace. He smells delicious, like lavender and mint, fresh out of the shower.

'Hey babe, cheer up!' she coaxes. 'I'm sorry your team lost but you played bloody well! I'm so proud of you!'

'Shit happens,' he replies, flippantly.

She rubs his arm, as if to assuage the pain of losing the game. He shrugs it off brusquely. Yandisa is shocked.

'What's wrong with you? You lose a rugby game and you act like the whole world is against you?'

'Not the whole world. Just my girlfriend.'

'What is that supposed to mean, Wesley?'

'I turn my back for a few minutes and there you are holding hands with some white pig.'

'Wesley, that was Gill …'

'I know who he is!' snaps Wesley, 'and I don't like the way he was looking at you and holding your hand. I wanted to bash his face in.'

Wesley's jaw tightens with anger as he speaks.

'Wesley he just wants to—'

He cuts her off abruptly, 'I know what he wants and I don't care. I've told him several times to piss off. I don't want you talking to him either.'

Yandisa sighs and her mood is soured. Wesley senses he has upset her and cups her chin so that she's looking him directly in the eye.

'Cheer up,' he says to her. 'It's not the end of the world.'

His lips curve into a smile. Yandisa smiles back. Then he kisses her in full view of everyone still lingering outside the stadium.

'Come on let's go home and screw,' he says, taking her by the hand.

She hesitates. 'But I was hoping we could go over to my parents' place. My sister is home from the British Virgin Islands and I know she'd love to meet you.'

Wesley is dismissive, 'I'll meet her some other time. Let's go home and screw.'

They walk to his car, his arms snaked possessively around her. They don't make it to the flat and start making love in his car. Yandisa straddles him like she is mounting a stallion, impaling herself on his engorged penis. She rides him with practiced ease, gyrating atop of him in rhythmic, circular motions. He reaches for her full breasts, squeezing and kneading them like putty. She throws her head back, enjoying the sensations coursing through her body. She picks up tempo, riding him harder and faster, grinding into him like a pestle. He thrusts his hips to meet her and they gallop towards explosive orgasms that await them at the finish line, steaming up the car windows in the process. They come together and it is a euphoric moment that leaves them both gasping. Afterwards, they collapse into each other's arms like deflated balloons.

Once they get home, they spend the rest of the weekend in bed together only getting up to eat before returning to one another with an insatiable passion.

Monday arrives as usual, heralding the start of a new week and reminding them that they have to come back to reality. After Wesley drops her off at work, Yandisa quickly flips through the newspapers because she won't have time during the day, sequestered in her cubicle. She's actually not at all interested in the news. She doesn't care that the Zimbabwean dollar is losing value against other major currencies. She doesn't care that the drought situation has worsened and threatens the livelihood of so many. Neither does she care for the increasing agitation between the two main political parties as the country edges closer to the 2002 presidential elections. Instead, she thumbs past all the major news until she lands on the back page. Her interest is focused on the 'Flats to rent' column. Wesley's landlord has served them notice and the cost of renting is astronomical. She sighs in despair. Even with their salaries combined most of the nice places are beyond their reach. She looks at the sports section of the paper and sees an article about Wesley, glorifying his prowess as an athlete.

Yandisa snorts and throws the paper aside. If only they knew how reluctant Wesley is in the pursuit of stardom.

The bank manager calls them to their morning meeting which always starts with a one-minute prayer. Yandisa hates that religion is shoved down her throat at work *and* at home. There is no option to be anything other than religious and she finds it stifling.

After the prayer, the manager outlines their goals and protocols for the day and the official work day begins. It's a busy day and Yandisa is tired after her and Wesley's weekend's activities. She is happy to break for lunch until she realises that she has no money and is meeting her sisters for lunch and there is no way she can cancel. She decides to help herself to the float. She'll make up the difference later, she tells herself. She always has a way of balancing things.

LIFE GOES ON

Zandile is sitting cross-legged on the bed, travel brochures scattered around her on the bed. The Heroes' Day holiday is coming up and she decided they ought to make a weekend of it. She's narrowed down her choices to a few self-drive places and wants to get her husband's input.

'Baby, are you alright in there?' she calls out. This is the not-so-glamorous part about marriage no one tells you about.

He grunts and when he emerges a short while later, he's clutching his stomach and looking pallid.

'It must be the food we ate at the conference,' he says, before collapsing on the bed and on top of all the brochures.

'Mind, baby,' says Zandile, pulling them out from under him.

She touches his forehead, 'Let me get you something for the runs.'

'No, I'm good. My system will clear itself,' he replies stubbornly, turning onto his side. 'What is all of this?' he says, motioning to the brochures.

'I was thinking we could go away over the Heroes' weekend,' suggests Zandile.

Since they got back from honeymoon, they haven't had one weekend to themselves as there has been something or other on every weekend.

'We can't,' he responds quickly.

'Why not?' she asks, creasing her brow.

'I forgot to tell you, Caleb's daughter is being lobola-d that weekend and we all have to be there.'

Caleb is Ndaba's first cousin; his father and Ndaba's father are

109

brothers. Ndaba continues and says they obviously need to support Caleb at the rigorous lobola negotiations.

'Have I met Caleb's daughter?' asks Zandile.

'Yes, you have,' replies Ndaba. 'Ntando was at our wedding.'

Zandile feels bad for not remembering her but there had been so many faces that day to remember and so many people she had never met.

'The whole family is going to congregate eMarula while we wait for *umkhwenyana* to arrive. *NgabakoNkomo.*'

'Nkomo? Which Nkomo? I might know them,' enquires Zandile.

'I didn't ask. I'll ask Caleb in the morning, he might already be asleep.'

Zandile is about to ask what her role is going to be at the negotiation but against her better judgement decides not to. She puts the brochures aside, resigning herself to the fact that she'll have to save them for another time.

'We can always spend the rest of the Heroes' weekend sleeping,' suggests Ndaba cheekily, snuggling close to her once she turns off the light. 'We need to start making babies.'

Zandile giggles, 'Isn't it a little soon? I thought we could wait at least two years before having babies.'

'Two years!' protests Ndaba. 'I want babies. *Now*. I want a cute little girl who looks just like you!'

'I thought you'd want a son!' she teases.

'I do but in a few years. First, I want a cute, little girl called Zanele who has big eyes and a kind heart just like her mother.'

Zandile is overwhelmed with emotion and hugs him fiercely. She's going to give him twenty babies if he wants them.

She is woken up the next morning by the aroma of bacon and freshly ground coffee permeating the air. The bedside clock tells her it is almost 10.30 am. Zandile slips on Ndaba's Van Heusen shirt which was discarded on the floor the previous night and follows the mouth-watering smells downstairs to the kitchen.

'Hey baby, you didn't have to go to all this trouble,' she says, hugging him from behind.

'I wanted to cook for my wife,' he replies, proud of his efforts.

'And then you are going to tell your family that I'm a bad wife who doesn't cook for you!'

'*Angithiwangiloya*. What can I say, you bewitched me!'

'*Owaloya omunye ngubani*? I'm equally bewitched,' she replies, gently kissing him on his collarbone.

'Hold that thought,' he says, and twists around to give her a quick kiss.

She slaps him playfully on the bum. Ndabenhle wearing her apron with nothing underneath is a moment she wishes she could capture on camera. They have already made so many memories together that she wishes she could stop time but they are relegated to memory forever.

She takes a carton of orange juice from the fridge and pours herself a glass. Ndabenhle always prefers to drink it directly from the carton, a habit she has stopped trying to undo. She sits up on the kitchen counter and observes Ndaba as he slices and dices tomatoes, onions and peppers for the omelette. He puts four slices of bread into the toaster. A wedding present from Sis Ntombi.

She has started assembling most of their wedding gifts in their new home. They had decided to move into the house, even though the interiors are not complete. Their voices echo through the house which is still largely unfurnished and there is a mountain of work to be done but Zandile has expensive taste so it is taking them some time. They never eat out and during the week Zandile makes them polony sandwiches for their lunches but unbeknownst to her Ndaba often sneaks across the road to have chicken and chips. Zandile doesn't mind the sacrifices though, after all, she's a homemaker now.

She's thrown herself into the task of decorating the house

and always combs the auction sites for paintings, vases or glass ornaments to add some pizzazz to their home. Now that Xoliswa is back in the country, they spend many Saturday mornings together at haberdasheries looking for fabric for new curtains and cushions. Followed by a long, lazy lunch with tall, pink drinks. Ndaba hates shopping and indulges her with his chequebook. He prefers to spend his Saturday mornings sleeping in and then watching local soccer matches at home or at the stadium when the Highlanders are playing. If there is a big English premier league match on, he goes to the pub with his friends or has them over to their place. He never goes out in the evenings and most nights they spend curled up in front of the television watching videos.

'How is Xolie doing?' asks Ndaba, almost like he knew Zandile had been thinking about her sister.

'She's fine, I suppose.'

'You know I have a lot of single guy friends I could set her up with!' he says, giving her a wink.

Zandile smiles, 'That's a brilliant idea. She needs to get Thulani out of her mind, she still talks about him all the time.'

'That reminds me, Ntando's fiancé is called Thulani. Caleb messaged me this morning.'

'Thulani Nkomo?' she says, hoping she didn't hear Ndaba correctly. Her stomach churns. It hasn't even been six months. How can Thulani already be getting married, she thinks to herself.

'Are you sure?' she says.

'Yes. I think that's what his name is.'

'That's Xolie's Thulani, Ndaba! Why didn't you say something before?' snaps Zandile.

Ndaba shrugs his shoulders, 'I didn't know it was the same Thulani.'

Zandile jumps off the counter. She's suddenly lost her appetite and decides to go back to bed. She has a morose look on her face when Ndaba marches in a short while later carrying a tray with her omelette and a single daisy floating in a fluted wine glass next to the plate.

'I'm sorry that I didn't realise it was the same Thulani but please accept my peace offering.'

Zandile's face dissolves into a smile. How can anyone stay annoyed in the face of such charm and wit?

The following day, Zandile decides to pop in and visit Xoliswa at the office so she takes the car that morning to make the drive out to the offices on the periphery of town. It wouldn't be appropriate to drop the Thulani bombshell over one of their lunches, especially since she is unsure of how her sister is going to react. At least in the confines of her office they'll have some privacy if Xoliswa breaks down. Zandile doesn't expect it to be an easy conversation.

'These offices are so much nicer,' says Xoliswa, ushering Zandile through the reception area to her office.

The offices are huge and much grander than their father's had been. Xoliswa has chosen more modern furnishings for the interior as well as pristine finishings.

'Who did this for you?' asks Zandile.

'Michelle Landers,' replies Xoliswa. 'We were at school together.'

'It's nice but I could have done a better job. For half the price,' says Zandile.

'I know but I am trying to cultivate relationships. Her husband gave me a tender to build a school hall so it's just business. Nothing personal.'

'Oh?' says Zandile, circumspectly.

'Look, Dad has put me in charge here and I'm really trying to grow the business. I mean none of you were really interested.'

Zandile is a bit surprised by Xoliswa's statement, 'Nobody ever asked if we were interested.'

'Well, sometimes you just have to show initiative,' says Xoliswa, condescendingly.

Zandile doesn't respond and Xoliswa shrugs her shoulders, an uneasy silence follows.

'So, what brings you here?' says Xoliswa, trying to break through the icy tension. 'I'm actually glad that you're here, I need you to fast-track a building permit approval for me.'

'I'm not here to discuss business, Xolie. I'm here to talk about Thulani.'

They are sitting in the cosy lounge area in the corner of Xoliswa's office, overlooking the garden. Zandile can see why her sister has chosen this set-up, it's quiet and the garden views are more tranquil than looking at populated city streets and hearing noisy traffic.

'Should I ask my PA to get you some tea or coffee or water?' offers Xoliswa.

'No, I'm fine,' says Zandile, keen to offload the news about Thulani. 'I heard Thulani is getting married and I wasn't sure if you'd heard …'

Across from her, Xoliswa looks unruffled by the news, only crossing and uncrossing her legs a few times.

'I heard from Ndaba yesterday,' continues Zandile. 'Apparently Thulani is marrying his niece and they are coming to pay lobola this weekend.'

Xoliswa stands up and walks towards the window.

'So it's serious with Ntando?'

Zandile is surprised, 'Oh, you knew?'

Xoliswa swings around sharply to face her sister and calmly says, 'I knew but I thought it was just a fling, I didn't know it was that serious.'

Zandile had expected raging anger. She'd expected her sister to throw things at the wall. To cry uncontrollably. *She* certainly would be acting differently if she was in Xoliswa's shoes.

'Look, he was going to move on, I just didn't expect it would be this soon. But hey, life goes on.'

'I won't go to the lobola negotiations. I feel betrayed as well,' says Zandile.

'Don't be silly,' says Xoliswa, dismissively. 'You must go, it's no big deal. Anyway, we need first-hand information when we meet for our next gossip session!'

Xoliswa laughs nervously and Zandile laughs with her. But their laughter is short-lived and is followed by a terse silence that makes Zandile nervous.

'You know if you want to talk or cry I am here,' she offers.

Xoliswa dismisses her with a wave of her manicured hand, 'I'm fine, Za. I've cried enough. This is actually a good thing, at least now I can move on with my life and I won't be wondering whether he's going to come back or not. Now I know he won't.'

Zandile stands up and hugs her sister tightly. Xoliswa is the strong one, she always has been. Whether it was bearing the brunt of their father's reprisal after getting home after curfew when they were younger, or covering for them if they snuck out, Xoliswa always took responsibility. When their mother was having one of her meltdowns, it was Xoliswa who took over the reins. She'd get her and Yandisa ready for school, she'd drop them off, she made sure they did their homework and she told the maids what needed to be done in the house. She just kept things going so it made sense why their father had chosen her to run the business.

THE PECKING ORDER

That evening, Zandile tells Ndaba about her visit to her sister. As she tells him about Xoliswa's reaction to hearing about Thulani, she thinks about the pecking order in their family. She's always been at the bottom just by virtue of the fact that she is the last born and Xoliswa is always at the top as the first born. She's always been the leader. The strong one.

'My sister is stronger than I could ever be. I swear I would have a nervous breakdown,' says Zandile.

Ndaba puts his hand on hers, 'You don't ever have to be. I will always be here for you. I'll never let you down.'

Zandile squeezes his hand. Her heart swells with indescribable love for the man seated across from her. He makes her feel like a beautiful rose cultivated with love.

'She really is doing a lot with the business but I feel a bit left out. I wish she had at least consulted me. I may not be qualified yet but I've got more experience in the building industry than she does.'

Ndaba shrugs his shoulders, 'I get the feeling that she's your dad's favourite.'

'And my mother's. Xoliswa's always been the golden child. She always got the highest marks at school and she was head girl. Yandisa and my achievements always paled in comparison.'

'That may all be true about Xoliswa but I definitely think you're your mom's favourite,' says Ndaba.

Zandile shakes her head, 'I'm nobody's favourite, I'm just there. *Nje.*'

'Well, you're *my* favourite,' says Ndaba, looking into her eyes

116

which sparkle radiantly back at him.

Zandile's eyes mist over with tears, 'I know I shouldn't be upset about the business but I am.'

'Maybe your dad felt she could handle the responsibility,' Ndaba says in an attempt to mollify her. 'Plus, she does have more work experience. I think it's a good thing that she's busy, it'll help take her mind off the whole Thulani situation.'

Zandile nods, 'You're right. I'm just finding my feet in my new job, I have this new house and I have a new husband!'

A huge grin spreads across Ndaba's face, 'And you know how much time I take up …'

He embraces her lovingly and says, 'You know what, you can set up your own business at a later stage. It'll be better to do your own thing anyway, family politics can get in the way of business. I'll help you get started when you're ready.'

The day of the lobola negotiations arrives and Zandile is wearing a long, floral skirt and black T-shirt and a stylishly wrapped *doek* that matches her skirt. Ndabenhle had said that she should dress demurely for the occasion.

'You know you don't have to come,' he'd said to her a few times.

He knows what a difficult situation this is for her. Being involved with the arrangements of her sister's ex-boyfriend marrying another woman in a space of six months after the break-up isn't an easy set of circumstances.

'I want to come.' She'd been adamant.

It's a fairly long drive to Marula but Zandile has queued their favourite R&B love songs which provide the soundtrack to their journey. They sing at the top of their voices, off-key, and make each other laugh. They reminisce, sharing the memories that each song evokes.

'We often travelled this road with my mom,' says Zandile. 'Every time things got tough at home, we'd be on the road to Plumtree.'

Ndaba is surprised, 'I would never have thought things were ever tough with your folks. I mean that tough that she'd want to leave.'

'Oh yes, they were some very rough times. At first I was too young to understand but as I got older I realised just how bad things were between them.'

She has vivid memories of good and bad times growing up. The parties that went on for days. Their mother was always the centre of attention while their father retreated to the sidelines. She vividly remembers not being able to sleep one night because of all the noise from a party that had spilled out to the poolside area. She had climbed out of bed to open her window and saw her father kissing another woman behind the gazebo. The memory stayed with her. Especially when their mother threatened to pack her bags and leave a few days later.

Ndaba glances over at her, 'I pray we never get to that place.'

Zandile smiles back at him, 'Me too.'

In sharing their memories, some painful and some happy, they reveal new things about themselves and it is like finding another piece of a jigsaw puzzle about that person.

On arrival at the farm, Ndaba's sister-in-law, Edna, welcomes them. She is a tall, buxom woman with wide hips and a generous smile. By virtue of being married to the oldest brother, she is the head *malukazana*, the head girl. There is something matronly about her and she fits the role perfectly. Her husband, Butho, is the father figure of the family and everyone calls him 'Baba'. His three children, Bukhosi, Bahle and Bongile step forward and greet Zandile and Ndaba respectfully and help them offload groceries from the car.

'We don't see you!' teases Butho, after they've dispensed with all the pleasantries.

'My wife is keeping me busy,' says Ndaba, deferring to Zandile with a nod.

Zandile smiles, 'We are still honeymooning but we will come and see you soon.'

Butho is amused, 'I want to see the results of the honeymooning! The next time you come here I want to see you pregnant!'

Zandile laughs good-naturedly, 'We're working on it.'

'I'll give her some tips,' says Edna, gently leading her into the house.

The farmhouse is not a traditional series of rondavels but a double-storey house with a thatched roof. Butho is a rancher and rears his own cattle. He also has a hunting concession for tourists and a number of antelope and zebra are mounted on the walls throughout the house. Edna gives Zandile a grand tour, culminating in the rustic kitchen fitted with solid, pine cabinets. Bahle is chopping cabbage on the pine table in the centre of the room and Zandile is immediately recruited to peel the butternut. Edna is overseeing the setting up of the pots outside in the braai area and delegating responsibilities to the women as they arrive. Chandelle, married to Ndaba's youngest brother, Maqhawe, is the next *makoti* to arrive. They live in Berlin, close to her parents, and in a vain effort to fit in she's wearing an Afro print pinafore, her wispy blonde hair escaping from the doek tied messily on her head. Chandelle and Zandile are introduced and Chandelle kisses her on both cheeks and apologises for missing the wedding.

'I bought you a lovely gift though! Mack and I will try and drop it off this week. Maybe we can all do dinner.'

'Sounds great,' says Zandile, excited about the idea.

Edna cuts their conversation short and asks Chandelle to decorate the tent and set up for the guests.

Hours later when Zodwa arrives, she comments that, 'Edna never does the dirty work like us!' Zodwa is pregnant and sporting a huge belly and professes that she can't do any work because the doctor is worried about her blood pressure. She's married to Nkululeko who, despite being the fourth born in the family, is supposedly the richest. Zandile has gleaned this from the talk she has heard about him from other members of the family. A CA by profession he is the CEO of a blue-chip company and has several other business interests.

'I have swollen ankles,' says Zodwa pointing to her feet. 'If anyone needs me, I'll be in the lounge.'

Sis Nandi, the second born, is the last to arrive and oversees that everything is in place. She speaks mostly to Edna, ignoring everyone else and Zandile is aware of the pecking order in their family and that once again, because of her status as Ndaba's wife, she is towards the bottom of the hierarchy in the Khumalo family.

'Where's Zodwa?' enquires Nandi when she arrives.

'She's crying about her blood pressure,' replies Edna, facetiously.

'If it's not her blood pressure, it's her back!' quips Nandi. 'She always has an excuse.'

'Don't worry, I'll sort her out,' says Nandi. 'She can shell groundnuts while she lies on the couch.'

Zandile almost chops her fingers off, paying more attention to what is going on around her than the cucumber salad she's supposed to be making.

'*Malukazana!*' she hears Nandi call out. 'Please finish up and start setting up for lunch. The negotiations are drawing to an end.' Nandi is the only woman who is privy to sit in on the lobola negotiations with the men.

Zandile goes outside and starts setting up the food on the foot-long buffet tables that Chandelle is still decorating with elaborate flower centrepieces. She sees Chandelle stop and take a sip from a flask. 'Do you want a drink?' she says to Zandile, reaching for a bottle of vodka under the table. But before Zandile can answer her, she's poured some into a coffee mug and hands it to her.

'Don't let Nandi see you, she's fucking uptight about drinking. But don't worry about Ma, she's fine about a lot of things including having a drink,' explains Chandelle.

Zandile bursts out laughing and takes a swig of her drink. She likes Chandelle already and figures she has at least one ally in the family. Another hour lapses and the lobola negotiations are nowhere near complete but it doesn't matter to Zandile as she's enjoying her vodka. Nandi reappears and tells Chandelle to light the chafing dishes and then points to Zandile, 'You can wash the hands of abakhwenywana. Don't forget to kneel, makoti. We kneel here.'

Zandile goes into the house to get hot water and when she returns abakhwenyana and the rest of the family are sitting outside under the tent. Judging by the pleased looks on their faces, the negotiations have gone well. She sees Thulani and there is a moment of awkwardness as he acknowledges her. Like the good makoti that she is, Zandile falls to her knees and Thulani leans forward and holds his hands out. But the hot water spills all over his trousers and he quickly jumps to his feet.

'Sorry! Uxolo bakithi!' she cries out. 'I made a mistake!'

She hands him a towel and he tries to dab the water. Nandi marches up to her, an annoyed look on her face and hisses at her, 'Why are you so clumsy?'

'It was a mistake,' says Ndaba, coming to his wife's defence.

He helps Zandile to her feet and feeling slightly light-headed, she leans into her husband. The vodka is definitely working its way through her bloodstream.

Butho offers Thulani a pair of trousers to change into and Nandi takes over the role of hand-washing, while Zandile slinks away to the tent to help dish up the food.

Chandelle chuckles, 'Are you okay, Sis?'

Zandile giggles, 'I'm very okay! I wanted to burn his balls but I missed!'

The two women giggle conspiratorially.

HEARTBREAK HOTEL

That Sunday, Xoliswa checks into the boutique establishment, Heartbreak Hotel. A six-star establishment rated according to the scale of pain. One star is mild to moderate pain while six stars is excruciating and debilitating pain. The proprietor, Heartbreak, is at the reception to greet her but there are no sunny smiles or warm hugs at Heartbreak Hotel. Only a cold, icy draught that chills you inside, awaits you. The dark interior of the hotel is like stepping into a Siberian winter with harsh winds and a frozen ambience. Heartbreak itself is a sexless, faceless, formless nuisance that seems to fit numerous descriptions depending on the circumstances. No one person has described Heartbreak the same but everyone agrees it is a painful encounter. Heartbreak is that person you go to painstaking lengths to avoid. That bad spirit we all try to fend off.

Xoliswa has tried to build walls to keep Heartbreak out of her life and she had been doing well, until that lobola announcement. Zandile's visit at the office got the ball rolling and after that she had received a few calls from friends about Thulani being in town. Being in a long-term relationship means you inevitably have friends in common. Your circles overlap, his friends are your friends. Your friends are his. Everybody is talking about Thulani and Ntando and how deeply in love they are, the wonderful things he's doing for his fiancée. And there's always that person who says how well *he* is doing.

'He looks *so* happy.'

What does that mean? That he had been unhappy with her? Those words are soul-destroying, especially as she feels herself spiralling into a dark pit of despair that she's unable to claw herself out of. She was completely unprepared to feel like this and there have been days when she's wished that she was dead. At least death is final. At least she wouldn't have to wake up every morning and encounter Heartbreak sitting at reception with a toothless grin.

Xoliswa is struggling to coexist with Heartbreak. To think that she met Heartbreak six months ago already but she feels like they are meeting for the first time. But this time around it feels like there is a permanency to their relationship. Lying in bed, staring at the ceiling, she feels like Heartbreak has climbed into bed with her and is curling beside her. Keeping close company. Silently mocking her, taking joy from her pain and discomfort. The rawness feels brand new and as if someone has lunged at her chest, cut a huge gaping hole in her heart and then tore at it, causing it to bleed again.

With all the strides made in the medical field, no one has found a cure for Heartbreak. Something to assuage that throbbing ache. The pain that started in her head and coursed through her body, down to her toes. She has felt every pang and lost count of the number of painkillers she has swallowed but the pain continues unabated. It refuses to be ignored. It has to make itself known all the time and be felt. She pulls the covers over her body, hugging them tighter. It's the middle of August, one of the hottest months of the year but Xoliswa feels an uncharacteristic chill in the air. Or maybe the cold is in her heart.

There is a loud hooting in the distance but she ignores it just like she has ignored her phone ringing and the messages that flood her inbox. She really doesn't want to be bothered. The hooting gets louder and more persistent, forcing her out of bed. Her parents have gone to church and she's not expecting them back until late afternoon. She traipses to the front door in her pyjamas.

As she gets closer to the door, she can see Thulani standing outside at the gate and she suddenly wishes she *had* decided to change out of her pyjamas. Instead, here she is looking like a hot mess. She runs a hand through her hair. This is not the image of herself that she wants Thulani to be left with. But it doesn't matter any more; it's over between them. He's married to someone else so why is he even here? Isn't he supposed to be with *her*? The new love of his life. His new wife. She never imagined that Thulani could be happy with someone else. She thought she owned his heart, his smile, his laugh. He had been her first love and she always thought he'd be her last. She foolishly believed it was impossible that he could ever have what they had with anyone else. She thought they were the real deal and that nothing would ever come between them.

'Xolie. I thought you might be home so I took a chance,' says Thulani when she nears the gate.

'Go away,' she says.

She realises that she doesn't have to open the gate or talk to him. His part in her life is over. Just like that. One day they were lovers and the next they were enemies. A few years from now they'll bump into each other and be like strangers to one another. Like the decade they spent together never happened. Like they were never intimate. Like they never shared their deepest secrets and darkest desires. Just like that. How sad.

'Xolie!' he screams. 'Please! Can you just hear me out?'

His voice is hollow and pained, she's not imagining it. She knew Thulani at his happiest and she also knew him at his worst. When he lost his dad, she held him through his heart-wrenching anguish and nursed him through his depression. She had been there, through it all.

'Xolie, please. Let me explain.'

She stops in her tracks. Does she really want to hear him out? Is this the closure she wants? That she needs? The neat and tidy ending that will conclude their love story? That will leave no unanswered questions, no loose threads from the frayed fabric of their relationship to haunt her. She exhales noisily and turns around.

'Are you going to let me in? 'he appeals to her.

She shakes her head vehemently, 'Just say what you have to say, Thulani. You don't need to come inside the house to say it.'

The steely, wrought-iron gate stands between them. Xoliswa is thankful for the barrier because she's afraid she might reach forward and scratch his eyes out. She doesn't trust herself or her emotions.

'Okay!' he says, a resigned look on his face, 'we'll do this your way then. It's always *your* way!'

Xoliswa takes a step back, shocked, 'What do you mean *my way*?'

'You know, Xolie, this is exactly why I married Ntando. She's not difficult. You are just *so* difficult.'

He grabs the gate and shakes it. The gate is resolute, unmoved.

'Our whole relationship felt like a competition. Being with you was exhausting, Xolie. I got tired. When you came home for your sister's wedding last year, I felt a sense of peace that I never felt with you. Ntando was there for me and she made me feel calm and happy. I don't have to try hard with her, Xolie. I really don't. It's easy to love her. So easy.'

Xoliswa is speechless. She stares at him, her mouth agape. It's like cymbals are crashing in her head and the pain reaches a crescendo.

'Aren't you going to say anything?' he shouts.

'Why are *you* angry, Thulani?' she shouts back. 'Why the fuck are you angry? How do you get to break my heart and be this angry? I gave you ten years of my life and you stand there and tell me I was a difficult lover!'

'You think I wasn't hurt, Xolie? You don't think you hurt me? But you wouldn't know would you, it's always about you and how *you* feel! I made sacrifices too, you know!'

'Fuck you, Thulani! Fuck you. If you were so unhappy why didn't you leave sooner? Why did you drag me along for ten years?'

'I didn't want to hurt you!' he shouts back. 'Honest to God I didn't!'

'Fuck off, Thulani. Just fuck off.'

He shouts out but she doesn't look back. She knows if she does her tears will cause her to collapse to the floor like a pillar of salt.

She sweeps into the kitchen like a hurricane. Her breathing is laboured and comes in short, raggedy gasps. She heads to the pantry, where she knows the leftover liquor from the wedding is stashed, even all these months later. Her parents had probably forgotten to give it away and she's glad they did. She hadn't had a drink since she arrived home, partly because she couldn't drink in their presence and didn't want to be disrespectful to them in their own home. And because she hadn't felt the overwhelming need to drink.

She's relieved to find a crate of assorted spirits and wine. She reaches for a bottle of Johnnie Walker Black, caressing the slim bottle tenderly. She unscrews the lid, takes a swig and it burns her throat. She coughs at first, spluttering a little but keeps going. She slides to the floor because her legs are shaking so much she can't support her own body weight. She takes another long swig from the bottle. A warm sensation spreads throughout her body but only too quickly the feeling evaporates, leaving her heart and body colder than before. She puts the bottle down on the tiled floor, where it lands with a loud clank, breaking the eerie silence that hangs over the empty house. Her hands are shaking uncontrollably. She draws her legs up to her chest, hugging herself tightly. She starts to cry, gut-wrenching sobs. She rocks back and forth, weeping uncontrollably. None of this makes sense to her. Had Thulani ever loved her or had it all been a lie? Their ten years together? Had he stayed with her all that time because it was convenient for him? Had all those years meant nothing to him? Had he just been going through the motion? And he had the gall to stand there and tell her she was a difficult lover! That it was difficult to love her! She cries even harder.

She finishes the bottle of whisky in-between floods of tears, feeling empty inside. Thulani's words stay with her, deeply etched into her heart. The voices in her head are screaming that she's not loveable, that she's a difficult person to love, that she's not worthy of being loved. Over and over again, the voices get louder and louder. She stands up, shaky on her feet and walks to the kitchen counter where the gleaming, silver, stainless steel knives hang. She reaches for one. She wants to transform her emotional pain into physical pain, that way it will be so much easier to deal with. She wants the memories to stop. She wants the voices in her head to stop. She cuts her left wrist. The blood flows, a brilliant, crimson red. She can understand this pain, it makes sense to her. She cuts herself again, feeling a sense of release with each welt she carves into her flesh.

BORN AGAIN

Xoliswa wakes and immediately smells that antiseptic smell that permeates a hospital. Isolated in her private room, her days are white, clean and sterile, filled with the nurses' mindless chatter and her regular doses of medication. The days seem inordinately long and lonely and the nights even longer, filled with torment and regrets.

'Hi,' says a familiar voice at the door. She recognises that deep baritone voice as Thulani's.

He's carrying a huge bouquet of bright, red roses interspersed with white lilies. The arrangement is so big it shields his face. He edges closer towards the bed, closing the distance between them. Her heart gallops like a herd of buffalo and she starts to panic.

'Hi Xoliswa,' he says, a little louder this time.

'I heard you the first time,' she snaps.

She glances at the clock on the side of the bed. It's only 3.30 pm. Visiting hours only start at 4 pm. She wonders how he managed to sneak past the beady eyes of the nurses at their station down the corridor.

'What do you want?' she asks, shifting awkwardly in her bed.

'I heard from Zandile that you were in hospital,' he says.

Xoliswa sighs. Why is Zandile spreading word of her hospital stay like she's preaching the gospel? She wanted this to be kept a secret. The less people know, the better.

He places the bouquet of flowers by her bedside.

'These are your favourite,' he pronounces.

'I don't want them.'

The dejection on his face is visible. He's never been good at hiding

128

his emotions.

'Xoliswa, this is hard for me. Please don't make it any harder!'

'Do you think I'm having a field day here?' she wails.

She wants to reach out and hit him but she's restrained by the drip in her arm.

He lets out a long sigh. 'You know, Xoliswa, whatever I say won't be right. It just won't be enough for you, will it? I'm sorry about all of this. You think it makes me happy to see you lying in bed like this? I blame myself and if I could make it right, I would. When I heard you were in hospital it made me realise just how much you mean to me. I don't want to lose you. Not like this ...'

'Thulani, spare me the bullshit, will you! I don't want to hear it. I've been to hell and back and I don't need your crap. At one point I wished I was dead. *Dead*. But you know what made me cling to life? The realisation that you're not worth dying over! I hate you! Do you hear me? I hate you! Take your flowers and get out! Just go!'

She cries out and feels herself kicking and writhing under the covers and then feels a gentle nudge on her shoulder. She opens her eyes and sees her mother is sitting next to the bed, coaxing her out of the nightmare playing in her head.

'It's okay, my baby,' she says tenderly, stroking Xoliswa's wet forehead. 'It's just a bad dream.'

Xoliswa feels flustered. She looks around and yes, she's still in the hospital but there's no sign of Thulani. It's just her mother in the room with her. And bouquets of beautiful pink roses, proteas and peonies. Flowers everywhere, all in full bloom. No roses and lilies.

'I thought he was here. I honestly did.'

'No, baby, it's only me,' soothes her mother.

Xoliswa starts to cry, 'Oh Mama, I don't know why I did this.'

Phumla throws her arms around her daughter and squeezes her tightly. Xoliswa looks so thin and vulnerable, so unlike the Xoliswa they all know. Phumla holds her and lets her daughter cry, rocking her back and forth. She cries until she is hoarse and has no tears left. Phumla holds her, comforts her and when Xoliswa is spent, she wipes her face gently with a handkerchief.

'You're going to be fine,' says Phumla reassuringly.

Xoliswa nods, 'I know, I just felt so shit that day. Like I wanted to die.'

Phumla holds her hands in hers and squeezes them.

'I am so ashamed of myself, Mama. I embarrassed the family.'

She's flushed with shame.

'There is nothing shameful about what you did, Xoliswa. It's going to be okay.'

Xoliswa nods in affirmation. She's grateful for her mother's presence and support. She's grateful that she can lean on her. Everyone always says that she's the strong one, the tough one but she doesn't want to be those things. It's too much of a burden.

'I'm just sad I wasn't there for you, Xolie. You shouldn't have had to go through this alone.'

'I know what I did was wrong, Mama but it felt like the only option at the time. Thulani said those things to me and I flipped ...'

Xoliswa's voice falters.

'Forget about Thulani,' instructs Phumla. 'He's not worth your tears. You deserve better, Xolie, and don't let that piece of shit tell you otherwise. Any man worth his salt would be lucky to have you. He isn't man enough for you, Xolie. And that's not your problem.'

Xoliswa manages a weak smile. Her mother is right. She *does* deserve better. She vows then and there that she will never again compromise herself in the name of love. To think that she risked everything for Thulani and he tossed her aside like a piece of garbage. She had compromised her relationship with her family and for what? He is in the arms of another woman and all she can do is lie back and lick her wounds. Never again will this happen, she avows to herself. Never again will she compromise herself over a man.

Mother and daughter sit together in silence. No words are needed.

That is how Yandisa finds them when she arrives for visiting hours. Her mother's face falls when she sets eyes on her and she is about to comment when the door opens and Abraham arrives with a coterie of followers of church elders and their wives. He glances at Yandisa and quickly looks back at her, realising what he's seeing. Yandisa wants to escape her parents but she can't get to the door so she has to stay and endure the sermon that Abraham preaches. He calls on them to remember the book of Job and how Job was assailed and afflicted but that even through his suffering he didn't lose faith in God.

'Good things happen to bad people,' he entreats, 'but don't ever forget, my child, his strength is made perfect in your weakness. Weeping may endure for the night but joy comes in the morning.'

This is followed by a resounding 'Amen' and everyone gathers close to her bed and lay their hands on Xoliswa. They pray fervently for an hour, calling on Jehovah to work his hand in her life.

Three days later, Xoliswa is discharged from hospital. The doctor has prescribed a cocktail of pills to help her deal with her depression but her father is adamant that she doesn't need them.

'We'll pray her out of it,' he insists.

Dr Filmore is an elderly doctor who has served the family for years and doesn't believe that things can be prayed away. He's been privy to the psychiatric evaluation which recommends continued therapy for Xoliswa. This angers Abraham.

'Are you saying my daughter is a nutcase?' shouts Abraham.

'No, Abraham, all I am saying is that people who cut themselves rarely ever want to kill themselves. It's a cry for help.'

'But you know Xoliswa, she is such a good daughter. She got good grades at school, she was always at the top of the class. And even her articles, she was in the top three qualifying CAs in her year. Before she left that island they were promising her a partnership. She's a trailblazer!' boasts Abraham.

'Maybe that's the problem,' responds Dr Filmore. 'Some people can't deal with failure after achieving so much in their life. You did say Xoliswa's relationship of ten years recently ended and that is a failure to her.'

Phumla shifts her weight from one leg to another. She can't really understand this all either. It's so unlike Xoliswa. If any of her daughters were going to kill themselves over a man it would have been Yandisa. Not Xoliswa. She's the strong one. The one who's always had it together.

'My husband is right,' says Phumla, speaking up. 'Let us deal with this our *own* way.'

Dr Filmore still gives them the prescription for the medication and also gives them a list of three psychologists that he suggests they consult. 'They all have a good reputation and are discreet.'

He knows Abraham wants to keep this quiet and understands the need for privacy considering his position in the community but he's far more concerned about Xoliswa's welfare. He had been in casualty when Xoliswa had arrived, bloody and unconscious and seeing what she had deliberately done to herself is more severe than Abraham understands.

'She'll be fine,' says Abraham firmly.

'God never fails us, doctor,' adds Phumla. 'This is yet another trial and we shall triumph.'

The doctor stares back at them unconvinced and merely mumbles, 'Amen.'

That seems to appease the Mafus and they usher Xoliswa out of the hospital.

When Xoliswa arrives home, there is a small congregation waiting. There is none of the grandiosity of previous gatherings but instead it is a sombre and spiritual event. Everyone prays for Xoliswa and she decides she is ready to give her life to Jesus. That she is going to be born again.

THE GOOD, THE BAD AND THE UGLY

Sis Ntombi is dying to tell her sister what has transpired in the Mafu household and the minute she gets home, she phones her. Sis Lungile is based in Harare so she is far removed from all the drama in the Mafu household and relies on her sister to keep her up to date with all the latest developments. Sis Ntombi loves assuming the role of the undesignated family spokesperson.

'Your niece is pregnant,' says Sis Ntombi. On seeing Yandisa at the hospital earlier, Sis Ntombi immediately suspects she is pregnant. Her belly was not contained by her A-line work skirt and was stretching and straining over her expanding stomach.

'So she fell pregnant and Thulani still refuses to marry her? *Ngumhlolo lowo*! It's a travesty!' says Sis Lungile, who has been listening to the story in dribs and drabs.

'No, sisi, it's Yandisa who's pregnant! Xoliswa attempted suicide,' explains Sis Ntombi, providing some clarity. 'Thulani married another girl two weeks ago. I told Xoliswa a long time ago that this is what would happen if you do wifey duties on a girlfriend allowance, you'll go broke or get broken. Now she's slitting her wrists in frustration.'

Sis Ntombi can hear Sis Lungile clap her hands twice and realises her sister must have her on speaker.

'Aww *bakithi*. It's not like her though. I spoke to her a few weeks ago and she sounded happy. She told me all about what she was doing for the family business and things seemed to be looking up for her.'

'It's all a pretence, sisi. My friend Annabel is the head nurse at Alma Mater Hospital and she said the psychiatrist there recommended Xoliswa be admitted into a clinic for depression.'

133

'Xoliswa? I don't believe it. What does Abraham say?'

'He won't hear of it. He insists they'll pray it out,' says Sis Ntombi.

'Hmm, it all sounds very suspicious to me. Are you sure there is no witchcraft involved, sisi? How does a relationship just end after ten years?'

Sis Ntombi disagrees, 'There's no witchcraft here, sisi, it's self-sabotage! We like to blame things on witchcraft when there isn't any. But let's talk about Yandisa. She's pregnant and she looks far along and I think you must talk to Abraham. I'm not interested this time.'

Sis Lungile has a soft spot for Yandisa and got to know her niece in the few months she lived with her during her pregnancy with Babalwa. As her sister carries on talking, Lungile pages through her diary to see when she can make a trip to Bulawayo. But unbeknownst to the sisters, Abraham already knows about the pregnancy after a confrontation with Yandisa.

Once Xoliswa was discharged from hospital, Yandisa knew she couldn't avoid her parents any longer. Her mother raised the subject of her pregnancy first and Abraham launched in with a harsh, reprimanding voice.

'Don't you have any sense of shame at all?' roars Abraham. 'Two children out of wedlock?'

Yandisa hangs her head in shame, 'I'm sorry, Daddy.'

'Sorry, huh?' smirks Phumla. 'A first child is a mistake but the second one is a bloody bad habit!'

'Who is this man?' asks Abraham.

'His name is Wesley Bhunu.'

'Bhunu? What kind of name is that? Have you ever heard of the Bhunus?

Yandisa lowers her head, resisting the temptation to look at her father, his bigotry always revealing itself in angry moments.

'Bhunu is a common name,' says Phumla softly, trying to calm her husband down.

'Well, *iBhunu lakhe* is going to marry her,' he says, looking at his wife over the rim of his glasses. 'This isn't a nursery school and I won't have Yandisa turn it into one.'

There was nothing more to be said and Yandisa makes a hasty exit. As much as she hates to admit it, her parents are right. It was careless of her to fall pregnant a second time. What could she possibly offer this child? The thought depresses her more than she cares to admit.

Her mood carries over to the next day and she wakes up feeling nauseous. She decides to skip work and lie in but feels sick the rest of the day and spends it doubled over the toilet seat. She wonders why it is called morning sickness instead of all-day sickness. She can't recall ever feeling this sick with her first pregnancy but then again she'd spent the best part of those nine months suppressing any emotion and feeling. She feels so exhausted and sleep comes too easily, seducing her into a deep slumber. When Wesley arrives home that evening, he finds her curled up in bed. Her senses are heightened because of the pregnancy and she stirs when she smells him walking into the room. The overpowering stench of grease and fumes is enough to make her retch and she wonders why he didn't shower at the workshop.

'Hey, sugar? How you feeling?' he asks, softly, staring down at her naked body.

'So-so,' she replies.

'Can I make you something? A cup of tea? A drink?'

Yandisa eyes him circumspectly. Why is he being so nice? Then she sees the bulging erection in his pants. He sits down on the edge of the bed and starts stroking her, his fingers brushing down her bare back. On another day she might have been turned on but today his overtures turn her off.

'Not now, Wesley. Please,' she implores.

'And why the hell not? We haven't screwed in ages!' he shouts.

'Ages' in Wesley's book translates to three consecutive days of non-activity.

'Wesley, I'm not feeling well. Please.'

'Yandisa, you haven't been in the mood since you went to visit your folks on Sunday. Every time you go there you come back acting bloody righteous!'

'Wesley, I'm just not in the mood,' replies Yandisa, becoming increasingly annoyed. She rolls onto her side, turning away from him. Why wouldn't he leave her alone? Why can't he masturbate in the bathroom and let her be?

He grabs her by the shoulder, 'Since when have you not been in the mood, Yandisa? You can usually never get enough and that's what I like about you. Why do you think we've lasted this long?'

'For crying out loud, I'm just not up to it!' she screams in frustration.

'You haven't been feeling up to it a lot lately. You're seeing someone, else aren't you? That would explain why you've been so offish. So who is the guy, Yandisa? One of your hoity-toity friends from your hood? You've decided to go back to your own kind, huh? Tired of roughnecks like me?'

Yandisa rolls onto her back.

'Fuck me, Wesley,' she says resignedly. 'Just fuck me and get it over with!'

'I want you from behind,' he says, quickly taking off his trousers before she has a chance to change her mind.

She gets on all fours and he grabs her thickening waistline. He makes no attempt at any form of foreplay and enters her roughly. She grimaces, her body dry and unreceptive, unyielding. As he thrusts into her, Yandisa's body jerks forward like a rocking horse. She can feel the bile rising in her throat.

'Stop, Wesley. Please stop!' she begs him.

The more she protests, the more he pumps into her. Suddenly she's that young schoolgirl again, fighting off Marshall. She tries to wrestle away from Wesley but it only serves to fire his passion even more. He holds her even tighter and carries on pummelling into her. He finally comes, ejecting his seed into her. Afterwards, he collapses on the bed, physically spent. Yandisa scrambles off the bed, semen trickling down her legs and barely makes it to the bathroom before spewing a stream of vomit all over the floor.

She's just finished rinsing her mouth when she looks up and sees Wesley's reflection in the mirror. He's standing in the doorway, a look of concern registered on his face.

'Are you alright?' he asks her.

'No, I am not alright!' she snaps. 'I've been trying to tell you that the whole time!'

What is wrong with men? she thinks to herself. First it was Marshall and now Wesley. Does she make bad choices in men? Or maybe it's her? Is she so bad at communicating? Is her 'no' not loud enough or clear enough? She wants to cry out but exhales noisily instead.

'Yandisa, are you pregnant?'

'Yes,' she replies, matter-of-factly.

'Is it mine?'

'Of course it's yours!' she snaps, running her fingers through her hair. Sometimes he makes her want to tear the tiny locks of hair sprouting out of her head.

In the mirror, she can see his face crease into a smile. He hugs her, burying his head into the crook of her shoulder. His reaction surprises her and she slowly relaxes in his arms.

'We're pregnant, Yandisa?' he asks, sounding unsure.

She nods, 'Yes, we are.'

He wraps his arms around her fleshy folds, 'I love you,' he says quietly and tenderly.

The knots in her stomach loosen, releasing the tension that has built up and she feels happy. She's ready to face the world.

She goes back to work the next day and her manager asks to see her in his office. The grave look on his face tells her it's bad news, even before he says anything.

'Mr Sibanda, I genuinely wasn't feeling well!' pleads Yandisa.

She knows what's at stake. She can't lose her job now, not with a baby gestating in her uterus.

'That's not the issue, Yandisa. The issue is that there is video footage of you taking money from your daily float.'

'I always put it back!' protests Yandisa. 'You know I've never been short!'

Mr Sibanda counters her protestations with a solemn look.

'That is irrelevant, the point is that you are not allowed to use the float. It's clearly outlined in the code of ethics and conduct you signed when you joined the bank.'

Yandisa feels like a little bird whose wings have been clipped mid-air and she's spiralling to the ground, landing with a resounding thud.

'The bank wants you for fraud, Yandisa. I asked that you be dismissed quietly as I don't want this to get out to your father.'

Yandisa's face flushes with embarrassment. She's already the black sheep in the family, she can't afford to have 'thief' added to her already controversial reputation.

'I am so sorry, Mr Sibanda,' apologises Yandisa profusely. 'Is there no way I can make this right?'

'Unfortunately not. And unfortunately, because of the circumstances of your dismissal, we can't give you severance pay either.'

'I'm so sorry,' she apologises again.

'So am I,' replies Mr Sibanda.

Yandisa has to pack her few belongings and leave the bank immediately. She decides to tell her colleagues that she's going on maternity leave. 'I'm leaving to have a baby', is better than, 'I'm leaving because I got fired for theft'. They are all congratulatory, wishing her the best. She goes home and collapses on her bed in a heap, not even bothering to remove her uniform. She's not sure what she's going to tell Wesley. She's not sure what she's going to tell anyone.

GROWTH

DAMAGED GOODS

Wesley is surprised that he is so excited about Yandisa's pregnancy. He proudly announces the news to his friends, Charles and JB, while they are having a few beers after work and they raise their glasses for a toast. It isn't the first time Wesley has made a woman pregnant but it is the first time he has contemplated becoming a father. He always insisted on abortions even though terminating a pregnancy is illegal in Zimbabwe. But for the right price many medical professionals would perform an illegal abortion.

'I think I'm ready to be a father,' says Wesley to his friends.

'I don't think you can ever be ready,' professes Charles, who is married with two children.

'Kids are a blessing,' declares JB, who has three baby mamas and prides himself on being a dad but insists he's not ready to tie the knot and maintains relations with all three women.

Wesley's friends agree that Yandisa is a great woman. They like her because she hangs out with them and is part of the clique and even with her posh upbringing, isn't pretentious. She is cool and easy-going and can outdrink them on a good day but they also agree that she is a bad cook and they always decline dinner invitations! They've often wondered whether she'll be a good mother but always keep these reservations to themselves. It's apparent that Wesley is enamoured with her so they're careful what they say. The fact that her and Wesley have lasted for over a year is a testament to her staying power. Most of his ex-girlfriends didn't make it past the probationary three-month period and after Natasha, he hasn't lasted with any woman.

'I'm going to see her aunt this weekend,' says Wesley.

Charles claps his hands, 'The man is *really* serious!'

JB is more subdued, 'What is your plan, mate? Are you doing the damages thing or are you going to lobola?'

'I want to do the whole damn thing,' replies Wesley. 'We've been living together for a while and we're cool together. We have our fights but I like the idea of coming home and her being there. She's good fun.'

'Let's hope she doesn't change,' comments Charles. 'I look at Rufaro and sometimes wonder who I married.'

They all erupt in laughter, Charles' extended belly heaving as he laughs heartily.

'You guys can go ahead and get married, that shit ain't for me,' says JB.

'Whatever support you need, we got you!' says Charles, punching Wesley gently on the shoulder.

'Yeah, we got you,' agrees JB. 'Being the pastor's daughter, he might charge you an arm and a leg!'

'Shit, that's true! I need to find out what the going rate is. I'll sell my car if I have to. We can downgrade until I get my shit together, I need to do right by my child. By Yandisa.'

They clink their glasses together for another toast. Wesley feels affirmed in his decision and knows he's doing the right thing. He can't really articulate what he's feeling but after his break-up with Natasha he never thought he'd feel this way about a woman again. But he's feeling it. Deep in his core.

Yandisa's aunt has requested an audience with him, as is the custom, to discuss what is expected and to apprise him on the cultural procedures. The morning of the meeting, Yandisa wakes up feeling sick so Wesley goes to Sis Ntombi's house alone. Yandisa is a bit apprehensive that he will be meeting with Sis Ntombi instead of Sis Lungile but she can't make it from Bulawayo that weekend. She assures Yandisa that her sister will do a sterling job.

JB and Charles offer to accompany Wesley but he's adamant that he has everything under control and is confident that it's going to be a perfunctory visit. He arrives at Sis Ntombi's home at the designated time, after almost getting lost in the winding roads of Fortunes Gate. He finally finds the house nestled behind some koppies in the fancy suburb, a reminder that he's marrying into money and that Yandisa is no location girl.

He takes a deep breath and starts to wonder whether he's made the right decision. He buzzes the intercom and the gates open like the Red Sea and he drives up the winding driveway. He's welcomed by Sis Ntombi's sons, Edward and Edmond, who recognise him immediately and tell him what big rugby fans they are and this makes Wesley relax slightly. Their older sister, Khethiwe, comes out to see what the hold-up is and so the brothers quickly usher him into the plush home, the opulence of which is not lost on Wesley.

'I see the boys were monopolising you!' teases Sis Ntombi, stepping forward to greet him.

She looks regal in a sweeping silk caftan and Wesley reckons she must have been a beauty in her day.

'They were just being friendly,' says Wesley playfully.

'Welcome to my home,' Sis Ntombi says, holding out a hand. 'This is my husband Ben.'

She looks around for her husband before screaming out his name and he eventually emerges from another room. He's full of apologies.

'*Nguye lo umkhwenyana*. This is the prospective future son-in-law,' Sis Ntombi says by way of introduction.

They shake hands and lead Wesley to the dining room where there is a huge spread laid out. Wesley suddenly feels underdressed.

'Where is Yandisa?' asks Sis Ntombi.

'She's not feeling well,' replies Wesley. 'The pregnancy is giving her a hard time.'

'It must be a boy,' declares Sis Ntombi. 'I was sick with my boys.'

'I don't buy the logic in that thinking,' says Ben, speaking up.

'Says a man who has never been pregnant,' says Sis Ntombi disdainfully.

Her comment silences her husband and Wesley realises he doesn't say much during lunch either. Sis Ntombi dominates the conversation, asking what he does besides playing rugby and what his plans for the future are. Wesley hadn't contemplated going to play rugby in England up to this point but he feels he needs to somehow impress Sis Ntombi so he tells her he's been made an offer and this earns him nods of approval. Ben breaks his silence and tells Wesley that going overseas will be good for his exposure and experience and starts to recount the time he spent overseas studying but Sis Ntombi quickly cuts him off.

'My husband fought in the liberation struggle. I'm sure you've heard of him, Brigadier Ntini. He was a high-ranking army general until he retired a few years ago.'

Wesley has no interest in politics and has only overheard the name but hadn't made the connection to Yandisa's family.

'He's no longer in politics,' explains Sis Ntombi. 'He decided to retire and focus on his businesses. Politics is a dirty game.'

'Marriage is even dirtier,' mumbles Uncle Ben under his breath.

Wesley stifles a laugh and pretends he hasn't heard the old man. After the meal, they move to the lounge and have a whisky before Uncle Ben excuses himself, leaving Wesley alone with Sis Ntombi. Wesley had started to feel like he had found some kind of kinship with the old man and is rather sad to see him leave. Ben assures him they will meet again in the not-too-distant future.

Sis Ntombi starts the conversation off by saying to Wesley, 'Well, I just wanted to meet you and apprise you of our family's procedures. You do know you will be required to pay damages?'

Wesley nods, 'Yes, I do.'

'Look, I doubt it'll be much, what with Yandisa being damaged goods.'

Wesley does a double take. He's not sure he has heard correctly and feels it might be impolite to ask Sis Ntombi to repeat herself but she senses his confusion.

'Oh, she didn't tell you? About her daughter?'

Wesley can't mask his surprise and swallows hard. Then he reaches for his glass of whisky and drains it quickly, trying to calm his nerves, if only momentarily. He wants to ask for another drink but it might be rude to send Sis Ntombi to refill his glass so he decides against it.

'So Yandisa had a baby when she was fifteen but it's something the family doesn't talk about. I thought you should know so that you know exactly what you're getting into, what you are marrying.'

Wesley feels his insides churn and fears the delectable lunch he's just had will soon find its way onto the carpet, that is so lush it almost swallows his feet up to his ankles.

'I'm straight up, *mkhwenyana*. Some call me a straight shooter but I believe in honesty. I believe we owe you that much,' continues Sis Ntombi.

Wesley nods gravely. He can't find the words to formulate a response and so Sis Ntombi continues talking, undeterred.

'My advice to you is that you declare upfront that you want to marry Yandisa, that way they will go easy on the damages. My brother is dying to get her married so don't worry about the price, they'll be reasonable.'

Wesley clears his throat, wanting to ask a question but he stops himself.

'So, we'll see you and your delegation month-end. Carry cash for the preliminaries. *Uvula mlomo. Ungangaziwe.*'

Sis Ntombi goes on to explain every detail of the customs involved but Wesley's mind is no longer there. He's there in body but desperately wants to leave. He's thankful when Sis Ntombi finally concludes her lengthy discourse and walks him out to his car. He thanks her graciously but has no intention of ever returning.

It's midnight when Wesley gets home and stumbles into the bedroom and wakes Yandisa up. He reeks of alcohol and she feels her insides constrict with anxiety and cusses to herself as she sits up, rubbing her eyes. She's anxious to hear how it went with Sis Ntombi.

'I've found someone who can help us with the abortion. I don't think I can go through with this,' slurs Wesley.

Yandisa is stunned, 'I can't. I've already told my parents. Besides I am too far along.'

'Well, you can tell them that you miscarried. These things happen,' he says dismissively.

Yandisa is quiet. What could have happened to make him have such a change of heart?

'I thought this is what you wanted, Wesley.'

'So did I until I found out you have a child that you didn't tell me about! I mean what the fuck, Yandisa? I don't even know the woman I'm supposed to be marrying!'

Yandisa gasps.

'How were you going to keep a whole child from me? What else are you keeping from me?'

Wesley opens his cupboard and starts flinging clothes into his tog bag.

'I'm going to sleep at JB's house for a few days and when I come back I want you gone. Do you hear me?'

'Wesley! I can explain!' implores Yandisa.

'What is there to explain? Your aunt told me everything! I can't believe I've been such a fool!'

'Did she also tell you that I was raped? That I was fifteen years old when it happened!'

'I didn't need to hear you had a child from her, I needed to hear it from you!'

Those are his parting words before he slings his bag over his shoulders and storms out. This is exactly what she had been afraid of, the judgement, the harsh reproach.

The following morning Wesley tells JB that he's calling the whole thing off with Yandisa. JB is shocked.

'But why man? I thought you were really into her.'

'She has a child,' he replies, clearing his throat. 'She had a child when she was fifteen or some shit. She's damaged goods.'

JB eyes Wesley circumspectly, 'Wesley, we're all damaged goods. Look at you and me, you're the last person that should be judging Yandisa. If you don't want to be with her, let it be for something else but not this.'

JB then leaves for work and Wesley drinks his tea and reflects on JB's words.

We are all damaged goods.

GHOSTS OF THE PAST

Xoliswa returns to work and is pleased to see the new sign has been put up outside the building: Askaheni Enterprises. She pauses for a moment and then makes her way to her office. She means business in her pinstriped suit and killer heels, her snakeskin briefcase matching her shoes. Her staff welcome her back with a huge bouquet of flowers and a get-well-soon card. Xoliswa is touched and remembers she needs to take things one day at a time.

The first thing she does is call for a morning meeting to touch base on all their projects and their progress. Joel, the quantity surveyor, who also doubles as a project manager reports that they have broken ground on the construction of a school hall. Xoliswa makes a mental note to visit the site later in the day. There are three tenders out on the market which Xoliswa suggests they go after but Joel complains that the workload is getting too much. Xoliswa reminds him they are in the process of bringing in two quantity surveying interns from the local university and there's a pile of CVs to get through. Her hospital stay has delayed the process but she assures Joel he will get some assistance soon enough. Xoliswa launches her day with zeal, working through the lunch hour. She gets so busy she forgets her lunch date with Zandile, who calls her sounding rather annoyed and suggests they do drinks instead. 'Ndaba is going to Harare for work and I'll be alone.'

'I can't,' says Xoliswa. 'I have a cell group on Wednesday night.'

'Friday night?' asked Zandile, sounding hopeful.

'I've got choir practice!'

'Breakfast on Saturday morning?'

'I've volunteered for a soup kitchen for an old-age home.'

'Well, when you're free, let me know,' says Zandile, dropping the call.

Xoliswa shakes her head, wondering why her sister is so sensitive. She pushes the thought aside and launches back into her work. It's well after 6 pm when she gets a call from Yandisa. She almost doesn't answer it but decides it might be urgent so she picks up. Her sister sounds upset.

'Do you mind picking me up from Wesley's place on your way home?' Yandisa asks.

'No problem,' replies Xoliswa. 'I'm leaving the office now.'

She packs up and leaves the office and drives to Wesley's flat in Fort Street. Xoliswa knows exactly how to get there but she's surprised Wesley still lives in the same flat and hasn't progressed from his one-bedroom bachelor pad. Back in the day it had been called 'The Slaughter House' and Thulani and his mates had shared a three-bedroom flat in the same building. Wesley had always been popular in high school and had been two years ahead of them but everyone knew him because he played for the first team rugby. He was one of those guys that everybody knew, or if you didn't know him, you'd heard of him. At some point, her friend Natasha started dating Wesley and he was no longer just that rugby jock but her best friend's boyfriend. Which is why she finds it rather unsettling all these years later that Wesley is now dating her younger sister. It feels slightly incestuous even. Plus, after the way he treated Natasha, she knows he isn't a good man.

She pulls into the vacant parking lot outside the block of flats and steps out of her father's Nissan Pajero which she's taken over. She's about to walk into the building when she hears someone call her name. She turns around and is surprised to see the voice coming from a bright yellow BMW.

'Xolie!' Wesley calls out again.

She looks closer and there he is. Xoliswa pauses, debating

149

whether to greet him or continue upstairs. She reminds herself that she's now attending church and ought to do the Christian thing. Civility is required in such instances so she walks towards the car. The Three Musketeers are sandwiched in the car. Their friendship is still intact and has certainly outlived all of their relationships. Thankfully, Wesley has upgraded his car from the Datsun 120Y he used to drive which often wouldn't start without a push. They had endured so many embarrassing moments in that car and once Wesley had beaten up Tash in the backseat while JB and Charles had manned the doors, ensuring that no one came to her assistance. Xoliswa remembers that night vividly because she had had to call a security guard to assist but he had refused to get involved.

'I had no idea you were back in town,' says Wesley, getting out of the car to greet her.

He puts out his hand but Xoliswa doesn't reciprocate. Wesley is a bit put out by her rebuff.

'Ah come on,' says Wesley. 'Don't tell me you're still nursing grudges.'

'I'm not nursing anything,' says Xoliswa curtly. 'Besides, you and I were never friends.'

'How is Tash?' he asks, ignoring her comment.

'Tash is great. She's getting married to a man who adores her.'

'And you? You were always such a snob. Did Thulani finally put a ring on it?'

Xoliswa wonders if he genuinely doesn't know about her and Thulani breaking up or if he's just baiting her.

'We broke up,' she says.

'I could have told you back then that you were wasting your time with him, he always cheated on you.'

Xoliswa feels her heart constrict painfully and holds her hands up in disbelief.

'Are you going to stand there and assume the moral high ground like you weren't cheating on Tash all the time? Like you weren't beating her all the time?'

'Listen, I never pretended to be anything else. What you see is what you get.'

Xoliswa shakes her head, 'I wonder how my sister got involved with you. Now that you've got her pregnant we're going to have to be family or are you going to run from your responsibility like you did with Tash?'

Wesley winces. It surprises Xoliswa that her sharp rejoinder has caused him to react.

'Tash aborted my child,' retorts Wesley.

'When it became clear you weren't prepared to be there for her. What did you want her to do?' says Xoliswa.

Xoliswa was there the day Wesley was supposed to pay damages to Tash's family. They had waited all day for him but he never showed up. She remembers how devastated Tash was not to mention the embarrassment it had caused Tash's entire family. The Mhlophes could not save face and Tash's mother found someone who quietly performed the abortion. Tash left for university in South Africa shortly after that and never looked back. Yet here is Wesley, still doing the same, except his victims are getting younger.

'I loved Tash,' says Wesley, suddenly feeling the need to explain himself.

'Oh fuck off,' says Xoliswa dismissively. 'You don't love anyone but yourself and I honestly don't know what my sister sees in a piece of shit like you.'

Xoliswa turns around sharply and makes her way into the building. Merely being there she is assailed by so many memories. Her past flashes before her. She gets into the lift and has a flashback to when her and Thulani had once stalled the lift and made passionate love, her legs wrapped around his waist as he rammed into her. She suddenly feels claustrophobic and gets out of the lift a floor earlier and takes the stairs to Wesley's flat on the fourth floor. She hesitates at the door. The sign is gone. The infamous sign that used to be stuck on the door.

She still remembers the exact wording: *Management will not be held responsible for any loss of virginity incurred on these premises.*

At the time, they had found the wording provocative and slightly amusing but in hindsight it is so distasteful considering how many young women were purportedly raped behind that door. She shakes her head as if to try shake the memories away.

She takes a deep breath, opens the door and walks in. She stops in her tracks, save for a picture on the wall, nothing about the place has changed. The same old, red velvet couch still occupies space in the centre of the living room except now it is falling apart. There's a round rug in the middle of the room and a TV set in the corner of the room on top of an old pine wooden cabinet filled with trophies. They had had some amazing parties in this room with the DJ set up in the corner, music blaring from the speakers, the room heaving with hot, sweaty, sexy bodies. Despite everything, Wesley had always thrown the hottest parties.

'Are you ready?' she asks Yandisa, as she walks into the bedroom. Xoliswa doesn't want to spend a minute longer than necessary in this flat.

'Very ready,' says Yandisa, not hesitating even for a second.

Xoliswa notices the suitcases on the floor and realises Yandisa is leaving for good.

'And now? What's all this?' she asks her sister, pointing to the suitcases.

'Sis Ntombi thought it might be a good idea that I go home now that Wesley wants to formalise things.'

Xoliswa eyes her suspiciously, 'And since when do you listen to Sis Ntombi?'

'She's right, Xolie. Just let me try do things the right way for once.'

'Pfft. I hope for your sake Wesley does right by you.'

Yandisa doesn't respond. They wheel the suitcases out of the room and leave. When she gets to her car, Xoliswa is surprised to see that Wesley and his friends have left. She shakes her head; he didn't even have the courtesy to say goodbye.

'Does Wesley hit you,' Xoliswa asks her sister suddenly on the drive home.

'What?' asks Yandisa, the question catching her off guard.

'Does he beat you up? I swear if he's laid a hand on you I'll kick his ass myself!'

'He's never hit me!' says Yandisa.

She doesn't know why she's defending Wesley. Is it love? Is this what loyalty is about? Maybe she's not admitting it because she knows that she'll forgive Wesley but her sister won't. Maybe that's why she was protecting him. Protecting their love which she's not sure even exists.

They get home just in time for dinner. Babalwa has set the table and their mother is dishing up food for their father who is sitting at the head of the table. They all hold hands and say grace. There's now a chef who prepares all their meals. Phumla says their church schedule no longer afforded her the time to cook or even supervise it.

'I paid my dues a long time ago,' she says.

'You did my darling,' says Abraham. 'You no longer need to impress me.'

Phumla smiles thoughtfully. Xoliswa is genuinely surprised how they've managed to keep it together all these years. She remembers all the times her mother had wanted to leave but here they are still eating meals together as a family. Xolie is pushing her beef stew and rice around her plate. What Wesley said to her about Thulani has stayed with her; their relationship had always been a farce. He had been unfaithful to her right from the start.

'Come on, Xolie you need to eat,' says Phumla, noticing she hasn't touched her food.

Xoliswa picks at her food, not wanting to draw unnecessary

attention to herself. She has assured everyone that she is fine and has to appear that way, even though deep down inside she knows she's not quite there yet.

Afterwards, they all go to the living room to watch the 8 pm news, an old family ritual. Babalwa recuses herself and kisses her grandparents goodnight. They remark what a well-behaved child she is. 'An angel if there ever was one,' adds Abraham. The snub doesn't go unnoticed by Yandisa.

'I've come back home,' announces Yandisa, during an ad break. 'Sis Ntombi said it would be best if I returned home now that Wesley has decided to formalise things.'

'How long do we have the pleasure of your company?' asks Abraham. 'You come and go as you please so I'm never sure.'

Abraham is in his armchair, his feet elevated on a footstool. Everyone in the family know that it is his chair and no one dares occupy it. Not even Babalwa. Phumla is on the settee, flanked by her daughters, happy to have them home with her.

'Sis Ntombi is right,' says Phumla, 'you need to do things the right way.'

Abraham grunts something inaudible under his breath. Yandisa hadn't expected a warm welcome from her father but his hostility stings a bit. She knows that hugs are reserved for his favourites and she had begrudgingly accepted her role as the black sheep of the Mafu household years ago.

'I'm glad you are back,' says Phumla, reaching for Yandisa's hand and clasping it in her own. 'At least now you can help me chauffeur Babalwa to school.'

'She has nothing else to do,' says Abraham pointedly. 'Seeing she was fired from work. Weren't you, Yandisa?'

The comment takes Yandisa by surprise. Nothing ever escaped her father's knowledge. Xoliswa and her mother turn to face her, both making her feel uncomfortable with their judgemental gazes.

'Yes, I was dismissed. It's true,' admits Yandisa.

154

'Did you tell them why you were fired?' continues her father.

'Dad, do we have to do this now?' says Yandisa defensively.

'Yes. Let it be known you were fired for theft. Is this what I raised you to be? A thief?'

'It wasn't like that!' shouts Yandisa.

Abraham holds his hands to his head to show his exasperation. Yandisa decides it will be best to end the conversation and rather go to her room before things get ugly with her father.

'We are about to go and say our prayers, Yandisa,' says her mother.

'I'll pray in my room,' snaps Yandisa.

'If anyone needs a prayer it's you, Yandisa!' shouts Abraham.

Her father's words follow her to her room and stay with her as she closes her eyes.

THE SINS OF THE FATHER

Alone in the sanctuary of their bedroom, Phumla reprimands her husband for being so harsh with Yandisa. He dismisses her, claiming she's always had a soft spot for Yandisa and that of all the girls, she lets her get away with murder. Phumla disagrees, saying she loves the girls equally and has no favourites.

'Don't sit there and act like you have never made mistakes in life, Abraham. You've made plenty!'

Abraham is defensive, 'Yandisa always takes it too far, Phumla. She's brash, impulsive and doesn't give a damn about the consequences of her actions. She needs to take responsibility for herself.'

Phumla laughs, 'Listen to yourself, Abraham. Just listen. You were like that too. Where do you think Yandisa gets it from? Don't try and act holier-than-thou with me, Abraham. I *know* you.'

Phumla pulls the blankets up and turns her back on her husband. He curls into her, hugging her from behind.

'Don't do that,' he says softly. 'You promised you'd never turn your back on me.'

She did promise him that so she turns to face him. No matter how angry they were with each other, they had vowed to never to turn their backs on one another.

There'd been many times when Phumla had been ready to throw in the towel on their marriage. The first time she contemplated leaving Abraham was in the summer of September, 1981. Abraham had been promoted to general manager at the bank and the role came with a bigger salary and more perks. He met Miss Bulawayo, a long-legged, slender beauty queen, after the bank proudly sponsored the beauty pageant. Abraham appeared to take his professional role further and they had embarked on an affair. Prior to this, he had always been discreet about his affairs but this time he flaunted Miss Bulawayo in Phumla's face.

'I am going to leave you, Abraham!' threatened Phumla one morning, having suffered enough public embarrassment. He was getting ready for work and she was getting ready for the morning school run.

'So then leave,' replied Abraham nonchalantly, tightening his tie.

Driving the girls to school a short while later, Phumla was distracted. For a change, Xoliswa and Yandisa aren't fighting and instead Xoliswa is trying to brush Yandisa's unruly hair. Zandile is strapped in her car seat, sucking her thumb. Phumla ignores them and turns on the radio to drown out any noise. She isn't paying attention and almost goes through a red robot, narrowly avoiding a terrible accident. People hoot furiously and she can barely see the road through the blur of tears.

Maybe if she was still employed she could afford to leave but she's a housewife. Abraham had convinced her to quit her job because he was making enough money to take care of all their financial needs. Too much it seemed because he now had a surplus to entertain whores. She drops Xoliswa and Yandisa at Whitestone, an exclusive private school, and bids them goodbye with a kiss. Now that Xoliswa is old enough, she relies on her to walk her sister to her class. Phumla doesn't want to face the other mothers and their judgments about her. She then drops Zandile off at nursery school and goes home. She lies on her bed, sobbing and falls asleep with swollen, puffy eyes. When she wakes up, she decides she is going to leave her marriage. That afternoon when she picks the girls up from school, she casually tells them that they are going on holiday.

'Without Dad?' asks Xoliswa.

They always travelled with Abraham so it seems odd that they would be going anywhere without him.

'It's just us girls,' said Phumla, trying to inject some boldness into her voice.

Phumla is determined to drive all the way to the Eastern Cape but they don't get far when the blue Pulsar splutters a few times and grinds to an abrupt halt. They only make it as far as Figtree and Phumla tries starting the key a few times but the engine refuses to purr to life. She gets out of the car and kicks the front tyre repeatedly. The girls watch her vent until she bursts into tears. Xoliswa, who is sitting in the front seat, quickly removes her seatbelt and gets out to try and comfort her mother. Yandisa is in the backseat with baby Zandile, who is getting hot and restless. Zandile then starts crying so Xoliswa opens the back door and takes her little sister in her arms and quietens her with ease. She reaches for her bottle in the cooler box and plugs it into Zandile's mouth. She suckles greedily.

'Why are we just sitting here?' asks Yandisa, who is getting agitated. 'And why is Mom crying?'

It is a sizzling hot day and they are stranded in the middle of nowhere.

'Yandisa, be quiet,' chided Xoliswa. 'Mama is upset.'

'I'm bored and I am hungry and I want to go home!' wails Yandisa.

'Mom, did you pack some food?' asks Xoliswa, looking in the boot of the car.

There is nothing but suitcases filled with clothes. Why had their mother not packed snacks or juice for them? Xoliswa thinks to herself.

'I forgot,' replied Phumla, meekly. It hadn't exactly been a well-thought-out trip.

Xoliswa stood on the side of the road, balancing baby Zandile on her prepubescent hips, trying to flag down cars to ask for help. Many whizz past without a second glance. Xoliswa's worry is that the sun is going to set and they are miles away from home. They're finally helped by a white farmer travelling with his farmhand. The men get under the body of the car, tinkering with the engine and finally emerge with grease-covered faces. It is 6 pm by the time they are back on the road to Bulawayo. No one talks on the journey home. Phumla plays The Manhattans but she doesn't sing along like she normally does. Zandile gurgles happily like nothing is amiss before falling asleep. She is a happy baby only crying when she's hungry or needs her nappy changed. They arrive home about an hour later and when she pulls up at the house, Abraham is standing outside on the patio, looking fraught with anxiety. He rushes to the car and embraces Phumla as soon as she gets out, apologising profusely. Nothing further is said as they offload the suitcases out of the car and there was no further talk of going on any holidays.

Things settled down in the Mafu household for a while until Miss Bulawayo arrived at the house one day with a three-year-old baby boy. She claimed Mandlethu was Abraham's child and that she was suing him for maintenance. Things got messy and the local paper even carried the story but the woman later retracted her story. The lawsuit was withdrawn and Abraham tried to move on and patch things up in his marriage by gifting Phumla a gold ring and a brand-new Mercedes Benz. But Phumla wasn't so easily placated and packed her bags and her girls into the brand new Benz and left. This time they made it as far as the Plumtree border post and were in the immigration hall when the passport official demanded to see an affidavit from Phumla.

'What affidavit?' asks Phumla, puzzled.

'You're travelling with minors so we need a signed affidavit from your husband giving you permission to travel with these children. Otherwise we can't grant you passage.'

Phumla's heart sinks as the official hands her back the four passports. Back in the car, she breaks down and bursts into tears.

'It's okay, Mama,' says Xoliswa, trying to console her mother. 'We'll go on holiday another time.'

Phumla cries even harder. At sixteen, Xoliswa knows what an impromptu 'holiday' means in the middle of the school term. She knows her mother is trying to run away.

The next time Phumla decides to leave, she decides to go alone. She deliberates over it for a while and concludes that the girls will be fine with their father. Before she leaves, she goes to talk to Xoliswa in her room one night. The light is on so she knows Xoliswa must be studying for her exams.

Phumla walks in the room and Xoliswa is indeed poring over her books. She is in the middle of writing her A-levels and anxious to cover all the work she needs to before her chemistry exam a few days later.

'I'm leaving,' Phumla announces.

Xoliswa looks up, annoyed by the interruption and sits back in her chair and stares at her mother. Phumla confides in Xoliswa a lot and in some ways they are more like best friends rather than mother and daughter. Phumla has come to realise over the years that there are very few women she can actually trust. She had formed friendships amongst the Xhosa community that were resident in Bulawayo, most having arrived with Cecil John Rhodes. Soon most of these friendships disintegrate as very often her so-called confidantes ended up sleeping with Abraham.

'We're not going with you this time,' states Xoliswa.

The last time the girls had gone anywhere with their mother, they had gone to eLindini, a small village outside Mthatha. The 'holiday' had been sanctioned by their father, who bought them one-way plane tickets to Johannesburg. They had then bussed to the Eastern Cape and spent that leg of the trip eating chocolates and watching the landscape change from flat terrain to undulating mountainscapes.

Two days later they arrived at their makhulu's house, 60 kilometres outside Mthatha. Aunt Phatiswa was a widow and lived alone on her homestead rearing livestock. Her three children, Nwabisa, Vuyelwa and Yoliswa were similar in age to the Mafu girls. During that trip, Phumla took her daughters to the Home Affairs Department office in Mthatha to apply for their South African ID books. Xoliswa then realised that they were never going back to Bulawayo.

In the beginning it was fun sleeping on the floor in the lounge with their cousins but after a week Xoliswa yearned for her bed. They missed the amenities of running water and electricity. They missed their own rooms and what they realised was a cushy life. Zandile was the only one who loved the life *ezilaleni*. She played with the other children in the village all day long. Xoliswa wanted to return home and be with her friends and Yandisa just wanted to go home. She hated that her makhulu made her fetch water at the well every day and the only thing Yandisa enjoyed was the freshly baked *isonka* Aunt Phatiswa baked every morning.

Phumla had a raucous fight with her sister one day and so the Mafus packed their suitcases and went back to Bulawayo. There were no plane tickets bought for them this time and they were on the road for a full week and finally arrived back in Bulawayo with swollen ankles and stiff backs.

'I know you're not going to come with me, Xolie but will you look after your sisters for me?' asks Phumla.

Xoliswa loses her temper and throws her pen at the wall.

'Do you have to go *now*, Mom? I'm in the middle of my exams and I *need* you here!'

'I can't live like this any more!' says Phumla, throwing her hands up.

Phumla paces the room, feeling troubled. She has deliberated over her decision to leave for so long and the girls are old enough to take care of themselves. Zandile is old enough to put a meal together for herself. Yandisa is moody and retreats to her room when she gets home from school and does her own thing anyway and Xoliswa has her driver's licence so she can ferry her younger sisters to and from school.

'What has Dad done this time?' asks Xoliswa, bored with the regularity of her parents' issues affecting her and her sister's lives.

But she realises it is a Sunday night and her mother has finally got tired of Abraham leaving on a Friday with a small suitcase and waltzing in on a Monday morning without any explanation for his absence. He used to mention business trips but he doesn't bother saying anything any more.

'*Selibona nya!*' he would say sarcastically as he walks into the kitchen on a Monday morning. They would be having breakfast and no one would respond. He would try and kiss their mother but she would turn the other way, his lips landing on her cheek. When Yandisa and Zandile were much younger they would run to their father, excited to see him and holding on to his legs. But the battle lines were drawn long ago and they all side with their mother now.

'I can't do this any more, Xolie! I'm forty-four years old. This can't be what the rest of my life is going to be. I deserve better than this!'

'We *all* deserve better than this, Mom! *I* deserve better than this! Damn it, we didn't ask to be in this mess!'

'Are you blaming me? Is this all my fault?'

Phumla starts to cry and Xoliswa feels bad for expressing her anger so brazenly. She reaches out to her mother and hugs her.

'Go, Mom. You do deserve better than this,' says Xoliswa.

Phumla decides to leave as planned, comforted by her daughter's words of encouragement. Xoliswa has always been the strong one and Phumla will be forever grateful for her support.

It's after midnight when Phumla arrives at Sis Ntombi's house and buzzes the intercom. Her and Uncle Ben are alarmed when they see

Phumla outside and immediately presume something terrible must have happened to Abraham or the girls.

'I'm leaving your brother,' announces Phumla defiantly.

Ben dismisses Phumla, turns around and walks away, annoyed to have been woken up. Sis Ntombi is equally annoyed.

'You've woken my family up in the middle of the night to tell me this, Phumla?'

'Well, I thought you should know. He's your brother,' says Phumla.

'And it couldn't wait until the morning?' asks Sis Ntombi.

'No, it couldn't.'

Sis Ntombi lets out a sigh, 'You know what, Phumla, I'm so tired of your histrionics!'

'My histrionics?' squeals Phumla. 'Your brother is a womanising bastard and no one says or does anything about it. You think I don't know that you entertain his girlfriends here? From the day I came into his life, Ntombi, you've been plotting to destroy me and my marriage!'

Sis Ntombi shakes her head, 'Don't play the blame game with me, Phumla, you knew exactly what you were getting into when you met my brother. He was a married man and it didn't seem to bother you when Sarah was the one crying foul!'

'He chose me!' screams Phumla. 'Your brother chose me, I didn't choose him!'

'Well, he's obviously chosen someone else now and it hurts, right? Get off your high horse, Phumla, get over it and move on.'

Phumla knows there is nothing more to be said and is seething as she walks away. Even after all these years, Sis Ntombi and Sis Lungile blame *her* for the breakup of Abraham's first marriage. How was it her fault when their brother was the one at fault?

Phumla gets in the car and drives away. She's tired of staying for the supposed 'sake of the children' and resolves to start taking care of herself so she decides to check herself into the Bulawayo Sun Hotel for the night. She sleeps soundly and wakes up at 10 am. She has the scrumptious buffet breakfast and checks out shortly after midday. A while later, she arrives in Plumtree and decides to put on the radio and listen to the local news.

'Local businessman, Abraham Mafu has been involved in a fatal accident ...'

Phumla doesn't hear the rest of the report. She brings the car to an abrupt halt and makes a hasty U-turn to go back to Bulawayo. The thought of the girls growing up without her and Abraham is unimaginable. Plus, there'll be nothing left of Abraham's estate once her sisters-in-law are done fighting over it.

LET THY KINGDOM COME

Abraham didn't die that day, though he often wishes he had. He survived the gruesome car accident but the woman in the car with him wasn't so fortunate. His Toyota Cressida sedan wrapped around a huge baobab and crunched up like a piece of paper. Those who witnessed the accident wonder how anyone could have emerged from the wreckage alive. He doesn't understand it either and save for a broken arm, punctured lung and a dislocated hip, he was fine. The doctor warns him that he will walk with a slight limp for the rest of his life but at least he's alive. Musa, a teenager just shy of her 19th birthday, died instantly.

'She was just a few years older than your daughter, Abraham! Aren't you ashamed of yourself?' asks Phumla.

'It wasn't like that, I promise you, Phumla,' Abraham attempts to explain.

'This is low, even for you, Abraham,' chastens Uncle Ben. 'This nonsense is all over the papers!'

Nobody will listen to Abraham's side of the story and only believe what they've been told. That he's a forty-five-year-old man who was driving drunk with a teenager in the car. But there is far more to the story.

The 1990s were lucrative years for Abraham as his business grew in leaps and bounds, as did his influence. During this time his womanising was at its peak. He was fraternising with a married woman, Thandiwe Mupoperi, whose husband was a local MP. She had been instrumental in getting her husband's sign-off on Abraham's latest project. Construction began on the project, a luxurious five-star lodge just outside Victoria Falls and because of its location, Abraham was on the road every week. Thandiwe was the general manager at one of the hotels he stayed at in the area and she always ensured he was upgraded to a luxury suite. She often joined him there and the arrangement suited them both and for the duration of the twelve-month project, their love affair intensified. So much so that Abraham was pressing her to leave her husband.

'I'll take care of you,' he said. '*Tshiyana leShona lakho lothuvi.* Leave that piece of Shona shit you are with.'

They were lying in bed after another passionate lovemaking session and Thandiwe was playing with her diamond ring. She wasn't sure she was ready to leave her husband and their two boys to play mistress to an up and coming businessman.

'I'll leave my husband if you leave your wife, Abraham. Unless there is marriage on the cards I am not leaving.'

'It's a deal. I'll end it with my wife.'

Abraham had left a marriage before and had no qualms about leaving again. He wanted to be with Thandiwe and it bothered him that she went home to another man. Thandiwe had assured him that her and her husband were no longer sexually intimate but Abraham didn't believe her. While they tried to see each other every week, it wasn't always possible and he doubted that a woman with a raging libido like hers could survive a week without a man.

Driving back home to Bulawayo later that evening, Abraham is determined he is going to end things with Phumla. He has his usual six-pack of beer for the drive and is just pulling onto the highway when he sees a young girl on the side of the road trying to flag down a car. He rarely picks up hitchhikers but the girl catches his eye in her tight-fitting T-shirt and bum shorts. Her perky breasts beckon and he brings his car to a stop. Other hitchhikers make a beeline for the car but he chases them away with a wave of his hand.

'I'm just taking the girl,' he says.

The young girl smiles and climbs into the passenger seat, giving Abraham a perfect view of her shapely legs.

'Where are you going?' he asks her.

'Luveve,' she replies. 'I work at the Falls and it's my week off so I'm going to see my child and my parents.'

'Aren't you too young to have a child?' Abraham asks.

She casts her eyes downward, 'It was an accident.'

Abraham quickly concludes that she must be of loose morals and will therefore probably be an easy lay. He offers her a beer and when she doesn't turn it down he knows he's in. When they stop in Hwange to refuel, he buys them more beers and some biltong to snack on. Abraham promises to buy the girl a proper meal at Chicken Inn when they get to Bulawayo but they never make it. The road is pitch black and Abraham doesn't see an animal standing in the middle of the road and hits the animal, driving into one of the portly baobab trees that line the road.

Abraham has no recollection of the accident and wakes up in the hospital with his arm in a cast and intravenous tubes in his arms. He's in hospital for two months and because of his injuries is unable to attend the girl's funeral. Musawenkosi was her name. God's mercy. He wonders why God has been merciful with his life and not hers. He is the one who deserved to die, not her. Her parents come to the hospital to see him and he is full of shame and remorse. His lawyer has warned him that the family might press charges and he could be facing counts of drunk driving and manslaughter. His lawyer does also point out that they are an impoverished family and can easily be bought; Abraham has already footed the bill for their daughter's funeral.

'Uxolo,' says Abraham. 'There is nothing I could possibly say to take away your pain except ask for your forgiveness.'

The father shakes his head, 'It was an accident. Accidents happen. We forgive you.'

'Could I at least give you some money?' says Abraham, beckoning to his lawyer.

'Money will never bring our daughter back,' says Musa's mother. 'She's gone and it was God's will.'

'Could I at least put your grandchild through school?'

They agree to the arrangement and Abraham's lawyer draws up the papers committing Abraham to educate the child for the rest of his life. Abraham knows this is not enough to begin to atone for all his mistakes.

Thandiwe comes to see him in hospital and is seething with anger. Even in his helpless state, she slaps him several times across the face. Her fiery temper was one of the things Abraham loved about her.

'So you want me to break it off with my husband but you were cavorting with a child?' she hisses.

Abraham knows there is no point in trying to explain himself and Thandiwe leaves the hospital and never speaks to him again. He cries for days and the nurses think he is reeling from the physical anguish of the accident but he's nursing a broken heart. He feels like a tree with no branches and in the winter of his grief, he sheds tears like falling leaves, leaving him naked and vulnerable.

Lying in hospital gives Abraham ample time to reflect on his life. He thinks about his mother and wishes she was there to nurse him. He misses her nurturing hand, especially now and even more so because none of the women in his life cultivate that feeling in him.

When Phumla comes to see him she is filled with hostility. She brings the girls with her so that her and Abraham are never alone. The girls have adopted their mother's aloofness and his conversations with them are stilted and awkward. Their visits only serve to amplify Abraham's discomfort and it's like his trunk is hollow with pain. He wishes he could fill the cavity with the love that once nourished him.

He is stumped and at a complete loss. He yearns for the soft reassuring touch of a mother and wishes she was still alive. Only she could alleviate this pain. He has no one.

Abraham was seven years old when his father died in a mineshaft collapse at Bushtick Mine. He remembers the funeral and how he held his sister, Ntombenhle's hand who was four at the time and had no understanding of what was happening. Lungile, just a tiny baby, was strapped to their mother's back and slept through the entire funeral. Afterwards, the family had undergone a cleansing ceremony and Abraham remembers the local *sangoma* cutting marks on their wrists and rubbing a black ashy substance into them. He said it was to ward off evil spirits.

Abraham's mother, Sakhile, never remarried and single-handedly and raised him and his sisters with the help of the nuns at the mission, who ensured they received the best education. He was born 'Mandla' but 'Abraham' was the name bestowed on him by the Catholic priests at the mission when he was baptised and so Catholicism was their default religion. He had never been particularly religious but was grateful for the Catholic missionaries who were instrumental in shaping his career path. Abraham was able to study at the Fort Hare Mission, while many of his cohorts chose to join the liberation struggle that took hold in the mid-1960s.

It was during this time that he met Phumla, a vivacious beauty who strutted around campus like a peacock. It had been love at first sight on his part but it was compromised by the fact that he had been promised to another woman, Sarah, who had grown up in the homestead a few metres from his family's.

He returned to Rhodesia with Phumla in hand and they began building a life together. His education afforded him the opportunity to secure professional jobs and he started in the clerical department at the Central African Building Society (CABS) and quickly worked his way up. Phumla was a teacher at St Patrick's Primary School and they lived in Makokoba Township, the first African township in Bulawayo. The name was derived from Mr Fallon, the native commissioner at the time who walked around with a walking stick or *ekhokhoba*.

It was a vibrant neighbourhood with a multi-ethnic population, drawing immigrants from Malawi, Mozambique and Zambia and others. The nightlife was electric and every day after work, Abraham drank at the Big Bar and fraternised with other working-class men. On weekends him and Phumla fraternised the shebeens, much to the chagrin of other men who believed that good women did not go to shebeens. They argued that shebeens were for *amawule* but Phumla was nonconformist and that was the very thing Abraham loved about her. She drank and danced the night away. It was the disco era and full of bright lights and starry-eyed dreams. They made a dapper couple and Abraham loved wearing loud, brightly coloured suits, replete with a bow tie while Phumla loved wearing her signature suede miniskirts with black stockings and platform heels always teamed with a blouse or cowl-neck sweater. They both sported huge afros which were like thick halos around their heads. They purchased their first gramophone and music filled their tiny abode and they often laughed that Xoliswa was conceived to the sound of Percy Sledge's 'Cover Me'. The O'Jays, The Manhattans, Bill Withers and Otis Redding and later Stimela, Dorothy Masuka, Hugh Masekela and Miriam Makeba became key members of their music collection. On some weekends they would go to Stanley Square and watch theatrical and musical productions and in those moments it was easy to forget that Rhodesia was a country under turmoil with a brewing battle for majority rule. There were painful reminders that they still lived in a segregated and unequal society. They were segregated in the way they lived. Blacks in the townships, while the whites lived in the suburbs. The segregation spilled over to schools, hospitals and even public toilets. There was no way Abraham could take Phumla for a drink at the Selborne Hotel because their bars were not open to both races. Their's was an unequal society, even in terms of income. Abraham was aware that his white colleague got paid a lot more for doing the very same job he did.

When Xoliswa was born in 1972, Phumla became a full-time mother and they hired a young girl who lived with them to assist with the daily chores. As Phumla settled into her mothering role, Abraham continued to party, much to his wife's growing resentment. Even more so when he came home with lipstick on his collar and reeking of cheap perfume.

A few years later when Abraham's sister, Ntombenhle, got a job in the city council she lived with Abraham and Phumla because women were never allocated their own houses. It was during this time that Abraham befriended Ben Ntini, a militant trade unionist who later became a struggle icon and was part of the ZAPU faction. Ben spent a lot of time in their home trying to stir political consciousness while eyeing Ntombenhle. He left a few years later for Zambia to join the struggle. They would later marry and have children together.

When Zimbabwe gained its independence, Abraham was one of the first blacks who could afford to relocate to the suburbs. They qualified for a mortgage and bought a three-bedroomed house in Hillside which they extended with further loans from the bank. It was during this time that Abraham's interest in development took hold and this led to the establishment of his construction company. The 1980s were a burgeoning time and Abraham's business started to grow.

On the face of it, the country appeared to be flourishing, with growing urbanisation and rapid development. It belied the underlying turmoil that shook the rural areas when the Gukurahundi skirmish that broke out in 1982. Most people in the urban areas were unaware that Zimbabwe was a country at war with its citizens. Every month-end, they visited Abraham's mother in her village and during one of their monthly visits they were stopped in a roadblock. That particular month they arrived to find the homestead smouldering with flames of hatred. They searched for the old woman and found her in the cornfields, chattering incoherently. They returned to the city with her and she narrated the atrocities for days, over and over again. Gogo Sakhile was never the same and she'd often wake up at night screaming about men in red berets coming for them. By this time, Sis Ntombi was living alone with her boys because Uncle Ben had been arrested and put in prison. Gogo Sakhile didn't live to see Uncle Ben get released from prison in 1987 after the Unity Accord was signed.

Lying in his hospital bed, reflecting on his life, Abraham vows to visit his mother's grave the minute he's discharged from hospital. He hasn't been to her grave in years. However, on the day he is finally discharged from hospital, Phumla has other ideas of what he needs to do and it doesn't involve visiting the dead. They've barely pulled out of the hospital parking lot when she lays down the law.

'As soon as you are well, I'm leaving,' she declares. She tells him that divorce papers have already been drawn up.

'Please don't leave me,' he begs.

'No, Abraham, I've had enough of your whoring and I can't carry on like this.'

'Please don't leave me, Phumla. I promise I will change. I will make amends.'

Tears are streaming down his cheeks.

'I don't want a new car or new jewellery, Abraham! I want my dignity back. I want my happiness back!'

'And I promise I will try to give those things to you, Phumla. I promise. I'll stop with the women, I'll stop drinking and all the other nonsense.'

Phumla sighs and in that moment she decides to give him another chance, not sure if conceding to his cries is the right thing to do.

Abraham takes a while to fully recuperate but when he does, he lives up to his promises. He stops drinking. He stops going out and he stops all the women. At first, Phumla doesn't think it will last but he then starts going to church. Initially, he goes on his own and Phumla reluctantly joins him after a few weeks. This becomes a routine and every Sunday after church, he takes Phumla out for lunch, just the two of them. They start reconnecting as a couple. Reaching for each other's hands across the table, his hand over hers, hands stroking like lovers, Abraham sees the sparkle start to come back in Phumla's eyes and he courts her like when they first met. They revisit the completed Victoria Falls project and make a weekend of it, alone, without the girls. They rediscover each other and reignite the passion that had gone dormant between them. Stoking the flames of a fire that has long gone out, they fan it with their love until the heat consumes them. They fall in love with each other all over again and nothing else seems to exist outside the intensity of their love. But then Yandisa falls pregnant and Abraham suffers an emotional breakdown and has to be admitted to hospital for treatment.

'God is punishing me isn't he?' he cries. 'The sins of the father are being revisited onto the children.'

'You are not being punished,' says Phumla.

'I have to do better,' he says. 'Look what nearly happened to us. Look at our girls.'

Phumla knows Abraham wants to do better for his family and when he's discharged from hospital he drives her to Matsheumhlope to share something with her. He shows her a huge piece of vacant land that he had bought from the council just before his admission to hospital. The land borders Stour Road, Aberdeen Avenue and Old Esigodini Road and he had been debating whether to use it to build a housing estate or a private school.

'I see a school here,' says Phumla when she sees it. 'There are no good schools in this area.'

'I see a church,' says Abraham. 'Maybe we can build the church first and then add a school later on which you can run.'

They both agree that it is a long-term project that will require a long-term vision. He asks if Phumla is in it for the long haul. Phumla takes his hand and squeezes it tightly to indicate her agreement. And that is how the Kingdom of God was borne.

COUNTING COWS

September draws to an end and Yandisa is pregnant with apprehension, both literally and figuratively. The date had been set aside for *abakhwenyana* to bring home the cows and her father's relatives arrive early that morning, ready to carry out their mandate. The uncles are ready to assume their role at the negotiating table and the aunties take out the three-legged cast-iron pots and light the fires to cook the lunch. The roles are clearly delineated with no overlap. Everyone is in a buoyant mood that morning and the family agree that Zandile's marriage has brought the family immeasurable good luck which has rubbed off onto Yandisa. Everyone is certain that Xoliswa will soon follow suit on the marital path.

Sis Ntombi advises them all that *abakhwenyana* will be arriving at 11 am to start the proceedings. As the only person to have met Wesley, Sis Ntombi is feeling smug and Abraham keeps asking over and over again, if he is a good man. Sis Ntombi replies smoothly, 'He is good enough for Yandisa.'

As the day unfolds, Yandisa continues to wrestle with her own anxiety. She hasn't seen Wesley since that fateful day when she had moved out of his flat and they haven't spoken to each other either. She's been too much of a coward to tell her family that Wesley called everything off. To tell them that he is not going to show up. She's tired of always being the failure in the family. First it was falling pregnant, then she was fired from work and now she's being ditched. She figures that if Wesley doesn't show up, her family might have more empathy for her as it's almost akin to being ditched at the altar. She plays along with the charade and the eleventh hour slides into the twelfth. When the clock strikes 1 pm, Sis Ntombi's patience starts to run thin.

'*Kanti*, where is your person?' she screams at Yandisa. 'The men keep asking me and I don't know what to tell them.'

Yandisa shrugs her shoulders, 'I don't know either. Maybe their car broke down.'

'Why aren't they communicating with you?' shouts Sis Ntombi. 'They've all got cellphones!'

Yandisa had called and texted Wesley but he hadn't responded which only added to her spiralling anxiety. Sis Lungile is equally tense because it isn't uncommon to be stood up by *abakhwenyana*. Some men get cold feet or if they feel they haven't raised the required amount of money they abscond from the negotiations.

'I'm not sure he's going to come,' Xoliswa confides to her mother.

Her mother stares back at her, horrified, 'What do you mean?'

'Wesley got my friend pregnant years ago. He stood her up.'

Phumla is dismissive, 'That was years ago. People change. Maybe he wasn't ready then.'

'And you think he is ready now?' shoots back Xoliswa.

'People *do* change, Xolie. Look at your father. Did you ever think he could become the person he is now?'

The question lingers in the air, hanging between them unanswered.

Phumla puts a gentle arm around her daughter, 'I know you've been through a lot with Thulani but don't let it make you bitter.'

Phumla takes Xoliswa by the hand and they walk into Yandisa's bedroom together. All the women are huddled there in solidarity and as per the custom, they are far removed from the lobola negotiations. No women are allowed to sit around the lobola-negotiating table and the discussion is held by the men in the family. They are all dressed for the occasion in *imibhaco*, traditional Xhosa regalia, replete with elaborate beadwork and headscarves. However, the splendour of their regalia can't detract from Yandisa's nervousness and the lump in her throat threatens to choke her. She's on the verge of disappointing her family yet again and it'll only take something small to trigger an avalanche of tears.

'Let's all pray,' instructs Phumla.

They all kneel, holding hands and Phumla begins the prayer for the proceedings.

It's 2 pm when Sis Lungile sweeps into the room declaring boldly that *abakhwenyana* have arrived. At first, Yandisa thinks she must have misheard.

'They're here!' says Sis Lungile excitedly.

The uncles are pacing restlessly, annoyed that *abakhwenyana* are so late.

'*Bayadelela*. They are rude!' is the agreed-upon sentiment.

Wesley's delegation is comprised of his Uncle Ndodana, the *dombo* or negotiator and Charles and JB. The four men are suited up and wearing shiny, pointed leather shoes and look like a quartet from a jazz band about to stage a performance. They stand at the gate, waiting expectantly to be let in but are ignored.

Twenty minutes later, Yandisa approaches her aunt telling her they should be let in but Sis Ntombi is unbothered.

'They kept us waiting, let them wait,' is her response.

Wesley and his entourage are left standing at the gate for another thirty minutes. By this time, they can no longer withstand the afternoon heat and remove their jackets to reveal their colourful, viscose shirts. It is then when Sis Lungile finally decides to open the gate and let them in.

Before the men are even allowed to state their case, a representative from the Mafu family requests '*Uvula mlomo*' which loosely translated means the 'mouth opener' and nothing can be said until this amount is paid. It is the icebreaker used to thaw relations between the Mafus and the Bhunus before they start the negotiations.

'What brings you here, gentlemen?' asks Uncle Scotch, opening the dialogue.

Because Abraham is the only male in his family, he has to rely on his cousins Scotch, Foster and Lizwe to provide support in the negotiations.

'We have come to ask for your daughter's hand in marriage,' responds Ndodana.

'My brother has three daughters,' says Uncle Scotch, 'which one have you come for?'

Yandisa and her sisters are called and are joined by Khethiwe, who is there almost like an afterthought but Sis Ntombi had insisted her daughter be included. Much as she had insisted Khethiwe had to be involved in Zandile's wedding. Khethiwe isn't wearing the black top and flowing white skirt with a black bead trim like the sisters.

The women are asked to sit on the floor with their heads bowed and their hands in their laps as it's important for the women to assume a posture of demureness. One by one they are asked if they know the Bhunus and Yandisa is the only one who professes her knowledge of the family.

'How do you know them?' asks Uncle Foster.

'I know their son, Wesley,' she replies, looking up for the first time.

Her eyes connect with Wesley and she quickly looks away, not wanting to hold his gaze for too long. She can see his lazy grin out of the corner of her eye and she finds it comforting. JB and Charles are trying to hold back their laughter and she knows they're going to tease her afterwards about acting so shy and demure.

Now that the elders have received confirmation of their relationship, the women are asked to leave.

'*Liwonile. Lilecala*,' says Uncle Scotch. 'As you saw, our daughter is with child.'

The severity of his tone conveys the severity of the crime. Impregnating a woman out of wedlock is considered a violation of womanhood as it means a young woman has been robbed of her virginity, causing disgrace to her family as a result of then falling pregnant.

'*Siyalivuma icala,*' says Ndodana confidently, taking full responsibility for the charge levied at their feet.

'For the crime you have committed we will require you to pay three cows,' says Uncle Scotch.

'Three cows?' says Ndodana.

'Yes, we demand three cows,' repeats Uncle Scotch and he then goes on to explain what each cow represents. 'The first cow is a fine. If you break the law you must pay a fine. The second cow is *inkomo yobulunga* to cleanse the family of the shame this act has brought upon the Mafu family. The third cow is to restore Yandisa's dignity.'

Ndodana asks for a few minutes to confer with his entourage. There is a brief exchange and he responds that they are adamant they are only going to pay one cow. Uncle Lizwe and Uncle Foster shake their heads in consternation and say that the Bhunus can't be serious about only paying one cow.

'We are serious,' maintains Ndodana. 'We have accepted responsibility for the crime levied against us as my son did impregnate your daughter so we agree to pay one cow for the fine. The rest we refuse to pay.'

'*Madoda liyabheda!* Gentlemen, this is preposterous!' hisses Uncle Foster.

'With all due respect,' counters Ndodana, 'Yandisa is not a virgin. She was robbed of her virginity long before our son laid a hand on her. Secondly, she already has a child so your family name was shamed a long time ago. We can't be expected to pay reparations for damages of the past.'

A hush falls over the living room like a curtain coming down on the first act of a theatrical performance. Uncle Lizwe loosens his bow tie and Uncle Scotch and Uncle Foster both shift uncomfortably in their seats. This is not part of the script they rehearsed and they ask for a recess to chew it over.

MARRIAGE IS AN ACHIEVEMENT

Sequestered in the living room, the men with creased faces confer with Abraham because they have reached a snag in the discussions. Voices are raised, accusations bandied about.

'I can't believe Yandisa told him about the child,' Abraham splutters angrily when they tell him the negotiations have stalled.

'Now they have the upper hand,' he adds and cusses under his breath. Uncle Scotch tries to appease him, appealing to Abraham to gain his composure.

The uncles return to the discussion, feeling defeated.

'*Siyavuma*. We are agreeable. We will accept the one cow,' says Uncle Scotch humbly.

Uncle Ndodana has a triumphant look on his face and Wesley and his crew breathe a collective sigh of relief. The negotiations are progressing much smoother than what they had anticipated.

Ndodana continues, 'Now that the issue of the fine is out of the way, we want to discuss the issue of *amalobolo*. It is our intention to marry your daughter and make an honest woman out of her. We want to restore her honour which I'm sure you'll agree was lost when she was first impregnated.'

An uneasy silence follows and none of the Mafu men offer a response, prompting Ndodana to continue.

'Our son has made it clear he will only lobola Yandisa. We don't want anything to do with the child from her previous relationship. Our son has made it clear that they are starting a new family and he wants nothing to do with Yandisa's past.'

'We are agreeable,' says Uncle Scotch.

179

It isn't uncommon for children borne out of wedlock to be raised by their grandparents when the child's mother's gets married in order to give the bride a future, one unencumbered by the past. But because Babalwa is being raised by Abraham and Phumla this doesn't make much of a difference and so the negotiations for Yandisa's hand in marriage continue. The Mafus request four cows for the *amalobolo*. Uncle Ndodana disputes this and says that four cows is too many and once again Uncle Foster goes to great pains to articulate why they are demanding that many.

'Yandisa is a beautiful and desirable woman. Have you not seen her? *Mhlawumbe,* you're not convinced!'

Yandisa is called in, flanked by her sisters and they are paraded in front of the delegation like models on the catwalk.

'Look at her!' enthuses Uncle Foster, *'isiqhabhobho esimhlophe.'*

He praises her light complexion and says she will light up the Bhunu homestead with her beauty. He admires her voluptuous figure and the men agree that Wesley will certainly have a trophy wife on his arm. After Yandisa and her sisters exit the room, Ndodana concedes that they will definitely present a heifer to celebrate Yandisa's beauty.

The second cow, argues Uncle Scotch, is for Yandisa's fertility. He indicates that it is clearly evident she will sire many offspring to grow Wesley's family. Nobody can dispute that having already given birth to one child, and pregnant with another, Yandisa will be able to sire more kids in the future.

The third cow is for breeding and gentility. Uncle Lizwe says that Yandisa comes from a good home. The Mafu name is counted alongside Ndebele royalty and is a name to be praised and upheld in the community.

The fourth cow is for the asset Yandisa is going to be to her new family. She's well educated and has a good job. Nobody makes mention of her non-existent qualifications or her misdemeanour at the bank, they just argue that her earning capacity will be of great benefit to her family.

After much discussion, the bride price is reduced to three cows. In addition, *inkomo yohlanga* is to be given to Yandisa's mother, to essentially thank her for her integral role in raising Yandisa. It is the only time the matriarchal role is acknowledged in the proceedings.

Uncle Scotch sums up the negotiations and says the Bhunus are expected to deliver the three cows upfront or the cash equivalent. The Bhunus pay a portion in cash immediately and indicate that the two outstanding cows will follow at a later stage. The Mafus also request that they want to have a 'white wedding' and that Yandisa will only leave the house in a 'white' dress. They are aware that the two 'lovebirds' had been living together 'in sin' and want things to be done the right way going forward. Uncle Ndodana agrees that this is a fair request.

Agreement is reached and there's a lot of handshaking and patting of backs and the uncles applaud each other on a job well done. Uncle Foster disappears to alert Sis Ntombi that food can be served and that the proceedings have gone well.

When Sis Ntombi walks into the kitchen, she starts ululating, signalling the success of the negotiations. Sis Lungile is the first to envelop Yandisa in a warm embrace.

'I'm so happy for you!' she gushes. 'It's not easy to get married when you have a child!'

'Praise God!' says Phumla, pulling Yandisa into her arms. 'God is faithful all the time.'

'Thank your ancestors,' enthuses Sis Ntombi. 'They worked for you. *Usebenzile* girl!'

Yandisa is passed around like a ball with everyone keen to congratulate her. Sis Ntombi calls them to order asking that the food be taken to the men, who are dying of hunger. Yandisa and her sisters are told to serve and Yandisa circles the room, on her knees, washing the men's hands one by one. They are full of praise for her, calling her *makoti* and her sisters follow with the plates of food. Bottles of whisky are opened and noisy toasts are made. The earlier tension has evaporated and has been replaced with immense jubilation.

The *bakhwenyana* leave shortly after the meal is concluded, even though it is clear the party is going to continue long after they have gone. Yandisa walks with the men, lingering a few steps behind with Wesley. They hold hands lovingly. They have barely spoken all day but his touch communicates so much.

'Why did you come?' she asks, before he gets into the car.

'Because I love you,' he replies, drawing her closer to him. 'I mean it.'

Yandisa throws her arms around him and hugs him fiercely. Uncle Ndodana prises them apart with his walking stick.

'This is how you got pregnant, *makoti*!' he teases.

JB and Charles are already in the car and both laugh playfully.

'I'm just joking, *makoti*,' Ndodana says with a naughty grin.

Yandisa is smiling from ear to ear and her heart is swelling with love as they drive away. Walking back to the house, she sees her father in the driveway and he pulls her into his arms and embraces her.

'I'm really proud of you, Yandisa. You have done me proud.'

The tears come. That is the nicest thing her father has ever said to her. All her life he has castigated her but today he is full of praise. Yandisa basks in his glowing admiration and for the first time in her life, she has done something right.

LOST AND FOUND

The euphoric mood of the lobola negotiations carries over to the next day and the family heads to church the next morning. Even Wesley attends the service which surprises the whole family and his presence causes quite a stir amongst the women in the congregation. This makes Yandisa's heart flutter but Wesley doesn't seem to notice and only has eyes for Yandisa.

Xoliswa can't mask her shock when she sees Wesley and he finds her seemingly supercilious attitude annoying, even more so now that he has proved himself to the family.

'You really are a changed man, Wesley. Even churching on Sunday?' quips Xoliswa.

'Us both,' he replies, matching her sarcasm.

She ignores his comment and instead gives him a hug, 'Welcome to the family.'

The gesture is unexpected but Wesley appreciates it and he's relieved they are finally putting the past behind them. Ndabenhle and Zandile step forward and embrace him warmly.

'Thanks for the support,' jokes Ndabenhle, 'at least now we can share the load!'

The mood is convivial as they all file into the church. Wesley immediately heads for the back row but Yandisa tugs him gently and leads him to the front where her family and the elders of the church are sitting. She quickly briefs him about the church's protocol of family and elders sitting in front and the hoi polloi sitting at the back. For a man who has never set foot in a church, sitting in the front row is daunting for him.

183

The service starts with praise and worship and the congregation take to their feet. A young woman with a melodic voice leads the choir and the music is rhythmic and upbeat. Wesley momentarily forgets that he's in church and gets caught up in the effervescent moment. People dance as they praise the Lord and when the music slows and the songs become more emotive, he starts to feel like the Holy Spirit is moving amongst them. He has never been religious and being forced to attend mass at school was the closest he ever got to experiencing religion of any sort. When the praise and worship episode ends, the congregation sits down and Abraham takes to the podium. His presence on stage is met with wild applause. Wesley understands that kind of adulation as he's often greeted with it when he runs onto the rugby field.

Abraham stands behind the pulpit and asks the church to turn to the Book of Matthew. He starts to tell the congregation the parable of the lost sheep.

'The story of the lost sheep is a dear one to me,' says Abraham, pacing across the podium. 'Many of you who know me, will know that I was a lost sheep. I was lost to the ways of the world and I sinned in every sense of the word. I was like a pig muddied with sin. I hurt my wife. I hurt my kids. I hurt everyone who was close to me. I hurt the women I sinned with. Sin brought me nothing but pain and disillusionment. It was only when I was involved in a car accident and had an encounter with the Lord and he said to me, "Abraham, I am giving you a second chance to change your ways. To make right all the wrongs", that I decided to change, *bazalwana*. I let go off my old self and my wild ways. I let it all go!'

The congregation all get to their feet, clapping wildly. When the applause dies down, Abraham continues with his sermon.

'Those of you with children know that children are a mirror of everything we do. Not what you say, what you do. They copy us, they imitate us. In your children you see your good traits and your worst ones too. Most of you know that I have three daughters but for the longest time Yandisa was lost to me. Not only was she lost to me, she was lost to the church, lost to the Kingdom. Yandisa is the daughter I have had the most difficult relationship with. And do you know why? Because she *is* me. I would see myself in her and get angry because she reminded me of myself at my worst. Last month she returned home, pregnant. She gave up her life of sin and decided to come home yet I was so angry. I couldn't look her in the eye or speak to her. Imagine living in the same house yet I can't even speak to my own child! Then my wife, in all her earthly wisdom, came to me, opened the Bible and reproached me gently with Matthew 7 verse 1 and 2. "Do not judge, or you too will be judged. For in the same way you judge others, you will be judged, and with the measure you use, it will be measured to you!"'

There is another rapturous applause that thunders through the church and shouts of 'Amen'.

'I had to take a step back and ask myself what right I had to judge my own daughter. Yes, she made a mistake but she was repentant. She said she was sorry but I was too angry to care. Have I not made mistakes? Have I not been forgiven? Even when I didn't deserve it? How many times have I wronged my wife and wronged my family? Do we not all sin and ask our Father for forgiveness? Does he not show us mercy? Yet I was behaving like I have never sinned and so in that moment I was humbled.'

Abraham looks directly at Yandisa. She has tears running down her cheeks.

'I then asked my daughter, "What do you want to do? What is your plan?" She's twenty-five years old, pregnant and has no husband. She told me she wanted to make things right. And you know what? Yesterday Wesley came home to pay lobola. These two young people said they want to do the right thing.'

There is another deafening applause. Abraham points to Yandisa and Wesley and asks them to stand up. The congregation cheer and clap and the choir sings a song praising the goodness of God. After the thunderous acclamation, Abraham continues with his sermon.

'I told Wesley yesterday that Yandisa is not leaving the house unless she is in a white dress. And I stand here, *bandla*, and tell you that we are going to have a wedding in December!'

This announcement is met with more ululating and another standing ovation.

'Wesley told me he doesn't have the money for a white wedding after the lobola proceedings but I told him God provides! We serve a mighty living God!'

This fires the congregants up even more.

'I pledge this church. They will be married in this church, in the house of the Lord, at no cost,' declares Abraham.

A woman stands up, 'I run a catering business. We will cook at the wedding for all the guests, free of charge!'

A man then rises, 'I have a farm. I am going to donate two beasts and a goat for the wedding ceremony so that the flock of the Lord can eat!'

And another, 'I run a transport service. I will pledge my cars to transport the bride and the groom on their wedding day.'

Then an elder stands up, 'I don't cook and I don't decorate but I have money and I will donate ten thousand dollars to the couple.'

Zandile stands up, 'I pledge to pay for the flowers for the wedding.'

And so the pledges continue, the ushers furiously writing the offers in their notebooks. Wesley is astounded at the generosity. These people were all strangers but here they are invested in him and Yandisa's union.

A SHOTGUN WEDDING

Wesley and Yandisa have a big wedding and it is featured in the *Sunday News*. 'Rugby Fly Half meets his Other Half' screams the headline, accompanied by several pictures from the reception.

At least five hundred people file into church that Saturday morning to witness their union. The Kingdom of God is a solid two-storey box structure with slashed windows to allow shafts of light to shine through. Were it not for the huge cross indented into the stone-faced façade, it could easily be mistaken for a AAA-grade corporate office building. Throngs of people make their way through the five-bay arcade, through the aluminium-framed sliding doors to the foyer of the church. Lush fig trees are positioned at various entrances to the church, greeting people as they walk in. On closer inspection, however, it is discovered that they are fake and used merely to add to the décor. The ushers work tirelessly, seating everyone in the church sanctuary which is illuminated by translucent, pendant lights. Metal-framed, blue-upholstered chairs are used instead of the traditional wooden pews found in most churches. The auditorium-style seating gives the feeling of being in a theatre as opposed to a church, the stage being the focal point. Church protocol has largely been observed with the first few rows reserved for close family members and the church elders. Every now and then there is a slight disturbance with a relative insisting they deserve to be seated in the front row.

The ceremony is slated to start at 9 am but it eventually only starts two hours later. No one can provide an explanation for the two-hour delay but by then a restless congregation is fanning themselves with the programme.

Wesley and his groomsmen strut into the church with a gentle swagger, accompanied by Jagged Edge's, 'Let's Get Married'. Initially, Xoliswa had flinched at the idea, thinking it was ghetto-fabulous but witnessing the furore the men have caused, raising the church to its feet, it doesn't seem like such a bad idea after all.

Wesley and his cohorts decided to ditch the traditional suit and tie and instead chose to wear cream shirts and khaki Bermuda shorts, replete with gold braces and pink bow ties. Leather moccasin shoes to complete the look.

The groomsmen include a right wing, hooker and loose head prop and with their muscled calves on display, the younger women in the congregation cheer the party on. Save for Charles, who looks portly in comparison, the rest of the guys are buffed and brawny.

It takes a while for the church to settle down as they wait for the bridesmaids to file in, accompanied by Tamia's, 'You Put A Move On My Heart'. The bridesmaids look vivacious in pastel-coloured, scalloped, lacy, crop tops teamed with flimsy, chiffon skirts and strappy pink sandals. The bridal party is made up of Yandisa's friends, including Dumile and Towanda from high school, Sunette and Shamiso, who used to work with her at the bank, and her cousin, Khethiwe, in order to accommodate Sis Ntombi's wishes.

Xoliswa had declined the role of maid of honour, having been too immersed in the planning and setting up of the wedding. Zandile took on the matron of honour role instead. Babalwa is also a bridesmaid and Wesley's two nieces are flower girls, their dresses mimicking those of the older bridesmaids. The pageboys are styled in cream shirts and Bermuda shorts just like the groomsmen.

By the time Yandisa walks down the aisle, flanked by both her parents, the church is hyped up. The elderly women are ululating, dancing and throwing their scarves in the air. Yandisa is a sight to behold and positively radiant with a crown of baby's breath on her head and tiny micro braids spilling down her back. She's wearing a Grecian-style gown with diamanté detail. The high-waisted bodice flows into a full chiffon skirt, draped over her curves and baby bump.

Three songs later, the ceremony begins. Abraham is in his element as he delivers the sermon based on the Book of Genesis.

'It is not good for man to be alone which is why God had created a help mate called Eve. Yandisa is your Eve. She is only here to help you achieve your vision but if you don't have a vision or agenda, Wesley, she will not be able to help you. Strong men lead. Strong men work!'

At this point, Abraham pauses and turns to his Bible and to Genesis 2 verse 15. '"The Lord God took the man and put him in the garden of Eden to till it and keep it". Did you hear that? Adam was not sitting on his laurels, he was working in the garden. It is every man's responsibility to work his garden to provide for his family.'

There is rapturous applause. Applause so loud that it jerks some of the groomsmen to attention as rumour has it the bachelor party the night before had been riotous. However, Wesley's demeanour doesn't show any signs of a lack of sleep or of being hungover and he holds his composure throughout the ceremony. The vows are recited and the rings exchanged and the long kiss that follows is met with a round of applause and more ululating. The marriage ceremony is concluded and there is a rush to get outside to congratulate the new Mr and Mrs Bhunu and to get a picture with the couple.

The reception is held in the church gardens, under a canopy of a few Musasa trees that were left during the construction process. Pastel-coloured voile fabric is wrapped around the tree trunks, creating the feeling and ambience of a midsummer daydream. You could almost expect fairies to dance across the garden. Opaque bottles filled with yellow and white daisies hang from the branches of the trees, adding to the overall ethereal feeling. The flowering perennials give the garden a burst of colour with deep pink magnolias, bright white jasmine and red roses. The heady, floral scents of flowers intermingle with the aromatic smells of soul food.

Wheelbarrows painted green and yellow are filled with bottles of cool drink and ice, providing refreshment points for guests. Wooden trestle tables draped with floral garlands are set up in the garden and people are able to sit where they like. Everyone is accommodated with no formal table seating. Pitchers of ice-cold fruity punch are placed on the tables. Some guests have brought their own alcohol-filled cooler boxes, easily concealed under the tables. Without much prompting, some of the guests remove their shoes and walk barefoot, their feet connecting with the lush grass. The bride herself is barefoot, having discarded her pumps which could no longer contain her swollen feet. Yandisa is carefree and content and pauses for pictures as she mingles and chats to the guests. A table has been assigned for her and Wesley and the bridal party at the front but she hasn't sat down since the reception began. Guests comment between themselves how good-natured Yandisa is and not as snobby as her two sisters.

'I was worried this was going to turn into a circus,' remarks Xoliswa, who is holding a parasol to shield herself from the hot December sun.

'So was I,' says Zandile, 'but people are actually being civilised.'

Lunch is served a little after 2 pm, by which time most guests are chewing their fingers off they are so hungry. There are several serving points and people are ushered table by table to get their food. It's not an elaborate menu and has been pared down to beef curry, tripe and offal stew and crispy pieces of fried chicken. The accompaniment is spicy yellow rice, dumplings and steaming hot *isitshwala*. The vegetables are butternut, creamed spinach, grated beetroot and coleslaw salad. Guests pile their plates high with food, forming mountain peaks, with the sauce from the stew running down the valleys.

'The food is really good,' says Uncle Ben, who already wants to go for seconds but Sis Ntombi gives him a scathing look, 'You know what the doctor said about your cholesterol,' she scolds.

'You only live once,' responds Abraham, encouraging his brother-in-law.

'Try the tripe, *bhudi*,' suggests Phumla, licking her own fingers.

'It's finished,' says Sis Lungile, who has just returned with her second helping.

Seated together at one table and forced to set aside their differences for the day, the mood between them is jovial.

'Have some more, sisi,' says Sis Lungile, offering Phumla some food off her plate. The meat has been cooked for so long it slides off the bone but as appetising as it looks, and as tempted as she is to get more, Sis Ntombi decides to save some space for dessert.

There is tricoloured trifle and a fruit salad with every fruit imaginable, whether in season or not and sliced watermelon on kebab sticks which proves to be extremely popular with the elders.

The bridal team perform their obligatory dances and receive standing ovations. This is followed by the cutting of the three-tier rose gold wedding cake with delicately crafted white and cream peonies, served to guests with tea and coffee. The gifting ceremony takes place and Abraham and Phumla are the first to stand. They gift Yandisa and her new husband a piece of land; no one can rival that.

'All Dad gave us was ten thousand dollars,' remarks Zandile begrudgingly.

'We didn't need the land,' says Ndabenhle, 'they need it more.'

Wesley's mom gifts them with two thousand dollars even though most guests feel that she needs it more. The gifts include a four-plate stove from Sis Ntombi and a fridge from Sis Lungile. Some guests announce what they have brought, especially if it is of monetary value. Ululating and clapping follow each announcement. At sunset, Abraham gives a thank-you speech before he launches into a feverish prayer. Many of the church guests leave after that, leaving family and friends to enjoy a more intimate evening together.

A VISION OF LOVE

Once the church folk leave, the party transitions from a religious celebration to a secular one. Those who had been drinking on the down-low, start to do so brazenly. Wesley's close friends, DJ Flavour and DJ Snaxx, set up their station and a huge spit braai is started and soon the smell of roast lamb fills the air. Corn on the cob, potato salad and a tossed green salad are laid out and Wesley and Yandisa open the dance floor with 'Dilemma' by Nelly and Kelly. Apparently it was the song that was playing the night they met. What surprises people is how vigorously Yandisa dances, especially for someone so heavily pregnant, and everyone comments that they have never seen such an active bride.

'It's a good thing the Bhunus only want us to take her there tomorrow afternoon,' remarks Sis Lungile, standing on the sidelines watching her niece.

'You're alone on this one,' says Sis Ntombi. 'I did Zandile's.'

'I'm happy to take her,' says Sis Lungile. She's always had empathy for her niece that no one else has.

'I don't know what they're going to do with Yandisa,' says Sis Ntombi, shaking her head in disdain.

'Even I'm worried,' says Phumla, picking up on the conversation. 'All my daughter knows is how to dance!'

The three women laugh together; it's one thing they can all agree on.

Xoliswa observes the wedding from the sidelines, glass of champagne in hand. She has finally removed her heels and is walking around in stockinged feet, happy to be able to finally relax now that all the hard work is done. There is nothing left on her to-do list. People are fed and happy. She exhales deeply. The culmination of all her hard work. The past two months have felt like *she* was the one getting married and Yandisa literally slept through all the preparations, only waking up to attend her big day.

It certainly might not have been as grand as Zandile's wedding but it certainly is more fun. Looking around she can see glowing happy people holding hands. She looks across at her parents' table and they also look happy. Even her father is relaxed, engaged in a boisterous conversation with Uncle Ben and Uncle Foster. Even though their mother is chatting animatedly to their aunts, she is lovingly leaning into Abraham. At the table next to them, Zandile and Ndabenhle are staring dreamily into each other's eyes and acting like they got married yesterday. The love between them is so palpable, she can almost touch it. She casts her eyes to the dance floor and Yandisa and Wesley are still the main attraction, everyone having formed a circle around them. Wesley is holding Yandisa close to him, his hands playing along her backside, squeezing and cupping her flesh. They are radiating enough heat to warm the ozone layer and the chemistry between them is so electric Xoliswa could easily draw sparks around them. Yandisa is laughing, throwing her head back and Wesley is twisting and contorting his face as he gyrates down to the floor.

'Do you want to dance?'

Xoliswa turns around and a man is standing just behind her, looking at her expectantly. He is so tall she has to look up at him and she's usually the same height as most men, if not taller. She often didn't wear heels when she was with Thulani, lest she overshadowed him.

'You mean me?' she says unsurely.

'Yes, you, Xoliswa.'

He speaks decisively and confidently. She is surprised that he knows her name.

'My name is Keith Ndiweni,' he says, offering her his hand.

She shakes his hand and he grips it firmly, holding it a little too long, she thinks.

'Which side of the family?' she asks.

'Neither,' he replies. 'I'm with the church.'

He leads her to the centre of the garden where another dance space has been created in the most illuminated area. Keith is quite the dancer, whereas Xoliswa moves awkwardly like her joints need oiling.

'Would you just relax?' admonishes Keith, taking her by the hand and swivelling her around.

Xoliswa laughs, surprised at his candour.

'You are *so* beautiful when you laugh! Seriously!'

Xoliswa laughs even harder, 'Are you coming onto me, brother Keith?'

'Maybe,' he replies with a naughty grin. 'Dating the pastor's daughter would be a blessing.'

His eyes light up and his face creases as he smiles at her. His chiselled cheekbones forming perfect contours. The Lord certainly took his time with Keith, pausing to iron out any flaws. She wonders how she has never noticed him at church before but with three services a day it is perfectly possible to miss people. Even someone as good-looking as Keith.

The Aaliyah song that was playing fades away and Mariah Carey starts crooning a beautiful ballad. Keith pulls her into his arms without any invitation and they rock gently, back and forth with the other couples being serenaded by the music. Through his suit, Xoliswa can feel the tautness of his body; firm, yet supple. She allows herself to rest her head on his chest.

He's making her feel things she hasn't felt in a long time. He holds her and she doesn't want the song to end. They dance together for the rest of the night and the party carries on into the early hours of the morning.

Luckily the Bhunus had said their *makoti* could come through at 2 pm so they can all sleep in until midday at least but Yandisa doesn't make it. She wakes up with a start that morning saying that her waters have broken. They rush her to the hospital and by 4 pm that afternoon she is cradling her baby in her arms. It is as if Jason Thabani Bhunu waited for his parents to be legal before making his entrance into the world. The baby is taken to the nursery and Yandisa passes out and sleeps.

Yandisa is thankful her son arrived when he decided to. She is spared the rigmarole of having to go to Wesley's home to *kotiza* and do all the other *makoti* rituals. Her sisters had gone, along with Maria, to stand in her for her but had not stayed long, saying they had to be with her in hospital. The Bhunus were of course extremely understanding and said Yandisa could always do it at a later stage. Yandisa has no intention of doing anything at any later stage.

It is her second day in hospital and her back aches and she's exhausted. Her hospital room is a hive of activity and there is a constant stream of visitors. After attending the wedding, the church folk feel like they have some kind of stake in her life and feel justified to visit her in the hospital and meet the baby. They come in droves, bearing gifts and money.

Her family are thrilled with the new addition and her sisters never leave her side. They are all enamoured with Baby Jason. He has a tag with 'Baby Bhunu. 3.8kg' attached to his wrist and is light in complexion with droopy cheeks like a bull terrier.

'He's huge,' marvels Zandile, holding his cherubic face to hers.

All she wants to do is envelop him with kisses and holding him in her arms makes her even more broody than she already is.

'Yeah and I have the stitches to prove it,' says an exhausted Yandisa. 'All the way up to my arse like a rag doll!'

'Can I hold him?' asks Xoliswa.

Zandile pretends not to hear her and Xoliswa has to repeat her request a little louder.

'I'm not done!' snaps Zandile, placing Jason on her shoulder and stroking his back lovingly.

'Have your own,' chastens Yandisa.

'I'm trying! You have no idea how hard I am trying. We are at it every night!'

Both her sisters burst out laughing as they imagine the frantic coupling going on in the Khumalo household.

'And Ndaba's mother is asking. Every time we visit her she checks me out and the last time I was so bloated just before my period, she looked at me and said, "*kule mpilo*. There is life in there"!'

They laugh even harder.

'I've started to wear caftans every time we go and visit!' continues Zandile.

'Well, good luck with giving birth,' jibes Yandisa.

Even though it was her second time around it hadn't been any easier because this time she anticipated the pain. In the delivery room she had cried and screamed during the labour. Her mother had gone in with her because when they called Wesley he hadn't answered the phone. No doubt passed out after the wedding day festivities.

'Ah, but he's gorgeous,' says Zandile, tracing a finger over his chubby face.

'Can I have him now?' demands Xoliswa, extricating him out of Zandile's arms. She inhales his scent; innocence infused with Johnson's baby powder. His eyes are tightly shut and he has so much hair, the silky strands escape from his tiny little hat. Everything about him is so perfect.

'He is so beautiful,' coos Xoliswa. She holds him close to her chest and is overcome with emotion.

She had been pregnant before. They had been doing their articles and had agreed that their work schedules were not conducive to becoming parents. The rigorous exam schedule meant having a baby would just not work. A feeling of hollowness comes over her and she feels tears forming at the thought of what could have been had she kept her baby. The guilt creeps up on her as well as the pain. She hands the baby back to Zandile.

'He's beautiful. Here. Take him.'

Suddenly she can't bear being in the room with her sisters and leaves, telling them she's left her camera in the car. Both sisters are too absorbed in the baby to realise anything is amiss.

Baby Jason starts to whimper and Zandile immediately passes him back to his mother. Yandisa plugs his tiny mouth onto her breast which is so big and swollen it looks like it is going to squash his tiny face.

'Is there any milk coming out?' asks Zandile.

'Not yet,' replies Yandisa, 'but the nurses said I should just let him suckle anyway.'

Yandisa strokes his head tenderly and makes funny faces and cooing sounds to engage with him. The love she has for her child is so apparent and you can see it in her eyes and in her smile. She had never been like this with Babalwa.

Wesley arrives and even though it's nearly the end of visiting hours, as the father he is allowed to visit his family anytime. Zandile decides to say her goodbyes and give them some time alone. Wesley is eager to hold his son in his hands.

'Did you bring me alcohol?' asks Yandisa.

'Alcohol for what? You're breastfeeding!'

'Oh come on, Wesley. I've been craving alcohol for nine months.'

'No, Yandisa,' says Wesley sternly. 'I want my son breastfed and alcohol is not good for breastfeeding moms. You survived nine months, you can survive another nine months.'

Yandisa pouts at him. Three days into marriage and Wesley is behaving like a fuddy-duddy. She only wants one drink.

'He looks like me, doesn't he?' Wesley says, marvelling at the baby's features.

'I don't think you can really tell at this point.'

'Nah, he looks like me,' asserts Wesley.

The baby wraps his tiny fingers around Wesley's forefinger and Yandisa feels so happy in that moment. They are their own little family. She can't wait until her and the baby can leave the hospital and they can start living like a family.

'I'm going to miss you guys so much,' says Wesley, still gazing at his son.

'Miss us? Where are you going?'

Wesley has decided to accept Gill Hornsby's offer to play rugby overseas. As the exhilaration of the wedding died down, reality has set in and he's going to be confronted with a whopping hospital bill. He is fully aware that it's no longer about him and Yandisa and now there's a third person in the equation. He's also very aware of the affluent lifestyle his wife's family lead and the expectations that are on him to provide. Although Yandisa says she doesn't care where they live, he cares. It matters deeply to him the impression he makes on the old man. All these thoughts had propelled him to search for the contract Gill Hornsby had given Yandisa all those months ago. When he had found the brown envelope, he had hugged it to his chest and spent the morning going through it. The bait is the signing-up fee; they are offering him two thousand pounds which after doing the conversions, he realises is a shitload of money. It's then that he decides to make the call that he hopes is going to change his life forever. Gill Hornsby doesn't answer and so after leaving a detailed message, he prays to God that he returns his call. As someone who is not used to praying, he falls to his knees and mumbles a few incoherent sentences. Gill

Hornsby does call him back and Wesley is just grateful that he calls at all.

'The rugby season has already kicked off so I'll have to leave as soon as possible. I promise I will arrange for you and Jason to join me as soon as I've settled.'

Yandisa's heart constricts. This was what she had once wanted but not any more. Not when they are just about to be a family. Wesley stands up and closing the gap between them hugs her, careful not to crush Baby Jason, who he is still cradling in his arms.

'This will be good for us,' he says reassuringly. 'It's going to be hard but we need to do it for Jason. My lease at the flat is up anyway so you can go and stay with my mother for a while and then you and Jason can come to the UK.'

'I'm not going to stay in Luveve,' says Yandisa firmly.

Wesley laughs dryly, 'Where the hell do you plan on staying then?'

'Can't I just stay at home with my folks?'

'No, Yandisa. You're my wife now, you are no longer a Mafu. You belong with us.'

When she is discharged from hospital, Yandisa returns to her parents' home for the customary period of confinement. Culturally, a new mother returns to her parents' home where she is confined for a month, learning the ropes of motherhood. She's not allowed to leave the house and if she does, she cannot take the baby with her as the baby is not supposed to leave the house during this time. Most women find this period claustrophobic and the loss of independence nauseating but Yandisa loves it. She now has a valid excuse to wander around the house in her pyjamas and slippers. Baby Jason is a night owl so she is usually awake with him in the early hours of the morning, only going to bed at 5 am. Being at home also means she has all her needs catered to. Sis May cooks and cleans and washes the baby's laundry so she just feeds the baby, eats and sleeps when she can. Wesley comes to visit during the day and because he resigned from his job and only leaves for the UK in a few days, he has lots of time on his hands. Sometimes he is accompanied by his mother, MaNyoni, who is looking much thinner since the wedding. She always brings Yandisa fresh fruit and vegetables from the market when she comes to visit. She holds her grandson for hours, the only time Yandisa sees her eyes come alive.

'When are you coming to live with me, *malukazana*?' she asks Yandisa every time she comes to visit.

'We are coming month-end, Mama,' replies Yandisa, even though she has no intention of fulfilling her promise.

Wesley flies to the UK at the end of the month. Before he leaves, Abraham holds a farewell ceremony for him and the elders lay hands and pray for what seems like hours. The family all go to the airport to bid him goodbye because it's never really a goodbye until you see the aeroplane taxi down the runway and take off.

KEITH AND KINSHIP

Keith didn't hesitate asking Xoliswa for her number at the end of the wedding but the rest of that weekend ends without her hearing from him. She was too preoccupied with Yandisa giving birth to notice but when she still has not heard from him by Wednesday she gets a sinking feeling in the pit of her stomach. She replays the night of the wedding over and over again, trying to think if she had missed something. Maybe she had been looking at the world through inebriated champagne-tinted glasses and maybe he was just being nice and she had read too much into it. Eventually she decides that he's clearly not into her and must have a girlfriend or a wife somewhere. What are the chances that someone like Keith is single and available anyway?

She attends an evening service during the week, her eyes scanning the congregation for his face but her heart sinks even further when the crowd filters out the church and he's nowhere to be seen.

During their routine Thursday morning meeting, he finally calls. As her phone lights up, so does her heart. While she can't be sure it's actually him, she excuses herself saying it is an urgent call she has to take. She hates herself for answering after only the second ring.

'Keith here. Unjani, Xolie?'

'Oh Keith. Hi!' she says trying to sound nonchalant. 'I'm good. You?'

'Could be better. I'm having a crazy week,' says Keith. 'Are you free for lunch today?'

'Let me check my diary,' she replies, not wanting to sound too eager and pretending to look at the calendar on her phone.

After a few seconds, she says that she is free to meet him. He suggests they meet at The Cattleman, known for its good quality steaks. Xoliswa is already salivating when she hangs up. She considers going home to change but quickly decides that the plaid pencil skirt and silk blouse she's wearing will have to do.

She arrives at the restaurant a little after one o'clock and Keith is already in the car park and getting out of a sleek, black Mercedes Benz. He waits on the pavement while she parks her car and is wearing beige chinos and a striped blue shirt. He draws her into his arms and hugs her.

'Good to see you,' he says, once he releases her from his warm embrace.

'Likewise,' she replies.

He leads her into the restaurant and the two of them make quite a picture. He's booked a table and seems to be very familiar with the staff.

'Do you eat here a lot?' she asks.

'I'm a Ndebele man through and through, I love my meat,' he answers.

'You've got great taste,' she flirts, as she starts perusing the menu.

He orders a huge porterhouse steak with chips and the comp-limentary creamed spinach and butternut while she opts for filet mignon with a rich, balsamic glaze. He orders them a bottle of wine; a signature red from the Mukuyu stable. As they wait for their food to arrive, they nibble on crispy breadsticks and get to know each other a bit more. Keith tells her he runs a string of businesses, ranging from internet cafes, supermarkets, bakeries and bottle stores in the townships. He explains that his father built his wealth on the back of a milling business and later diversified his interests into retail.

'So did you grow up in Bulawayo?' asks Xoliswa. 'I'm surprised our paths have never crossed.'

'No, they wouldn't have. I went to Peterhouse Boys in Marondera. My dad sent me there when he made a lot of money and because he didn't have an education himself, I think it made him feel good being able to say I was at the best private school.'

There used to be an unwritten rule about dating and that was that private school students only dated other private school students. Public school students had to cavort amongst themselves. Even years after school, some still stuck to that 'code'.

'How big is your family?' Xoliswa asks.

'It's big. My mom was my dad's third wife and she had my sister and me.'

Xoliswa nods slowly, taking it all in.

'But I don't want to be a polygamist. I am a one-woman man,' says Keith quickly.

'So I take it you're not married then?'

'Eish! I haven't had luck in that department. I broke up with someone a few months ago and I'm still recovering.'

He draws his lips into a tight smile, indicating that it had been a rough break-up.

'Tell me about it,' says Xoliswa. 'I came out of a ten-year relationship a few months ago and it hasn't been easy.'

'I know, hey. That's why I started going to church. I was like "God help me!"'

Xoliswa throws her head back and laughs. They are alike in many ways. Their food arrives and they both tuck in.

'I was with my ex for four years and when we broke up, I told myself that the next woman I date I would marry after four months.'

'Four months?' says Xoliswa, arching her eyebrow.

'Why? Do you think that's too soon, Xolie?'

Xoliswa shrugs, 'I'm not dating you so it's not really important what I think, is it?'

'I want us to date,' says Keith. 'Listen, I'm thirty-three this year and I want to settle down and start a family. That's what I'm about, Xolie. My ex was all about "finding herself" and she said she wasn't ready but I'm ready, hey. I'm very ready.'

Xoliswa is warmed by his words. It's refreshing to meet a man who knows what he wants.

'So are you with me on this one?' he says, looking her in the eye. 'I don't want to waste your time if you're not going to be invested in a relationship with me.'

Xoliswa nods, 'I'm with you.'

'So you want to be my girlfriend?'

'Yes. Yes I do.'

Keith takes an onion ring from his plate and puts it on her finger. 'That's a girlfriend ring.'

They both laugh. If anyone asks Xoliswa when she thought Keith was the one, she would easily point to that moment. Lunch is over too quickly and when the waiter brings the dessert menu, Keith says he has to get back to the office for an afternoon meeting and asks for the bill.

'We can split the bill,' suggests Xoliswa.

He disregards her offer. 'I'm not here to split things fifty-fifty, Xolie. I invited you to lunch, remember?'

He reaches into his trouser pocket but he can't find his wallet. An awkward moment follows as he searches frantically.

'I swear, I thought I had it with me. This is so embarrassing.'

'Don't worry, I'll get it,' says Xoliswa, reaching into her handbag for her purse.

'I swear I'll make it up to you, Xolie! This is not how I wanted our first date to end!'

Xoliswa reassures him that she doesn't mind and whips out her NMB cheque book and quickly writes out a cheque. Keith thanks her and continues to apologise profusely and she keeps reassuring him that it isn't a problem. They leave the restaurant hand in hand and walk to the car park, both commenting what a wonderful time they've had. He opens the car door for her.

'So, do I get a kiss?' he asks hopefully.

She tilts her head towards him, her lips red like a flowering hibiscus. His lips land on hers like a butterfly drawn to nectar and he kisses her softly and gently like she's being caressed by a balmy breeze. Her lips tingle, parting, allowing him to probe further. He tastes of berries, fruity and spicy like the Merlot they had over lunch. Then he pulls away and she gasps in surprise. She hadn't anticipated the kiss ending so quickly. So abruptly and without warning.

'I don't want us to get arrested for public indecency,' he whispers in her ear.

Xoliswa laughs, 'Of course not.'

He holds her hands and they stand and look at one another for a while, not moving.

'I really must get going,' he says eventually.

She gets in her car and he kisses her forehead through the open window. She drives away with butterflies in her stomach. The question of his missing wallet gnaws at her a bit. Was he being truthful or was he just broke and trying to get out of paying the bill? She quickly dismisses her doubts. Keith certainly doesn't look broke and he is an established businessman after all.

She returns to the office in buoyant spirits. Her lips are still tingling with the memory of that kiss. She's distracted and Gertie and Mike come into her office needing her to sign off on a costing for a new project and she does so without so much as a second glance. She settles down at her desk and is about to start working on a project costing when her phone rings. She's tempted to ignore it but it's a South African number so it's probably Mpho or Natasha. It's the latter.

'Hey friend! So good to hear from you!' enthuses Xoliswa, pleased that her friend has called because she can't wait to tell her about Keith and share some of the nitty-gritty of their lunch date.

'Is it really?'

Natasha's voice is scratchy on the other end and Xoliswa isn't sure if it's a bad connection or her friend has a cold.

'Babes, are you okay?' she asks, deferring her good news for a bit later in the conversation.

'I heard about your sister's wedding. How could you let her get married to Wesley?'

'I have no control over my sister's decisions,' replies Xoliswa.

'Oh, that's rich coming from you! For years you said Wesley wasn't good enough for me but he's good enough for your sister!'

Xoliswa wonders if she's missed something and exhales noisily.

'Wait a minute, Tash. Why are we even talking about Wesley? I thought you were over him. You two went out years ago and he was abusive towards you. He isn't abusive towards Yandisa!'

A strained silence follows and Xoliswa is keen to end the conversation. She lies to Tash and tells her she has an urgent call coming through and cuts the call. She doesn't need anything ruining her good mood.

That evening, while she's setting the table for dinner, Xoliswa casually asks her mother about Keith.

'You mean that guy you were dancing with at the wedding all night?' Yandisa pipes up as she spoons the food into serving dishes.

Xoliswa flushes, she hadn't realised anyone had really noticed them.

'Yes, him,' says Xoliswa, careful not to sound too interested.

'He hasn't been coming to church for too long but I know that he tithes a lot. His name always appears on the register,' explains Phumla.

'Oh,' says Xoliswa, pleasantly surprised.

Yandisa whistles animatedly, 'He's got money, he's got money!'

'Shut up,' hisses Xoliswa, 'that's not what I was asking!'

'I don't know too much about him but he seems like a good man,' adds Phumla, 'and he's single,' she adds with a sly wink.

Yandisa jabs Xoliswa playfully in her side, 'Go get him, sis!'

Later that night when Yandisa and Xoliswa are sitting in front of the TV, watching *Top Gun* for what must be the hundredth time, Yandisa brings up Keith again.

'So, do you like this guy?' asks Yandisa mischievously.

Xoliswa giggles, 'Yes, I think I do.'

'Well, I'm happy for you, sis,' says Yandisa. 'You deserve to be happy and maybe Keith is the one.'

A lazy smile appears on Xoliswa's face, 'I hope so.'

Yandisa reaches over and puts an arm around her. Xoliswa decides not to raise her conversation with Natasha. There's no question that if she ever *had* to choose, she would choose her sister over her friends, every day and every time.

HUMBLE BEGINNINGS

Yandisa watches the mass exodus of children as they throng the car park. Babalwa is the last to appear, her long spindly legs almost dangling out of her uniform. She's going to be tall just like the father who denied her, Yandisa thinks to herself. Her bushy hair is secured in two ponytails, kept in place with bright, blue ribbons. Now that she is living at home again, Yandisa has taken a liking to doing Babalwa's hair every day. Yandisa waves frantically so that Babalwa sees her.

'Hi Yandisa!' she says, as she gets into the car, throwing her suitcase onto the back seat. 'Where's Mama?'

'She had to attend a lunch-time prayer meeting so I said I'd pick you up.'

'You left Jason at home?'

'Yes, he was sleeping and I didn't want to disturb him so Sis May is looking after him.'

'He's *so* annoying. And he cries all the time!'

'Babs, he doesn't cry *that* much!' says Yandisa, slightly surprised. By all accounts, she had thought her son was a good baby. He only cries when he's hungry and the rest of the time he sleeps.

On a whim, Yandisa decides to stop at Eskimo Hut for lunch. Babalwa orders a hamburger and chips and a large chocolate milkshake. Yandisa opts for the same but what she's really craving is alcohol. Every now and then she expresses some milk for a bottle for Jason so that she can have a few drinks on the sly.

Throughout lunch, she listens attentively as Babalwa regales her with stories about her school and her friends. After she's paid the bill, Babalwa thanks Yandisa a few times.

'It's nothing really, Babs.'

'No, you don't understand, it means a lot to me, Yandisa. Ever since Baby Jason came home everybody has been ignoring me.'

'Oh Babs, come on!'

She starts to cry and Yandisa's heart constricts with guilt. It never occurred to her how the arrival of a new baby would affect Babalwa. She pulls her daughter into her arms and holds her and for the first time feels an affinity of sorts towards her.

Three months go by and Yandisa is still firmly entrenched in her parents' home and showing no signs of leaving. She's a new mom receiving a pound-denominated allowance from her husband and this suits her just fine. She's relishing her new role and enjoying being back home. Every morning, she drives Babalwa to school and then comes home and goes back to sleep. In her absence, Sis May takes care of Jason because Phumla sleeps till about 10 am. The routine is that Phumla and Yandisa have breakfast together out on the patio, a bonding moment of sorts. Phumla then leaves to attend to any church business, otherwise they lie on the patio on blue-and-white striped chaise lounges, soaking up the sun. They take turns in picking up Babalwa from school and if there are no errands to be run, they go for a long leisurely lunch somewhere in town before heading home where they then become preoccupied with Baby Jason.

Yandisa often does her mother's hair and has a knack for it. In high school she was well known for being able to do good cornrows. She manipulates her mother's hair into fine lines and Phumla's grey hair with its silver streaks, adds character. Yandisa relishes the time she's spending with her mother and for the first time they are actually conversing and relating and not embroiled in messy arguments. They have really bonded over Baby Jason and Phumla is besotted with him. Yandisa's experience of being at home since she got married and had Baby Jason is very different to what it was like when she used to live at home. She feels like she is being treated with more respect, like she has earned a seat at the table.

'When are you guys leaving?' asks Abraham one evening during dinner.

Yandisa is taken aback by his question. They are all getting along so well, why would they leave?

'Leaving for where?' asks Phumla. 'Their visas haven't been processed yet.'

'Yandisa needs to go to her husband's family, Phumla. She's a married woman. *Walotsholwa.*'

'Please *Tata*, I don't think anyone minds that she is here. The baby is happy here,' says Phumla, holding Baby Jason on her lap.

'It is not right,' says Abraham. 'Remember the Book of Ruth, "you go where I go"?'

'Please don't tell me about the Book of Ruth, Abraham! I'm just enjoying my grandson,' snaps Phumla.

'And I'm sure the Bhunus would love to enjoy him too. It's not right, Yandisa needs to go.'

'Dad, I don't see what the big deal is,' says Xoliswa.

It is one of those rare occasions when she is actually home for dinner. If she is not at a church meeting, she's on a date with Keith. 'I don't think the Bhunus mind that Yandisa and Jason are here,' adds Zandile, who happens to be supping with them that night.

'Why aren't you at home with your husband?' barks Abraham.

'He's gone away on business,' says Zandile calmly.

'She has to go,' says Abraham, in a tone that makes it clear no further comment or argument is needed. 'I don't think Wesley is happy with this situation. I certainly wouldn't be if it was my wife and child.'

Abraham throws his napkin down and leaves the table. They are all annoyed but know better than to argue with him. They discuss it at length and by the end of the evening, Yandisa has reconciled herself with the fact that she has to leave her parents' house. Before they go to bed, Phumla phones Maria and tells her to catch a bus into town first thing in the morning as Yandisa is going to need help with the baby. Filabusi is only about 100 kilometres from Bulawayo so she will be able to make the trip easily.

The next day, Yandisa and Phumla are packing. Abraham has made it clear he does not want Yandisa in his home a day longer. The bus Maria is travelling in is delayed and so they can only leave the following day. Xoliswa and Phumla prepare to accompany Yandisa and Baby Jason to their new home. They do so with heavy hearts and complain bitterly about how Abraham is being so dogmatic.

'I could understand you living with his mother if Wesley was around but he's not even here!' moans Phumla.

'And Wesley doesn't mind. I told him it was more convenient for me to stay in Hillside because it's close to the paediatrician and I'd have more help,' says Yandisa.

'But you know how Dad is with everything having to be done by the book,' says Xoliswa.

Yandisa and Maria drive together in the Beetle and Xoliswa and Phumla follow suit. The car had been a bone of contention with Abraham arguing that Yandisa should leave it behind.

'I bought her that car! Wesley should buy her a new one.'

'Then how does your grandson get to the clinic for his jabs? You want him sandwiched in some taxi with people with TB?' quips Phumla.

That is enough to swing the pendulum in Yandisa's favour so her father concedes defeat and allows her to take the car.

They get to the township and drive past rows and rows of shoebox-sized houses. Most of the houses are uniform in their design and appearance, with a small patch of vegetables in the front. A few have been extended on the tiny stands until there is barely any space.

They finally arrive at the Bhunu home. Yandisa hoots until MaNyoni appears with a brood of dirty children in tow. Xoliswa wonders why they aren't in school but then looks at her watch and realises it is well after 2 pm. They all get out of their cars and MaNyoni greets them with reverence. She pushes open the creaky gate that is almost coming off its hinges.

'Welcome home, *malukazana*,' she says to Yandisa. 'I'm so excited. Today my *malukazana* will cook for me.'

Phumla and Xoliswa exchange knowing looks. MaNyoni takes hold of Baby Jason, who is fast asleep and wrapped in a muslin cloth. Her creased face is lined with joy. MaNyoni hollers at the top of the voice for the children to help unload the car and this wakes the baby up but she's quick to quiet him again. MaNyoni apologises that there is no reception to welcome Yandisa home. She feels that they should have done something as Yandisa still hasn't been duly initiated into the family. MaNyoni invites them all into the house for a cup of tea but Xoliswa says she has to rush back to work. 'Just one cup,' MaNyoni coaxes.

'I'm sure you can take the rest of the afternoon off, Xolie' says Yandisa, walking behind Maria.

'I actually have a three o'clock meeting,' snaps Xoliswa. 'Some of us work, you know.'

They walk down the stone gravel towards the house which speaks of abject neglect. The paint is weathered and peeling off the walls like onion peels. MaNyoni ushers them inside into the living room which is cluttered with an assortment of furniture donated by her various employers over the years. A 1970 WRS radio, that has long since stopped playing, sits atop a table. A rickety old display unit crammed with glasses and crockery.

'Please sit down,' MaNyoni says.

Phumla settles down on the sofa which is covered with crocheted doilies. She is almost swallowed into the sofa and has to hold onto the armrest so as not to sink into it completely. Her heart sinks as she realises how much Yandisa has given up by marrying into the Bhunu family and how they will never be on her level. Xoliswa sits next to her, looking equally uncomfortable. Maria sits down in an old armchair but it breaks and gives way and she falls to the floor. MaNyoni apologises profusely while Yandisa stifles her laughter. Having visited her mother-in-law before she is over the initial shock of the humble abode. Phumla's eyes dart around the room and save for one picture on the wall of Jesus Christ, the walls are bare, marked with dirty handprints of children and marks of posters long removed. Shafts of sunlight peep through the gaps in the heavy brocade curtains and Phumla is tempted to draw them open to let more light into the room.

MaNyoni retrieves teacups from the wooden display cabinet in the corner of the room. Phumla can see the fine layer of dust on the glass shelves and after the cups have been removed, they leave a clear mark. She could write her name in the dust that is on those shelves! What shocks her even more is when the cups are placed on the table without even being rinsed. MaNyoni then reaches into her bra and pulls out a ten dollar note and sends one of the children to go and buy a packet of biscuits and a 2-litre bottle of Fanta. 'So, do you live here alone?' asks Phumla, initiating small talk while they wait for the kettle to boil.

The house is not much bigger than the servant's quarters their maid, Sis May, stays in at home. MaNyoni explains that she lives with her eldest daughter, Evelyn, who is widowed with three children.

'Hluphekile is the oldest,' she says, pointing to a boy strapped into a wheelchair. He is immersed in a book and hasn't looked up from the time they walked in the house.

'Can you greet the visitors, please!' she reprimands.

He grunts something inaudible and returns to his book, leaving his grandmother to continue with the introductions.

MaNyoni explains that her younger daughter, Primrose, works in a restaurant in South Africa and so her granddaughters, Linda, whose skin is as dark as midnight and Rochelle, who is coloured, live with her.

'I remember they were flower girls at the wedding,' says Phumla.

'You have so many grandkids so at least you are never alone.'

'You have Babalwa,' says MaNyoni pointedly. 'You can never be alone with grandkids.'

The children arrive back with the biscuits and MaNyoni pours the tea. Phumla and Xoliswa sip on theirs politely but struggle to drain their cups. They thank MaNyoni and then leave Yandisa to settle into her new home and new role.

The sleeping arrangements are awkward. Yandisa is given Wesley's old room to share with Jason and Maria while MaNyoni, Evelyn and the children sleep in her bedroom. Hluphekile sleeps on a sponge mattress in the living room. Yandisa is thankful to have a room to herself, as stuffy as it is. A stale air hangs over the room and she immediately opens a window to allow fresh air to sweep through the room. She can hear the neighbours and is quickly reminded of how they are now living in close proximity to other people. She puts the baby down on Wesley's old bed, the only piece of furniture in the room. The floor is cluttered with wedding gifts and Maria quickly starts to try and organise the room, while Yandisa sits on the bed, disinterested.

'When you are done, assemble his camp cot in the corner, Maria. If you can find the space!' Yandisa says sarcastically.

'It's not so bad,' says Maria, trying to find the positive in the situation.

Yandisa sneezes three times in succession, 'Even my sinuses are flaring up. Can you imagine what this will do to the baby?'

She stands up and goes to the bathroom, if you could even call it that. There is no bathtub, only a shower which has neither tiles nor character and threadbare towels hang on the wall. Yandisa slides down to the floor and starts crying. 'For better or for worse,' her father's voice reverberates in her head.

THE LAZY MAKOTI

Jason is unsettled that first night in their new abode and they all eventually fall asleep at 3 am only to be rudely woken up two hours later by Evelyn. She sweeps into the room with authority.

'I want to show you how things are done around here,' she says to Yandisa.

Yandisa rubs her eyes, a confused expression on her face.

'Show Maria,' says Yandisa, turning to shrug Maria awake.

Evelyn stands with her hands on her hips, staring at Yandisa, mouth agape.

'*Kanti*, who is married to my brother? You or her?' demands Evelyn.

Yandisa sits up in bed and looks at Evelyn squarely in the eyes.

'*Kanti*, sisi, what is your problem?'

'You are my problem! I'm trying to show you how things are done here and you're giving me attitude!' Evelyn shouts at Yandisa.

'I told you, that's Maria's job. I don't know which part you are failing to understand.'

'So, what exactly is *your* role?' asks Evelyn. 'Last night you didn't cook supper and I can see you don't intend to cook breakfast this morning either.'

'Sisi, I'm sure you have been surviving just fine without me. Continue doing what you were doing. Like I said, if you need extra help with stuff, Maria is here.'

Their shouting rouses Baby Jason and Maria quickly gathers him into her arms. By this time, MaNyoni has come to see what all the commotion is and Yandisa is now having a standoff with her *mlamu*.

215

Evelyn, who is tall and lithe, is talking down to the much shorter, Yandisa. Yandisa doesn't back down and points an accusatory finger at her sister-in-law. As she speaks, her bosom heaves with anger and her rump shakes in concurrence.

'I demand respect here!' hisses Evelyn.

MaNyoni quickly lodges herself between the two women and tells them to calm down. Evelyn leaves the room, seething with anger and aggravation. Her mother follows close behind her.

'Don't harass our visitor please, Evelyn!' warns MaNyoni.

Evelyn turns around and stares at her mother, 'Visitor? Is that what she is?'

'Hayi, Evelyn! She was raised differently. She doesn't know these things.'

'Every woman knows these things, Mama. Are you trying to make an exception because she is light and pretty?'

'No, Evelyn, I have been to their home a couple of times and their mother raised them differently. Try to understand where she is coming from.'

'What does she know then? How to get fucked?'

MaNyoni shakes her head, 'Don't be vulgar! Not in my home.'

With that harsh reprimand, MaNyoni returns to her bedroom and calm is restored. Evelyn puts a huge pot of mealie meal on the stove then goes to have her bucket bath. Later, she wakes up her children and bathes them. This is a noisy process but once they are bathed and dressed, they all sit down to eat their porridge. One child complains that there is no peanut butter while another complains that the sugar has run out. Evelyn screams and tells them to all shut up. A deafening silence ensues and a short while later, Yandisa and Maria hear the front door slam as Evelyn and the children leave the house. Only then does Yandisa try and catch up on some sleep.

Maria gets up and starts the daily chore of cleaning the house, asking for direction from MaNyoni. When Baby Jason wakes up, Yandisa calls for Maria to take him so she wraps him on her back and continues the household chores. Later, MaNyoni relieves her and takes charge of her grandson. When Yandisa finally wakes up at midday, she joins her mother-in-law out on the veranda, still in her pyjamas. MaNyoni is sitting, legs outstretched on a grass mat, Jason in her arms, chatting to her neighbour across the fence. Yandisa greets them both before sitting down next to her mother-in-law.

'I was tired, Mama. The baby was so restless last night, I think he might be teething.'

'Oh *bakithi*,' says MaNyoni apologetically. 'I'm so sorry about Evelyn this morning. Don't mind her, she has her own stress.'

'It's nothing,' says Yandisa dismissively. 'Have you eaten, Mama?'

'I had porridge in the morning. We don't eat much here, *malukazana*.'

'You must eat, Mama,' says Yandisa.

Yandisa stands up and goes to the kitchen to see what they can rustle up for lunch. Maria tells her there is nothing in the cupboards and opens them to show Yandisa the dearth of food in the house. The fridge whistles with emptiness. Yandisa is hollow with hunger and breastfeeding has given her an intense appetite.

'Let me change and we'll go to the shops,' says Yandisa to Maria.

Maria straps Baby Jason into the car seat and as they are about to leave, MaNyoni decides to join them. She says she needs some fresh air and Yandisa is grateful she is with them because they need directions to the shops. She's sure they would have got horribly lost. They fill the trunk of the car with groceries and even the seats are covered with food items.

They have spaghetti and mince for lunch and when the kids get home from school, they polish off the leftover mince with bread. Afterwards, they thank Yandisa for the food and although she finds it a bit embarrassing, she feels good that she has made them happy. They then go out to play on the streets, returning only at dusk. MaNyoni insists that she will cook supper that evening and Yandisa obliges her. MaNyoni marvels at the packets of brisket, blade steak and other cuts of beef from the butcher that Yandisa purchases for them. It's not often they get to eat meat in their house.

She delights in cooking them a meaty stew and Maria assists her with chopping onions, tomatoes and vegetables. Yandisa flops in front of the television with Jason on her lap and that is how Evelyn finds them when she gets home in the early evening. Enraged, she goes straight to the bedroom, slamming the door angrily. Yandisa and Maria look at each other and shake their heads.

TURNING HEADS

With time, Yandisa settles into the routine of township life. It is a simple one without any of the luxuries she has been accustomed to. During the mornings spent sitting out on the veranda with her mother-in-law, Yandisa gets to know her a bit better and about the tough life she has led. She isn't an old woman, probably the same age as Phumla, but the hardships of life have aged her.

'Mama, can I do your hair?' offers Yandisa one morning, wondering why her mother-in-law hides her crown of thick hair under a doek all the time.

'This old hair? I really should shave it off but I just haven't got round to it.'

'No, let me fix it,' says Yandisa.

Yandisa plaits her hair into neat cornrows and afterwards, MaNyoni looks at herself in the mirror and smiles.

'Where did you learn to do hair like this?' asks her mother-in-law, surprised at Yandisa's talent.

'I taught myself. I'd practice on my sisters and my friends and I guess it's just something I have a knack for.'

Yandisa starts to plait the children's hair when they get home from school and word quickly spreads about her prowess with hair. Soon, she has people lining up to pay to have their hair done and so she plaits their hair on her mother-in-law's veranda. Whether it's cornrows or braids, she meets so many different women every day who all regale her with colourful stories. There is never a dull moment in her day and every evening her and MaNyoni talk about some of the stories and laugh together.

Some women pay her mid-month and others pay her month-end and Yandisa uses the cash to spoil the children. She is shocked to learn that until her arrival they had not tasted ice cream before and the things she takes for granted are alien to their palates. One evening Yandisa is lying on her bed when there is a knock on the door. It's Evelyn.

'I just wanted to say thank you,' says Evelyn.

'You don't have to thank me Evelyn, we are family,' replies Yandisa.

'You don't understand,' says Evelyn. 'For years I've been struggling on my own with *uMama*. Wesley has never done a damn thing and even though Primrose is working in Johannesburg she doesn't send much. She just sends clothes, does she think the kids will eat Ackermans and Pep?'

Evelyn tells Yandisa that she works in a factory in Belmont. Her salary is meagre yet she has to try keep the lights on and the water bill paid. She also has school fees to pay and needs to make sure there is food on the table too.

'Hluphekile had to drop out of school because I couldn't afford to keep him there. He needs to be in a special school and I know he resents me for it but I was struggling.'

She exhales deeply as she tells Yandisa her hardships. Then she caves and starts crying.

'Let me help where I can, Wesley sends me money,' suggests Yandisa.

Evelyn is sobbing, 'You've done so much already by putting food on the table.'

Yandisa stands up and hugs her. That is the turning point in their relationship and they quickly transition from foes to firm friends.

One night, while sharing a bottle of wine which Yandisa introduced Evelyn to after her curiosity was piqued, the older woman confides in her. 'If I ever have enough money one day, I want to have my own stall at the flea market.'

She raises her glass which makes Maria laugh as it is the first time she has seen Evelyn this relaxed.

'How much do you need?' asks Yandisa. 'I can loan you the money.'

Evelyn's eyes light up. 'Really? I can't believe you would do that for me! I promise I'll pay you back, Yandisa!'

Yandisa has a wad of money she keeps in a stocking under her mattress and she gives half to Evelyn. The following morning, Evelyn resigns from her job and is given her paltry pension. She catches a bus to Johannesburg the next Friday and returns with a sack full of merchandise ranging from cosmetics to shoes. She hires a stall at the flea market and two months later, has repaid Yandisa the money she lent her, plus a bit extra for interest. Yandisa is so impressed and sees how happy it makes the children to be spoilt a bit by their mother.

'Why don't you open your own salon?' suggests Evelyn to Yandisa one day. 'You have so many people queuing up here to get their hair done anyway.'

'Do you think so? I mean, do you think I could do it?'

'Yes, of course. You are good at this hair thing, Yandisa. One day my brother will stop sending you money and then what?'

'You don't have much faith in him do you?' says Yandisa.

Evelyn shakes her head. She has no faith in either of her siblings.

'I can buy you the hair chemicals the next time I'm in Joburg. All you need to do is get some premises. I'm sure your family knows someone who has space to rent somewhere.'

'You know what, I've got a better idea,' suggests Yandisa. 'The next time you go to Joburg, I'll come with you.'

She has no qualms about travelling and leaving Jason behind because she knows he will be in the capable hands of Maria and his gogo.

And so the idea of 'Turning Heads' is borne. Yandisa approaches

Xoliswa for some retail space as she knows Askaheni Enterprises owns some commercial space in town. At first Xoliswa is sceptical but Yandisa is so passionate and enthusiastic about her ideas, that she agrees to give her a six-month lease on a space.

The following month-end, Yandisa takes her accumulated savings from the money Wesley has been sending her and converts it to rands on the black market. Armed with cash, her and Evelyn catch a luxury liner to Johannesburg. The ten-hour journey reminds her of the gruelling journey they had taken to visit her mother's relatives in the Transkei when she was young. But this time the trip goes a lot quicker because she mixes some brandy into her 2-litre Coke bottle, even though no drinking is allowed on the bus. She eventually passes out and when she opens her eyes, they are pulling into Park Station as the sun is setting on the skyscrapers lining the Johannesburg CBD. They disembark from the bus with their rucksacks on their back, their only luggage.

Evelyn is fairly street smart and takes Yandisa to wholesalers and light manufacturers in City Deep. That evening, they spend the night with Aunt Phindile, Phumla's older sister, in Soweto. Meeting Yandisa's aunt helps Evelyn understand why Yandisa looks the way she does with her light skin and voluptuous frame. When she walks with Yandisa they rarely get harassed by officials.

Aunt Phindile is very helpful and directs them to where they can purchase hair dryers and other equipment for the salon. Everything is packed into striped Shangaan bags and offloaded to *omalayitsha* who will ferry the merchandise across the border. After a successful trip, they return to Bulawayo, exhausted and happy. It was a productive trip and Yandisa and Maria spend the week cleaning the new premises. In all honesty, Maria does most of the cleaning while Yandisa gives the instructions, reclining from a chair, drinking wine. The walls are repainted in a pastel palette and the floors refitted. Zandile directs the shop-fitters until Turning Heads looks like the chic establishment she wants it to be. There is a lounge area in the front of the shop where clients can look at magazines or watch TV. Even Xoliswa is impressed with what Yandisa has managed to do with the space.

A month later she has a launch to celebrate the opening of Turning Heads. Yandisa has a staff complement of six hairdressers, all of whom she's poached from other salons, decked out in blue jeans and peach blouses. She wants her salon to be associated with style and elegance. From the day it opens its doors, the salon is packed. Phumla punts it to all the ladies at the church and despite the fact that the prices are high, most women want to get their hair done there. Clients also love the ambience and that they are offered a hot beverage or juice while they wait. Yandisa is aware the prices are steep for her township clientele so on Sundays when Turning Heads is closed, she attends to those clients on MaNyoni's veranda. They still get her services for a quarter of the price. Soon, Turning Heads establishes itself in Bulawayo as the premier hair-grooming salon for the young and trendy.

DOMESTIC BLISS

Perched on a stool, Yandisa has an unrestricted view of the activity on the street outside. It's a Monday and business is slow and even the hairdressers have tired of doing each other's hair. Even the gossip has run out. Yandisa paints her nails and repaints them out of pure boredom. Her mood picks up when she sees Ndaba's car pull into the vacant parking space outside the salon. She watches as he goes around to open the passenger door for Zandile, who is six months pregnant and sporting a bump that she is extremely proud of. Ndaba is the only black man Yandisa knows who does that sort of thing. The couple walk into the salon, hand in hand, madly in love and joined at the hip. Yandisa gives them both a warm hug.

'Sisi, if I didn't come here to get my hair done, I'd never see you,' teases Zandile.

'I'm so busy! This is the first slow day since we opened.'

Yandisa is very hands-on and opens the salon at 7 am and often leaves as late as 6 pm. Saturdays are jam-packed and they open at 6 am to cater for ladies wanting to get their hair braided and only close once the last client has been served which is sometimes as late as 10 pm. The only thing she wants to do when she gets home is sleep.

'I haven't seen you for months,' says Ndaba. 'You must come over to the house sometime. How is Jason?'

'He's fine. He's walking all over Luveve!'

'I miss my nephew,' says Zandile. 'You need to tell him his cousins are on the way,' she adds, pointing to her belly.

'I won't lie and say I'll come and visit soon,' says Yandisa. 'it's just too hectic these days.'

224

Even Sunette, Towanda and Dumile complain that she has disappeared off the radar socially.

'But we really want to spend time with you and Jason,' insists Ndaba.

He reaches out and gives Yandisa a hug and tells Zandile he'll be back in a few hours to fetch her.

'Aren't you at work today?' asks Yandisa.

'I took the day off and Ndaba insists on driving me everywhere now.'

'He's such a sweetie,' says Yandisa, watching her brother-in-law walk out the salon.

'He is,' agrees Zandile. 'How is your man?'

'He's fine, I guess. Moaning about the cold and saying the training schedule is rigorous.'

'Shame, it must be hard for him being away from you and Jason,' says Zandile.

'It's hard for all of us,' says Yandisa.

'Now that you have the salon and it's doing so well are you still planning to move to the UK?' asks Zandile.

'Wesley says he's not sure if his contract will be renewed so he wants me to sit it out here for a bit.'

Not really wanting to talk about it any more, Yandisa takes her sister to the sink to shampoo her hair. She squeezes apple balsam shampoo onto Zandile's hair and works the creamy fluid into a thick lather until her hands disappear into the foam. She massages her scalp in slow, circular movements.

'Aaah, that feels so good,' murmurs Zandile, closing her eyes.

With Yandisa's gentle touch, she's lulled into a sleep and only wakes up when Yandisa is rinsing her hair before patting it dry. After lathering in some leave-in conditioner, she coils Zandile's hair with rollers. The sisters chat non-stop, catching up on everything from mothers-in-law to sisters-in-law and everything in-between including Xoliswa's blossoming romance with Keith the Christian, the nickname the family has given him. Then Yandisa leaves Zandile to recline underneath the hairdryer and she falls asleep again. When she wakes up, Yandisa's dexterous hands are styling her hair into waves.

When Ndaba picks Zandile up a while later, he boasts that he is going home with the most beautiful woman in the world. He pays for his wife's hair and Yandisa charges him a little bit extra, as she does with those she considers 'premium clientele'. She makes a note of the transaction in the cash book, as Xoliswa has taught her to do, and she always deposits the salon's takings from the previous day at the start of each new day. Xoliswa has warned her about the dangers of keeping too much cash on hand. As she's closing the shop that day, Sunette arrives and insists they go to Bulldogs Pub for a drink. To think it was Marshall who had first introduced her to that place many years ago. 'Eish, babes I can't,' replies Yandisa. 'I'm so broke!'

She's resisting the urge to spend that day's takings.

Sunette arches an eyebrow, 'Isn't Wesley sending money any more?'

'He is, but we're starting to build our house. My dad gave us that piece of land in Riverside and we've started with the foundations. *Yhu, mngane,* it's expensive!'

'It's on me! Come on, Yandisa,' urges Sunette.

As tempting as the idea seems, the prospect of driving home drunk is scary and walking into her mother-in-law's house drunk would be disrespectful. She's also fairly certain Wesley wouldn't approve.

'Some other time, Sunette. I promise.'

Sunette pouts petulantly, 'Marriage has made you such a wet blanket. Fuck, Yandisa!'

Yandisa shrugs her shoulders, 'Some other time. I promise!'

She goes to TM supermarket and buys a few basics and standing in the queue she reflects on how her spending habits have changed. She had to fight the temptation to buy the gleaming pair of shoes displayed in the window at Truworths or the red lipstick at Edgars or the jeans on sale at Ramjis. Instead, she is buying bread, milk and a few slices of polony for the children's sandwiches. She buys MaNyoni her favourite chocolate, a Nutlog, and a bottle of wine for her and Sis Evelyn. Every time she feels the urge to spend money she reminds herself that she has to be responsible. Her and Wesley are now building their house and the sooner the house is up, the sooner she can move out of her mother-in-law's home.

Arriving home, the children run out to the Beetle to welcome her home. She loves the ritual and they always ask her what she has bought them and when she jokes and tells them there's nothing, they giggle and scurry away like little rats.

Jason is always the last and she lifts him up into her arms. He is stocky and short and every time she picks him up she realises how heavy he's getting. MaNyoni feeds him mealie meal porridge and peanut butter in the mornings and pap and gravy in the afternoon plus he has his bottle in-between.

'Ma-ma! Ma-ma!' he mouths at her, happily.

Her heart fills with joy. Motherhood the second time around has been so fulfilling for her. She is besotted with Jason and every time his little face twitches into a smile, she is overwhelmed with emotion. When he laughs, she laughs with him. He is such a happy baby.

Her mother-in-law comes out to the car and as always, asks after her day. She tells Yandisa how her and Jason spent theirs. His antics around the house are legendary, causing havoc wherever he goes. He tries to poke his stubby little fingers into sockets and pulls at anything within reach. Evelyn's children have to hide their schoolbooks away from him because he scrunches and tears the pages.

They sit together in the living room for a while before having supper at 6 pm when Sis Evelyn arrives home. That night they have *isitshwala* and spinach in peanut butter sauce. There's no meat to accompany the dish and Yandisa has accepted that they can't afford to have meat every day of the week. The construction is taking a huge toll on her finances. Every other day, the builders call to tell her they have run out of cement or that they need more bricks. Cement is not always readily available and she has to pay exorbitant prices for it on the black market. MaNyoni is understanding and has them on a vegetarian diet some nights, alternating between kale, okra and pumpkin leaves. Only on weekends do they have a meaty treat. After the meal, Maria does the dishes, the children are put to bed and the adults then go into the living room and wait for *Generations* to start. Yandisa bought a new colour television set and a decoder. Yandisa and Evelyn have their obligatory glass of wine before heading off to bed. On some evenings, Wesley calls and they chat for a bit. Yandisa's life has changed dramatically but she welcomes the change. She's grown fond of her husband's family, as they have of her. And now they are her family too.

FIGHTING TEMPTATIONS

The Kingdom of God has a clear and succinct policy about dating and what it should look like. According to the church, a date must involve two unmarried couples meeting at a designated public venue to partake in recreational activities. The strict nature of the definition means that couples can't meet in a private space, like a home, unsupervised. Chaperoned dating is encouraged and it is not uncommon to see couples double-dating accompanied by church elders or married couples. Dating within the church is strongly encouraged.

'Keep it in the family! Let's grow the Kingdom!' Abraham intones. 'As couples you must be equally yoked. Not just in spirit but in social standing too.'

Every other weekend there is a wedding at the Kingdom of God. After Yandisa's wedding, it has become a popular venue and, for a fee, couples can get married there. Dating is considered a serious pursuit in the church and people don't just date for 'fun'. They date with the express purpose of getting married and the dating process is merely a way to get to know each other at 'arms length'.

If marriage is not considered to be the main objective of dating, it is discouraged. Sex before marriage is a complete taboo. Abraham preaches fervently against fornication which is considered to be consensual sex between unmarried people. He also preaches against adultery which is consensual sex between a married individual and an unmarried one. Notwithstanding this, there have been a few scandals in the church including the choir master getting the praise and worship leader pregnant. Then there was the issue of the deacon who had been cavorting with one of the ushers and when his wife got wind of it, attacked the usher after the main morning service one Sunday. Then the youth pastor made two girls in his cell group pregnant.

It is a Thursday night, and Pastor Mlilo is preaching about premarital sex. 'The problem is that if the relationship becomes physical, a person becomes emotionally invested. This makes it difficult to break things off when you discover things about the person you don't like or if you have differing ideologies. Get to know the person on an intellectual and spiritual level first. You will have the rest of your life to get physical.'

A hand is raised and a young man stands up to question the pastor.

'So why would God give us these desires if he didn't want us to act on them?'

There are murmurs of agreement around the congregation.

Pastor Mlilo explains, 'When you are born again, you are born in spirit not the flesh. You need to control your desires and like the Apostle Paul said, it is better to marry than burn with passion. Sex is meant to be enjoyed in the confines of marriage.'

He dims the lights and asks everyone to turn their attention to a video on the screen that will provide further teaching and explanation on the subject. Keith turns his attention to Xoliswa. She's wearing a short, pin-striped skirt that has been distracting him from the moment he laid eyes on her earlier that evening. He casually starts stroking her thigh, his eyes fixated on the screen. Xoliswa can feel his hand moving upwards, igniting her passion inside. She wants to tell him to stop but she doesn't want to draw attention to herself. Luckily they are seated near the back after both arriving late for the evening youth meeting. The few rows behind them and in front of them are vacant. She feels his hand move further up, gently pushing her thighs apart until his fingers touch the silky fabric of her underwear. She is wet and receptive and feels betrayed by her own body. He slips his finger under her panties and starts to stroke her tenderly, like a man strumming his guitar, stroking the chords of her ardour. Xoliswa bites down on her lip to stop herself from shouting out. Keith is looking ahead, pretending to be unaware of the turmoil he's creating. Xoliswa's body pulsates with pleasure as an orgasm grips her. When the lights come on, she feels like there is a spotlight shining on their misdemeanour and she quickly stands up and goes to the bathroom to clean herself up. As she walks out, she wonders if anyone can smell the sex on her. When she returns, she perches a few seats away from Keith. 'You were avoiding me,' he says to her afterwards when they're standing together in the parking lot.

'You're such a bad influence,' she teases. 'You heard the pastor!'

'I couldn't resist. Could you?' pulling her into his arms and kissing her slowly and intensely. She quickly pulls away.

'I have to go, it's getting late,' she tells him.

'Do you really? I feel like we have some unfinished business,' he says, tracing his fingers over her quivering lips.

'Keith, you know how it is with my parents,' she says, her voice thick with longing.

Much later when she's alone in her bedroom, she masturbates furiously and thinks about Keith as she has another fierce orgasm which lulls her to sleep.

Rumours start flying that Keith is dating the pastor's daughter. Abraham secretly approves of the union but continues to profess ignorance of the relationship even though Xoliswa is regularly absent from the dinner table.

Keith wines and dines Xoliswa at fancy restaurants like Maison Nic and Les Saisons and spoils her with gifts and flowers. After church he usually takes her to the Churchill Arms for Sunday lunch but that particular Sunday is different because he suggests they go to his house for brunch. She has never been to his house so Xoliswa welcomes the invitation even though her father would have insisted there be a chaperone with them.

They drive up a winding driveway to Keith's home which is elegantly perched on the hills of Mqabuko Heights. The house is situated on acres of sprawling lawns, interspersed by rocks and bordered by colourful perennials and shrubs. Xoliswa is stunned. Keith parks the car alongside a Land Rover cruiser and they get out the car. The front doors open into an entrance hall that welcomes visitors to the house in all its splendour. An antique oval-shaped table, two leather wingback chairs and an exquisite Persian rug are perfectly placed and hanging above the space is an ornate chandelier. The table is covered with framed photos of Keith as a child, Keith as a teenager, Keith graduating from university, Keith with his sister, Keith with his parents. Keith's whole life is on display. There is also a picture of Keith and a woman, presumably his sister, and two children who look about eight and nine.

'That's my niece and nephew; Tim is seven and Tamara is ten,' says Keith, almost as if he had been reading her mind. 'Welcome to my humble abode.'

'Humble? My God, it's beautiful, Keith' exclaims Xoliswa, unable to hide her admiration.

She realises she could be the mistress of this all. She can already picture herself floating down the staircase in her morning gown.

'There are four bedrooms upstairs but I'll show you those later,' says Keith leading her into the sitting room, replete with a library. Adjacent to that is a study which Keith says doubles up as his office when he's at home. They prepare brunch together in the pristine kitchen with its stainless steel finishes and modern built-in appliances. The wooden cabinets and mahogany shutters give it a warm, homely feel and there is nothing about the kitchen that Xoliswa would change. She can imagine herself cooking breakfast for Keith and the kids. It's a nice image. He sees her smiling.

'What is it?' he asks.

She laughs, 'Nothing serious, I was just thinking how serious this could get!'

He laughs, 'Funny because I was staring at you cutting the onions and thinking to myself that she's the one.'

They eat out on the sandstone patio, ensconced in comfortable rattan chairs, enjoying a glass of Chardonnay from the private cellar. Xoliswa feels so relaxed and happy.

'So do you sit here and eat alone?' asks Xoliswa.

'I don't actually. I eat in front of the TV but when I built the house I had a large family in mind. I still do.'

Their eyes meet and she holds his gaze before leaning across to kiss him. It starts to rain, a light persistent rain that forces them indoors. Keith leads her into the TV lounge where they spend the rest of the afternoon nestled on the sofa. Xoliswa is comfortably lying between Keith's outstretched legs and thinking to herself that having this life might not be such a bad proposition. They are watching *The Bourne Identity* and she falls asleep halfway through with her head resting on Keith's chest. She is roused when she feels Keith's fingers flitting in-between her legs. Her eyes flutter open and he slides his finger in and out of her silky wetness. He strokes her till she reaches orgasm. She lies back in his arms, and he smothers her with kisses. It's her turn to pleasure him so she gets off the couch, down on her knees and takes him in her mouth, sucking him hungrily until he comes in her mouth.

'I can't hold out any longer,' says Keith, cupping her face and looking deep into her eyes.

Xoliswa is overwhelmed with passion and desire.

'Neither can I,' she replies.

Up until that moment they agreed that sex before marriage isn't right but he wants her and she wants him and it feels right. He leads her upstairs to his luxurious bedroom and pushes her down on the bed. He turns her over and takes her from behind. Xoliswa holds onto the velvety headboard as he thrusts wildly into her, his balls slapping against her bouncy buttocks. Then they collapse together on the downy bed. Keith buries his face in her tangled muff. Her anxiety about not shaving dissolves, along with her inhibitions, as Keith licks and laps at her womanly folds. This is unexplored territory for her as it was something Thulani never did. Xoliswa comes again and again until she thinks her head is going to explode from the pleasure. She tries to roll away but Keith pins her down.

'You're mine,' he declares.

They wrestle and roll around on the bed with unbridled passion. They continue to ravage each other with unrestrained desire. Afterwards, in the bathroom, Xoliswa marvels at the marble tops on the vanity with his and hers basins. The finishes are immaculate. As she immerses herself in the oval, freestanding bath, she has a perfect view of Keith in the doorless shower. Afterwards, they stand together on the balcony, wearing white terrycloth gowns, drinking coffee and admiring the sweeping view of the lush gardens below. The canopy of indigenous trees and flowering agapanthus, azaleas, hydrangeas and day lilies make for beautiful scenery.

'It's not a sin,' he says to her, 'if we are planning to get married, right?'

'No, it isn't,' she replies, 'our hearts are in the right place.'

Keith snakes a protective arm around her and she lays her head on his shoulder.

It's 5 am when Keith eventually drops Xoliswa at home and she creeps into the house like a thief. She feels like a teenager sneaking in after her curfew, not a grown woman of thirty.

Her heart is thudding as she makes her way down the passageway to her bedroom to quickly change into her work clothes. She's startled when she sees her mother sitting on the bed, her hands folded in her lap.

'Morning, Mama!' she yelps.

Her mother shakes her head, 'This is not how we do things. Xolie. You are the pastor's daughter.'

Xoliswa is flushed with shame and wonders if her mother can smell Keith on her. His scent lingers and she's wearing him like a thousand-dollar Armani perfume. Her flesh is tender from being pinched and pulled, nibbled and suckled as he left no part of her body untouched. It felt so good to be wanted like that.

'Behave yourself, please!' her mother admonishes her, and with those stern words, Phumla walks out the room.

ONLY FOOLS RUSH IN

It's not long afterwards that Keith decides to bring home the cows. The urgency is further amplified because Xoliswa is pregnant and they are both adamant that they can't have a repeat of Yandisa's situation. They make the obligatory visit to Sis Ntombi and Keith gives Sis Ntombi a bouquet of red, arctic roses and a box of chocolates. She is duly impressed as she welcomes them into their home. This time, her children are not around so it is just her and Uncle Ben. Uncle Ben professes that he knew the late Ndiweni Snr and comments to Keith what an astute businessman he was. This endears him to the man vying for Xoliswa's hand in marriage. The date is set and is just shy of Xoliswa's 31st birthday.

As they clear the plates after the meal, Sis Ntombi compliments Xoliswa on her choice of a husband. She goes on to enounce that the Ndiweni family were Ndebele royalty and praises her niece on the choice she's made.

When Xoliswa tells her sisters the good news about the wedding, over lunch the following Monday, they're ecstatic.

'Your timing though! Couldn't you and Keith wait?' complains Zandile, who is due to give birth then.

'No, we can't,' replies Xoliswa. 'I'm pregnant.'

She whispers it, prompting Zandile to put her hand over her mouth. Yandisa can't contain her joy.

'Ooooh! This is so exciting!' she gushes.

'So that's why we need to do it before I start showing,' explains Xoliswa.

Zandile nods conspiratorially, 'I understand.'

Xoliswa's pending nuptials bring a lot of excitement to the Mafu household and the family now have a lobola ceremony to plan in addition to Zandile's baby shower.

It's the Thursday afternoon before the lobola proceedings when a distressed Keith arrives at Xoliswa's office. She stops what she's doing and takes him into her office.

'I was on the phone with Sis Ntombi a short while ago and she tipped me off that your uncles are going to ask for forty thousand dollars, Xolie.'

Xoliswa's face falls, 'Shit! That's a lot of money.'

'It is and I only have twenty thousand in the bank. I've just committed fifty thousand in a mining investment and I'm not liquid.'

'Oh no!' says Xoliswa, aghast.

'We could postpone things and I'm sure I will have raised the other twenty thousand in a month or two. I've done some side deals and I think that money will cover the rest,' says Keith.

Xoliswa takes Keith's hand and places it on her stomach.

'In a month or two I will be showing and you will then have to add damages to that forty thousand.'

Keith looks at her anxiously, 'So what do you think we should do?'

'Look, I have twenty thousand in a savings account and I can loan you the money. You can pay me back when you get your cash.'

Keith lets out a big sigh, his anxiety evaporating.

'Baby, thank you!' he says, throwing his arms around her.

She hugs him back, 'You don't have to thank me, we're a team. You and I.'

They go straight to the bank and arrange for the withdrawal of the cash.

That Saturday morning, Xoliswa wakes in buoyant spirits. Finally her day has arrived. Keith and her have barely slept, chatting excitedly most of the night about the rest of their lives and their child. As the day unfolds, they text each other heart-warming endearments.

Counting down to you being my wifey

Can't wait to call you hubby

I love you xoxo

I love you more

Her mother pops her head around the door and tells her that the cooking ladies have arrived. Xoliswa jumps out of bed and goes to welcome them in her pyjamas. She's hired a cooking club from Luveve to do all the cooking. They are led by a lady by the name of MaTshuma and Xoliswa discovered them at a colleague's wedding a month ago and was impressed with their food. She had been clear that she wanted everything done professionally, especially considering the calibre of Keith's family. Sis Ntombi agreed and reiterated to her brother that the Ndiwenis were a well-to-do family and they had to make sure they put on a superb spectacle of Mafu hospitality.

A team arrives to set up a marquee in the garden and set the tables for lunch. Chandelle arrives much later to do the flowers. Zandile, who is now in her ninth month of pregnancy, plonks herself down on the daybed next to the pool and asks not to be bothered as she basks in the sun. Phumla joins her and massages Zandile's feet, escaping the flurry of activity inside and outside the house.

'Xolie is such a perfectionist,' she says to her daughter.

'I know, Mom! Can you imagine what the wedding is going to be like!'

Yandisa is visibly absent and apologised to Xoliswa for not being able to be there because she is too busy at the salon. She promised to come after lunch, saying she would close the salon a bit early.

'I told her not to bother,' says Xoliswa, feeling quite affronted. 'I'm always there for her events. I planned her entire wedding and she can't even close the salon for one day and be here for mine!'

'Even when you had your welcome-home party she didn't show up. She always has other things,' Sis Ntombi chips in.

'She needs the money. Saturdays are her busiest days,' says Sis Lungile, coming to Yandisa's defence.

All eyes fall on Sis Lungile with glowering contempt. She excuses herself and decides to see how the food is coming along.

Time goes quickly and Xoliswa doesn't realise how late it is until she gets a text message from Keith.

Running late. Waiting for malume to arrive.

Okay baby. See you soon. I love you.

I love you too.

She's thankful for the delay because in all the preparations and trying to oversee everything, she's forgotten to have a shower. Eventually her aunts chase her away insisting she has to be a glamorous *makoti*.

'Phew, if this is the lobola, imagine what the wedding is going to be like,' says Sis Lungile.

'It's going to be classy,' lauds Sis Ntombi. 'The Ndiwenis have money. Xoliswa wants a big wedding and she's thinking of having it at the Elephant Hills Hotel in Victoria Falls before the end of the year.'

'Oh wow!' gasps Sis Lungile. 'I didn't know they were planning the wedding so soon.'

'Oh yes,' says Sis Ntombi authoritatively, pleased to be the one with the inside scoop. 'Keith is very eager. He says he wants his wife as soon as yesterday!'

Sis Lungile laughs, 'I suppose if there is money you can get married overnight.'

The women continue to sit and chat about the supposed grand wedding plans but two hours later the *abakhwenyana* have still not arrived and Xoliswa is genuinely worried. Keith is no longer responding to her text messages or her calls. Sis Ntombi tries calling him too but to no avail. Yandisa arrives and is relieved to see nothing has started.

'Looks like I am just in time,' she says as she walks into the kitchen. She can't understand why everyone is so tense.

She helps herself to the food in the chafing dishes and has a little bit of everything, from the lamb stew to the chicken curry.

'Don't mind me,' she says, 'I haven't had anything to eat since this morning and the salon was *so* busy.'

'Go ahead,' says Sis Lungile. 'You've lost so much weight. I can see you are on your feet all day working hard.'

'It's hard work but I'm enjoying it,' says Yandisa. 'Auntie, if you get a chance tomorrow you should come and see how far we are with building the house. We're at roof level already.'

'That's wonderful,' exclaims Sis Lungile. 'Your mom told me that Wesley sends you a lot of money.'

'He's trying, shame. We want to try and finish the house as soon as we can because they've only renewed his contract for one more year. They're off season now but he decided it would be better for him to do some odd jobs over there and make some extra money rather than spending money to make the trip home.'

As she's talking, she shoves mouthfuls of food into her mouth and when she's finished, she goes to the bedroom to look for her sisters. They are huddled on the bed, gathered around a concerned-looking Xoliswa.

240

'Maybe they were involved in an accident,' says Zandile.

'Let's not be negative,' says Phumla. 'Let's try and stay positive.'

Xoliswa's cellphone suddenly beeps to life and they all look at it apprehensively.

Sorry baby. I can't do this any more. I am so sorry.

Xoliswa throws her phone at the wall and runs into the bathroom. They can hear her crying behind the locked door. Yandisa and Zandile bang on the door, pleading with her to let them in.

Phumla goes outside to break the news to everyone that *abakhwenyana* will no longer be coming. The announcement comes as a shock and she tells them to all help themselves to the food.

'What happened? *Kwenzakaleni*?' asks Sis Ntombi.

'I don't know,' replies Phumla. 'He just sent a message to say he is no longer coming.'

Sis Ntombi puts her hands on her cheeks and shakes her head. She can't understand why Keith has had such a sudden change of heart.

Abraham is equally perturbed but gathers himself and says: 'God has a good reason for this. We shall know in time.'

When Xoliswa finally emerges from the bathroom, puffy-eyed and red, she asks to be left alone but none of her family comply with her request and she knows why.

'I won't cut myself. I promise.'

Feeling reassured that she won't hurt herself, they vacate her bedroom leaving her to succumb to her tears. She calls Keith over and over again but he doesn't answer. She sends him a text message that merely says:

'Why? Why me?'

KEITH AND KLOSURE

The following morning Xoliswa doesn't go to church with her family. Instead, she drives to Keith's house in Burnside. He owes her an explanation. He's not going to get away with sending her a flimsy text message. She's relieved to see his car parked in the driveway. She knocks on the door and is surprised when a light-skinned woman with a pixie-cropped weave opens the door. She's wearing a tight-fitting, JLo tracksuit and Xoliswa can't remember the last time she saw someone in one of those.

'Hello!' says the woman confidently. 'Well, if it isn't one of Keith's whores.'

'Excuse me?' says Xoliswa, taken aback.

'You heard me,' the woman responds.

Xoliswa has a feeling that the reason for Keith's no-show at the lobola negotiation is standing right in front of her.

'I don't know who you are but you have no right to disrespect me like that!' says Xoliswa angrily.

'Ah please sisi, you're disrespecting me by sleeping in my home. This is *my* home, in case Keith told you otherwise. The maid told me you've been here every other night behaving like the madam of the house.'

'Look, I'm sorry. I didn't know Keith was married, he didn't tell me he had a wife,' says Xoliswa.

The woman laughs loudly and heartily, 'Come inside. You've already been in my home so it can't make things any worse.'

Xoliswa steps into the house cautiously, not sure what to expect. The woman leads her to the kitchen and offers to make them a cup of tea which Xoliswa declines and then offers her a seat which Xoliswa accepts.

'My name is Katherine. I'm Keith's sister. I wouldn't be stupid enough to marry a man like Keith.'

Xoliswa holds her hand up to her head in amazement. She's really not sure what is going on.

'I don't know what my brother told you, or didn't tell you but Keith is an old hand at this game. He's forty-three years old but acts like he's thirty-three and he is married with two kids. His wife kicked him out of the house last year because he got another woman pregnant and she then had him deported. We've been trying to fix his mess and to cut a long story short, they are back together. So, while he was trying to sort things out he has been living in my house. This is *my* house.'

Xoliswa is speechless.

'So what did my brother promise you? Marriage?'

Xoliswa doesn't respond and Katherine carries on unperturbed.

'My brother promises so many people so many things,' she says. 'He has a few other children all over the place.'

'I'm pregnant,' Xoliswa blurts out.

'You know what I would do, sisi *wami*? Abort that child. Keith won't do jack for you or your child and frankly, I'm tired of supporting his bastards. *Banengi.*'

Xoliswa starts to cry and Katherine hands her a paper towel.

'I'm sorry if I'm angry but my brother is bad news. If you know what's good for you, you'll stay the hell away from him.'

'Where is he now?' asks Xoliswa. She wants to see him one last time and give him a piece of her mind.

'Keith left for the UK yesterday.'

Xoliswa realises then that she has been scammed. Of her heart and of her money. She stands up and says goodbye to Katherine. She sits in the car for a long time, immobile. How is it that she's back here again? Screw Keith. Screw him. She's not going back to Heartbreak

Hotel. She refuses to check into that place again. She turns the key in the ignition and drives home.

MISSION ABORTED

The conversation about the abortion happens one afternoon when the sisters congregate for lunch. They have just placed their lunch orders when Xoliswa announces her intention.

'Ten years with Thulani and you couldn't fall pregnant! How do you fall pregnant from this prick you've known less than a year?' berates Yandisa.

'Can you spare me the judgement, please? I need your support!' implores Xoliswa.

'Why are you doing this?' asks Zandile.

She has just birthed two gorgeous twin girls and that afternoon is a rare occasion when she has left them at home.

'The whole thing with Keith was a mistake. This pregnancy is a mistake.'

Zandile then quotes the prophet Jeremiah, '"Before I formed you in the womb, I knew you. And before you were born I consecrated you." Nothing is a mistake with God.'

'Please Zandile, hold off on the sermon! You sound like Dad right now.'

'I agree with Zandile,' says Yandisa. 'You're carrying a human being inside you. You can't feel it now but you'll feel it soon.'

'It's easy for both of you. You have your husbands to stand by you, I have no one.'

'You have us,' says Zandile. 'Don't ever say you have no one.'

'Yes, we're here for you,' adds Yandisa.

'Yandisa, don't force it!' hisses Xoliswa. 'When have you *ever* been there for me?'

'I'm here now, aren't I?' Yandisa shoots back defensively.

'Are you going to help me or not?' she says, looking at her one sister and then the other.

'I want nothing to do with abortions,' responds Zandile, 'as a matter of principle.'

'I'll help you,' says Yandisa.

By the time their meal arrives, none of them feel like eating and they stab at their food disinterestedly and distractedly.

Yandisa organises the doctor for Xoliswa's abortion. A hairdresser at the salon knows someone, who knows someone, who performs abortions. She insists that it is safe and hygienic. Xoliswa has to go to Dr Muti's surgery after hours, as requested. It is not something that can be done in the normal course of the day, evidence of the illegal nature of the procedure. She sits in the waiting room, nervously tapping her heels and aside from the receptionist, who seems to be filing, she is alone.

Her thoughts transport her back to September 1994. The year she had an abortion. Thulani was adamant that the timing was wrong. He knew a friend of a friend whose girlfriend had recently had an abortion.

'It's just a foetus, Xolie. It doesn't have any feelings,' said Thulani reassuringly.

Xoliswa had done enough biology to contest his theory. She had read that at seven weeks they can discern a heartbeat, even though the baby is about the size of a blueberry. That at this stage, the facial features start to take shape.

'Thulani, this baby *is* alive.'

'Xolie, we're not going to debate this. We have no choice. The timing is off. With exams and our workload we can't factor a baby into this equation.'

The methodology of Thulani's argument was sound yet Xoliswa could not help thinking that his decision-making process was somewhat flawed. It lacked any emotion and that is what kept her awake at night. Was it her rigid Catholic upbringing that made her so averse to having an abortion? She wasn't religious and hadn't been to mass in years but did she think abortion was a sin? Her parents would steadfastly be against an abortion but she doubted they would embrace her pregnancy either. She had seen what had happened with Yandisa and the embarrassment that had surrounded her pregnancy. How their father had collapsed under the stress. Her parents had great expectations of her and she couldn't disappoint them. Besides, one Yandisa in the family was enough so she finally agreed to have an abortion.

'You're making the right choice,' said Thulani when she told him her decision.

But she never felt convinced that she was making the right decision. Her and Thulani had gone to the surgery together to see Dr Simbi, a pleasant old man, wearing a sterile white lab coat and a stethoscope around his neck. He asked her a few rudimentary questions like when it was that she had her last period and how far along she was, and then did an ultrasound, almost like he was verifying her responses. He confirmed that she was indeed in her first trimester and so the procedure would be a simple one. Thulani then left the room and told her he'd wait for her in the reception.

Dr Simbi told her to undress completely and then did the strangest thing. He fingered her.

'It's just to make you relax,' he reassured her, seeing the bewildered look on her face.

Xoliswa instinctively knew it was wrong. But it was also wrong when after inserting a pill in her vagina, he patted her like he was petting an animal. He told her to expect to feel moderate pain followed by profuse bleeding but that it would all be normal. He lied on both accounts. The pain had been crippling and Xoliswa had bled so heavily it went through to the mattress that night. Thulani had called the doctor and he told them to get to the hospital immediately. She was booked into theatre straight away for a dilation and curettage to clear out all the tissue in her uterus. Sweeping her clean of any evidence of the life that had begun to form inside her.

'So is this your first pregnancy?' asks the receptionist, in an attempt to make small talk.

Xoliswa replies that it is her first. She's not about to tell this stranger her life story.

'Ah sweet,' she says, 'I have four kids. They are such a blessing.'

There is an uneasy silence. Xoliswa clears her throat,

'My boyfriend isn't ready.'

'And you? Are you ready?' asks the woman bluntly.

'If he's not ready I guess I can't be ready, can I?' responds Xoliswa.

'It's your body, sisi,' continues the woman, 'and you get to decide what happens in it. If you want the baby, have it. It's yours and it's your decision to make. It doesn't matter if he's ready or not.'

'But surely it's a joint decision,' says Xoliswa. 'It takes two people to make a life so surely each one must agree to bringing a child into the world?'

'No, it's *your* choice. You are no greater than your choices and you will choose what you value in life. If you value your relationship, you will choose your boy —'

Before the woman can finish, the nurse appears and asks Xoliswa to follow her; the doctor is ready for her.

On entering Dr Muti's consulting room, the first thing he asks her is if she has the US dollars. He had been explicit on the phone about needing payment in foreign currency. 'No forex, no abortion,' he had stressed over and over again.

'I've changed my mind,' says Xoliswa. 'I don't want to go through with this any more.'

He's visibly annoyed, 'Well, thank you for wasting my time. I could have been at home already. I had to pay my secretary overtime *and* I had to ask the nurse to come in after hours to assist.'

Xoliswa reaches into her handbag for a few crisp dollars with Benjamin Franklin's face on them and throws them at him. 'For the inconvenience,' she says and walks away. She might have lost a few dollars that day but her life would be invaluably richer with Owami in it.

TOO POSH TO PUSH

Xoliswa is well into her second trimester when she tells her parents that she's pregnant. She tells them it was the 'Ndiweni boy' when they ask who is responsible. His name has not been spoken in a while, not after the aborted lobola negotiations. Phumla isn't surprised and says she had suspected it.

'It's God's will,' mumbles Abraham.

'A blessing is a blessing,' says Phumla matter-of-factly, 'it doesn't matter how it comes.'

At her baby shower, the question of 'Who is the father?' lingers in the air and goes unanswered. Xoliswa isn't willing to humour anyone's inquisitiveness and even Sis Ntombi, who would normally be the one to ask, doesn't pry and congratulates Xoliswa instead. And then offers, 'At least you will have someone to look after you in old age.'

A child is considered a retirement plan, like an annuity that will pay out at a later date.

'At least you have a child,' says Sis Lungile sympathetically. 'A child will always be yours.'

A child is also viewed as somewhat of a consolation prize. If you don't make it into marriage by a certain age then at least you have a child to fall back on.

'At least you won't be buried with a rat,' says another aunt.

That is the supposed fate suffered by single, childless women who die alone. But judging from everyone's reactions, there is clearly a big difference between being unmarried and pregnant as a teen and unmarried and pregnant in your thirties, because the reception

Owami receives, even before he's born, is overwhelming.

Yandisa throws a huge baby shower for Xoliswa at her house. She really wants to prove to Xoliswa that she is there for her even though she might have not been in the past. She goes all out, paying for the huge luncheon she has catered by Holiday Inn and a full bar. Sis Ntombi thinks that Yandisa is just using the shower as an opportunity to showcase her new home.

The house is beautiful and filled with furniture that Wesley bought in London and had shipped to Durban and transported to Bulawayo. He might not be around but his money certainly makes itself known.

When Xoliswa arrives at Yandisa's house, she is met with a boisterous surprise. The planning had been flawless on Yandisa's part and Xoliswa hadn't got a whiff of the plans. She is even more surprised to see Mpho, Natasha and Rutendo who all flew in for the celebration. Between them, they bought the whole of Baby City, Babies R Us and Woolworths.

Xoliswa feels so touched and bursts into tears when she sees everyone. She blames the pregnancy for making her soft. After a hearty lunch, she unwraps her presents with glee. Every little item the baby could possibly need has been gifted to her and every present comes with an explanation on what it is, how to use it and some sound words of advice. Zandile moans that she didn't receive so many gifts and she had twins! Everything is blue and yellow as everyone has been told that she is expecting a baby boy.

Afterwards, Rutendo and Natasha take all the gifts into the house and get a good look at the interior of the house. There are huge portraits on the walls: Yandisa and Wesley from their wedding, Yandisa and the children, Yandisa and her parents.

'It's a beautiful home,' says Natasha as they put everything down in the sunken lounge.

'Nah, it's all Ikea furniture, it's cheap,' counters Rutendo. 'Wesley has always been a cheapskate, I wouldn't expect anything less from him.'

'Well, it's certainly an upgrade from his Fort Avenue flat,' says Natasha.

'He could have gotten himself a better wife though. I mean Yandisa isn't all that.'

They hear a baby whimper and unbeknownst to them Zandile is in the sun lounge breastfeeding one of the twins. She ambles into view with the baby on her hip. They aren't sure how much of their conversation she's overheard and both smile uneasily.

'You guys were on your way out, right?' says Zandile pointedly, giving them no room to respond or explain themselves. Natasha has no rejoinder and Rutendo quickly apologises and they both leave the party with haste, leaving all the women to debate and discuss childbirth.

'You're going natural aren't you?' asks Sis Ntombi, with a hint of bias in her tone.

Xoliswa hasn't even thought about how she's going to give birth. 'I had to have a emergency C-section,' interjects Zandile.

The women around the table express their pity but Zandile doesn't need any, she's perfectly content the way things worked out with her birthing experience.

'I had an elective C-section,' says Zodwa, Zandile's sister-in-law, who has been invited at Zandile's behest.

'Too posh to push, hey,' remarks Edna. 'You're just as good as someone who hasn't given birth at all.'

'Does it matter how you give birth to a child?' shoots back Chandelle. 'The important thing is having one.'

'It does matter,' replies Sis Ntombi with authority. 'Real women push.'

'Not to mention the innumerable advantages for the child from a vaginal delivery,' continues Mpho, who goes on to elaborate about her water birth, replete with a midwife and her hubby looking on intently.

She insists that it was painless and that natural is *always* best.

'My C-section babies are just fine,' says Zodwa, without apology. 'Plus, I'm still intact down there.'

This comment elicits some gasps from a few of the women.

Sis Lungile's forthright rejoinder, 'I had vaginal births for all my children and I can assure you that it does come back,' causes murmurs of agreement around the table. And so the debate continues until dusk when the party finally wraps up and Xoliswa goes home feeling exhausted and happy.

Xoliswa opts for an elective C-section after hearing the gruelling accounts of labour and decides to choose what is considered the 'easy way out'. But nature gets the better of her and she goes into labour while out on a construction site, a week before her scheduled caesarean. People are not surprised she goes into natural labour having worked well into her ninth month of pregnancy.

She goes straight to the hospital and her gynae takes a while to get there so by the time he arrives, her labour has progressed very quickly and there is no time for a C-section and she gives birth naturally. After all the gory stories she'd heard, she anticipated excruciating pain but it is less debilitating than she imagined. Phumla is in the room beside her throughout the birth, sponging her forehead and holding her hand in encouragement. A short while later, Owami announces his presence with a resounding cry. As he's laid on Xoliswa's chest, it ceases to matter how he arrived, she's just thrilled he's arrived. She's immediately smitten by the tiny baby boy who plugs onto her breast straight away. Theirs is a different kind of love affair. He is hers. And she is his.

MATURITY

TILL DEATH DO US PART

Abraham and Phumla decide to celebrate their 32nd wedding anniversary by hosting a grand party. Not since Yandisa's wedding has there been such a big celebration in the family. For the three months preceding it, the sisters plot and plan every detail of the special occasion with Phumla overseeing the finer details. They decide to hire the huge banquet room at the Holiday Inn, after deciding that the church is too small to accommodate everyone on their guest list.

Abraham and Phumla still make a dapper couple after more than three decades of marriage. Phumla goes to the salon every month to get her silver-grey hair relaxed and styled into a neat bob that frames her face. At sixty years of age, she looks at least five years younger. Money is one of those underestimated anti-ageing solutions and those who have it can delay the ravages that come with age. Abraham's hair has whitened with age and his face is lined with wrinkles, adding to his wisdom. He's looking a bit frail, having suffered a mild heart attack. Dr Filmore put him on a stringent diet of vegetables and fish and the result is that he has lost a lot of weight so the extra folds of flesh hang loosely on his frame like dressed tripe. Phumla eats to her heart's content even though Dr Filmore has warned her that it's time she cut down on the calories.

'We're not young any more,' he warned her during a routine check-up.

'If I die, I die,' was Phumla's flippant reply.

For Abraham, death is no longer something remote and something

257

that will only happen far in the future. Laying Uncle Ben to rest the previous year has made his eventual death seem closer to home. There is an urgency now in the way he does things and he has drawn and redrawn his will a few times. The chaos that ensued after Uncle Ben's death is testament to the fact that Abraham can no longer take anything or anyone for granted.

Uncle Ben's death was most unexpected. It wasn't a long protracted illness which often gives people time to prepare themselves emotionally for the eventuality. Uncle Ben was taken suddenly one Sunday morning. Abraham had just finished delivering a fevered Sunday morning service when he got a call from Uncle Ben's young brother, Obed. When he started the conversation with 'Sokuwonakele' Abraham knew that something bad had happened. He just didn't realise how bad. Obed asked Abraham to come to the house immediately, where everyone had gathered.

When Abraham arrived at the house, there was a red cloth tied to the gate, a symbol to indicate that someone has died. Obed was standing at the gate waiting to receive him, his face ashen.

'Ubhudi has passed on,' he said to Abraham, solemnly.

Even though Abraham had officiated over many deaths, there was something far more intimate about the death of somebody close to him. In that moment, his heart stilled as the reality of Uncle Ben's passing sank in. He hugged Obed and clung to him, seeking to be consoled at this time rather than consoling others. As they disengaged from one another, Abraham offered his heartfelt condolences and Phumla did the same, her sombre face indicating the solemnity of such an occasion. They both attended so many funerals that it had become second nature to switch into a character of sorts but this time no character was required. Only after all the formalities did they enquire about the details of what had happened to Uncle Ben.

'He collapsed this morning. uMaMoyo called an ambulance but by the time they arrived at Gallen House, ubesephel' umoya.'

Phumla and Abraham exchanged puzzled looks. Clearly anticipating their next question as to who MaMoyo was and sensing their confusion, he quickly proffered an explanation.

'*Umam'ncane,*' Obed said.

No further explanation was needed. They both understand what that word meant in this context. She was a paramour. Or what the Europeans would call a mistress. 'Girlfriend' wouldn't do justice to her role because that would imply that her role is fleeting, a mere infatuation. The word enunciated the permanence of her position. A certain respect came with '*umama*' but '*ncane*' indicated that she was junior in ranking to the affections of the wife of the house.

'Where is my sister?' Abraham asked, sensing that the situation would kill her, if not physically, then in spirit.

'She is on her way home,' said Obed.

Sis Ntombi had travelled to the United Kingdom to assist her daughter, Khethiwe, who had recently given birth. As per the custom, she would be with Khethiwe for the weeks following the arrival of her child, a grandson. Khethiwe had married a seemingly nice German man two years before in an intimate wedding celebration at Victoria Falls with the majestic waterfall as the epic centrepiece. Khethiwe was the first of the Ntini children to get married so it had been quite the occasion. Uncle Ben and Sis Ntombi had made a formidable pair, posing for photos with the bride and groom and other members of the family, as could be seen in the pictures hanging on the walls of their home.

Sis Ntombi had left for London two weeks before Khethiwe's expected due date and when baby Karl arrived, she was elated to assume her new role as a grandmother. Uncle Ben had escorted her to the airport and bade her goodbye. As with many goodbyes, often said with careless consideration, they had mouthed the words to each other, taking it for granted that they would see each other in six weeks time.

When Sis Ntombi heard the news that her husband of twenty-five years had passed on, she collapsed under the weight of her grief. She forced herself to contain her tears as she boarded the plane heading to Zimbabwe, Khethiwe and baby Karl with her. Thirteen hours later they landed at Harare Airport and took a connecting flight to Bulawayo.

Sis Lungile, Phumla and Abraham, all clothed in black, denoting their state of mourning were all there to welcome them. She had managed to maintain her composure throughout the two flights but gave into the tears as her siblings enveloped her in a hug. The last time they had cried like that was when their mother had passed on.

When she got to the house, as more people assailed her with their own grief, the cycle repeated itself. It was only later, in the privacy of her bedroom, that Sis Ntombi had demanded to know exactly how her husband had died. Abraham excused himself from the conversation, deferring to Sis Lungile to try and explain to their sister the circumstances surrounding Uncle Ben's death, as sordid as they were. He heard Sis Ntombi's strangled screams when the situation in the home was revealed to her as he'd closed the bedroom door behind him. He stood frozen, choked with emotion.

The mourning period was a time filled with much activity. Relative calm prevailed during the day and family and relatives descended on the house for the evening prayer led by Abraham. Tradition dictated that the widow assumed her place on the mattress that she had shared with her husband and her sisters and other female matriarchs occupied the space with her. Sis Ntombi refused to take her position on the mattress, defying the tradition, opting for the couch instead.

The reason for the mattress tradition is unclear but some say it is because a widow doesn't have the strength to get on and off the bed during the mourning period. Others say that a bed is a luxury and that mourning is a time of grieving and therefore getting a good night's sleep is not considered in line with the mourning process. Whatever the reason, Sis Ntombi was not interested in the tradition and refused to comply.

'You need to sit on the mattress. *Abantu bazothini?* What will people say?' chided Uncle Ben's side of the family, mostly the older female matriarchs who had occupied that space themselves.

'Fuck the people. What were they saying when Uncle Ben was fucking around?' Sis Ntombi snapped. She was resolute in her stance and sat on the couch, cross-legged at times, receiving condolences from people as they walked in the house. She shed no tears, stoic in her grief. At first, mourners who arrived to pay their condolences were baffled by her stance but no one said anything directly to her. Private conversations were had and everyone agreed that *umfelokazi* was very dignified.

Every morning, Sis Ntombi woke up and got dressed in her two-piece suit and opaque stockings and a strand of pearls around her neck. Her aunts tried to force her to wear a chitenge, a traditional Zambian garment worn like a sarong with the remaining fabric used as a doek but she refuses to wear both and instead covers her head with a black lace scarf. She is calm and composed.

After Abraham's prayer every evening, supper is served. Xoliswa organised MaTshuma and her cooking club as Sis Ntombi was insistent that she didn't want *isiphithiphithi* in her fully fitted kitchen or random relatives cooking up a storm in her backyard. The cooking club make lunch and supper every day and Sis Ntombi ensures that meat is served at every meal despite the fact that everyone is feeling the strain on the economy. Often when people pass away, they are buried as soon as possible so the family can avoid the costs associated with feeding people every day but money is clearly not an issue with the Ntinis and mourners take the opportunity to socialise. Sis Ntombi has two beasts slaughtered for the occasion but she herself abstains from eating meat. Tea and scones are served at around 10 pm for those still lingering at the house.

Uncle Ben had several funeral policies that were taken out to cater for the mourning period and in addition, Khethiwe brought British pounds which when converted into Zimbabwean millions, go a long way. The boys also arrive with their foreign currency, with Edmond flying in from Singapore and Edward from Sweden.

Uncle Ben's body is brought home on the Friday night and this triggers further displays of sorrow from mourners. MaMoyo arrives at the house with her two children, Ben Junior and Benita, who are eighteen and sixteen respectively. Sis Lungile whispers her arrival to Sis Ntombi, who immediately confronts her.

'I've come to pay my last respects!' wails MaMoyo.

Sis Ntombi looks at the ordinary looking middle-aged woman dressed in a white tunic with a java print sarong wrapped around it and a white doek. Her eyes are puffy, swollen and red and she looks like she has been crying for days.

'You need to get her out of here!' barks Sis Ntombi.

'He collapsed in my arms. *Uphel'amandla. Uphel'umoy' ezandleni zami!*'

'If you had any shred of respect you would not have come here!' says Sis Ntombi.

'Please!' MaMoyo pleads. 'This man died in my arms. He took his last breath in my arms, please allow me to say goodbye.'

This riles Sis Ntombi even more and she calls on Obed and some of the other men to remove her from the premises. Phumla comes to MaMoyo's defence.

'Sis Ntombi, just allow her to say goodbye. Uncle Ben is gone, what difference will it make?'

Sis Ntombi gives her sister-in-law a contemptuous look: 'Are you serious?'

Phumla puts her hand on her shoulder but Sis Ntombi's shrugs it off brusquely.

'I know you are hurting now but you need to forgive. The same way Jesus forgave our sins we should also allow the same gratitude to others.'

'Phumla, if you keep this up I will bar you *and* Abraham from the funeral!' hisses Sis Ntombi. 'Don't come here acting pious with me. I said I don't want this bitch here. Save your happy-clappy nonsense for another day. If she wants to mourn Ben, she can do so on her own turf.'

Abraham quickly barges in to quell the rising animosity and leads his wife away from the brewing confrontation. Sis Ntombi goes to her room, accompanied by her daughter and Sis Lungile and Edmond, Edward and Obed escort a hysterical MaMoyo to the gate, making it very clear that she is not welcome. The children are allowed to stay and mourn their father, even though no one had known of their existence until that day.

The following day, the funeral procession leaves Fortune's Gate to give Uncle Ben his final send-off. It isn't a small gathering and political stalwarts, high-ranking army officials, both retired and sitting, attend the funeral. Members of the business community and social activists also attend and while the president isn't there, one of his deputies attend and he speaks about Uncle Ben's illustrious career and his liberation struggle credentials. Other war veterans and political activists speak fondly of him, professing their admiration for Brigadier Ben, as he was called. Edward and Edmond give moving tributes to their father. Khethiwe chooses not to speak, instead preferring to sit with her mother, holding her hand.

Sis Ntombi stands tall and unflinching as they leave the church. She is the epitome of regal, dressed in a two-piece black suit and matching black lace head wrap. Her eyes are shielded behind black sunglasses, protecting her from the glorious sun. She sets the tone for the day and everyone is impeccably dressed. The women totter to the dusty graveyard in their nine-inch heels and fan themselves furiously with the funeral programme, as everyone sits under the tent next to the grave site. The men are decked out in immaculate suits or army regalia. There is a five-gun salute as Uncle Ben's white coffin, draped in the Zimbabwean flag, is lowered into the ground. A strangled cry escapes from Sis Ntombi. Her body quivers as she finally gives into the pain she has been suppressing. Uncle Ben is finally laid to rest, as is Sis Ntombi's anger.

AFTER TEARS

After Uncle Ben was laid to rest, mourners gather at the house for the After Tears. This is where Xoliswa formally meets Chengetai Chihore. He is one of the many dignitaries that had flown in from Harare to pay his respects. She first catches him eyeing her out standing under the tent watching as Uncle Ben's body is lowered into the ground. While everyone has their eyes on the coffin, his eyes are on her. His gaze is so intent and she stares back at him, their eyes locked, before quickly looking away. When she looks at him again a few minutes later, he is still staring at her. She nudges Yandisa.

'He's probably one of those CIO types,' says Yandisa, from behind her Gucci sunglasses.

Afterwards, after shaking Sis Ntombi's hand and offering her aunt his condolences, he shakes Xoliswa's hand and holds onto it longer than necessary. He approaches her later in the VIP tent reserved for family and dignitaries, when lunch is served.

'I'm Chengetai Chihore,' he says. 'I saw you at the grave site.'

'I remember,' replies Xoliswa.

He has rough features and a chiselled jaw that juts brutally from his face and when he removes his sunglasses, they reveal a pair of hawkish eyes that rest on her with keen interest. He holds his cleft chin up proudly. He is well dressed which is probably his only redeeming feature when it came to his appearance.

Once again, he takes her hand and then says, 'I'm so sorry about your uncle. He was such an asset to the revolution and to our founding forefathers. We are eternally grateful.'

Xoliswa has always hated these revolutionary ZANU–PF types.

She despises them more now that the economy is in the doldrums. Of course, they blame it on the Western-imposed sanctions but she blames it on corruption, ineptitude and mismanagement of resources.

'It was his time,' says Xoliswa, wanting to disengage her hand from his.

The demure gold band on his left hand glistens as it catches a bit of the sun. It is dull and lacklustre, just like its owner. Xoliswa thinks he is probably in his late forties, if not early fifties.

'And you are?' he asks, prompting her for her name.

'Xoliswa Mafu.'

'And you are beautiful just like your aunt. I can see beauty runs in the family.'

'Thank you,' she replies.

'Can I call you sometime, Colie?' he asks, stumbling over her name.

It seems to be a bit of a tongue-twister for him and she has to hold back her laughter.

'I'd much rather call you,' she says quickly.

He hands her a business card which Xoliswa doesn't even bother reading and tosses it in the bin later that night and forgets all about Chengetai Chihore.

Xoliswa is surprised when Gertrude puts a call through to her office from Chengetai early Monday morning. He hasn't even waited for her to settle into the day.

'Where did you get my number?' she asks, even more convinced that he must be a CIO.

'There aren't many Colie Mafus in Bulawayo,' he says smoothly.

Xoliswa laughs even though she hadn't intended to. This 'Colie Mafu' business is going to be a comedy.

'So what can I do for you, Chenge?' she asks.

'I want you to be my girlfriend,' he states.

'You're a married man,' she responds.

'My marriage is my problem. Not yours.'

'Chenge, I'm not interested,' and she abruptly hangs up the phone.

He's unperturbed and tries calling her back several times that day. She won't take his calls and tells Gertie not to put him through and again fobs him off. He's undeterred by her rejection and rebounds by sending her a huge bouquet of red roses. Gertie and the others in the office ooh and aah over the elaborate arrangement when she arrives the next morning. They hover like vultures over her when she reads the card that is attached to the arrangement.

You are giving me sleepless nights.
CC

She is unmoved and puts the card back into the envelope and throws it into the bin, together with the flowers. An hour later Chengetai calls to find out if she received the flowers.

'I didn't like them,' she replies candidly.

Two hours later, an Interflora van arrives and delivers an elaborate arrangement of pink orchids to the office. Xoliswa is at a loss for words. It would be dishonest to say she wasn't impressed.

He doesn't stop there and makes sure flowers are delivered to her at the office every day for the rest of the week. He's converting her office into a mini florist and she's eventually forced to call him and thank him for his rather wild exhibition of intention. He's hard to get hold of but finally returns her missed calls. After failing to get hold of him on his cellphone, she googles him. This exercise reveals he is the Permanent Secretary in the Ministry of Public Works. Xoliswa curses herself; she had no idea he was this influential or powerful. She chides herself for being rude.

'I see the flowers are working; you went to great pains to call me.'

She can visualise his lips curving into a self-satisfied smile.

'You don't give up easily do you?'

'I wouldn't have got this far in life if I did,' he replies. 'Persistence is my middle name.'

She laughs because there is a very real possibility that his name could actually be Persistence Chihore.

'Chenge, I'm not interested. I only called to say thank you and to tell you to stop with the flowers. My hay fever is out of control!'

'Colie, don't break my heart!' he says and laughs. 'Hey, I am only trying to light up your life.'

'And what do you know about my life?' snaps Xoliswa, feeling defensive.

'I've done my research. I have a dossier on you. 36. Beautiful. Intelligent. Unmarried. One child ...'

'Chengetai, I'm going to hang up on you.'

'Well, you've mastered that pretty well, haven't you?'

Xoliswa sighs in exasperation, 'So, how do I get rid of you then?'

'Have lunch with me tomorrow at Amanzi in Newlands. I'll book us a private table.'

'Chenge, in case you've forgotten, I'm in Bulawayo.'

'I haven't forgotten. Be at the airport for the 6 am flight, there'll be a ticket waiting. You'll be here in time for lunch and you can fly back in the evening.'

'I have meetings,' protests Xoliswa. 'I can't just up and leave ...'

'Cancel them. You can reschedule them for Thursday. I'll see you tomorrow.'

He cuts the call and Xoliswa is speechless. She sits and stares at the phone and slowly starts to smile to herself. This is how Gertie finds her when she pops her head into Xoliswa's office a while later and tells her she's running late for a 3 pm site meeting.

'Thanks, Gertie. Please cancel all my meetings tomorrow. I have to go to Harare for an urgent meeting.'

'Is it about that government office building tender?'

Xoliswa nods distractedly, 'Yes. Please arrange for the driver to pick Owami up for school. I'll be gone all day.'

She gathers her folders into her briefcase and leaves for her site meeting.

She flies into Harare the next morning and because the flight is slightly delayed she only arrives at around 10 am. Chenge has organised for a driver to pick her up, who has been given stern instructions to be at her disposal. The driver hands her bricks of cash, still wrapped in plastic. Millions and millions of Zimbabwean dollars for her to spend as she pleases.

'The boss said that's money in case you need to do a few things.'

Xoliswa looks at the money and looks at her watch. She can definitely squeeze in a few hours of shopping before their lunch date. The driver takes her to Greatermans where she frantically combs the clothing racks making the most of the time she has left. She shops for herself and Owami and then for her sisters. She goes up to the next level and buys a few pairs of shoes. Her last stop is at the cosmetic counter where she has her make-up touched up and stocks up on the entire Clinique cosmetics range. She is well aware of the curious glances she gets when her purchases are rung up and when she stacks bricks of money on the counter. It's 2007 and the Zimbabwean economy is in the throes of a depression but you wouldn't know it by looking at her extravagant purchases which give no indication of the hardships suffered by most of the population She feels a slight pang of guilt. The trunk of the car is brimming with all her shopping bags by the time the driver loads everything in.

Chengetai is the perfect gentleman over lunch. When she is ushered into a private wing of the restaurant, he stands up to greet her and kisses her chastely on the cheek. He pulls a chair out for her and compliments her on her outfit. She does the same as he looks debonair in a dark brown suit and yellow shirt that brightens his dark complexion. They have a long leisurely lunch and talk about everything from the economy to the building industry. He asks her about her company and her future plans. Not once does he try and come onto her. Not once do his hands even stray across the table to try and touch her. When lunch ends, he tells her he has to rush to a cabinet meeting.

'Thank you once again for agreeing to meet me for lunch. I know we got off on the wrong foot but I'd really like us to start over.'

'I'm sure we can,' she says.

'I'm sorry I won't be able to see you off at the airport but my driver will take you wherever you'd like to go.'

'It's fine, Chenge. I know you are an extremely busy man.'

Another chaste kiss is planted on her cheek and he leaves Xoliswa to linger over her dessert and her thoughts of him. He's not a conventionally handsome man but his rough features are softened by his polished exterior, wit and intelligence. She starts to think that maybe she had been too dismissive of him. He could be a good companion plus he clearly has loads of money.

She spends the rest of the afternoon at Sam Levy's Village shopping centre and Chengetai doesn't leave her thoughts. She keeps replaying their conversation in her head and starts to wonder when she might see him again.

When she lands in Bulawayo, she doesn't go straight home and instead goes to the office. She's surprised to find all her staff are still there and Gertrude is brimming with excitement as Xoliswa walks in.

'We won the tender to build the new government precinct!' she announces.

Xoliswa throws her briefcase down and gives Gertie a hug. This was the biggest project they had ever tendered for and had been up against giants like Murray & Roberts. They had worked diligently to get the contract but in the back of her mind Xoliswa can't dismiss the nagging feeling that Chengetai Chihore has had a hand in their good fortune.

MOM KNOWS BEST

On the morning of Abraham and Phumla's anniversary party, Zandile wakes with a start after a fitful night's sleep. She's anxious about the arrangements for the party and wants it to be perfect for her parents. She takes Ndaba's hand from around her waist and gets up. He mumbles something incoherent before sinking back into his reverie. She pulls on her nightgown and goes to attend to the children. She knows Maria is there to help but she feels guilty for offloading them to her all the time. As she makes her way downstairs she can hear their voices coming from the playroom. She peeps around the door and they rush towards her.

'Hi Mummy!' they squeal in delight.

Zanele and Zinzile, the twins, are almost five. Zwelihle is the accident that happened a year later.

'Come see what we're doing!' commands Zanele who is more assertive than Zinzile, who tends to be soft spoken and gentle. Unlike the girls, who are small in stature, Zwelihle is round like a teddy bear. His white T-shirt is tight around the chest and his white shorts are creeping up between his legs. He has yoghurt on his cheeks, a telltale sign that he has already started eating.

Maria is in the kitchen cleaning up. Zandile co-opted her into full-time employment a few months after the twins were born as Yandisa no longer needed help because she had her mother-in-law.

'We're building a house, come build with us,' says Zinzile.

Zandile glances at the clock on the wall and decides she has a few minutes to contribute to the Lego effort. Zwelihle jumps up excitedly to join in but his sisters don't want him to help because he constantly

271

tears down their efforts and giggles with glee when he does so.

Zandile plays with the children for a few minutes and then tells them they need to go and bath and get ready to go to Gogo and Khulu's house.

The children normally abhor bathing but the mention of 'Gogo' and 'Khulu' is a major drawcard. They are even more delighted to hear that Zandile is bathing them as it is a daily chore Zandile usually delegates to Maria.

Zandile's mother-in-law can't understand why she needs to employ Maria to help her.

'You don't work,' criticises Selina. 'What do you do all day besides spend my son's money?'

'Who else must spend it?' replies Zandile flippantly.

Ndaba has made a lot of money and his position in the banking sector means he has access to lucrative foreign currency deals. Rumour has it that he has a team of Vapostori women working for him, changing foreign currency on the black market. Zandile always pleads ignorance when it comes to her husband's work and she has a simple mantra: He makes the money, I just spend it. And spend it she does. She flies to Johannesburg to do her groceries at Woolworths. They fly in on a Friday and return on the Sunday and the groceries follow with *umalaitsha*. She always makes provision for her parents in the grocery bill so that when other women complain about food prices going up or the raving shortages, her mother is never part of that conversation.

On the outside, Zandile appears to be a pampered housewife but inside she is a frustrated one. Raising children is hard work. After the twins were born she'd quit her eight to five job. The labour had been long and finally the doctor decided she needed an emergency caesarean section. At that point Zandile was exhausted and in extreme pain, so she welcomed it. The twins came into the world an hour later. When the doctor placed the girls on her chest she didn't feel anything. What was supposed to be such an euphoric moment was an anticlimax. She was so exhausted that all she wanted to do was sleep. Ndaba was over the moon about his daughters and camped in her room and constantly checked on the girls in the nursery. He never left her side, slept in the chair next to her and even helped her pee which was difficult and painful after the surgery.

'You are babying her too much,' complained Selina to her son.

'If you don't become active those stitches won't heal,' admonished her sister-in-law, Sis Nandi.

When did you ever give birth? Zandile wanted to scream at her but restrained herself.

She was tired of people offering unsolicited advice. She was tender from the operation and her breasts were engorged with milk and she was failing at breastfeeding her girls. She hadn't realised how challenging it would be to get a child to latch. Let alone two. It always seemed so natural when women whipped out their breast and the child immediately suckled. She struggled and was frustrated when after countless attempts, she still wasn't successful.

'You'll get the hang of it,' said Sister Bettina encouragingly.

But the babies wailed and Sister Bettina said it was because they were hungry. Ndaba was anxious and worried about his daughters not feeding and kept appealing to her to try harder. She started expressing but the sister cautioned against the girls getting used to the bottle, lest they never wanted to breastfeed again.

'Don't breastfeed,' said Zodwa one morning when she was visiting Zandile in the hospital. 'That nonsense that breast milk is the best is not true. You don't want to have droopy breasts, do you? Ndaba will leave you.'

'I breastfed all my babies,' countered Edna, who was also visiting. 'All three of them. Breast milk strengthens their immunity and it's free.'

'That's probably a consideration with unplanned motherhood but my husband could afford formula,' responded Zodwa.

Zandile certainly didn't want droopy breasts but on the other hand, she wanted the twins to grow up strong and nourished. When she raised the issue with Ndaba he made his position clear.

'Those are *my* breasts, Zandile. Perky or not, I'll still cherish them,' he said reassuringly.

So she persevered with the breastfeeding until their tiny mouths latched onto her breasts. Ndaba looked on with pride as they suckled but because she didn't produce enough milk she still had to supplement with a bottle. This meant that Ndaba could help with the night feeds while she was still in the hospital. Selina was disapproving of her son doing night feeds as well as about giving the girls the bottle.

'You are here all day and he has to go to work. It's not fair on him,' scolded Selina.

He doesn't mind doing it, Zandile wanted to say but she kept quiet.

'The problem is that you don't eat,' lamented Selina. 'Drink tea. Loads of tea and you will see the milk will come.'

When she was discharged from hospital, she went home with her 1.8-kilogram babies. All Zandile could think of was how tiny they were; smaller than a 2-kilogram bag of sugar. Ndaba had been adamant that he didn't want her to go to her parents' house for the traditional six-week confinement period and argued that Phumla could easily come to their house and help. Phumla hated that she was uprooted from her own home but what she hated even more was that Selina was there too. It was like watching *Clash of the Titans*. The two women never agreed on mothering methods and it always seemed like they were trying to outdo each other with parenting advice.

The first week went fast and Zandile spent most of it breastfeeding and changing diapers. When the babies woke for the night feeds, both mothers insisted she sit up even when she was drowsy with sleep. They told her horror stories of mothers who had fallen asleep while breastfeeding lying down and their babies had choked to death or being suffocated by the breast. Although she couldn't ascertain the verity of the stories, they had instilled enough fear into her that she sat up while she breastfed. She loathed burping the babies after their feeds and luckily whenever she struggled, Selina came to her rescue and took one of the babies on her lap and rubbed her back with her knotted fingers, until she belched noisily.

When the umbilical cords fell off, Selina took them, telling Zandile there was a custom as to how they were disposed of. The same way she insisted there was a reason why she shaved the twins' silky, black hair which had angered Zandile immensely. She had planned to take the twins for a newborn photoshoot but had had to shelve that idea. Selina, through pursed lips, merely said it was their culture.

Ndaba shrugged his shoulders when Zandile told him about it and said, 'Mom knows best. She raised me, didn't she?'

THE GOOD WIFE

There were other customs that Zandile did appreciate however like the fact that she wasn't allowed to cook because she was still considered 'unclean'. She was happy for the mothers to take over that responsibility and to do all the cooking and take over her kitchen. Phumla left after a fortnight, delegating all responsibilities to Selina. Although she didn't say it, Zandile felt betrayed by her mother's abrupt departure. Selina continued to cook diligently and was very hands-on and made sure Zandile ate three meals a day and drank tea in-between. There was always an urn of milky tea ready, not just for Zandile but for the constant stream of visitors who came to the house to see the babies. The visits tired Zandile out and disrupted the routine she was trying to establish with the twins. They slept a lot during the day and Zandile tried to sleep when they did but whenever she was about to put her head on the pillow, there would be an announcement that a visitor had arrived.

At least when her sisters visited, they *always* brought food. When the rest of the family arrived, they ate whatever food was available.

'I have tea leaves coming out my arse,' whispered Zandile to Xoliswa when she was visiting one evening.

They were cloistered in Zandile's bedroom but Selina would barge in if she heard so much as a whimper from the twins.

'When is she going?' asked Xoliswa.

Zandile shrugged her shoulders, 'It's not like I can ask her.'

Things often came to a head between Zandile and Selina when it came to the girls. Zandile nearly always felt that the girls were overdressed.

Selina would dress them in a vest and rompers and then swaddle them in plush blankets, even in the searing October heat. Selina threw out all the pacifiers, saying they would harm the babies and stop them from breastfeeding properly. So for the duration of her mother-in-law's stay, Zandile puts her feelings one side and doesn't consult Google, and let the older woman take over. Occasionally she would ask Yandisa, who would baulk at some of the suggestions.

Selina finally left after Zandile's six-week check-up at the doctor. Ndaba took her to the gynae because she still couldn't drive. Leaving the house felt liberating for her even if it was just to the doctor. Her appointment was at 9 am but she only got to see the doctor at 11 am because there had been an emergency. Doctors were never on time. The long wait made her anxious but thankfully the twins had slept the entire time. The gynae then examined her and told her that she was healing well and was ready for sex. Zandile had been dreading hearing those words.

After her appointment, she visits the paediatrician who is in the same building. The twins are weighed and they both weigh 4.5 kilograms. She had felt proud.

That night when she climbed into bed after bathing at 10 pm, because the twins had fallen asleep late, she collided into Ndaba's erect manhood. He snuggled closer to her, telling her she smelled good. She knew what was coming next and even though she was exhausted, she gave into his strokes. She fell into a deep sleep only to be woken up two hours later by the twins ready for their feed. Ndaba slept soundly every night and didn't even hear the twins when they cried so she did the graveyard shift alone. She would sometimes fall asleep at 4 am only to be woken up by him getting ready for work.

She was quietly resentful but also felt bad for feeling that way because he had to go to work. She still made him breakfast every morning and sat with him while he ate. When he left for her work she would try and sleep before the twins woke up. She'd bathe the girls which wasn't easy and then feed them and they would all fall asleep.

She tried to tidy up around the house but there was never enough time and so she often neglected her duties.

Selina and her sisters-in-law liked to visit in the afternoons. Zodwa was the most frequent visitor because she didn't work and lived in the neighbourhood so she often popped in on her way to the shops or on her way back from picking up the children from school. One afternoon she arrived with a beef stew, armed with heaps of advice.

'You look terrible, Sis,' she said, placing the ceramic pot on the kitchen table.

Zandile self-consciously ran her hand through her dishevelled hair. She hadn't relaxed it since she had given birth and the growth was showing. She was still wearing her nightgown and pink stokkies and it was 2 pm in the afternoon. She hadn't bathed and smelt of milk and talcum powder.

'Do you know this is the most dangerous time in your marriage?' Zodwa warned her. 'This is when men start looking at other women because their wives let themselves go. The house is a mess, get a maid, Zandile.'

Motherhood was overwhelming for Zandile and she felt the true magnitude of it once Selina left. As annoying as she'd been, she'd also been extremely helpful. She often sat in the bathroom crying and hated herself for not coping and transitioning into her new role as a mother. She felt like such a failure. Worse, her nipples were cracked and swollen and breastfeeding was becoming an extreme sport. Never mind the house being a mess, she was a mess.

Edna arrived at the house one Friday morning to find Zandile and the twins all crying. Every Friday, Edna came into town to buy groceries and supplies for the farm and she often travelled with her maid. On a whim, she decided to pop in and see Zandile and the girls.

It had been a trying night with both girls restless and both refusing to be put down. Zandile was drained. The babies hadn't been sleeping well and she was lucky if she could manage to snatch one or two hours of sleep here and there. Edna had swept into the house, drawing the curtains in Zandile's bedroom to let the sun in.

'Zandile, give them to me,' said Edna with authority.

Edna told Zandile to have a bath and get some sleep and that she and Phathisani would take care of the children. Zandile didn't argue. She took a long leisurely bath which she wasn't accustomed to any more because the minute she stepped into the water, one of the twins would start crying. It was like they were programmed to sabotage her every move. After her bath she changed the linen and climbed into bed and slept.

She didn't realise how long she slept for until Edna woke her up for lunch. Phathisani had cleaned the house and it was sparkling and fresh.

'Thank you so much for your help,' said Zandile.

'Don't be silly. If you need help, say so,' replied Edna. 'Motherhood can be overwhelming. Especially in the beginning.'

Zandile nodded but didn't say anything. She couldn't help feeling like a failure. She thought of the shame she would feel when Edna relayed her ineptitude as a mother to Nandi and the rest of the family.

'I also struggled in the beginning,' said Edna. 'And Bongani was so colicky. Yeyi! He wouldn't sleep. And Butho moved out of our bedroom because he said the baby was making too much noise for him. Can you imagine?! It was his kid too!'

Zandile suddenly felt appreciative of Ndaba's efforts, as meagre as they seemed.

'You can afford to get help; we couldn't afford it. We were living with his mother who didn't seem very helpful at the time but now I can see that she actually was. Get someone to help you, Zandile. You don't need to suffer in silence.'

'I just feel so useless,' confessed Zandile.

'Don't be silly. You're doing great. Those little minions are growing well.'

Zandile managed a weak smile. She was always on the verge

of tears. Whenever she tried to confide in her mother, Phumla was dismissive.

'Stop complaining and count your blessings,' she told Zandile.

Sis Ntombi was worse: 'Just pull yourself together. You have always been the weakest link.'

Edna was the first person to offer an empathetic shoulder. She continued, 'I'm not in a rush, go and get your hair and nails done. We'll watch the twins.'

'Are you serious?'

'Yes, of course I am.'

For someone who hadn't left the house alone in eight weeks, Zandile felt liberated to drive by herself. They still only had one car so she borrowed Edna's sporty Toyota Hilux. She drove around for a while, enjoying the freedom of being alone. She finally pulled into an empty parking space outside Turning Heads. For the first time in months, she dressed up. She wore a fashionable pair of bootleg Levis and a tiny cropped vest, revealing her flat belly which one would dispute had produced two kids and showed none of the obvious telltale signs of pregnancy.

She had lost almost all her pregnancy weight, attributing this to the stress of motherhood, more than a diet and exercise regime which she definitely didn't have time for. It didn't matter how much she ate, those twins would suck her dry until she felt a hollow emptiness in her stomach.

When she walked into the salon she was greeted by Yandisa, who was coiffing a client's hair, and all the familiar faces of the ladies who worked there. They praised her on her appearance which uplifted her spirits immensely.

'I know I don't have an appointment ...' chirruped Zandile, kissing her sister on both cheeks.

'It's alright Sis, I'll make space for you,' replied Yandisa. 'How are you and my babies doing?'

'They're fine but it's all about me right now and it feels so good!' said Zandile.

She settled into the couch in the lounge area and texted Edna to check if the girls were okay. Edna replied that everything was fine and not to worry and just enjoy herself. She picked up a *Hair* magazine and thumbed through it looking for ideas as to what to do with hers. She settled on a long mahogany weave which she hoped would be low maintenance and quick to style.

While she waited for Yandisa she had a manicure and a pedicure and then decided to have a full body massage. Later, as Yandisa weaved her hair into cornrows, they chatted about their families. And gossiped. It felt so good to laugh and catch up. When Zandile finally left the salon she felt so invigorated. At home, the twins were already fast asleep. She couldn't thank Edna and Phathisani enough and hugged them both.

'That's what family is for,' Edna told her.

When Ndaba gets home that evening the twins were still asleep and he was full of compliments for Zandile. How good she looked, how nice she smelled and what a welcome change it was to see her dressed up and smelling of J'adore instead of milk. Edna had already cooked supper for them so they ate together. It felt so good to have a meal made for her and not worry about the girls. Afterwards, they even relaxed on the couch and cuddled. She realised how much she had missed the intimacy of their relationship.

'Do you think we can squeeze in a quickie?' whispers Ndaba in her ear.

'I think so,' she replies.

She takes his hand, placing it between her thighs and he needs no further prompting. She pushes him back and makes love to him with an intensity that even surprises her. Her libido had been dead for a while but it has been reawakened. When he's inside her, their bodies merge with a mutual desire.

Afterwards, they are lying on the couch revelling in the afterglow when they hear a loud wail.

'Duty calls,' says Zandile, as she stands up.

'Damn it!' says Ndaba, who had been hoping to squeeze in a second round. That's parenthood for you; a few stolen moments here and there.

The twins continued to be demanding and Zandile's heart sank when she discovered she was pregnant when the twins were only six months old. She even contemplated having an abortion but then felt guilty for even thinking about it. At the annual Christmas celebration that year at the Khumalo house, Butho teased them.

'You two are really playing catch-up!' he said playfully.

Ndaba laughed but she didn't. The twins were crawling and into everything and now she had a new baby burgeoning inside her.

'It's actually the best way to do it, to have them one after the other,' said Edna, who was always full of encouragement and positivity and had become a constant source of strength for Zandile.

'And you have help this time round.'

At this point Zandile had recruited Maria to help her with the children. The only good thing about being pregnant was that Zandile was excused from *makoti* duties. She missed drinking though and yearned for a vodka and lemonade. Chandelle and Maqhawe were quizzed as to why they weren't pregnant yet.

'Look at Zandile,' says Selina. 'She's born to breed.'

'We don't want kids,' responded Maqhawe matter-of-factly.

'You're right not to want them,' said Zandile, 'they're overrated,' only half-jokingly.

Looking at her kids in the bath this morning of the anniversary party, Zandile smiles. She is proud to be a mother. They are splashing about in the water and playing happily with one another. She laughs with them as she soaps their small bodies. Afterwards, she dresses the girls in pretty lacy frocks and Zwelihle in a miniature suit. She gathers them together and takes a picture and her heart swells with love.

Maria takes over, while she goes to her bedroom to get dressed. Unexpectedly, Ndaba is running a bath for her, emptying Radox Bath Salts into the water. He tells her they are going to bath together and so they both climb into the tub, water spilling over the sides. They giggle playfully.

'I also want to be bathed,' he purrs in her ear.

She straddles him, pressing her breasts into his chest. 'I can do more than bathe you,' she says, reaching for his erection in the soapy water.

'Oooh,' he moans, 'start there.'

It's no wonder they're late for the party but it was worth it. Driving to her parents, Ndaba lovingly steals glances at her. The children chat and play contently in the back.

He reaches for her hand.

'You're a good wife,' he says.

'I'd better be,' replies Zandile cheekily. After seven years of marriage she hopes she's somewhat perfected that role.

A FAMILY AFFAIR

The anniversary celebrations kick off with family brunch at the Mafu home. They all agreed it would be an intimate gathering for the immediate family only, excluding all the extensions and simply didn't tell any of the other family members it was taking place.

Xoliswa is the first to arrive at the house early that Saturday morning. MaTshuma and her club are doing all the cooking but she's anxious that everything goes according to plan and is breathing down the women's necks making sure they are doing everything correctly. Owami, her four-year-old son, is a ball of energy and is darting in and out of the house, pinching strawberries and grapes from the spread that has been set up outside.

'Owa!' she chides, as he collides into her for what must be the third time that morning. He is already looking ruffled and untidy and she realises she should have waited to change him into his suit and tailcoat. He runs into the living room and finds refuge with his grandfather.

'Dad, please keep an eye on him,' she asks.

Abraham is comfortably seated in his chair, immersed in his newspaper when Owami bounds onto his lap like an excited puppy. Abraham immediately takes off his glasses and sets aside the newspaper to give his grandson his attention.

'Owami, behave yourself,' admonishes Abraham, in a sort-of stern voice.

'Okay, Khulu,' Owami replies, tugging at the old man's ears.

Abraham laughs and Xoliswa can't help notice what a walk over her father is when it comes to Owami. The boy literally rules the roost he was born into.

284

It was always her intention to move out of her parents' home but when Owami was born it didn't seem practical so she told herself they would move out when he turned a year old. She had been working on a townhouse complex at that time and decided to reserve one of the units for her and Owami. But they still didn't make the move and another year passed, and that morphed into three. When she started dating Chengetai he started pressuring her to move out and said it wasn't ideal for them to have to keep meeting at hotels so she finally made the move, very much against her parents' wishes.

'An unmarried woman living alone is not a good look,' insisted her father.

'Dad, it's 2007 not 1867,' replied Xoliswa flippantly.

The idea had been to move into her townhouse but Chengetai complained that it didn't offer him the discretion he required so he bought her a house in the leafy suburb of Burnside, replete with bodyguards. She lives down the road from Zandile and some mornings they go for a brisk walk or jog together. It is convenient because when she travels for business she leaves Owami with her sister.

Owami, who has never met his own father, delights in Uncle CC's visits. His grandfather, Uncle Ndaba and Uncle CC have become substitutes for the father he has never known. Keith is never mentioned.

'I don't want CC at the anniversary party,' declared her father, as he went through the final guest list a few days before the party.

Xoliswa wants to tell him that CC is paying for most of the party but decides not to.

'He is my friend,' replied Xoliswa defensively.

'Well, I don't want that friend of yours at the party,' says Abraham, peering at her over his reading glasses.

'*Tata*, he is a good man,' interjects Phumla, who is very much aware of the monetary donations CC is making to the Kingdom.

'Listen, Phumla. I wish you wouldn't encourage her, CC is a married man.'

'So was King David and King Solomon,' Phumla shoots back.

Abraham hits his hand down on the table, signalling that he no longer wants to partake in the conversation. Phumla is under no illusion about the church's precarious financial position. Yes, they have grown in size but the tithes have reduced drastically with most people's earnings diminished by the high cost of living. Many congregants no longer tithe and Xoliswa is one of the few that still tithe religiously. The church stays afloat because of the benevolence of people like her. Even beyond the church, Xoliswa takes care of her parents and makes sure their lights stay on. That their water bill is paid. That their servants are paid. That if anything breaks, it is repaired. Xoliswa pays the car insurance and makes sure their cars are regularly serviced. When the rigorous load-shedding began, Xoliswa bought them a generator and makes sure there is diesel to run it. Xoliswa pays Babalwa's school fees every month and buys her uniforms and all her clothes. Yandisa doesn't contribute anything towards her own child's costs, or her parents', whereas Zandile makes sure there is food on the table.

Phumla knows better than to antagonise Xoliswa and so after her husband takes CC's name off the guest list, she puts it back. Although he won't be welcome at the house for the family brunch, he certainly will be at the reception. Blessings come in different guises and Phumla knows CC is a blessing in disguise for their family.

'Is Mom *still* getting dressed?'asks Xoliswa.

'Yes,' replies Abraham, 'she's acting like a crazy bride!'

'Let me go and check on bridezilla,' she says, marching to her parents' bedroom.

Upon entering, Xoliswa is met with her mother's imposing reflection in the mirror. Phumla is scrutinising herself and the stylist and make-up artist are standing beside her, appraising her appearance. Phumla is wearing an olive-coloured, lace gown with cuffed sleeves that sweep the floor. Her hair is swept up in a bun secured with gold pins. Xoliswa applauds her.

'You look stunning, Mama!'

Phumla's smile lights up her eyes which sparkle like the emeralds around her neck. Xoliswa, who towers over her mother, puts her arms around her.

'You could easily be twenty-something and getting married for the first time, Mama.'

'Xolie, I want you to find someone and get married,' replies her mother, 'it's been too long.'

'Mom,' says Xoliswa dismissively, 'today is about you, not me.'

She kisses her mother on the cheek and leads her out of the bedroom. As they walk down the passage, they can hear raucous chatter and know it means Zandile and Ndaba and their noisy brood have arrived. The grandchildren are in awe of their grandmother's transformation but not more than Abraham who is staring at her like she is an angel.

'No jumping on Gogo today!' declares Phumla, sidestepping the children before they try and pounce on her.

'You look gorgeous, Mama,' enthuses Zandile, embracing her mother.

'My queen,' declares Abraham, opening his arms out to his wife.

He gives her a chaste kiss on the cheek, before pulling her into his arms. He is in a three-piece tuxedo, complete with a tailcoat and they make quite a couple all these years later. Phumla often tells them all that they never had a 'white' wedding because they couldn't afford it at the time and had merely done a court signing, followed by a lunch with friends. Had Uncle Ben been alive, he would have been officiating the formal ceremony all these years later, having been their friend for so many years. Sis Ntombi has insisted she can fill his shoes but they don't have the guts to decline her offer.

A foot-long table has been set up in the garden, with Abraham and Phumla the anchors seated at the heads opposite each other.

The children and grandchildren fill the spaces between. By the time Yandisa arrives, her three children in tow, brunch is well underway and she is full of apologies. She looks miff but everyone is too caught up in the moment to pay much attention to her foul mood. She says Wesley will be coming later that afternoon.

'Did you tell him we are taking pictures?' asks an annoyed Xoliswa.

'He'll be here,' stresses Yandisa.

She excuses herself a short while later and walks to the bottom of the garden to call Wesley. His phone rings continuously without being picked up and she sighs heavily and crosses her fingers that he does actually show up.

PORTRAIT OF A FAMILY

The mood is buoyant and light-hearted during the meal and Abraham and Phumla joke and reminisce on days gone by. The grandchildren are having their own conversations and creating their own memories. Wesley arrives as they are about to finish and he is wearing a brown suit which Yandisa scolds him about. The family had agreed on a specific dress code of black suits for the men and emerald green for the women. Phumla's dress was imported from a boutique in Johannesburg and the sisters opted for lacy, emerald-green body suits and flared skirts buoyed with layers of netting. It had been the one style flattering to all of them, although Yandisa had argued that she looked like a meringue.

'I can go home and change,' says Wesley.

'It's too late now we're about to take the photos,' snaps Yandisa. 'I don't know how you didn't see the suit that I put out for you to wear today.'

Wesley had seen the suit but had deliberately chosen not to wear it. He hated conforming to the Mafu way of doing things. He notices Ndabenhle is dressed correctly but Ndabenhle is the conformist in the family. The good son-in-law who always shows up and does what he is told.

'You are going to ruin the pictures,' says Xoliswa, acidly.

'I can stay out of them,' says Wesley.

The professional photographer is lining them all into position when they realise Babalwa isn't there. She often goes unseen, skulking in the background.

'She's probably on a hunger strike,' says Phumla sarcastically.

289

'I'll go and get her,' says Yandisa, rushing to Babs' room.

Yandisa knocks but there is no answer. She pushes lightly on the door and is surprised when it opens. Babalwa is lying on the bed, earphones on.

'Babs! Everyone is waiting for you!' shouts Yandisa. 'Why aren't you dressed?' noticing that Babalwa is wearing a T-shirt and shorts.

'I'm not coming,' Babs replies sulkily.

Yandisa breathes noisily. Her mother has often lamented recently that Babalwa is becoming extremely difficult but Yandisa thought it was her mother just being her mother.

'Babs! This is a big family celebration,' yells Yandisa.

Babalwa sits up and removes the earphones from her ears.

'Yandisa, didn't you hear me? I said I'm not coming!'

'I'm sorry but you have no choice, Babs. You are part of this family!'

Babalwa stands up and is a foot taller than Yandisa.

'Don't you dare talk to me about family! For years you all lied to me about who I really am, this whole family is a scam.'

Yandisa is stunned and feels like she's been slapped across the face. There's a knock on the door and Wesley peers in and tells them to hurry up.

'Your sister is going to have a hernia if you don't come outside.'

He gets an eyeful of Babalwa's long smooth legs but looks away quickly and shuts the door.

Yandisa looks at her daughter pleadingly. Her eyes have misted over with tears.

'*Please*. Please come for the sake of Mom and Dad.'

Babalwa begrudgingly agrees but she doesn't change into 'something more appropriate' as Yandisa suggests.

They pose for a huge family portrait in the garden and Abraham and Phumla are seated in the middle surrounded by their children and grandchildren. The dogs even creep in without an invitation. A few family shots, without the sons-in-law, follow and then a few of the parents and their daughters. Then some with the parents and sons-in-law and then just the parents, in various locations and in different poses around the house. Once the pictures are taken, they all pile into their shiny new cars, all German brands, with Wesley in his new BMW 3 series leading the convoy.

The guests are all seated in the grounds outside when the Mafus arrive. The grandkids march in first, followed by the grandparents, and the daughters and their spouses trail in behind them. Xoliswa walks in alone after Babalwa refused to be part of the parade. There is a huge applause as Abraham and Phumla take their position at the front of the gathering. Deacon Nyathi opens the proceedings with a prayer and people applaud, both for his brevity as well as for the celebration. Abraham and Phumla stand under the makeshift arch and recite their vows, reaffirming their commitment to one another. There is much ululating and cries of jubilation and after the congratulatory hugs and confetti throwing, the procession moves into the banquet hall.

The guests take their seats and Sis Ntombi takes to the podium and welcomes everyone. Many guests last saw her at Uncle Ben's funeral and are quite surprised by her overall sunny demeanour and appearance. She's wearing a two-piece floral suit from Bloomingdales that Khethiwe sent especially for the occasion.

'It is an honour for me to be standing here to introduce the family. You all know how we adore my brother and the immeasurable sacrifices he has made for us and the family. So often we wait for people to die before we celebrate them but today I want to celebrate you and your wife, Abraham!' she says looking directly at her brother and sister-in-law.

This introduction heralds a noisy applause and some guests stand up. Sis Ntombi continues unphased.

'I know most of you know the Mafu family but I'm going to begin with a formal introduction. I'm going to start with the children. Can all the Mafu kids please stand up?'

Xoliswa, Yandisa and Zandile all rise to their feet. Yandisa signals

291

to Babalwa to stand up but she remains seated, her hands stubbornly folded over her chest. Two men seated at a table on the far right of the room, also stand up. Xoliswa is too far away to tell them that Sis Ntombi is referring to children and not cousins, the words so loosely applied in their culture.

'As you can see,' continues Sis Ntombi, 'my brother has five children. The first born is his son, Vumani, followed by Wandile.'

The two men wave at the audience.

'Followed by Xoliswa,' adds Sis Ntombi.

Xoliswa raises her hand hesitantly, not quite sure what is going on. She looks to her mother, who looks equally confused. Their father is unmoved, his face expressionless.

'Then follows Yandisa and Zandile.'

There is more applause.

'We have a joke in the family,' says Sis Ntombi. 'The Mafu kids are VWXYZ. My brother has always been a methodical man, even in the way he named his children!'

More laughter emanates from the audience.

'I'm going to ask the firstborn of the Mafu family to take to the podium and say a few words.'

When Xoliswa included 'Firstborn Speech to Parents' on the programme, she had done so with herself in mind. She has no idea where this hat-trick Vumani has come from and he confidently strides to the podium. He is tall just like their father and equals him in stature. The sisters look to one another for an explanation, unsure of what to think.

'Good afternoon everyone. I am Vumani and I am the firstborn in the Mafu family. I know a lot of you don't know this but before my father became a man of God, he was a man of the world. It is with profound pleasure that I have been included in this family affair.'

Vumani pauses to look at Abraham, whose lips twitch into a nervous smile. Phumla's face has tightened and her brow is anxiously furrowed.

'Wandile and I were born to uMahlangu, who is not here with us today. Our mother passed on last year and we decided it was time to reconcile with our father. That is why we are here on this auspicious day to celebrate this moment with the family. Thank you for having us.'

And just like that, the Mafu siblings go from three to five.

THE AFTER-PARTY

When the anniversary party celebrations come to an end, Wesley suggests they all go to the nightclub, The Zone, for the unofficial after-party. Of course, the invitation is not extended to the 'church people' as most of them shun clubbing and drinking. Zandile looks to her husband for approval but Ndaba says he's tired and wants to go home but she eventually persuades him and they decide to go along. 'Come on, it'll be fun,' she says.

They've all already had too much to drink and are drunk on alcohol and the revelation that accompanied the days' celebrations.

'Maybe I should have invited the Mafu brothers too?' jokes Wesley in the car.

'That's not funny, Wesley' says Yandisa.

'Come on, be a sport. You've got big brothers now. I'm not surprised, your dad is good at keeping secrets. He tried to pull a fast one on me with that kid of *yours*.'

'Wesley!' berates Yandisa. 'I wish you wouldn't say that about my father!'

'It's the truth, isn't it? Bab' Mfundisi was a "man of the world". That was your brother's choice of words!'

Wesley laughs and ignores his wife's growing exasperation.

'Look on the bright side, Yandisa, at least you got to meet your brothers now and not at your father's funeral.'

'This culture of meeting siblings at funerals needs to end. I don't want that for my children. 'I've been thinking about it and maybe it's time Babalwa comes and lives with us. She needs to form a relationship with her siblings.'

'I want no part of that mess, Yandisa. Where is her father? Let him take care of her.'

Yandisa purses her lips in annoyance and stares ahead. She suddenly has no desire to go to the club. Wesley opened The Zone after he was forced to retire from professional rugby after a severe collarbone injury. He received a hefty pound/dollar payout and decided to open a nightclub with some of the money. Her father had always been against the business, saying it encouraged sin and depravity but Wesley opened it anyway, causing a massive fallout between him and Abraham.

The nightclub was very profitable when it first opened, especially considering it was one of only a handful of clubs in Bulawayo. But with the economic situation in the country, it isn't making nearly as much money. Wesley had used the rest of the money he was paid out to set up a car dealership importing second-hand cars from Japan. They serviced and sold cars in the back and sold fuel in the front. The fuel station was what was keeping them afloat. Petrol tankers brought in fuel from Botswana and most of it was then sold on the black market at double the price. They got the foreign currency from Ndaba, who had worked his way up to the position of GM at the local branch of the bank, and who also had women changing forex on the black market on his behalf. None of it was ethical but that was how they all survived. Parallel lives. Parallel lies.

It was month-end so the club was packed. Wesley drives around to the back entrance to the VIP parking. They all park their cars and go inside. Yandisa isn't surprised to see JB and Charles sitting in the VIP section; the two of them are there so much they're like the wallpaper. JB is sandwiched between two women that he introduces as Leona and Tabitha. They make space for the new arrivals and soon they are the biggest and the noisiest table in the club. Wesley makes sure CC is served the finest cognac in the house and takes out the Cuban cigars which are reserved for very special guests.

'Today we have VVIP!' bellows Charles, eliciting laughter.

'Does anyone want to dance?' asks Wesley, jumping to his feet.

No one obliges him as they are all happy to sit, drink and smoke. Wesley takes Yandisa by the hand and pulls her onto the dance floor, even after she says she isn't in the mood. Everyone watches as he pulls Yandisa into his arms and kisses her. Everyone cheers and this spurs him on and he gropes her, making her visibly uncomfortable.

'Wesley! Not here!' she reprimands and pulls away from him.

'Why the *hell* not? No one is looking!'

'No, Wesley,' she says, pushing him away and returning to her seat.

'When did you become so boring?' he screams after her.

Yandisa ignores him and is relieved to be back at the table. She reaches for a drink but when she sees the glass is dirty, she orders the waitress to bring her a clean one. She enjoys clubbing less now that she is the owner and not a patron.

'Not dancing any more?' remarks JB. 'You used to be quite a dancer, Yandisa.'

'I guess I grew out of it.'

'Well, Wesley is dancing with Jezebel over there,' comments Charles.

Everyone laughs and Yandisa looks over and sees that Wesley is dancing a little too intimately with a lithe-looking girl, who is wearing next to nothing.

'That's not dancing!' shrieks Zandile, as the girl rubs her bum suggestively into Wesley's groin.

They all look on as Wesley grabs the woman's waist and simulates sex. Yandisa is heating up with humiliation and wants to escape outside for a breath of fresh air.

'Go and rescue your man,' urges Xoliswa.

'He's a big boy,' replies Yandisa, 'he can take care of himself.'

Her pride won't let her get up and fight for Wesley. Not in this way. Her drink arrives and she takes a swig, trying to wash down the rising mortification inside her. Then she stands up and excuses herself and says she's going to the bathroom. Zandile and Xoliswa follow suit. Wesley continues to make a spectacle of himself on the dance floor and when another woman joins in, he is sandwiched between the two women.

'That is why we men cheat. Women don't know how to have fun,' says JB to the men at the table.

'How is *that* fun?' retorts Ndaba.

'Wesley wants to dance so his wife should dance with him. Otherwise, another woman will fill her shoes. It's that simple,' explains JB.

'So what are we saying, gents? That whatever we can't get from our wives we outsource?' asks Ndaba, interrogating JB's assertion.

'It makes sense to me,' replies CC. 'I have my wife and my kids but my wife will never be able to give me everything I need. I'm not saying she's a bad woman, she's lovely and she takes good care of the kids and makes sure we have a lovely home but she doesn't satisfy me sexually. She never has. So should I divorce her and be that dad who only sees his kids every second weekend? Cheating makes marriage tolerable.'

As CC is talking, Ndaba is shaking his head vehemently to show his disagreement with the men's explanations.

'But how can you be so sure you are everything to your wife?' says Ndaba. 'Maybe you aren't but she has decided to compromise. I don't think for one minute that I am everything Zandile wants in a man. She certainly isn't everything I want in a woman but I'm not going to try supplement the missing parts. I'm happy with my choices.'

'How do I handle not having enough sex?' counters CC.

Before Ndaba can respond, Zandile and Xoliswa get back from the bathroom and return to their seats. Yandisa told them she had a headache and was going to sit in the car. Ndaba quietly says to Zandile that they should leave because this isn't his 'thing' and not the type of company he wants to keep. Xoliswa and CC decide to stay, with CC declaring that he is having a good time enjoying his cognac and his woman.

Yandisa eventually falls asleep in the car and doesn't hear Wesley knocking on the window. She is woken by a loud crash as a brick hits the window, shattering the glass, splinters and shards of glass landing in her lap.

'What the hell, Yandisa?' screams Wesley. 'You trying to lock me out of my own car? Who the fuck do you think you are?'

Yandisa is still half asleep and trying to work out what has happened when Wesley grabs her hair, tugging at the roots. He tries to pull her out through the broken window, resulting in cuts and scratches all over her face and upper body. A security guard and other revellers intervene and pull Wesley off Yandisa. She is sobbing uncontrollably with sharp incisions engraved on her face. The cuts and scratches are visible and painful but the scars inside hurt a lot more.

THE POST-MORTEM

As per their family tradition on a Sunday, they all converge at the Mafu household for lunch. They dissect the proceedings following the big occasion the previous day. Since there are no leftovers, Xoliswa has again called on MaTshuma and her cooking club to cater, otherwise all the cooking would have been her responsibility. She wanted to sleep in after the rowdy night at the club but had left CC fast asleep when she left for her parents' house. She parks in the driveway, behind Sis Ntombi's Benz. As she walks into the house, she sees Vumani and Wandile sitting with Abraham in the living room. She greets them cordially. As they shake hands she wonders if hugging them might be more appropriate but they are complete strangers and one announcement is not going to evoke fraternal feelings in her just yet. She thinks of how many times she might have passed them on the street, not knowing they were remotely related.

'Come and sit with us,' says her father, patting the seat beside him.

Up until then she had always known she was her father's favourite child but with the arrival of the brothers, she doesn't know how long she will be able to lay claim to that. Overnight she has gone from first born to third born.

'I'll join you in a few minutes, let me go and greet everyone,' she replies, hearing raised voices coming from the kitchen.

She doesn't want to miss out on any drama and as she gets closer to the kitchen, the voices get louder and angrier. She can hear her mother and Sis Ntombi and when she walks in the kitchen, she sees that her aunt and her mother are in a noisy altercation with one another.

'You wanted to show me up last night didn't you, sis?' shouts Phumla.

'You would think like that wouldn't you, Phumla?' scoffs Sis Ntombi. 'That's something you would do, the same way you tried to show me up at my husband's funeral.'

'I did no such thing, Ntombi. I only asked that you find it in your heart to forgive MaMoyo and allow her to attend Ben's funeral.'

'Yet you can't find it in your heart to embrace Abraham's kids? Spare me the hypocrisy, Phumla. You destroyed that woman's marriage and now you don't want her kids to have a relationship with their father!'

Abraham appears in the doorway and tells the women to stop arguing but Sis Ntombi won't be contained.

'Somebody has to tell her, Abraham. She's a hypocrite!' says Sis Ntombi.

'She didn't destroy my marriage, Ntombi. I did. I was the one who left Sarah.'

'Who is Sarah?' asks Xoliswa, immediately regretful for interfering in adult conversation. She knows it's rude to eavesdrop but she's also an adult and deserves some kind of explanation.

Sarah was Sis Ntombi's best friend at school. They lived three homesteads apart and often walked to school together. Sarah caught Abraham's eye and their romance blossomed under the shade of an acacia tree. They spent their days out in the veld where Abraham courted her while Sarah shyly drew patterns in the sand with her feet. Abraham wooed her with syrupy sweet words of endearment and when it was in season, he would take her *uxakuxaku* or 'snot's apple'. They sat on the riverbank and chewed the fruit until all the juice ran out and then spat out the stringy remains. Organic chewing gum, if ever there was such a thing.

Sarah sat and nervously plucked out all the grass around her, a telltale empty patch would be all that was left behind when she stood up. Sometimes the grass would be flattened where they made love. They would have been called 'high school sweethearts' and many watched their budding romance from afar. Sarah was sixteen when she fell pregnant with Vumani. Abraham took the last of the cows in his father's kraal to pay for the damages and Sarah dropped out of school and moved in with him and his family and tended to the homestead. Every morning at sunrise, Sarah would rise with Abraham's mother, Sakhile and go into the fields to plough. In the afternoon, they sat under the sparse shade of an acacia tree shelling groundnuts. In the evening, Sarah cooked supper over an open fire and at night she lay beside her husband, who was still a senior in school. It was not an anomaly in their community to be married young as very few parents wasted time educating the girls in their family because they knew they would get married anyway. It was considered enough if the women had an elementary education.

When Abraham was awarded a scholarship to study further after school, Sarah was dismayed. They had lain awake many nights discussing how Abraham was going to find a job at the nearby mine and rebuild his father's homestead, once he finished school.

'South Africa is so far away,' she lamented, as she traced circles with her fingers around the knotted hair on Abraham's chest.

'It won't be for long,' he replied. 'Once I get my degree, I can come back and work in the office at the mine and I'll earn more money.'

'But four years is a long time.'

Abraham stroked her face tenderly, 'The time will go by so fast you won't even notice.' He kissed her tenderly, rubbing her distended belly.

'I just want the best for you and our child. *Sizawuvusa umuzi kababa.*'

Abraham started at the University of Fort Hare and wrote to Sarah diligently. Long letters that she often had to read with a dictionary next to her.

20 June 1966

My darling Sarah

*It is after great consideration that I decided to pen this
missive to you. I cannot find the words to describe to you
the beauty of the Eastern Cape. The beauty is almost as
breathtaking as you. It is filled with undulating mountains
which remind me of the curves of your body. We travelled
a great distance to get here. I feel like I am at the corner of
Earth. I am so exhausted and I spent two days recuperating.
Did you know that Robert Mugabe also studied here at Fort
Hare? They speak highly of him. To think that he's now
languishing in prison. There is much hostility here but I
will not dwell too much on it. I must not lose focus on why I
am here. Send my regards to Vumani and Mama. I love you
dearly and miss you terribly.*

Ngimi ngothando

Mandla Abraham

Sarah reads these letters with baby Vumani plugged to her breast. He
was born in December the previous year. In the beginning, Abraham
wrote often and consistently but by the second year, the letters tapered
off in frequency to one every quarter. By the time he was in third year,
they had stopped completely and Sarah would read his old letters to
keep the memory of him alive in her head and to continue to foster the
love she felt for him. Her mother-in-law and Sis Ntombi encouraged
her to not feel despondent, saying he was probably consumed with his
studies and too busy to write letters.

Abraham graduated the following year and returned home but by
then they were like strangers to one another and even their coupling

was awkward, like two teenagers fumbling in the dark. Wandile was conceived like an afterthought to their lacklustre sex. Abraham didn't stay in the village long and said he had to go into the city to find a job. Every time Sarah insisted on visiting him in the city, he turned her down and told her that Makokoba wasn't ideal for a woman with children. He said city life would corrupt them and so she remained in the village and saw him only over the Easter holidays and Christmas break.

It wasn't long before rumours started circulating that Abraham had another woman. Sarah knew it in her heart to be true because even when he was with her, he didn't hold her like he used to. It was almost as if he despised her and the sex was always rushed and felt like an obligation on his part. He wouldn't kiss her or even bring his eyes to connect with hers and their lovemaking always left her feeling diminished and unfulfilled. But she couldn't confide any of this to Sis Ntombi or her mother-in-law as they both told her to remain steadfast, in what she considered a loveless marriage. By this time, Abraham was employed in a bank and could adequately provide for the family. Whenever he came home, he was laden down with bags filled with clothing for her and the boys from Sales House and Edgars and groceries and toys for the boys.

Unbeknownst to Sarah, it was Phumla who picked out the dresses for her, presuming she was buying them for Abraham's mother and sisters. Phumla also chose full cotton panties with a lace trim from the Dolores clothing store for Sarah.

'It's time you two got married,' said Sakhile to Abraham on one of his visits home. 'You can afford it now.' Sarah was pregnant with their second child and Sakhile couldn't understand what the hindrance was. Abraham was dismissive and told her he was trying to save for a house.

'Marriage can wait, Mama.'

So the plans to solidify Abraham and Sarah's union with a white wedding were again put on hold. Sakhile was impatient with her son so she arrived in Makokoba unannounced and was confronted by Phumla, who was pregnant and would later that year give birth to Xoliswa. It was the biggest exposé of her son's other life and a huge family meeting was held at the homestead. Uncles were invited and Abraham's intentions were thoroughly questioned. He announced that he was going to end things with Sarah and start a new life with Phumla. When Xoliswa was born, she was given her name as an apology to the family for the anguish that had been caused before her birth. She was a peace offering of sorts.

Phumla was officially introduced into the family and later Abraham, in the company of a few uncles, travelled south to lobola her. Phumla always wanted a big wedding and because she would be the first person in her family to get married, it was going to be a big deal. She had grand ideas of waltzing down the aisle in a white dress similar to the one Winnie Mandela wore when she married Nelson. But all her dreams were dashed when Sakhile blankly stated that if there was going to be a wedding, she would boycott it. Abraham could not have a wedding if there was a possibility that his own mother wouldn't show up, as that would herald an entire life of bad luck. So the white wedding was shelved and they were joined together in a small court ceremony.

Phumla was never liked and was always viewed as the reason Abraham left Sarah. Comparisons were always made between the women and where Sarah was studious, Phumla was considered lazy. Sarah was generous whereas Phumla was supposedly stingy. Phumla alienated herself from the family which earned her the reputation of being aloof and snobbish. Her mother-in-law refused to visit their home and Phumla was blamed for Abraham's neglect of his sons, whom he rarely saw more than twice a year.

After him and Phumla bought their house in Hillside, Abraham gave the house in Makokoba to Sarah, even though it was registered in the boys' names. This always seemed like an olive branch he extended to Sarah and she always thought it was Abraham's way of reconciling with her, yet he never sought her or her affections out. When he came to see the boys, she would bath for hours, put perfume on and wear one of her special dresses but he didn't even notice. He would chat to the boys for ten minutes, play with them distractedly and then leave. He never ate any of the food she went to great pains to prepare and once he was gone, she would be sick for days. She would reread all the letters he had written to her in the early years of their relationship and lie prostrate praying to God to restore their relationship.

Sis Ntombi set aside at least one Saturday a month to visit Sarah. Even though her status had been greatly elevated when she married Ben, she never forgot about her friends or her nephews. When the boys saw her, they ran to her and relieved her of the groceries she was sometimes carrying, as she often took it upon herself to buy them food because Abraham often shirked his responsibilities. It wasn't that he couldn't afford to support the boys, but when he fell out of love with their mother, he had little regard for their children. Compared to his three daughters, the boys' upbringing was very basic and without any frills and they received a government school education. The girls were treated like princesses and all went to a prestigious private school.

During the holidays, Sis Ntombi brought her nephews to her home, exposing them to life beyond the township. Vumani aspired to that life, whereas Wandile rejected it. He loved the township life and the strife that went with it and rejected the order and discipline of school in favour of unruliness. Vumani was determined to excel and was a brilliant boy just like his father and received all the accolades. Sis Ntombi was there for the momentous occasions and awards, egging him on to do better. But where Vumani excelled, Wandile floundered.

He dropped out of high school and no one could persuade him otherwise. Sis Ntombi reached out to Abraham to try and talk some sense into his youngest son because everyone else had failed.

'I don't have time,' Abraham barked down the phone to his sister. 'I'm trying to build an empire and you want me to waste my time and try knock some sense into that dunderhead? He takes after his mother!'

'If you gave those boys a fraction of the time you gave to your whores, you'd have time to talk to him.'

'*Zwana*, Ntombi. Learn to mind your own business.'

He hung up, as he often did, and Sis Ntombi had stopped trying to appeal to Abraham to take more interest in the boys.

'Don't they have a mother?' said Phumla, her voice full of contempt. '*Ndingenaphi mna?*'

'Yes but they need money for food and clothing, Phumla! Can you speak to your husband, please?'

'You speak to him. *Ndithe ndingenaphi mna?*'

So the boys grew up estranged from their father, who they grew to resent. Sarah painted a picture of a man who abandoned them and did nothing to care for them.

Vumani was in sixth form when he walked past his father's offices in town one day after school. He decided to go inside and visit him and Abraham's reception towards him had been warm. He had paraded Vumani around the office, introducing him as his son and Vumani glowed in the admiration. In one afternoon, all the bad things his mother had said about his father were obliterated from memory. It also helped that his father gave him a few sheaths of money for him and his friends to spend. When he told his mother about the impromptu visit, she was bitter and angry.

'How can you betray me like this!' she screamed.

'He is my father! Our father,' replied Vumani.

306

'What has he ever done for you?'

'You say that like you've done everything for us but what do you do other than lie in your room and cry all day?'

'Get out, Vumani, and don't come back!'

Vumani threw a few things into a bag and they caught a taxi into town and another one to Hillside. When they arrived at their father's house, the street was lined with cars. They walked up the driveway, lined with balloons, and followed the excited voices to the garden where they saw a birthday party was taking place.

It was Xoliswa's 10th birthday and children of all age and races were singing to her while standing around her and her birthday cake. Yandisa and Zandile, who were seven and four at the time, looked on as their sister blew out the candles on her cake. Abraham was standing behind the birthday girl and their stepmother was beside her. Everyone applauded as Xoliswa blew out the candles and Phumla looked up and saw the boys standing on the periphery of the garden. She nudged her husband and he looked up and his eyes met Vumani's. Abraham quietly excused himself and walked towards the boys. He draped his arms around their shoulders and ambled away with them, the sound of children's laughter and cheering in the background.

'What are you doing here, boys? Did your mother send you?'

'No,' said Vumani, 'we came on our own.'

'You can't be here,' explained Abraham. 'We're having a party. It's a family affair.'

He quickly reached into his pockets and pulled out a few notes that he shoved into Vumani's hands.

'Please go and don't ever come here again. If you want to see me, come to the office.'

Wandile was confused, 'But I want to stay at the party.'

In a stern voice, Abraham told them to leave and Vumani understood that their father didn't want them there. He took his brother by the hand and led him away and they never sought out their father ever again.

The first time they saw him since then was at the anniversary party, years later, after Sis Ntombi insisted they attend. She bemoans their alienation from the family and says Abraham is not getting younger and they must be reconciled to the Mafu clan. They only agree because Vumani feels he owes her a lot after everything she did for him and Wandile when they were growing up. But it is their father who approaches them at the anniversary party and invites them to come to the house.

TAKING RESPONSIBILITY

Yandisa, Wesley and their children are eating lunch out on the patio. The tension between them is palpable. Yandisa's face is cut and bruised and she had been to Dr Filmore earlier in the day to have the wound cleaned and dressed. Her light complexion makes it easy to see the vivid bruising and fresh cuts. Wesley had been with her during the examination, holding her hand a little bit too tightly.

He had apologised for the incident the night before saying he had had too much to drink and had smoked weed with Charles and JB. In a contrite tone he assured her it would never happen again but that was what he had said to her a few months ago after she arrived home late one evening and he dragged her across the front lawn, accusing her of whoring. Rodney the gardener had had to intervene and suffered a few blows in the process; he resigned the next day.

She has accepted Wesley's sporadic bouts of violence and they tell the children that they had a minor car accident. They haven't exchanged a word during the meal and Yandisa only speaks to Jason and Nicola, while coaxing Ethan, who is sitting on her lap, to eat.

In the space of six years, Yandisa has had three kids. When Wesley visited from the UK in the off season, every June to August, he made sure he left her pregnant. It was his way of making sure she didn't fool around. By the time she weaned one baby from the breast, she was pregnant with the next. The kids are very close in age and after Ethan was born, Xoliswa advised Yandisa to get her tubes tied before she fell pregnant again.

'Are you competing with Zandile or what? Give your womb a rest. *Usuhlala nje umdidi umanzi ngendaba zokuzala!*'

309

When Xoliswa had said that Yandisa was deeply offended but looking at her three children she is thankful for her sister's intervention. She definitely doesn't want any more.

She picks at her food, not feeling hungry. Her body is aching and her head is pounding. Midway through the meal, Wesley's phone rings. He answers and responds curtly, his body stiffening and when he puts down the phone, he tells her that he has to go.

'There is some urgent business I need to handle.'

'On a Sunday?' says Yandisa, addressing him for the first time that day.

Jason and Nicola start protesting. Ethan is indifferent and happiest when he's on his mother's lap, resting his head on her bosom.

'Daddy! You promised you'd swim with us!' wails Nicola.

'I'll be back soon and we'll swim, I promise.'

'We have to go to my parents' house or have you forgotten?' says Yandisa.

'Like I said, something's come up.'

He bids the children goodbye and tells them he'll be back soon.

'Let's hope it's before midnight,' Yandisa mumbles as he walks away.

He throws her a scathing look and she's tempted to throw the teapot at him but restrains herself. The children suspect something is wrong because their father leaves without even giving their mother a perfunctory kiss. They have become adept at gauging the mood and can tell whether their dad is happy or sad by the tone of his voice.

After they've finished eating, Jason and Nicola help their mother clear the table and Yandisa piles the plates into the sink. MamTembo can tend to them the following day, she thinks. Yandisa checks her phone and sees there are several missed calls, mostly from her sisters. She doesn't bother returning their calls and decides not to go to her parents' house for the obligatory post-mortem following the anniversary party. There's no way she can show up at a family gathering covered in cuts and wearing sunglasses to hide her black eye. Her abuse is a closely guarded secret and she wants to keep it that way.

She basks in the sun, swims with the children and dozes on and off when Ethan has a nap and the older kids are playing inside. Her phone suddenly vibrates to life, interrupting her attempts at relaxation. It's Xoliswa. She declines the call and switches off her phone.

The kids finish swimming for the day and she puts them all in front of the TV. She dozes off on the couch and when she wakes up, the house is immersed in darkness. She piles them all into her Jeep and they go and buy pizzas which they eat while watching Cartoon Network. By 7 pm, it's time for Nicola and Jason to go to bed so after they have a bath, she settles them in their rooms. She can hear they are still wide awake but after a while things go quiet. She curls up on the sofa with Ethan and he eventually falls asleep so she carries him up to the nursery. Once he's down, she goes back downstairs to carry on watching TV. She's too tired to pick up the toys strewn all over the house and opts for a glass of wine instead. She ends up drinking the entire bottle and then decides she really needs something stronger and helps herself to some whisky from Wesley's collection.

She carries her glass upstairs to her bedroom and has a lukewarm bath. Her body is tender and bruised and she finds the bath soothing. Afterwards, she slips on a blue satin camisole with matching pants and climbs into their king-size bed which always looks so empty when Wesley isn't there, which is often. She props herself up against a satin continental pillow and turns on the TV. She puts on E! News, her favourite channel and starts watching an E! true story chronicling the life of Faith Evans, one of her favourite R&B singers. She's barely five minutes into the documentary when the landline rings. It's Phumla, complaining bitterly about their absence at the house that afternoon.

'The whole family was here, even your brothers. How do you think they felt when you two didn't bother to show up?'

Yandisa wants to tell her mother that she doesn't give a rat's arse about her 'brothers' and she can't understand why Phumla, of all people, is so excited about her half-brothers sudden appearance in their lives.

'We were involved in a small car accident last night and I'm still pretty bruised, so I didn't feel up to it.'

'Well, why didn't you call? Everyone was worried about you,' says Phumla.

'I didn't want people unnecessarily worrying. It wasn't a serious accident.'

She can hear her father in the background.

'They were drunk, weren't they? I told you nothing good would come out of that nightclub.'

'*Tata*! Be nice!' Phumla says to Abraham, before carrying on talking to Yandisa.

'Tell Dad the nightclub pays the bills!' says Yandisa loudly down the phone, annoyed by her father's comment.

'What bills?' shouts Abraham, 'You don't even pay Babalwa's school fees!'

Her father snatches the phone from her mother.

'Yandisa, your mother and I have decided that it will be best if Babalwa lives with you and Wesley from now on. Ever since she found out that you are her mother, she has become impossible to deal with. It is beyond our scope of responsibility any more.'

'Dad, please, this isn't a good time,' Yandisa tries to appeal to her father.

'*Khawume, Tata*,' she hears her mother say. When Phumla switches to isiXhosa, Yandisa knows things are about to get heated. She's back on the phone, her voice now a high-pitched shrill.

'*Jonga pha sana lwami. Ndimdala mna. Uyeva?* Listen hear, my child. I'm your elder so you need to respect me! What do you mean it's not a good time? When will it be a good time? You're not sixteen any more; you need to start taking responsibility.'

'Mama, you know how Wesley feels about Babalwa. He made

it clear that he didn't want anything to do with her when we got married.'

'So what must happen to Babs? Huh? Find her father and tell him to take care of her. I'm sixty years old, Yandisa, I'm not dealing with this teenage drama any more.'

Phumla hangs up.

It's not that she doesn't want to take Babalwa but Wesley is completely opposed to it. He's her husband and she has to respect his wishes so how is she even going to broach the subject with him?

GROWING PAINS

Babalwa is twelve years old when she finds out that Yandisa her sister is actually Yandisa her mother. Her and Phumla are registering her for Grade 7 exams and need to supply her birth certificate. She asks, who she always thought was her mother, where the document is and Phumla tells her where to find it. Babalwa reads the birth certificate. Mother: Yandisa Mafu. Father: Unknown. She takes the certificate to Phumla and asks her to explain.

'I thought my mother dumped me?' she says accusingly.

That was what she had been told all her life. That she had been orphaned. Phumla asks her to sit down and she tells her exactly what happened. When she finishes telling her the real story of her birth, Babalwa is horrified.

'So Yandisa dumped me?'

'No, she didn't,' says Phumla.

'Oh yes she did! She's married and living with her *other* kids. What about me? Doesn't she care about me?' shouts Babs.

'It's complicated,' says Phumla. 'When your mother got married, Wesley's relatives didn't want her to bring a child into the new family.'

As she says it, Phumla wonders to herself whether she should be divulging all the details to Babalwa.

'And Yandisa didn't fight for me?'

Phumla sees the look of dejection on her granddaughter's face and wishes she could do something to spare her the heartbreak the discovery of this information is causing.

'You have always been *our* daughter, Babalwa. From the time you were born you were ours,' Phumla tries to placate her.

'What's my father's name?'

'His name is Marshall Munyoro,' replies Phumla.

'Why isn't his name on here? Didn't he want me either?'

Phumla scratches her head, flecks of dandruff landing on the table. She doesn't think it will be appropriate to tell Babalwa the circumstances surrounding her birth so she decides not to and pulls Babalwa into her arms but the young girl worms her way out of them.

'Don't lie to me, Gogo. It's enough lies.'

'It's complicated,' Phumla says.

Babalwa is not the same person after that and Abraham said it is to be expected. She spends most of her time locked away in her room, refusing to talk to anyone or join them for meals. Abraham has seen her nibble on the food they leave at her door at night so he's mollified that she isn't going to starve herself to death. He says she'll come around and they pray for her every night.

Babalwa also prays. She prays that she will find her father. She makes a list of all the Munyoros in the Bulawayo telephone directory and calls all of them, asking to speak to 'Marshall'. This takes her a week but she doesn't manage to find him so she finds the Harare directory and does the same thing. She's about to give up when someone answers her call and tells her that Marshall isn't home but that she can call back later. Babalwa is ecstatic and nervous; this must be him! She's found her father! What is she going to say to him? She suddenly realises that he probably doesn't even know she exists and that Yandisa and her grandparents must have hidden her from him her whole life. It might be better to go and introduce herself to him personally. The thought of meeting him excites her and she lies in bed wondering what kind of a person he is and what he looks like. She wonders if he'll come to her school one day like the other dads. She has so many questions and no answers.

For the rest of the month, Babalwa saves her pocket money. She does random chores around the house and calls her Aunt Zandile and offers to babysit her nieces and nephew. Two months later, she's saved enough money to buy a bus ticket to Harare. She decides to leave after school one day so she packs a few extra clothes into her satchel because she's not planning on coming home. Ever. She's hopeful that her father will buy her brand new clothes when she gets there.

She makes a note of the number and street address from the telephone directory. It is well after 8pm when the bus arrives in Harare and it is pitch dark and she feels vulnerable as people quickly filter out of the bus station. She quickly hails a taxi and arrives at the house a short while later. The house is beautiful and she imagines her dad to be a wealthy man who is going to be so excited to meet her and take her in. After she pays the taxi driver and he drives away, she stands at the gate and buzzes the intercom.

'My name is Babalwa,' she announces, 'and I'm here to see my dad.'

'Who?' a woman's voice asks.

'I'm here to see Marshall. Marshall Munyoro.'

Nothing happens and Babalwa stands at the gate wringing her hands anxiously. She hopes her dad is going to like her. She's wearing a long scotch dress that she usually wears to church and her hair is plaited in neat cornrows. Lots of girls at schools are using relaxers on their hair but her grandmother won't allow her to. She wonders if her dad will let her.

A stout woman wearing a maid's uniform like the one Sis May wears comes to the gate and quizzes her.

'I'm here to see my father. Marshall Munyoro.'

The maid goes back inside the house and a few minutes later, a man appears. The moment she sets eyes on him, she knows it's her father.

'Dad!' she calls out. 'Daddy!'

As he catches sight of her and she calls out to him, he stops dead in his tracks.

'Daddy! Open the gate!' she urges.

A woman comes outside and they both stare at Babalwa. She can't understand why it's taking them so long to open the gate. All she wants to do is give her dad a hug. They finally open the gate and she throws her arms around the man. He is tall like her and they have the same nose. She is so excited to meet him but the feeling is not mutual and he's stiff in her embrace. She ignores the awkwardness between them. The woman continues staring at her but doesn't say anything. They invite her inside and offer her some juice and something to eat. She wolfs it all down.

'Who is your mother?' asks Marshall.

'Yandisa,' says Babalwa. 'Do you remember her?'

The woman walks out the room, leaving them alone. Marshall looks at Babs and knows there would be no need for a DNA test to confirm that she is his child. They look so alike that the resemblance between them is uncanny. He has two children who both look a lot like her. The twelve years that have passed, flash in his mind.

'I don't know who Yandisa is,' he says. 'You look like a really sweet girl but I'm not your father.'

The expression of happiness on Babalwa's face quickly fades and she drops the glass she is holding.

'Daddy, *please*,' she says, her face crumpling up as she starts to cry.

'There must be some kind of mistake, I'm not your father.'

I was the mistake, Babalwa thinks to herself.

'Is there someone we can call?' he asks her.

The woman walks back into the room at this point and suggests that they should perhaps call the police.

Babalwa fears the police and begs them not to and gives them her grandparents' number instead. She is handed the phone and starts sobbing.

'I was just looking for my father,' she cries when she hears Phumla's voice.

The phone is taken from her and Phumla asks Marshall for his address and explains that her sister-in-law, Sis Lungile, lives in Harare and will collect Babalwa. Sis Lungile arrives an hour later. Babalwa is expecting a harsh rebuke but Sis Lungile is empathetic and doesn't mention what has transpired and assures Babalwa that everything will work out.

Babalwa has so many unanswered questions but doesn't know who to ask. She knows she will always be alone in the world and that even God is not on her side because if he was, he wouldn't have watched and allowed this to happen to her. She feels betrayed by everyone. By her parents who didn't want her in the first place and by her grandmother and grandfather.

The next day she is on the bus back to Bulawayo and her grandparents and Yandisa are there to meet her.

'We were so worried about you!' cries Abraham, enveloping her in his arms.

'Why did you run away from us?' sobs Phumla.

Yandisa hangs back as her parents smother their granddaughter in an embrace. She tries to reach out to her but Babalwa recoils away.

'Don't you dare touch me,' she hisses. 'You abandoned me.'

'Babs, I can explain,' says Yandisa pleadingly.

'What's there to explain? You've been playing mother to your other kids but you never cared about me! I hate you. Do you hear me, Yandisa? I hate you!'

From then on, Babalwa becomes a troublesome child.

BLENDED FAMILIES

She tosses and turns all night as she tries to think of a way to bring Babalwa into the fold without causing too much of a stir. She's awake when Wesley finally gets home well after midnight and she feels the weight of the bed shift as he clambers onto it. She feels his hand groping her breast and the other between her legs. She keeps her eyes tightly shut hoping that he might let her be but then she feels guilty so she forces herself to turn around and kiss him. She kisses him passionately but her body is not co-operative. She is as dry as a desert when he enters her. As he plunges into her, she looks past his heaving shoulder and thinks of all the challenges ahead. She hears him grunt and knows it is over. He lies panting on top of her before falling into a deep sleep. She expertly worms herself out from under him and goes to shower, rinsing herself of his smell and the sperm he's secreted in her. Returning to bed, sleep evades her and she eventually gets up and starts to fervently pray. She prays for some kind of solution about Babalwa.

She wakes up the next morning feeling down and rushes the kids to school and then rushes to the salon. She uses Wesley's BMW with the broken window so that when she tells people about the supposed car accident, people will really buy into it. The teachers at school are sympathetic as are the other mothers she bumps into. Even the ladies in the salon buy into it and suggest she takes the day off but she decides against it. It's a slow day and she manages to catch a nap here and there throughout the day. Her mother comes to have her nails done and she tells Yandisa that Babalwa has to go.

319

That afternoon when Yandisa gets home with the children, she's surprised to see her RAV4 parked in the driveway.

'Daddy's home!' squeals Nicola.

It's Monday so the club isn't open so Wesley obviously doesn't have other plans if he's at home already. The minute she parks the car, the children bounce out and race into the house to see their father. There's a novelty factor when it comes to having their father home. In some homes, children sit down to eat dinner with their fathers every night but in their house it's a rare occurrence. Yandisa opens the trunk of the car and hollers for MamTembo. Hiring the middle-aged maid was a strategic decision on Yandisa's part. The younger ones tend to challenge her and almost always develop a crush on Wesley. That is another reason she is wary of bringing Babalwa into their home. She doesn't trust Wesley around Babs but she can't vocalise that to her parents. She hates herself for even having these thoughts but she has often seen Wesley ogling young girls in an inappropriate way. In a way that makes her uncomfortable.

She reaches for a can of Esprit from one of the grocery bags and opens it as she totters into the house, leaving MamTembo to unpack the car. It's been a long day and she really needs a drink. Entering the living room, she finds Wesley in front of the TV, children clinging to his back, interrupting whatever he was watching. He doesn't seem to mind the intrusion and judging by the number of empty beer cans lying around, he's been home a while.

'Hey, babe,' he says, as she walks in, patting the space next to him on the couch. She sits down and they kiss each other hello. The children look at each other and giggle. Yandisa wonders why Wesley is in such a good mood but it doesn't matter, the tone has been set and if Wesley's in a good mood they all will be.

'You're home early, did you get dumped?' she teases.

He smiles, 'Don't be silly. I was just tired. I had a late night last night so I decided to stay at home today.'

He takes her hand and strokes it gently. Yandisa tells MamTembo to bath the kids so her and Wesley can have a few minutes alone. She sits outstretched on the couch and puts her feet in Wesley's lap. He massages them tenderly and asks after her day. He then apologises for not going to her parents' house the previous day and for being an arsehole.

'Apparently Dad invited the boys to join the rest of the family for lunch,' comments Yandisa.

'This whole thing with your dad and the brothers has got me thinking. Maybe Babalwa should come and live with us. You're right, she needs to form a relationship with her siblings.'

Yandisa is reluctant to say anything in response. She's curious as to what has brought on Wesley's change of heart but whatever the reason she feels like a heavy weight has been lifted off her shoulders. Silently she thanks God. Her prayers have been answered. She throws her hands around his neck excitedly. Wesley is not such an unreasonable person after all.

She has to look at the bigger picture. Wesley loves her and he loves his children. She has a beautiful home, a nice car and a successful business. It might not be perfect but no one has a perfect life. So what if he fools around once in a while. What man doesn't? They're happy. At least some of the time which is more than most people can say.

CHRISTMAS WITHOUT YOU

Nothing heralds the advent of Christmas like eager retailers hanging up their Christmas-themed décor. Christmas carols become the default background music and 'Joy to the World' is played on repeat. In the oppressive December heat, faux Father Christmases sit on sleighs in shopping centres, waiting for children to want to have their photo taken with Santa. Xoliswa notices that all the Father Christmases look decidedly thinner than previous years. They aren't fat and jovial like they used to be and clearly 2007 has been a trying year for everyone. It seems to have brought more hardship than joy but everyone soldiers on in their lives, doing their best.

The spiralling inflation has rendered many of the company's projects that were feasible at the start of the year, unviable by the end of the year. Many projects stalled due to cost overruns and in some instances it was easier to down tools than try to continue with a job. A simple bag of cement is becoming a prized commodity in the construction industry. Connections are more important than ever and even buying a loaf of bread is about who you know.

Xoliswa has lost track of the number of businesses that have closed in Belmont, only to be replaced by all sorts of churches which seem to sprout up everywhere nowadays. Evangelism is also a tough business, her father laments. He complains that pulpits are being overtaken by rogue pastors.

They closed the Askaheni offices for the holidays with a Christmas luncheon which had boosted the morale of the staff slightly. The company had stayed afloat because of the government tenders they'd been awarded and she was able to give her staff bonuses but there would be no pay increases in 2008.

However, the overall hardship being experienced in the country is not uniform and CC had casually informed her that he was taking his family to Malaysia for the Christmas holidays. With the current crop of sanctions, travel to the West is off limits for many government officials but CC is unperturbed because they can still travel to the East. Xoliswa has tried to be blasé about the whole thing but it grates on her nerves. He left on the 20th of December and only gets back in the new year, and to say that she's feeling jealous would be an understatement. Not a minute goes by when she's not thinking about what him and his family might be doing. They say there are three seasons of loneliness for mistresses: Easter holidays, Heroes' Day holidays and Christmas holidays.

'Christmas without you. White Christmas and I'm blue ...' croons Dolly Parton and Kenny Rogers on the CD playing in the living room. That resonates so keenly with her and she thinks about how much she misses CC. She wants to turn the music off but her mother is singing along, even though she is off-key. Her father comes in the room and draws her into his arms and they waltz clumsily across the living room. Owami giggles as he watches them.

Christmas has always been a festive time in their home. The mood is set at the front door which is beautifully adorned with a green wreath, festooned with red ribbons and berries. She remembers Christmases gone by with such fondness and she's looking forward to this Christmas with equal eagerness. It's compounded even more because of Owami's excitement as he puts up decorations all over the house. The mantelpiece is adorned with candles and stockings and the Christmas tree has been pimped with string lights, red bows and gold ornamental balls. The presents are packed beneath the tree, the fruits of her and her mother's exuberant shopping spree.

Two weeks prior, Xoliswa, Phumla, Owami and their nanny

had flown to South Africa to do their Christmas shopping. Xoliswa was flush with cash as CC had given her what he called a Christmas 'bonus' but she thinks the money was just to ease his conscience for going away for so long.

They flew to Johannesburg with their long shopping list which included everything from groceries to clothes. They stayed at the Sandton Sun, overlooking the cosmopolitan metropole, and Phumla insisted she wanted to be waited on hand and foot.

'Please, *mntanami*, none of that self-catering *nton nton*,' she had said to Xoliswa.

Xoliswa thought her mother was being a diva but indulged her anyway. During the day they shopped and in the evenings they wined and dined in style at one of the restaurants at Nelson Mandela Square. The highlight of Phumla's day was getting dressed for dinner every night. She'd do her make-up and look impeccable in a different dress every night. On the first evening, Aunt Phindile joined them for dinner and spent the first thirty minutes complaining about why they weren't staying with her at her home in Soweto. And then the last half hour complaining about how sinful it was to spend so much on food. After dinner, Xoliswa slipped her aunt some money which seemed to placate her slightly. Uncle Songezo and his family joined them on the second night. He always referred to them as 'Mugabe's people' and wondered how they were surviving up in Zimbabwe. Uncle Sonwabile joined them on the third night and ran up a huge bill with his expensive whisky demands. Xoliswa decided she had had enough of her mother's relatives after that and spent the last few evenings hanging out with Mpho and Natasha. It was a tearful reunion as Natasha was going through a harrowing divorce.

When their time in Joburg ended, they parcelled up all their shopping and sent it to Bulawayo using *omalayitsha*. Unencumbered by luggage, they flew to Cape Town. Phumla only stayed a few days before catching a flight to the Eastern Cape to visit her other sister, Phatiswa. Xoliswa made it very clear that she was not going to be roughing it up *ezilaleni*. She uses the expensive flights to the Eastern Cape as an excuse to get out of the trip. Her mother had suggested they drive but Xoliswa refused because she knew she would end up doing all the driving and would be exhausted by the end of the trip. So her mother flies out alone, leaving them to holiday in Cape Town.

She stayed in Cape Town and spent a few days being a tourist. She took a guided tour up Table Mountain. She went on a hike and took a boat cruise and she went snorkelling which Owami loved. He was such a daredevil that it actually scared her because he had no sense of fear. In the evenings, the two of them would have a quiet dinner together and after Owami had gone to bed, Xoliswa lay in bed and thought about CC and how much she missed him. When she saw couples strolling along the beach hand in hand, she wished he was there to hold her hand. When they went snorkelling, Owami had said he missed Uncle CC and how much he would have enjoyed snorkelling with them. Uncle CC did so many activities with Owami and had taught him to ride a bike, took him horse riding, played soccer and did so many other fun activities with him.

'Can we call Uncle CC when we get back to the hotel?' asked Owami one evening.

'He's probably sleeping already,' replied Xoliswa, trying to let her son down gently.

As much as they both missed CC, she couldn't call him. It was one of the unwritten rules of their relationship and she had to wait for his calls which only happened when he was able to. The time difference didn't help and he ended up calling her at crazy hours in the night. She slept with her phone on her chest so that she always heard the call and during the day, she always had her phone next to her in case she missed his call. It didn't matter where she was or what she was doing when he called she answered. He called her once during a church service and she had stood up to go outside to talk to him, only for him to cut the phone a few seconds later because his wife had apparently walked into the room. She often wondered about CC's wife and what kind of person she was. CC often said she was a nice woman but Xoliswa would get cross when he made comments like that because if she was so nice then what the hell was he doing with her!

Before he left for his holiday, she had told him how hard it was not being able to see him and he had said to her, 'You know I also feel guilty, Xoliswa. It was never my intention to get this serious with you and I'll often be sitting at home with my family watching TV and all I'm thinking about is when I will see you again. It tears me up too not being able to see you. Do you think I enjoy the lying and sneaking around?'

He'd hung up the phone and Xoliswa wondered how she had even gotten herself into a relationship with CC in the first place. And her concern was how she would ever get out.

After their mini vacation, they flew home to get ready for Christmas. The flight to Bulawayo was full, with returning residents all keen to celebrate the holidays with their families. It made Xoliswa realise just how many people had left Zimbabwe and how many more were making that exodus.

'I didn't know Xolie was living in Johannesburg now,' remarked one of her mother's friends to Phumla at the airport, as they were checking in to fly home.

'She's not,' replied Phumla. 'We just had a holiday.'

She said it so proudly and it made Xoliswa feel so good that she had been able to do that for her mother. If only her father had come too but Abraham said he would only come if he could carry the church on his back.

FATHER CHRISTMAS AND HIS SONS

Xoliswa makes it clear that after buying the groceries she cannot be expected to do the Christmas cooking. As *umnikazi wempumphu* the position comes with perks which exclude hard labour. She's once again hired MaTshuma and her club to do all the heavy lifting. The women agree to work on Christmas Day because there isn't much for them to celebrate and not much money to celebrate with. So they are able to earn a bit of money in the morning and have something to take home to their families in the afternoon. Xoliswa pays them extra and organises Christmas hampers for each of them.

Christmas lunch is always a big deal in the Mafu household and Xoliswa is determined to carry on the tradition even though times are tough. She's happy to be able happy to sponsor the Christmas cheer. Abraham says they are going to slaughter a cow in honour of the boys, who will be joining them this year. When she had heard that Vumani and Wandile would be joining them, Xoliswa had balked at the suggestion. What bothers her is that they could usurp her position in her father's heart, having already taken her position in the family as firstborn.

'Mom, why didn't the boys ever stay with us or visit us when we were growing up?' asks Xoliswa, as she sets up the lantern centrepieces on the table.

'Well, they had their mother,' replies Phumla defensively. 'If she was dead, I might have taken them in but they were not my responsibility.'

Not since the altercation with Sis Ntombi has Xoliswa raised the issue of Sarah and the boys as it's still clearly a touchy subject all these years later.

327

'I know you're probably thinking that I'm a homewrecker but I'm not,' says Phumla. 'Your father never told me he was married. Do you really think I would have left my home in the Eastern Cape to go and live with a married man?'

Does anyone ever aspire to fall in love with a married man, Xoliswa wonders to herself. It nearly always seems like a mistake, like something a person falls into like tripping and falling into a ditch. Being with CC wasn't a mistake. It had been deliberate and she'd always known from the get-go that he was married. Initially that had been a deterrent but she had been swayed by the money. She had told herself it would just be a fling and flung herself into it willingly. His marital status then became an attractive feature and she knew the relationship could never progress into anything beyond her being his mistress. Did that make her a Jezebel?

'Find a man of your own, Xolie. I say this from a good place. Even if CC left his wife, would you really be able to take on his four kids? Or is it five? Even if he left his wife of his own accord, people would always blame you. You will always be the home wrecker, the woman who destroyed his marriage. You'll never live it down. Until her death, your father's mother hated me. Why do you think she never came to stay? I know you are in love, Xolie but is it worth it? Find a man without the complications.'

'Mama, I'm not dating him for marriage,' she replied. 'I'm dating him for companionship.'

Why can't two people date without the expectation of marriage? Did marriage always have to be the be-all and end-all? Growing up, Xoliswa vividly remembers playing dress-up with her sisters and putting on their mother's dresses and pretending to be wives or brides, because that is what girls aspired to be. No alternatives were offered beyond marriage and being single was never sold as an acceptable choice for a woman. She often questioned her own motivation for wanting to get married. Did she want to get married because that was what was expected of her? She had truly wanted to marry Thulani and marriage had felt like the natural progression in their ten-year courtship.

When she met Keith, she had buckled under the weight of the pressure to get married and she had been desperate to tie the knot. Desperate to meet those expectations imposed by society. Now she is in a relationship with CC that isn't going anywhere and she's fine with that. She isn't burdened with any future prospects and expectations, things that brought her a lot of heartbreak in the past. She just wants love and commitment, or some semblance of it, without the heartbreak.

Her mother continues. 'Your relationship is superficial and one day it won't be enough for you, Xolie. Don't you want more kids and a man you can parade at family functions? Surely you must want more for yourself. What you've settled on with CC seems like a raw deal to me.'

Her mother's words stay with her. They haunt her and she makes up her mind to end the affair with CC. The minute he gets back from his holiday she's going to tell him it's over between them. Her phone suddenly vibrates to life in her pocket and CC's name flashes across the screen. She walks into the scullery and locks the door behind her. She finds herself quietly mouthing, 'I love you too,' in a muffled voice.

'And I can't wait to fuck you,' he growls. 'It's all I can think about since we got here.'

As he says that she feels her groin tingle and hates herself for being under his spell.

They all leave for church and Abraham delivers the 10 am service with much vigour and enthusiasm. The mood is festive as they all sing Christmas carols and the Sunday school performs their own rendition of the nativity play. After the service, they bump into Yandisa and all her offspring, who are excitedly running around and having fun. Xoliswa presumes that Wesley must still be at home sleeping; he last featured at church when him and Yandisa got married.

'What is your plan for today?' asks Xoliswa, after they've exchanged all the pleasantries.

She presumes they will be spending Christmas with Wesley's family as is the age-old tradition for many married women.

'No real plans. I'm just taking MaNyoni, Evelyn and the kids out for lunch. Wesley has abandoned us,' says Yandisa.

'What do you mean he's abandoned you?'

Apparently Wesley left home on the 22nd of December and Yandisa got a call from him the day before informing her that he'd be spending Christmas with his sister in Durban. Xoliswa holds her hand up to her cheek, thinking where Wesley gets the gall.

'Well, you can join us,' says Xoliswa feeling sorry for her sister.

'Thanks but I've already made the lunch booking and my mother-in-law is so excited. So are Evelyn and her kids.'

'Why do you even bother with them?' asks Xoliswa.

Yandisa shrugs her shoulders, 'They are still my family. And they're good people.'

Zandile decided to dispense with all family tradition that year and they were having a white Christmas in Europe and visiting Eurodisney. She said she was asserting herself and breaking with tradition which meant they would no longer be doing Christmas with the Khumalo clan.

'I want to establish our own family tradition,' she had said to Xoliswa. 'This business of congregating at people's farms and being used as slave labour is not for me.'

They had flown to Germany with Chandelle and Maqhawe who were spending Christmas there with Chandelle's family. They were using their home as a base to explore the rest of Europe. Xoliswa could have travelled and taken Owami somewhere but she knew how much it meant to her parents that they were spending Christmas with them.

When they get back to the house, Vumani and his family and Wandile are already waiting. They have bought gift-wrapped presents for everyone which Xoliswa thinks is a nice gesture. Vumani introduces them all to his wife Yothando, who Xoliswa remembers from high school was a prefect when she was in form one. Yothando tells them that her and Vumani met at university and have three boys. Nqobile, their oldest son is thirteen, followed by Thabani who is ten and Vukani who is eight. Owami is immediately taken with Vukani and by the time they all sit down to eat, they are inseparable. Vumani is an actuary by profession and Yothando is an investment banker. They live in Johannesburg and seem to be doing very well for themselves by the look of things. Vumani makes it clear that he is not after any Mafu family jewels and his only desire is to have a relationship with his father and for his kids to nurture one with their grandfather.

Wandile, on the other hand, doesn't say much. He wolfs down his food while telling them that he's 'between things' at the moment and doing 'this and that' shuffling back and forth between Johannesburg and Bulawayo. His accent doesn't have the private school refinement that Vumani distinctly picked up along the way. His mannerisms are very different to his brother's and it's hard to believe they grew up in the same home. While Vumani has moved away to establish his own home, family and career, Wandile still lives in Makokoba. He's not married but indicates that he has a live-in girlfriend.

'You need to do the right thing, son,' says Abraham sternly. 'You don't want her falling pregnant. You're a Mafu, you must marry the girl.'

'Dad, please,' intervenes Xoliswa, seeing how uncomfortable Wandile is talking about his personal life.

After lunch, Wandile clears the plates and washes all the dishes. He seems quite happy to be in the kitchen and sips on some vodka that Xoliswa offers him. Yothando and Vumani don't drink but Yothando is not at all uppity and helps dry the plates and stack them away. Xoliswa carries on drinking her wine and once the last dish is packed away, she suggests they all sit outside. Wandile was hoping to disappear into the lounge with his nephews who are on the PlayStation but he joins them outside. They have mince pies and gourmet fruit cake for dessert, imported from Woolworths.

'We can get the groceries for you next time,' volunteers Vumani.

'And I can bring them,' says Wandile. '*Ngiyalayitsha.*'

He whips out a few business cards and puts them on the table.

'We need to find something for you to do,' says Abraham. 'You can't be driving up and down.'

'Dad, please,' interjects Xoliswa, knowing how condescending her father sounds. 'Why not invest in Wandile's business rather?'

'*Hayi hayi!*' refutes Abraham. '*Omalayitsha yizinto zabantu abanga-fundanga.*'

'*Angifundanga phela mina, Baba,*' responds Wandile cockily, surprising everyone. Abraham quickly suggests that he'll sponsor the rest of Wandile's schooling but he's horrified to discover Wandile doesn't have his O levels. Wandile says he's happy doing what he's doing. Even the sweet dessert can't salvage the souring conversation between father and son.

'We need to do this again,' says Xoliswa, trying to break the tension. 'Let's not be strangers.'

'Yes,' agrees Yothando. 'Easter is around the corner.'

Wandile doesn't commit himself to joining them for Easter and says he has already made other plans.

'You can always change them,' says Vumani. Wandile looks at this brother, visibly annoyed.

'And bring the kids anytime,' adds Phumla. 'Our home is open to them.'

Xoliswa puts her arm around her mother, knowing that her offer is a huge concession on Phumla's part. That she too is trying to make amends for the past by authoring a different narrative for the future. The lunch has really changed Xoliswa's perception of the boys and she's beginning to appreciate how hard it must have been for them growing up out of the fold, without a father. She has had her father all her life. She feels the resentment she was feeling towards them being replaced with empathy.

MARRIED VS UNMARRIED

A new year is ushered in with vigorous countdowns and excessive drinking in some quarters but in the Abrahamic quarters an all-night vigil prayer is held, with the fervent hope that the coming year will be better than the last.

But three months in and it's proving to be worse than the previous year. Economists make theoretical year-on-year comparisons and the population feel the pinch of those statistics.

But even in the most dire of circumstances there is always something to celebrate. It's a Friday night at La Gondola, a Venetian restaurant on the corner of Fort and Main Streets in Bulawayo. Most of the patrons are probably not familiar with the flat-bottomed boat used on the canals in Venice that the restaurant is named after but they don't care, they're there for the food, not the history. Everyone is sipping Prosecco and lingering over their hors d'oeuvres while Xoliswa is on the phone, trying to call Yandisa for what must be the eighth time that night.

'Her phone is still on voicemail,' says Xoliswa irritably.

It was 8.15 pm and they had all agreed to meet 6.30 pm for Zandile's 30th birthday celebration. Ndaba is taking her on a weekend away to Vumba so they decided to do a dinner for her the night before. Two generations of women are represented with Zandile the youngest and Phumla the oldest. At Zandile's insistence, Xoliswa made sure to invite Zandile's sisters-in-law, Edna, Zodwa and Chandelle as well as Ndaba's sister, Nandi. Out of courtesy and politeness, she also invited Vumani's wife, Yothando, who couldn't make it for obvious reasons but she had sent a gift for Zandile. Xoliswa had even extended the invitation to Zandile's mother-in-law, Selina, who politely declined and explained that she would be babysitting all the grandkids that night. Xoliswa is thankful she couldn't make it and can't understand why Zandile insists on having Ndaba's family at her 30th when she doesn't even like half of them.

'One has to be politically correct and keep the peace,' Zandile had said to Xoliswa. To balance things a bit, Xoliswa also invited Sis Lungile and Sis Ntombi from the Mafu side, much to her mother's displeasure but the three women are sitting together and getting along well.

The women at the table are not strangers to one another and all met at Zandile's bridal shower and then again at her wedding. They rallied together for Ndaba's 40th birthday bash and had been at both of Zandile's baby showers. But this is the first time they have all congregated together in a more intimate setting and sat together at one table.

'Yandisa was never good at keeping time,' says an exasperated Zandile, picking at crumbs of focaccia bread on her plate.

'Maybe we should just order our mains,' says Xoliswa. 'She'll catch up.'

As she looks up to signal to the waiter, Yandisa struts into the restaurant, donning a pair of thigh-high snakeskin boots and a little black dress. Her arrival sparks a lot of interest from the other diners as well as some of the ladies at their table. Yandisa is full of apologies as she hugs and kisses everyone hello.

'*Ukunona ke?*' chastens Sis Ntombi, referring to Yandisa's size. 'You look like a pig!'

'I'm getting fat on my own account. Why should it bother you?' says Yandisa snootily.

Even after all these years, there is no love lost between the two women and if anything, their antagonism has grown.

'You look fantastic,' says Sis Lungile kissing Yandisa on both cheeks, trying to mollify the frown on Yandisa's face caused by Sis Ntombi's remark.

A Family Affair

'She does, doesn't she,' agrees Phumla, seeing how crestfallen her daughter was after Sis Ntombi's hurtful comment. Yandisa has gained weight, especially after having Ethan, and she hasn't been able to shake off the extra pounds which make her look like a cuddly bear with a few extra layers.

'Trust you to make a grand entrance!' teases Xoliswa.

'The salon was busy,' says Yandisa. 'I can't turn away business and walk away from money these days.'

She hugs Zandile and wishes her a happy birthday and settles down at the head of the table, opposite her sister. She flips through the menu and settles on ossobuco with rice.

'Why don't you have a salad instead of the rice?' suggests Zandile.

'Mind your own waistline, Sis!' quips Yandisa, the flesh under her arm wobbling in collusion as she holds up her arm and points at her sister.

'Honestly, Yandisa, you don't always have to pig out,' remonstrates Xoliswa. 'You need to watch your weight.'

'And where did being thin get you in life, Xoliswa?' snaps Yandisa. 'I'm the married one!'

'If you still call that thing of yours a marriage,' Xoliswa retaliates.

'Let's see how long you'll stay married with those love handles!' adds Sis Ntombi.

Yandisa is not phased, 'If a man loves you, he'll put up with love handles and saddlebags.'

'I make the effort for my husband,' says Zandile, playing with the caprese salad on her plate. 'I go to the gym and make sure I look like I did ten years ago.'

'And you look amazing,' says Sis Ntombi pointedly. 'That's why your husband is smitten with you!'

Their main courses arrive and the dishes are all infused with the smells of oregano, basil and sage.

The vigorous conversation continues and a discussion ensues about a friend of a family relative who is embroiled in a very public divorce. In their circles, the word divorce is still a dirty one. Nobody ever gets divorced. You get married and you stay married. It's as simple as that.

'I don't understand how Lindiwe can walk away from all those millions,' says Zodwa.

'What millions?' remarks Nandi. 'Apparently Tom is bankrupt.'

There are surprised gasps around the table and Nandi is glad her comment has caught everyone's attention. In family circles, she's known as the unmarried and barren aunt while in corporate circles she's known as the first woman to become CEO of a listed entity on the ZSE.

'I knew Tom in a personal capacity,' continues Nandi. 'I worked with him a few years ago on the delisting of Rio Tinto. His life is a mess. He has about four mistresses and twenty kids and Lindiwe decided she wasn't going to put up with it any more.'

Everyone at the table is craning their necks in Nandi's direction so they don't miss a word of the inside scoop on the story.

'Besides *uLindiwe ufundile*. She's educated. She is a qualified doctor and doesn't have to put up with that nonsense,' says Nandi, using her manicured hands to make her point.

'I'd also leave,' agrees Xoliswa.

'It's easy for you to say that because you're not married,' counters Zodwa.

'I'm married and I would leave,' says Zandile. 'No woman has to put up with that kind of disrespect.'

'Men cheat all the time. What's important is that he comes home to you,' says Sis Ntombi, putting her two cents in.

'Not *all* men,' levels Chandelle. 'I really hate that assumption because there are some good men out there.'

Sis Lungile is quick to counter with, 'Black men cheat, sisi. Maybe in your white community it doesn't happen but black men cheat.'

Chandelle is visibly offended, 'I'm married to a black man and he *is* faithful.'

336

'*Ubani? UMaqhawe? Liqhawe lokufeba!*' says Yandisa vociferously.

Everyone laughs and Chandelle is confused. She looks to Zandile to translate.

'They're just saying he's a hero,' she says, trying to downplay the true meaning.

Chandelle joins in the laughter which makes everyone laugh even harder. When the laughter subsides, Zandile comes to her friend's aid.

'Not all black men cheat. My husband is faithful and I can say that with all my heart.'

Yandisa is dismissive, 'Rather say you haven't caught him yet.'

'No! I *know* my man!' avows Zandile.

'*Hayi*, sisi,' cuts in Sis Ntombi. 'Don't ever say you know a man. *Umuntu ngek' umconfirmer.* Remember that song by Brenda Fassie?'

'My man cheats,' says Yandisa. 'I'm not even going to try and lie about it. He would cheat with the dogs if he could.'

The table erupts into more laughter. As heartbreaking as Yandisa's assertion is, her delivery is comical and makes it seem like she is unperturbed by his behaviour.

'And I suppose you stay because of the financial support?' adds Nandi.

She's eyed Yandisa up and down and is pretty sure she doesn't amount to much in terms of net worth.

'No. I could support myself. I own a salon,' replies Yandisa.

'Just one?' says Nandi circumspectly. 'You might as well stay put, sisi.'

'Look, I am not staying for the money. I'm staying for my kids. I don't want them to grow up in a broken home. I don't want to imagine the trauma it would cause if Wesley and I were to split up.'

'But have you considered the trauma of them growing up in an unhappy home?' levels Chandelle.

'I'd rather my kids grow up in a stable home than a broken home,' says Zodwa.

The older women around the table nod in affirmation.

'There were many times I could have left your father but I stayed,' says Phumla, 'Look at my girls. Were any of you traumatised?'

Xoliswa wants to say that she was, forced to step up when her mother had her meltdowns meant that she was forced to grow up too soon. As a child, she should have been spared the vagaries of her parents' relationship.

'I totally disagree,' continues Chandelle, 'my parents got divorced when I was ten and it was definitely for the best. I lived with Mom during the school term and Dad had me over the holidays. My parents both remarried and everyone is happy.'

'Our society is not as kind to divorced women,' points out Nandi. 'It's actually considered better to be a widow than a divorcee.'

Many women are mentioned who were once unhappily unmarried but went smiling to their husbands' funerals. This elicits much laughter.

'Nandi's right,' says Xoliswa, 'that's why many women prefer to stay in miserable marriages.'

'Getting married is hard enough,' says Yandisa. 'Why would anyone go through the trouble of getting divorced?'

There is more unbridled laughter but Chandelle is the only one who doesn't find Yandisa's comments funny. 'I would never stay in an unhappy marriage. I'd rather be divorced and alone,' she says in response.

'I'd rather be married and miserable,' says Yandisa. 'You have no idea how much respect comes with having this ring,' and she fingers her gold ring to emphasise her point.

'I completely agree,' concludes Zodwa. 'You might be educated and successful but if you aren't married you've failed in life. Marriage is an achievement. I don't care what anyone says.'

Out of the corner of her eye, Xoliswa can see Nandi rolling her eyes.

'Marriage is an achievement only when you have nothing else to your name. I have plenty,' counters Nandi, determined to have the last word on the subject.

EXTRAMARITAL AFFAIRS

The waiters clear the plates away and the dessert menus are placed on the table. No one even glances at them and the lively discussion quickly resumes. Wine glasses are topped up and the conversation continues to flow, unabated.

'Marriage is overrated,' says Edna, surprising everyone with her statement. She hasn't said a word all night.

'You reckon?' challenges Zodwa.

'Yes. If I were given a choice to get married, I wouldn't and I've probably been married the longest. Three kids later and I think it's a scam!'

They all laugh, all except Edna, who reaches for a sip of her Irish liqueur.

'I've never been married and I don't have any regrets,' says Nandi. 'I just live my life to the fullest.'

'Yes. *Angithi yin'elidla amadoda wethu,*' says Yandisa volubly. 'All the single and happy women are fucking married men.'

'*Labo bafuna ukudliwa,*' counters Xoliswa. 'Why are married men dating single women?'

'Because you are all easy prey. Single women need to learn to say no when they're approached by married men. Where is their dignity?' asks Yandisa, looking directly at Xoliswa.

'Where is his?' says Nandi. 'It takes two to tango!'

'Listen, if I catch a bitch with my husband, I'll maul her,' says Yandisa aggressively.

'Keep doing that babe, and one day you're going to meet a bitch that will maul you back!' jokes Xoliswa.

There is more laughter but it's cut short when the waiters wheel in Zandile's birthday cake, an Italian ricotta cassata cake. The waiters sing 'Happy Birthday' in Italian and the ladies join in with the English version. Zandile makes a wish before blowing out all the candles and the cake is cut.

'It's so presumptuous to assume that single women want your men,' continues Nandi, looking around the table. 'Just because your man rocks your boat doesn't mean he'll rock mine.'

'Have you seen *my* man?' counters Yandisa. 'Wesley is hot!'

'I don't need to see him. From what I've heard I wouldn't want him.'

'I don't think he'd want you either,' snaps Yandisa.

Xoliswa taps her glass with a spoon, signalling to the birthday girl that it is time for her to say something. She's trying to deflect everyone's attention away from the brewing war between Nandi and Yandisa. Zandile stands up and thanks her mother for being there and for bringing her into the world. She tells her sisters how much she appreciates them both and how their closeness as siblings is so important to her. She thanks her aunts for being pillars of support.

'And finally, to my sisters by marriage, I appreciate you all. Aunt Nandi, thank you for welcoming me into the family.'

Phumla has already started yawning at the head of the table and is the first to leave shortly after Zandile's speech. She is followed by Edna, who says she has a long drive back to Marula. Chandelle then leaves, telling everyone she's meeting Mack for drinks. That's just an excuse but she's becoming more and more annoyed with Yandisa with each passing minute. Once she's left, Zandile chastises Yandisa for the comment she passed about Maqhawe.

'It was uncalled for, Yandisa. Just because you're miserable in your marriage, don't presume everyone else is too.'

'Listen Za, I work in a hair salon so I hear all the latest gossip.'

'Just stop it, Yandisa! We don't want to hear it.'

Zodwa then leaves, saying she has a midnight curfew and can't afford to violate her visa conditions. Nandi leaves and swaps numbers with Xoliswa. They promise to meet up for coffee the next time Xoliswa is in Harare.

'She's lovely,' says Xoliswa, after she returns from walking Nandi to her car.

No one else agrees with Xoliswa though and everyone says she is stuck-up and full of herself.

'She said her and I should do business together, the company are looking to empower female-run businesses.'

Sis Lungile snorts, 'Nandi has never empowered anyone but herself. She's a gatekeeper, that one. I know many women who've worked with her and quit. I've read the reports in the HR industry, she's a bully.'

Yandisa agrees with her aunt and is glad Nandi has left.

Now that the Khumalo side of the family have left, they cosy around the table and feel more at ease. Sis Ntombi and Sis Lungile are sharing a bottle of wine and since Uncle Ben passed away, Sis Ntombi has loosened up somewhat, even drinking alcohol on occasion.

'What next?' asks Xoliswa, keen to take the party somewhere else.

'We can go to the club,' suggests Yandisa.

'I'm going home,' says Zandile. 'I want to get some birthday sex. I'm tipsy and horny.'

They all laugh and tell her to go home to her husband. She says her thank yous and goodbyes and flounces off.

'Count me out of the nightclub,' says Sis Ntombi. 'Come to my house and we can have some more drinks.'

Xoliswa likes the idea of going to her aunt's house but Yandisa doesn't and suggests they part ways. Xoliswa calls for the bill and Sis Lungile frowns when she sees how much the evening has cost. Xoliswa doesn't bat an eyelid, pays the bill and they then all make their way outside, still chatting animatedly about the evening. They're standing outside saying goodbye to each other for what seems the hundredth time when Yandisa spots Wesley's BMW 3 series with its personalised number plates. She walks towards the car and knocks on the tinted window on the driver's side. The window rolls down and sitting behind the wheel is a young girl. Her face is familiar and Yandisa backhands her. The girl gasps and her hand goes up to her stinging cheek. Yandisa's fingers are adorned with chunky gold rings and they leave an imprint on the young woman's face. Yandisa then grabs the girl by her weave. Sis Ntombi and Sis Lungile run over to see what is happening and seeing the older women approach, the girl opens the door, jumps out of the car and tries to make a run for it.

'Yandisa, stop it!' shouts Xoliswa, as Yandisa runs after the girl and starts hitting her.

'Beat her!' Sis Ntombi eggs on. '*Bayajwayela.*'

'*Tshay' inja!*' says Sis Lungile, spurring Yandisa on.

'Miss me with this mess,' says Xoliswa, walking away.

As she gets into her car, she sees a security guard and the restaurant manager running towards the fight.

WHEN THE CAT IS AWAY

Babalwa suspects something is wrong when Yandisa is not there when they all wake up that Saturday morning. She wonders if her mother has left Wesley as she often threatens to. She has heard their fights and has many times been woken up by their shouting. She hears Wesley bellowing on the phone and he says, 'It is your fault. You're the one who took her out jolling in the first place, Xoliswa.'

Babs realises Wesley is talking to her Aunt Xoliswa. She can't hear what she is saying but Wesley responds, 'She isn't my girlfriend, she works for me. We ran out of wine at the restaurant last night and I asked a member of staff to take my car and go and get a few bottles from the guys at La Gondola. I've got a relationship with the manager there.'

She doesn't know what Aunt Xoliswa says in response but Wesley swears at her as she obviously tells Wesley they need to pay the bail to get Yandisa out of jail. 'I'm not bailing her out,' he says. 'She can rot in jail for all I care, *you* bail her out. Don't make your problems mine,' and he cuts the phone call.

He picks up his car keys and slams the doors as he leaves the house. She hears him pull out and not long after that, Xoliswa arrives to take them all to her house.

Babalwa refuses to go with her aunt and says she needs to study for exams on Monday. The minute Xoliswa has reversed out of the gate, Babalwa gets on the phone. She's home alone and she's not going to waste it. She calls her friend Bernice and they started plotting and planning the night ahead.

It is a balmy night in March and a good reason for Babs to wear as little as possible to go out. She's wearing a red jumpsuit with a low back, that clings to her lithe body. Her hair is in neat cornrows, accentuating her beautiful big brown eyes and pert nose. Her high-heeled sandals elevate her even taller then she already is and she stands shoulder to shoulder with her boyfriend, Anesu Gabe. Bernice and her met him and his friend at a bar one night when they snuck out. Bernice is dating his friend, Pepukai, and the four of them often go on double dates.

The guys are much older than them but that is the appeal. They always have money to spend but they also have more demands, including sex. Having grown up in a religious family, Babalwa knows that there is no sex before marriage. There is always a voice in her head that keeps her from going all the way with Anesu.
Her Aunt Zandile tries to reinforce the message all the time and stresses how sex is something to be enjoyed with your husband one day and that it is worth waiting for the right man. Aunt Xoliswa, on the other hand, is very pragmatic and suggests Babs goes for the injection, if she's fooling around.

'She is too young to be fooling around! Don't encourage her, Xoliswa!' says Zandile.

'I'm not encouraging her but you don't know kids these days,' says Xoliswa.

'I am not fucking around!' screams Babalwa.

She's tired of her aunts talking around her and about her and not *to* her.

'Well, AIDS kills,' says Zandile, 'and people are dying like flies.'

Babs has oral and anal sex with Anesu and he agrees they will save her vagina for marriage. He penetrates her arsehole and plays with her clitoris until she comes and he comes so hard that his sperm trickles down her thighs. They're both happy.

Anesu is hell-bent on marrying her one day but she's not even sure she wants to get married. Especially if marriage looks like what her mother and Wesley have. School isn't appealing either. Her aunts want her to go on to get a university education but she's not keen. Not with her grades anyway.

That night they decide to go to The Barnyard, a new nightclub in Bulawayo. Like anything new, everyone flocks to it when it first opens. The four of them sit at a table outside on the balcony and have a few drinks. There is a vibe of excitement in the air.

'Your stepfather's club is going to go out of business,' says Anesu to Babs, looking around at the crowd.

'It's about time that club closed down anyway, it's become so dodgy,' says Pepukai.

Yandisa won't let Babalwa go to any nightclubs, especially The Zone, and Babs can't wait to leave Bulawayo as soon as she can so she can party wherever and whenever she wants.

After the second round of drinks, Babs goes to the loo and as she's walking out of the bathroom, she bumps into Wesley. She's horrified and he is equally shocked to see her.

'What are you doing here, Babalwa? Who are you with?'

'My friends,' says Babs, pointing towards the table outside.

'Does your mother know you're here?' asks Wesley.

She's about to answer when a young girl comes out of the bathroom and latches herself onto Wesley like a tick.

'Does Mom know *you* are here?' says Babalwa cockily. She knows she has the upper hand.

'I won't say anything if you don't,' he replies.

Babalwa puts out her hand, indicating that she expects some money to keep quiet. Wesley begrudgingly reaches into his pocket and shoves some notes in her hand. With a self-satisfied smile, Babalwa walks back to the table and Wesley and the woman disappear into a dark corner of the club.

'Isn't that your stepdad?' asks Anesu when he spots Wesley. 'Just ignore him,' says Babalwa, signalling for the waiter to bring them another round of drinks. 'He doesn't own this club. Or me.'

Babalwa gets home at midday the next day and walks into the house confidently. Wesley and her greet each other but say nothing else. An unspoken alliance of sorts has formed between them.

A MANIC MONDAY

Yandisa is featured in an article that appears on the third page of the *Chronicle* the following Monday morning.

> *Local businesswoman and salon owner, Yandisa Bhunu*
> *(33) was involved in a skirmish with a ZRP policeman*
> *and Christabel Bizure (23), who is allegedly having an*
> *extramarital affair with her husband, Wesley Bhunu, the*
> *retired captain of the national rugby squad. Customers at a*
> *top Bulawayo restaurant were treated to a live version of a*
> *WWE wrestling match ...*

Next to the article is a picture of Yandisa standing outside her salon the day it opened a few years ago. Beside it is a picture of Yandisa and Wesley on their wedding day as well as a recent picture of Yandisa from Facebook.

Xoliswa tosses the paper aside as she leaves the office to post bail for Yandisa. She could have tried to get her out of jail over the weekend but she decided it was time Yandisa learns to deal with the consequences of her actions.

Yandisa's eyes are bloodshot, she looks exhausted and she's fuming when she comes to the front of the station.

'Xolie! They put me in a cell with prostitutes!' shouts Yandisa.

'They're just trying to earn a living,' is all Xoliswa says.

She takes her sister home and Yandisa is nervous and not looking forward to the conversation she is going to have to have with Wesley.

347

She asks if Xoliswa wants to come inside for a coffee, thinking her presence might help dissolve the tension. 'I have work to do!' snaps Xoliswa, annoyed that Yandisa can't appreciate the fact that she had to leave work to bail her out of *jail*!

'Please just come in with me!' pleads Yandisa.

Yandisa reasons that there is no way Wesley will beat her in front of her sister. If Xolie comes inside, it will buy her some time and hopefully by the time Xoliswa leaves, his mood might be slightly calmer.

'Are you even listening to me!' shouts Xoliswa. 'I had to postpone a meeting because of you.'

She tells her she has to go and speeds off. Yandisa lingers at the gate, trying to muster up the courage to go inside. Wesley will undoubtedly be home as he typically only goes to the service station in the afternoon. She finally plucks up the courage and buzzes the intercom. He answers.

'Who is it?'

'It's me,' she says, in a small voice.

'Go back to where you came from,' and he slams down the handset.

He doesn't open the gate and she buzzes again. This time he ignores her. She texts him but he doesn't respond to her message. Yandisa calls out to MamTembo and Dube, the gardener but there is no answer. Thirty minutes later, she's still standing outside the gate. People pass by and eye her curiously. She looks out of place in her little black dress, barefoot and holding her snakeskin boots in her hand. She wishes she had dressed more conservatively for Zandile's birthday dinner. A neighbour then walks up and pauses, 'Yandisa, are you okay?' she asks.

'I'm fine Deborah, thanks for asking,' says Yandisa. 'I don't have my house keys so I'm just waiting for someone to open the gate for me.'

Deborah has been their neighbour for a few years and has been witness to some ugly incidents on the other side of her high wall. Once

Deborah and her husband had been standing on their balcony which overlooked Wesley and Yandisa's backyard and had seen Wesley stomping on Yandisa's body like he was crushing grapes underfoot. Deborah had called the police and when they arrived, Wesley had fobbed them off and told them it was 'a domestic affair'. The second incident was when Yandisa had come to their gate, stark naked, in the middle of the night, seeking refuge. Deborah had covered Yandisa with a towel, brought her inside and called the police. Deborah was the one who helped Yandisa press charges against Wesley, only for Yandisa to later withdraw the charges. Deborah encouraged Yandisa get a restraining order against Wesley, only for Yandisa to rescind the application after Wesley expressed remorse. Deborah isn't sure if Wesley has stopped beating Yandisa, or if he had just become more discreet about it but Yandisa no longer appears at their gate for help.

She doesn't want to interfere so she takes Yandisa's word for it and keeps walking.

An hour later, the gates open and Yandisa walks up to the house. She passes Dube as he is cleaning the pool. He had been told to get back to work and mind his own business when he alerted Wesley to Yandisa's calls. He greets her politely and she can see the pity in his eyes. She doesn't want to be pitied, she's a strong woman. Doesn't he admire her resilience? How many women could have survived what she has?

MamTembo lets her in the house, asking after her well-being. She makes her way upstairs and to their bedroom and walks straight into Wesley. There are no hugs or kisses and instead, he grabs her roughly by the shoulders and pushes her up against the wall.

'Please don't hit me, Wesley! Please!' she grovels.

He backhands her and she slides to the floor. He kicks her in the abdomen and the pain is sharp and crippling.

'That'll teach you not to go around beating up innocent young women!'

'I'm sorry,' snivels Yandisa. 'Wesley! I said I'm sorry!'

He pinions her to the floor and pummels her body with his fists. He's careful not to injure her face because he wants to conceal the beatings. He covers her mouth with one hand and undoes his belt with the other. He starts to penetrate her and she bites his hand. This incenses him further and he plunges into her even harder and she digs her fingernails into his back, drawing blood. He thrusts his way to an orgasm and her screams are drowned out by his groans of pleasure. He comes quickly and intensely and collapses onto her.

'I miss this,' he says.

'What?' she shouts. 'Using me like your punching bag or raping me?'

'Don't be like that,' he says, rolling off her. 'You used to be so much fun, Yandisa. You used to like it rough. What happened to you?'

'I grew up.'

He stand up, kicks her in the stomach and walks away.

She manages to drag herself to the bathroom and gets in the shower to clean herself up. She is so relieved that all the children, including Babs, are at school. A voice of doubt creeps into her head and tells her that maybe she deserved this all and that Wesley is right, she has no business fighting people in public and embarrassing him. She is his wife and she needs to start acting like one instead of a two-dollar whore. Those were his words, not hers but she accepts them. She has embarrassed her whole family with her inability to control her temper. She cries until all her tears dry up and MamTembo eventually comes into the bedroom, after Wesley has left the house, and helps her. Yandisa allows herself to be vulnerable with her because MamTembo doesn't judge her. She dabs her wounds with antiseptic. Some of their previous maids used to sometimes mock her after Wesley beat her and would no longer listen to her instructions or respect her. MamTembo says nothing, her touch speaking volumes.

MIND YOUR OWN BUSINESS

As the Easter holidays begin, it reminds Xoliswa that a quarter of the year has already gone. The year has been off to a slow start, mostly because of the uncertainty surrounding the elections. Like most people in the business community, she is waiting on the outcome of the elections. Growing the business seems on track as they submitted a few tenders at the beginning of the year and have been awarded two of them. One is for the proposed construction of a private hospital and another for a proposed university. She is nervous about starting the projects until all the votes have been counted. CC is dismissive and says ZANU–PF will win and Mugabe will serve yet another term. Although she has tried to convince CC that change will be good, he argues that Zimbabwe needs stability and that the MDC cannot provide that. He would then start raising his voice and extolling the virtues of ZANU–PF and the liberation struggle. At this point, Xoliswa backs down because he becomes very passionate about his politics and reminds her that she was in business because of the benevolence of the ruling party.

The two contracts mean that at least they have work for the remainder of the year. Her staff have been worried about the future and about job security as many companies have closed their doors and others are retrenching.

Wandile has joined the firm at her father's insistence which has placed some extra pressure on the company in terms of finances but she had no say in the matter. She looks at her watch and sees that it is after ten o'clock and Wandile still hasn't arrived for work. She dials Gertie and asks her to let her know when Wandile gets there.

351

He finally arrives an hour later. Xoliswa stands up and saunters to his office which is across from hers. She greets him and casually reminds him that their business hours are 8 am to 5 pm.

'I had a meeting,' he replies offhandedly, settling in at his desk.

'A meeting with who exactly?' she asks.

'Potential investors. There are some guys from South Africa who want to invest in supermarkets so they're looking for land.'

Xoliswa nods, 'I see. Is that it?'

'For now but if there are any concrete developments, I'll let you know.'

He adjusts his tie self-importantly. He wears crisp white linen shirts and tailored suits every day and is clean-shaven and has had his hair trimmed. But unlike Vumani, who has a lean physique, Wandile's stomach spills over his pants. He is a very different Wandile from the one they all met on Christmas Day a few months ago. He's developed an air of confidence, rooted in nothing but arrogance.

He whips out a copy of the *Chronicle* and starts reading the paper, ignoring the fact that Xoliswa is still standing there.

'Are you done with the revised costing for the hospital project?' she asks.

'I assigned it to one of the boys, I'm too senior to be doing stuff like that.'

Xoliswa sighs, turns around and marches out of his office. He has been there three months and every day acts more and more like he owns the business.

Later that day, Xoliswa calls for an urgent meeting after CC emails her a tender and says they need to submit as soon as possible. Wandile declines the meeting and says he has other urgent issues to attend to. When Xoliswa comes out of the meeting, she walks into his office and finds him playing Solitaire on the computer.

'Wandile, why didn't you attend the meeting? I sent an email saying that it was urgent.'

'You're not the boss of me. I don't report to women.'

Xoliswa is caught off guard and visibly shocked, 'Are you serious?'

'I'm very serious. Your father hired me so I report to him not you.'

'Excuse me, Wandile, unlike you I've earned my place in this company. I'm a qualified CA and not here just because it's Dad's business. I'm here because I worked hard to be here.'

'Well, who knows what I could have become if our father had sent me to private school like you. Don't think you can bully me with your Engrish, Xoliswa. I don't care how educated you are. Like I said, I don't take instructions from women. I'm older than you.'

'Only by a few months,' says Xoliswa, fully aware that they were born in the same year.

Xoliswa storms out of his office realising she has possibly been prematurely generous with the empathy she felt for her half-brothers. Wandile is an asshole if there was one. He doesn't follow instructions, he can't execute even the simplest of tasks like getting price quotations and he comes to the office to read the newspaper and make a few calls. He leaves the office at lunchtime and returns at around 3 pm and tries to look busy on the computer for a while. She has tried to raise the issue with her father but Abraham had been dismissive. In the end, she decides to pay Wandile a basic salary that reflects his contribution to the company. He stopped coming to work once he got his next pay cheque and her father had called a meeting and forced her to reinstate his higher salary as well as other perks.

'Dad! He doesn't deserve to be paid that much. My interns do more work than him!'

'I don't care,' shouts Abraham. 'How much do you earn and nobody questions your salary?'

'I bring in the work, Dad. If I didn't, this company would be closed.'

'Just pay him, he's family. And while you are it, get him a new car. I can't have my son driving around in a beat-up old Isuzu.'

So Wandile got a huge pay hike and a company car. Then her

father insisted that he move into one of the townhouses which were part of a housing scheme they had built a year ago. The uptake of the properties had been slow so her father argued that Wandile could live rent-free because the townhouses were sitting vacant anyway.

'And don't complain,' admonishes her father. 'He grew up with nothing and you grew up with everything.'

Xoliswa wants to ask how that is her fault and why she has to work her fingers to the bone so Wandile can be comfortable but she keeps quiet.

A few weeks later, Abraham marches into the office, seething with anger and waving the *Financial Gazette* in her face. An article has been written about SMEs receiving business through fraudulent tenders. Askaheni Enterprises are fingered in the report.

'You're bringing my business into disrepute!' shouts Abraham.

'Dad, please,' says Xoliswa, trying to calm her father down. 'Those are unsubstantiated claims. Please don't believe what has been written about us.'

'Is it a lie that you are in bed with the Minister of Public Works? Do you think people don't know? That people don't talk? People see you, Xoliswa!'

Xoliswa is hot with shame. She never expected her father to throw her affair in her face.

'I've told you time and time again to end it with that man. I don't want ZANU–PF in my things. That was Uncle Ben's turf, not mine.'

Her father sits down, trying to regain his composure. He looks so frail and Xoliswa feels bad for causing him such angst.

'I'm sorry, Dad. I'll fix this. I will get legal on it.'

'No, Xoliswa. This has nothing to do with getting legal and everything to do with morals. What you are doing is unethical! I want you to resign as managing director and I want you to end your affair with CC.'

Xoliswa feels her face turn ashen.

'Dad, are you serious?'

'Very. I want you to draft your resignation letter now and I will tender it to the board on Friday. How you end things with CC is your problem, just do it.'

'Dad, I have given my *all* to this business! When I took over you weren't even breaking even and for the first time in years the business is profitable.'

'I don't care! I'd rather be making a clean million. *Ngeke ngidle imali yomlenze Xolie. Ngeke.*'

Xoliswa looks at her father, stunned. He has called her a whore and insinuated they are surviving on money generated from her thighs. No credence is given to the hard work she has done all these years. She met CC only a year ago and her father is behaving like the company had been on its knees prior to that.

'That's not a fair indictment, Dad and you know it.'

'Xolie, I don't mince my words.'

Gertie walks into the office and offers Abraham a cup of tea which he refuses. He instructs Gertie to set up an emergency board meeting and then gets up and leaves. Xoliswa follows suit and tells Gertie she's taking the rest of the day off.

By the end of the following day, Xoliswa has submitted her resignation. The office is devastated when they hear of her pending departure. So is she. She feels like she is breaking up with her lover and for over six years she's been in a relationship with this company and suddenly she's leaving. Gertie organises a farewell lunch a few days later and during the lunch, Abraham announces that Wandile will be taking over the reigns as the new CEO.

RESIGNED TO FATE

The last time Xoliswa remembers crying so much was when Keith stood her up on the day of the lobola negotiations. Her eyes are puffy and sore and she cries until she physically can't cry any more. She pulls herself together and calls CC to tell him what has happened.

'I always told you that family businesses are a problem, Xolie. Your dad is ungrateful, especially because you have been keeping the family afloat for so long.'

'I have,' agrees Xoliswa. 'I've done everything for them *and* that church. It would have closed its doors if it weren't for me!'

'Listen babe, just walk away. Don't fight your father, you know you've done your part,' encourages CC.

'But that business was my baby, CC. I put so much into it.'

'I know you did, babe. I was so impressed when you submitted your first tender and I didn't even know you then. Don't doubt yourself, Xolie. Don't doubt your capabilities.'

Xoliswa sniffs and wipes away the tears that are threatening to consume her again. She feels considerably better after talking to CC, he always has a way of making her see the world in a slightly more rose-tinted light. She decides to take a nap and when she wakes up, it's dark and her phone is ringing. CC is waiting outside. She looks out the window and sees him in his chauffeur-driven car. She runs downstairs and opens for him and runs into his arms. He has a tendency to arrive unannounced and she wonders if it's always to surprise her or if he sometimes wants to check up on her.

'CC!' she squeals. 'What are you doing here?'

'You sounded so upset on the phone earlier on and I knew I had to come and see you,' he says softly.

'Ohhh baby!' says Xoliswa, hugging him harder.

'Anything for my baby,' he says.

He's arrived bearing gifts. Lots of gifts. He's bought her perfume, jewellery and sexy lingerie and bags laden down with toys and clothing for Owami. CC's son is Owami's age so he knows exactly what to buy him. Xoliswa puts the gifts aside. She'll attend to them later but first she wants to attend to CC. She offers him food but he tells her that he'd much rather eat her. Afterwards, lying in his arms, drawing circles around his nipples, she thanks him for coming.

'It's a pleasure,' he purrs.

Her lips curve up into a smile, 'I meant coming coming ...'

He laughs, 'I know what you meant.'

She snuggles closer to him and falls asleep in his arms.

The next morning, Owami bounds into the bedroom dressed and ready for school. 'Uncle CC! I didn't know you were here!' says Owami, elated to see CC in the bed. 'When did you get here?'

'I arrived last night but you were already fast asleep,' says CC.

'Mummy! It's not fair, you should have woken me up!'

'It was too late, Owami!' says Xoliswa.

Owami manoeuvres himself between CC and Xoliswa. Sometimes she wonders whether he is more enamoured with CC than her. If she were to break up with CC, Owami would also lose him too and she often wonders if it was a mistake introducing him to CC. Sis Lungile says it was a mistake and her boys never met her long-time boyfriend, Saul. All their lives, she had given them the impression that she was a lonely widow and never entertained men at their home. Sis Lungile is the only one who understands Xoliswa's predicament. After her husband died, she never considered remarrying because motherhood was a full-time job that she couldn't delegate to anyone else. Dating with children was not an option for her, so when an opportunity to be with a married man presented itself, she took it. Twenty years later, she's still in a relationship with Saul Mbambo and their arrangement suits her just fine.

'How many uncles is he going to meet, Xolie? Uncle John? Uncle Jim? Uncle You-need-to-give-a-veneer-of-respectability. Men are judgemental. You are raising a boy and that boy will grow up and call you *sfebe* to your face.'

'Don't ever fall pregnant,' she cautions Xoliswa. 'He has a wife and kids at home, that's not what he's looking for with you.'

But Xoliswa starts to question the validity of this advice when CC brings up having a child. After Owami leaves for school that day with CC's driver, they stay in bed, relishing each other's company. CC lovingly strokes her exposed belly.

'Since you're now a lady of leisure with lots of time on your hands, maybe we should have a child.'

Xoliswa is unable to mask her surprise, 'CC, how can we bring a kid into this complicated equation?'

'Why not? Are you questioning my commitment to you? I can't give you marriage but I'm here aren't I?'

Xoliswa can't dispute his presence in her life. They might not coexist on a daily basis but he's fully committed to their union.

'I bought you a house, Xolie. What other assurance are you looking for? I funded your business and made sure you had work when other companies closed down. What are you doing to show your commitment to me? I want to have a child with you. One child.'

He lets his question hang in the air.

'Are you doubting my capacity to take care of you and a child, Xolie?'

'No, CC, not at all.'

'So let's get pregnant then,' he says, shifting his weight onto her body. As he prises her legs apart, Xoliswa knows there's no going back.

And that is how the idea of a baby was conceived. In an illegitimate moment of happiness.

DESPERATE HOUSEWIVES

The usual picture of domestic bliss in the Khumalo household is uncharacteristically disrupted when Ndaba marches into the kitchen demanding to know where his blue Savile Row suit is. Zandile is making pancakes for the children's breakfast.

'I forgot to pick it up from the dry cleaners yesterday,' she replies, not taking her eyes off the batter sizzling in the pan and starting to set around the edges.

'Zandi! I told you I wanted to wear it for my big meeting today!' he shouts, feeling exasperated.

'I'm sorry. I forgot,' she says.

'That's not good enough,' he shouts. 'How could you forget? It's not like you have a thousand things to do.'

She knows the implication of that statement and it always boils down to: I make the money while you stay at home and sleep. Ndaba storms out of the kitchen, leaving her to finish the pancakes. Zwelihle wants honey with his and the twins demand strawberries and cream with theirs.

'I don't have strawberries,' snaps Zandile.

Who do these kids think they are? Where the hell would you get strawberries in Zimbabwe at this time of the year anyway?

'I'm not eating this,' says Zinzile, crossing her hands over her chest in defiance.

'Me either,' says Zanele, copying her sister.

'Gimme! Gimme!' cries Zwelihle, quite happy to relieve his sisters of their pancakes.

Zinzile throws her pancake, and then her plate, on the floor.

360

Zanele again copies her sister. Zandile gives them both a smack and they burst into tears. Maria comes flying into the kitchen to see what the commotion is about and Zandile takes off her apron and leaves Maria to handle the children and clean up the mess on the floor. As she walks into their bedroom, Ndaba is putting on his tie and she tries to help him with his cufflinks but he pushes her away. He's still angry with her about his suit and has settled on a striped, charcoal Armani one instead.

'I said I'm sorry!' she shouts, not actually feeling sorry any more.

One small oversight on her part and he's acting like the world is caving in. She can't understand why he's still hanging onto his anger. He calmly explains that the big bosses are coming to Bulawayo for a meeting and it was important for him to look good. She listens to his explanation and wishes him luck.

He leaves for work and she changes into her gym attire and gets ready to drop the girls off at nursery school. Zwelihle stays at home because Ndaba insists he is too young to go to school, and there's nothing she can say to convince him otherwise. She straps the girls into their car seats in the BMWX5 and sees the fuel gauge indicator is on empty when she starts the car, so she unstraps them and loads them into Ndaba's Mercedes Benz. He had taken the other car, a Pajero, to work. As they back out of the driveway, the girls start quarrelling with one another. Her mornings wouldn't be complete without a performance from one, or all, of them.

Gym is her saving grace and she goes four times a week and jogs with Xoliswa on the other days. They were supposed to have gone for a jog early this morning but Xoliswa texted to say CC is in town and Zandile knows that when CC is in town Xoliswa drops everything, panties included, to entertain him. Zandile disapproves of their relationship and has done so right from its inception but she has had to learn to keep her condemnation to herself. That morning, her personal trainer puts her through a gruelling workout and afterwards, while stretching on the mat, he asks her if she's okay. She admits that she's not having a great day.

She goes to shower and gets dressed quickly, trying to avoid getting caught in the strident changing-room gossip. Just like her, the other women who come to gym at this time are either unemployed, self-employed or stay-at-home moms. They are all desperate housewives, maybe not as desperate as the wives on the series but they all watch it religiously anyway, trying to model their own lives on the wives of Wisteria Lane.

They are competitive in all aspects of their lives. Whether it be the size of their waistlines or the size of their engines. They buy their groceries in South Africa or from a supermarket in Bradfield, owned by a woman by the name of Anne, that is stocked with imported items catering to their expensive taste. The children all go to private schools and they all go on overseas holidays every year. When Zandile went to Paris and didn't go to the gym for two weeks, a woman had piped up, 'That's nice but have you been to Switzerland? You haven't lived until you have skied at Klosters .'

Zandile knows the competition extends to the size of their backyards so she's never invited any of them to their house and never socialises with them outside of the gym. Most of them consider her a snob which she's fine with as it keeps her sane.

She leaves the gym and picks up Ndaba's infamous Savile Row suit and then pops in at Turning Heads to have her hair and nails done but Yandisa is not there. She called in sick that morning so Evelyn is manning the shop having joined the salon after her flea market business was no longer thriving. Zandile tries calling her but her phone is off so she decides she'll see her another time as it's almost time to pick the twins up from nursery school. They are on the half-day option because Ndaba says they are too young to spend the whole day away from home. He only says that because he doesn't have to spend the afternoons with them. Thinking about the afternoon ahead of her, she can feel the stirrings of a migraine coming on.

As she arrives at the nursery school, she gets a text from Yandisa asking her to pick up her kids and she'll then pick them up later. Nicola is almost the same age as the twins and they will all be overjoyed to be going home together. After she's strapped them into the car, she gets a call from Xoliswa who wants to know if she is free for lunch.

'Yes, I'd love to!' says Zandile, welcome for the reprieve.

They decide to meet for lunch at a nearby horse farm so that the kids can play and they can have an uninterrupted conversation.

'So Dad fired me this week!' says Xoliswa, once they are sitting alone at the table.

Zandile is shocked, 'You're kidding?'

'I kid you not!'

'Why? The company has done so well since you took over.'

'He says I am bringing the company into disrepute because of my association with CC.'

Zandile rolls her eyes. 'Is that the real reason or does he want to give it to one of the boys to run?'

'Yes, he's already announced that Wandile is taking over. Can you believe it?!'

'What are you going to do? I suppose you could just be a kept woman!'

Xoliswa laughs, 'So I can sit at home all day and go for manicures and to the spa?'

'You say it like it's a bad idea. You're CC's mistress, why don't you just embrace that?'

'I don't know if I could be that reliant on a man, Zandile.'

'That's true, you don't know what it's like,' says Zandile. 'Selina told Ndaba she needs new couches and when I questioned it because the ones she has are still pretty new, Ndaba told me it is his mother and his money!'

'Are you serious, Zandile?'

She nods. Her eyes mist over with tears, 'I'm very serious. We haven't really been talking and when he tried to have sex the other morning, I told him it's my body and my vagina!'

363

Xoliswa laughs and throws her head back. Zandile shakes her head.

'Ndaba gives me money for lunch. For my hair. For my nails. But he doesn't give me any say when it comes to big-ticket items and doesn't even talk to me. I'm his wife and the mother of his children!'

'Have you thought of opening up your own business, Zandile? You can make your own money and not be dependent on him.'

'I don't have any start-up capital. I've asked him to loan me money to start something but his response was "Zandi, it's too risky, especially in this climate",' says Zandile, imitating Ndaba's voice.

'I can loan you the money,' says Xoliswa, feeling empathetic towards her sister.

'Nah, it's fine. I have to consider Ndaba's ego. He does so much for me and I don't want to seem like I'm being an ungrateful wife. But back to you, Xolie. How are you going to occupy yourself?'

'I don't know. I haven't really thought about it yet but I'm not sure what I *could* do after years in the construction business.'

'What about event planning? I think you'd be so good at it.'

Xoliswa's eyes light up, 'You know, I've never even thought of that.'

'You'd be great, Xolie. The way you organised Yandisa's wedding, my baby showers, Christmas lunches, birthday parties, you're a natural!'

'You're right, I do enjoy it. I actually might just consider it. Thanks Zandile.'

Driving home after their lunch date, Zandile is energised by Xoliswa's excitement and wishes she could be so excited about her own life. The only thing that's plaguing her thoughts is what to cook for supper. The children are easy and always want spaghetti and meatballs. They could eat that every day of the week. Ndaba is fussy and doesn't like spaghetti, he doesn't believe in being served breakfast for dinner and doesn't eat leftovers. When he's away on business, they get away eating baked beans on toast, bacon and eggs and spaghetti bolognaise.

She's out of ideas and combs the deep freeze, finally settling on fish fillets. She's making the batter for the fish when she sees Ndaba's car pull into the driveway. It's early for him to be home already and as he walks into the house, he looks defeated. He doesn't stride in with the self-assurance he usually does and pulls out a chair and sits down. She pours him a cold glass of water but he asks for a whisky instead, telling her he's had a tough day.

She presumes the meeting with his bosses didn't go well.

'They're closing the bank, Zandi. The ZW division is loss-making and all our positions are going to be retrenched.'

Zandile pulls out another chair and sits down next to him.

He continues, 'They're offering us lucrative packages but how long will that last us?'

'At least the house is paid off. You'll get another job, babe,' and she puts her arm around him.

'I'm not so sure, Za. It's hard out there, really, really hard.'

'We'll make it,' she reassures him. 'We'll just have to cut back.'

He strokes her cheek lovingly, 'No more holidays in Europe for us, babe.'

She puts her hand over his, 'We'll survive. For richer or poorer.'

She leans forward and hugs him. They'll be fine. Life has its ups and downs and this is just one of the downs.

DECLINE

CAUGHT IN THE ACT

That Saturday afternoon, Yandisa leaves the salon at 3 pm which is pretty early for a Saturday but she's been invited to Sunette's baby shower. She still maintains ties with her friends but they aren't that close any more. It wasn't a deliberate decision, they've all just drifted apart over the years with the advent of marriage and babies and life in general. They don't have much in common any more, or the time to enjoy the few things they do have in common. Dumile told Yandisa she was going with Towanda so she really wanted to make an effort to be there.

Driving into town, the streets are deserted. Most shops close at 1 pm so it's only eateries, hair salons and bars that are still open. She's steering her car along Fort Street when she spots Wesley's BMW parked outside a dingy hotel. She carries on driving, deciding it's best to ignore it but she quickly changes her mind and makes a speedy U-turn at the next robot. She drives back at breakneck speed, her temper rising like the dial on the speedometer. She pulls into the parking space next to his car and marches into the hotel. It's one of those 1-star establishments that was last rated in the 1980s. The place smells of damp and disease and Yandisa wonders what kind of woman would agree to be bedded in such a place. Her skin crawls as she looks around. She demands to see Mr Bhunu and the young lady in the blue uniform at the reception desk looks down at the ledger listing all the guests' names. She looks back at Yandisa and tells her there is no one there by that name.

'Are you protecting him?' screams Yandisa.

'Madam, we don't have anyone here by that name,' replies the

369

woman, trying to be polite.

'Do you want me to cause a scene?' threatens Yandisa. 'I'll strip naked right here if I have to, I've got nothing to lose. Do you hear me?'

The security walks over to the reception desk and asks if everything is okay.

Yandisa takes out her wallet and shows the man a picture of Wesley.

'My husband's car is parked out front and I know he's here. I just want his room number.'

The security guard hesitates, 'We're not allowed to give out that information.'

Yandisa pulls out a wad of crisp bank notes from her wallet and shoves them in his hands.

'Room number?'

'Twenty-one,' he says, this time with no hesitation.

Yandisa doesn't trust the look of the caged lift that looks like it hasn't been serviced since 1976 so she takes the winding staircase which creaks as she climbs each step. As she races up the staircase, her blood pressure is escalating. She reaches a landing and takes another set of stairs to the second floor. By the time she knocks on the door, she's breathless.

'Wesley!' she screams, banging frantically on the door. 'Wesley!'

She turns the brass doorknob and to her surprise, the door opens, giving her a perfect view of the extent of Wesley's adultery. There is a naked woman straddling him, her pert breasts beckoning. He's lying on his back, his eyes closed in ecstasy. The woman sees her first and screams and jumps off him. Yandisa realises it is the same woman who was in Wesley's car at Zandile's 30th birthday party. The same woman she mauled in the car park. The same woman who landed her in jail.

Yandisa sees red and goes berserk. She charges towards the bed like a raging bull and scrambles onto the bed. What follows can only be described as an action sequence in a movie. The woman dives off the bed, picks up her clothes from the floor and runs out the room.

Yandisa lunges onto Wesley, strangling him, his face stoking her anger even further. He manages to remove her hands from around his neck but she carries on pounding her fists into him with all the fury she can muster. He finally manages to shove her away and she falls back onto the bed. He pounces on her and they fight, grappling with each other. Wesley easily overpowers her and they roll off the bed and land on the parquet flooring with a loud thud.

Wesley reigns his fists into her. Blow after blow until Yandisa loses count. Lying there it occurs to her that she might die in this confrontation. She tries to wrestle away from him and crawl away but he grabs her by the ankles. She manages to wriggle free.

By then a few guests have come out of their rooms to see what the noise is all about. Yandisa isn't sure what happens next and whether Wesley pushes her or she falls but she bounces down the staircase like a ball until she reaches the bottom. Where she lies rigid and unmoving.

Yandisa wakes up in hospital. Her body is bruised, her face a bloody pulp. She can see Abraham pacing the floor in her room. He is so angry and unable to process what has been inflicted on his daughter. He looks up and Wesley is casually walking down the corridor towards the hospital room. Abraham runs and launches himself on him and lets his rage loose. Wesley retaliates and the security guards have to prise the two men apart.

'I have done bad things in my life,' shouts Abraham vehemently. 'But the one thing I have never done is beat up a woman.'

Wesley is unrelenting, 'Maybe that's the problem, old man. If you'd disciplined Yandisa better maybe I wouldn't be dealing with this shit.'

Abraham tries lunging at Wesley again but the guards restrain him. Abraham tells them Wesley is barred from seeing Yandisa but Wesley is insistent that he has a 'right' to see his wife.

'You won't have any rights in jail,' says Abraham, adamant they need to press charges against Wesley.

Sis Ntombi steps in and tries to calm Abraham down and discourage him from making any rash decisions.

'Bhudi, your daughter has a mouth on her. I've experienced it first-hand!'

'Are you saying she deserved to be beaten like this?'

'I'm not saying anything. All I'm saying is hold off on the charges until you've heard his side of things.'

'I've seen Yandisa's side,' replies Abraham. 'I don't need to hear his. No man has the right to hit a woman. No man.'

Sis Ntombi merely shrugs her shoulders. Uncle Ben hit her a few times during the course of their marriage but she blamed his rage on his military background and he was a strict disciplinarian. Of course she'd never been hospitalised because the beatings were never *that* bad but it wasn't uncommon in their circles for men to slap women around. It was never so bad that you'd think of leaving a marriage or getting the police involved.

'I'm going to leave him,' says Yandisa, a few days later, her words barely audible. Her lips are cracked, swollen and bloodstained. She has lost a few teeth and can't open her mouth properly so she's being fed with a tube. Zandile, Xoliswa and Phumla visit her every day and cry at her bedside. They don't say much and Yandisa is worried she's paralysed and that the doctors haven't told her yet.

'How long has this been going on for, Yandisa?' asks Xoliswa. Her eyes misting over as she says the words they've all been dreading to say.

'Too long,' says Yandisa meekly.

She can't remember exactly when it started. Was it the night he slapped her outside the club? Was it the night he hit her when she refused to make him dinner? Was it when he kicked her in the stomach when she was seven months pregnant with Nicola? She flinches when she starts thinking about all the incidents, too many to even try and remember. She realises just how long Wesley has been beating her and how regular the beatings became. She's sustained so many injuries, she lost count along the way.

FOR THE CHILDREN'S SAKE

When Yandisa is discharged from hospital, she goes to her parents' house. With a broken arm and dislocated hip, there's very little she can do for herself. She asks Xoliswa to bring the children to her but Wesley won't allow Xoliswa in the house. They fight over the intercom.

'They are my kids!' he screams. 'You're not taking my kids!'

'Wesley, the kids need to be with their mother,' says Xoliswa.

'Fuck you, Xoliswa! What do you know? You're raising a bastard and you're trying to tell me about what's best for my kids! If Yandisa wants to see the kids, she must come home.'

Xoliswa almost rams her car into the gate but common sense prevails and she drives away. The schools are closed for the holidays so she has no way of getting to them. Kidnapping will get her into all kinds of trouble anyway. She had consulted a lawyer and he had explained that there are laws stipulating that every parent has an inherent right to their children. He also explained that biological fathers have full rights and parental responsibilities.

'The only way your sister can get full control of the children is through litigation. She would have to prove in a court of law that Wesley is a bad father and that because he is abusive, it is in the best interests of the children that they reside with her.'

'The law is an arse. Maybe if we kill him it might speed up the process.'

When she arrives home that day without the children, Yandisa is crestfallen and her body is wracked with sobs. Xoliswa can't hold back her own tears and hates seeing her sister in so much pain. They all do. Abraham and Phumla desperately want to help but they feel

374

so helpless.

'I want my babies, Daddy! Do something!' Yandisa cries.

'There's nothing we can do,' responds Abraham. 'He's their father and the kids aren't in any danger so our hands are tied.'

She curls up on her bed, the numerous cracked ribs make breathing an excruciating task. Her mother bathes her every morning and softly sponges down her damaged and bruised body. She pats her body dry and Yandisa winces in pain. She only has the use of one arm and the family rallies to help and support her. Zandile helps Evelyn in the salon, making sure everything runs smoothly. Phumla helps nurse the physical scars while Yandisa wrestles with the emotional ones. The women from church come to the house every night and pray for her. Prayers of strength, courage and restoration.

Zandile decides to appeal to Wesley because unlike his relationship with Xoliswa, theirs is much more cordial. When he allows her access to the house, she considers it a mini triumph and a step closer to Yandisa seeing her children again. She pulls up the driveway and Babalwa comes out to greet her. It always amazes Zandile how grown-up she is; a young woman and no longer a child.

Babalwa is wearing a tiny denim skirt, a skirt so tiny it looks like a belt barely covering her pert ass, and a boob tube over her buxom breasts. She takes after her mother in that department. It bothers Zandile that her niece is so scantily dressed, especially around Wesley. She puts the thought aside, hating herself for even thinking that Wesley might harm her but the thought still niggles at her.

'Hey Aunt Za,' Babalwa says, giving her a hug.

'Hey Babs, how are you? Is everything good?'

'I could be better,' says Babalwa. 'I thought maybe you were bringing Yandisa home.'

Zandile knows Babs has been calling her mother by her first name all her life but it sounds strange and somehow impertinent. She realises it's a big ask for her to make the switch after so many years.

'It would be nice if you went to see your mom,' says Zandile.

'Does she want to see *me*?'

'She wants to see *all* her kids,' says Zandile pointedly, even though Yandisa hasn't actually said anything specific about seeing Babalwa.

'Are the kids inside?' asks Zandile.

'Yes. You can tell my mom that I'm taking good care of them and being a responsible big sister.'

Zandile throws her arm around Babalwa as they walk into the house. Wesley is sprawled on the couch in the living room, his T-shirt on the floor, playing with the children. When the children see Zandile, they run over to her and jump into her arms. Wesley slips on his discarded T-shirt.

'Where is Jason?' she asks, looking around the room.

'In his bedroom,' says Babalwa, 'he loves playing by himself.'

Babalwa sits down on the couch opposite Wesley and puts her feet up on the coffee table. The way she's sitting, Zandile can see her underwear but she bites her lip and keeps her disapproval to herself.

'Hello, Za,' says Wesley, standing up to greet her.

He asks after Ndaba and the children. She can't see much point in asking how he is because he seems quite content.

'I came here to ask you to bring the kids to see Yandisa.'

'If Yandisa wants to see the kids she can come home,' he says. 'What's this nonsense of her staying at your parents' house anyway?'

Zandile asks Babalwa to take the kids to play outside. She hates having confrontations in front of kids and her and Ndaba always try and make a mindful effort not fight in front of their own and while they don't always get it right, they try.

'Wesley, you're being difficult. Yandisa is afraid to come home.'

'Afraid of what? She ambushed me that day, Zandile. I was just trying to protect myself, you can ask all the witnesses who saw it all happen. I was afraid for my life. You have no idea how crazy your sister is when she gets into a jealous rage.'

Zandile restrains herself from calling him a liar and fights the anger rising.

'Tell Yandisa that if she doesn't come home, it means she wants to end this marriage. Which is fine because we'll go to court and do things the right way and I'll fight for my kids. I love my kids, Zandile and no one is going to take my kids away from me!'

'Wesley, nobody wants to take the kids away. Yandisa just wants to see them.'

'Tell her to come and see them here. One of you can escort her if she's so afraid but you can tell that father of yours that I'm not bringing my kids to his house and he must never try and set foot in mine.'

After a few more futile attempts at appealing to Wesley, Yandisa has no choice and goes to visit her children at the house. They have been told she was in an accident and definitely spared the ugly truth. Accompanied by her mother or one of her sisters, seeing their faces again and holding them close, helps her heal. They cry when she has to leave so she tries to convince Wesley to let her take them for a few days but he refuses, so the visits continue for more than a month. Yandisa shuttles back and forth until Xoliswa arrives at her parents' house one evening and Yandisa is not there. She's moved back home for the sake of the children. They all feel utterly betrayed by her decision.

THE HOMECOMING

Yandisa finally finds the strength to return home. She can't hide at her parents' home forever and knows that sooner or later she's going to have to pick up the pieces of her broken life. It feels strange walking back into her house after such a prolonged absence. Nothing has changed and everything is in its place, it's like she never left. She sees the look of relief on Lovemore and MamTembo's faces. MamTembo assures her that the household has been running smoothly and she's made sure the children have been well taken care of. The children are thrilled that she's home and Ethan is incredibly clingy. He hangs onto her legs and won't leave her side, worried that she's going to leave again. Babalwa is indifferent towards her and continues to harbour unspoken animosity.

They all sit down to supper together that night and Jason says grace: 'Dear God. Thank you for the food. Thank you for bringing back our mom home. We love her so much. Thank you God.'

They all join in the noisy chorus of 'Amen' and it takes Yandisa a few minutes to compose herself. She's so happy to be home and to be able to tuck the children into bed. She reads to the girls and then to Jason. Ethan eventually falls asleep after she straps him onto her back. MamTembo confesses that she too had to soothe him to sleep that way in Yandisa's absence.

She finally goes to her own bedroom and stands in the doorway, for what seems like an eternity. The bathroom door still has a gaping hole in it from when Wesley kicked it open. He had dragged her out of the bathroom by the hair. She touches her head. The doctors had to shave her hair to be able to stitch where her scalp had split open. It feels liberating not having to worry about her hair or a weave, there is

378

nothing Wesley could hold onto any more. She recalls an incident when he pulled out a tuft of her hair, like he was uprooting weeds. She shakes her head, trying to shake away the memory.

She glances at the phone next to the bed and it evokes yet another painful memory of her trying to crawl towards the phone, hoping to dial for help after another violent clash. Wesley had tried to strangle her with the cord. Even the bed is triggering because as much as they had made passionate love on it, the violent episodes overshadow any good memories. Like when he was choking her while he raped her. Yandisa decided she's not going to sleep in their bedroom. Everything in it elicited a memory she would much rather forget. The walls remind her of being bashed into them. The mirrors always caught her at her worst; the bloodied reflection of her pain.

She decides to sleep in the spare room and empties her closets and moves all her clothes. It's after midnight when she finally finishes moving everything and Wesley is still not home. She's relieved as she's not ready to see him. When she wakes up in the morning, she's startled to see him standing in the doorway, looking at her strangely.

'It's good to have you back,' he says. 'Welcome home.'

I wish I could say the same to you, she thinks to herself.

'I've had problems sleeping alone, I missed having you in our bed.'

She can't help herself and says, 'Why didn't you call Christabel to keep you company?'

'Yandisa, I'm sorry about all of this. I got us into this mess and I'm sorry. I don't know what to do to make things right but I need you. I can't do this without you.'

Yandisa stares at him long and hard and for the first time sees what a pathetic man he is. She feels the anger threatening to explode inside her like a volcano erupting but she doesn't give into it and instead looks away.

'Come back to our bed,' he says.

'I need space, Wesley. Give me space.'

Yandisa turns over on her side and pulls the blankets tight around her. It's not a cold day but there's a distinct chill in the air. She has no desire to return to their bedroom or sleep beside him and she's glad to hear the footfall of his steps down the passage as he walks away. The children come into the room a short while later and jump into the bed. They snuggle under the covers with her. She's so happy to be close to them again.

'Why aren't you sleeping with Daddy?'asks Nicola.

'I just need to be by myself,' replies Yandisa. She doesn't know how else to explain the concept of privacy to little children who often ambush her when she is in the toilet. Jason looks at her, not convinced by her explanation.

'Well, when you are tired of being by yourself can we sleep with you?' he asks.

Yandisa laughs and hugs them all close.

Wesley continues to appeal to Yandisa to move back into their room and she continues to rebuff his advances. He buys her flowers. He buys her chocolates. But she's unmoved. He soon runs out of ideas and decides to reach out to Sis Ntombi. Culture demands that marital conflict be resolved by respected third parties such as aunts and uncles. Resorting to marriage counsellors and psychologists is unheard of. Priests and pastors are the next best thing for strict members of the church. But as the fabric of extended family has started to fray, many have resorted to privately outsourcing paid assistance. Moreso, some feel that they cannot trust their aunts or uncles and so 'keeping it in the family' is not an option.

Sis Ntombi is touched that Wesley reaches out to her. Yandisa would never talk to her and would definitely confide in Sis Lungile if she ever needed help.

'I didn't know who to turn to, Sis Ntombi,' says Wesley. 'You were my first point of contact when I joined this family so I thought I should come to you.'

'Wesley, my door is always open when you need me,' replies Sis Ntombi.

She offers him tea but he declines and instead asks for a whisky. Uncle Ben's collection is still intact, one of the only things left that belonged to him.

'Yandisa no longer sleeps with me, Auntie,' says Wesley after a gulp of a single malt.

Sis Ntombi exhales, 'That *is* bad. Marriage is sex and if you don't have that then marriages fall apart.'

'She denies me sex, Auntie, and when I start sleeping around she complains. What am I supposed to do? I can't live without sex. She's my wife and it is her duty to satisfy me. She's even moved out of our bedroom.'

Sis Ntombi shakes her head in disbelief. The idea of Yandisa denying her husband conjugal rights is despicable. She's ashamed to hear what Yandisa is doing in her marriage and remembers that she didn't get 'the talk' after her wedding.

'Listen Wesley, I'll speak to her. Then I'll possibly call you both here to talk about this issue openly and honestly.'

Wesley accepts Sis Ntombi's advice and pours himself another whisky. Sis Ntombi encourages him to stay for lunch and he eventually leaves well after three o'clock when he has to fetch the children from school. As soon as he leaves, Sis Ntombi calls her sister and they chew over the matter. She then calls Yandisa and demands an audience with her.

'I'm busy,' says Yandisa. 'What's so important that I have to come to your house?'

'Your marriage. Or don't you care about salvaging it?'

'Sis Ntombi, you know nothing about my marriage so stay out of it.'

'I know that you're not sleeping with your husband. He was here and told me all about it. Do you know the fastest way to lose a man is to deny him sex, Yandisa!'

'So is that why Uncle Ben died in the arms of another woman?'

Sis Ntombi is speechless and quickly hangs up.

FINDING MYSELF

Zandile is angry at Yandisa's decision to return to her dysfunctional marriage and she knows Yandisa deserves better. She is plagued by guilt as she considers leaving her own marriage. By all accounts, her and Ndaba have a good marriage. Ndabenhle loves her and the children and has never raised his hand.

She feels stifled. The feeling of being trapped that she felt on her wedding day has returned. Her home feels like a prison and she feels oppressed by the institution of marriage.

After Ndaba's retrenchment, she's spent a lot of time online doing research. The bank gave him three months notice and being part of senior management, he had been promised a lucrative retrenchment package. They've indicated that it will be paid in US dollars. Ndaba is considering opening his own business but Zandile is sceptical, not that she doubts his ability, she doubts the economic climate in Zimbabwe. It's not conducive for business, for new opportunities and so many people are struggling to stay afloat.

The bank closes its doors after three months and Ndaba waits patiently for the package, that has not yet materialised. There is some complication about repatriating funds to Zimbabwe, they say but the bigger issue is that they might not be able to withdraw the money as foreign currency. While Ndaba stresses over the issues surrounding the package and how to circumvent them, Zandile tries to convince Ndaba to consider moving abroad. Maqhawe and Chandelle relocated to Germany and while Mack found it hard and the language difficult to learn, they are sticking it out. His family are critical of him; why didn't he stay and make things work here? But Ndaba is adamant that he doesn't want to live in Europe or the UK, despite having permanent residence there.

Zandile had always thought Ndaba's family had been well-off knowing that he had studied overseas but that wasn't the case. Ndabenhle told her that his dad, the late Mongezi Khumalo, was a chef at a local hotel. As a result of his dad's cooking career, their house was always filled with intoxicating smells as their dad tried replicating recipes at home when they had money to buy the ingredients. Ndaba was obsessed with freshly baked bread and scones because of his memories from that time. His father would often bring home leftover food from the hotel buffet.

Selina, Ndaba's mother, was a clerk at the city hall and Ndaba has fond memories of how she loved wearing stilettos and bell-bottom trousers. She had a crown of hair in those days but she'd lost it in her old age so her bald head is now always covered with a colourful doek.

Ndaba always spoke fondly of his childhood spent playing on the streets of Lobengula township. Butho was the oldest child, followed by Nandi and then Ndaba. For years it was just the three of them and then Nkululeko and Maqhawe were born years later in quick succession. Almost like an afterthought. The older siblings teased them and called them 'pension babies'. Except their father never received his pension and was robbed of his life just shy of his 51st birthday.

He didn't live to see his firstborn graduate from the local polytechnic college. Butho, just like his father, chose to work in the hospitality industry. He secured a job at the same hotel his father had worked at all his life and was very aware that he had to step into his father's shoes. The title of Khumalo Snr was levied on him, along with the responsibility of educating his siblings and helping his mother with the bills and general upkeep of the home.

When Butho met his future wife, Edna, he was still living at home and she understood, having come from a large family herself, about growing up on the benevolence of family members. When they got married, she moved in with him and his family as he always said that he had no intention of moving out until all his siblings had left. Thankfully this process happened slightly quicker than he antici-pated.

Nandi, who was two years younger than Butho, had just finished high school. She was a brilliant student and the nuns from her school managed to secure her a scholarship to study in London. She completed her degree in banking and finance and later did her masters in the same field. At that time, Ndaba had just finished his A levels and found work in a bank as a teller. After a few years, once Nandi established herself in a secure job in London, she sent for Ndaba and was able to fund his tertiary education. When Ndaba completed his studies, he then got a job and put his two younger brothers through university, relieving Nandi of the burden.

Ndaba had told Zandile about a woman by the name of Shelley Keyes, that he had been in love with. They met at university and he had been captivated by the sheen of her blonde hair that cascaded down her shoulders and her blue eyes that sparkled like sapphires.

'I'm sure she was captivated by your dark skin and big dick!' teased Zandile.

Ndaba laughed, 'Don't be jealous, Zandile!'

They dated for over a five years and he had always put off asking her to marry him because of his obligations to his brothers and taking care of his family back home. Shelley could never understand this as it was just her and her brother, Sebastian, living in a pretty borough in Buckinghamshire and they didn't have the complication of supporting an extended family. Shelley couldn't understand the obligation the family felt to contribute to buying Selina a house in the suburbs. Or the reason why they all contributed to Butho's hunting concession.

'Why didn't you marry her?' Zandile had asked Ndaba.

'She got tired of waiting and maybe deep down I knew I wouldn't fit in.'

'You wouldn't have had to fit in, Ndaba. She would've married you and like Chandelle married Maqhawe, she fits in with him.'

Maybe Ndaba married her because she fitted in, because she was the blueprint for the perfect wife. She had been the love that made sense to him but not necessarily the love that made him lose all his senses. Zandile realised that Ndaba had really lived life before he met her. He'd travelled the world and gone to places she'd only ever dreamt about and all these years later, she's starting to feel half alive.

These thoughts never leave her as she combs through websites looking for job opportunities in Johannesburg and Cape Town. One day he peers over her shoulder while she is on the computer.

'What are you doing?' he asks.

'I'm job hunting,' she replies.

'Zandile, please don't undermine me. I will take care of you and the kids, you don't need to work.'

'I want to work,' she replies. 'This is not about you, it's about me.'

'You'll never get a job. You think people are crawling to employ someone who has been out of the job market for over eight years, Zandile?'

His barb makes her more determined to find a job to prove him wrong.

She spends hours submitting online applications, populating forms and submitting her CV. Luckily she has a South African ID, that her mother insisted her and her sisters needed to get. So while visiting Aunt Phatiswa at eLindini in the Eastern Cape when they were kids, Phumla marched them all to the Home Affairs Department in Mthatha. Having the ID, also meant Zandile had been able to study in South Africa and apply for funding.

The document makes her job-hunting process slightly easier as she doesn't have the bureaucratic headache of having to apply for a work permit. A few days after submitting an application, she receives a call from an architectural firm in Cape Town. This is followed up by a telephonic interview and they had lauded her on her academic achievements. It reminds Zandile what a brilliant student she was and how her achievements and talent had been overshadowed by the demands of becoming a wife and mother and keeping a house. A letter follows with a job offer for a candidate architect and to say she felt elated, would be an understatement. When she shows the letter to Ndaba he doesn't share in her sentiments and dampens the celebratory mood she was in. She had secretly been hoping he would pop a bottle of champagne later in their bedroom and really celebrate with her.

'South Africa is so dangerous,' he said. 'I don't know if I want to relocate there with the kids.'

'What country isn't dangerous? Come on, Ndaba! This job means a lot to me and the fact that they even considered me after being out of the job market for so long is a big deal.'

'What would I do there?'

'You'll find something. Maybe not straight away but you will,' she says encouragingly.

'But I told you that I'm thinking of establishing a small micro-finance thing. We'll make a plan, I promise. Besides, this job of yours is only offering what, R20k a month?'

'Don't belittle me, Ndaba. It's not about the money, it's about my dreams. I didn't spend four years at university so that I could sit at home and do the school run. This is not what I signed up for!'

'So what are you saying? Are you not happy with us? With this?'

'Ndaba, allow me to live my dream. I've lived yours and now it's my turn.'

'But Zandile I have given you everything! How many women can say they have what you have?'

'Ndaba! I told you, this is not about you it's about me and what I want. Are you even listening?'

By now, Zandile is shouting in untold frustration. He holds his hands up in resignation and tells her he can't speak to her when she's like this when she gets crazy and irrational. He says they'll talk about it in the morning but she insists there is nothing more to talk about. She tells him she's accepting the job offer but he doesn't respond and disappears into the bathroom. That night they go to bed without talking to each other and with unresolved issues between them.

Zandile is unable to sleep. Why can't he understand how much she has lost of herself trying to build a life with him? Why can't he recognise that she needs to find herself again? She's got so lost in the Mrs so-and-so that all she knows is how to be a wife and mother. She doesn't know how to be Zandile any more and she's scared that if she doesn't try and reclaim herself now, she never will.

The following morning, she makes breakfast in silence. He eats without saying a word and the children come into the kitchen, breaking the silence with their boisterous banter.

'So when do they want you to start this job?'

'Next month,' she replies.

'But that's two weeks away,' he says.

'Yes, I know that.'

'So what is going to happen with the kids?'

'You'll be here, won't you,' she says. 'They're *your* kids too.'

She feels a twinge of guilt about leaving the children behind. Maybe she is being too rash.

'So you've got this all figured out then?'

'I do. I'm moving to Cape Town to start working and when I'm settled, you and the kids can join me.'

'What if I don't want to join you?'

'Then I guess it will be the end of our marriage as we know it.'

She leaves the house to escape the anxiety and meets up with Xoliswa at the gym. They do the circuit together, chatting between the punishing reps. Xoliswa admires her sister's resolve when she tells her what she's decided.

'So you're willing to throw away your whole marriage for this career thing?'

'Yes, I am,' says Zandile, with conviction. 'For the first time in my life, I'm filled with a sense of purpose.' Xoliswa isn't convinced Zandile is going to carry out her plan.

Tensions are high in the Khumalo household and Zandile is due to leave in a few days and Ndaba doesn't believe she is going to actually leave until he sees that her suitcases are packed. 'Where are you staying?' he asks.

'I've arranged to stay with some friends.'

Zandile has reconnected with some of her old university friends in the days leading up to her departure, including Kirsten, who has offered her the use of her studio in Cape Town because she is currently staying on a wine farm with her parents.

'You are still my wife, Zandile,' he says when she tells him the details. 'I can't have my wife living alone in some studio in Cape Town.'

'Ndaba, it's not a big deal. It's only until I get on my feet.'

'No. You're going to stay with my cousin Ntando and her husband. What do you think the family will say if they hear you are roughing it up in some studio?'

Zandile agrees only because she doesn't want to antagonise Ndaba even further a few days before she leaves. But staying with her sister's ex-boyfriend and his wife is not exactly the kind of living arrangement that sits well with her. It's arranged that Ntando will pick her up at the airport and she'll stay with her and Thulani until she's settled.

Zandile feels a pang of regret when she says goodbye to her children but she knows she's doing the right thing. They think she's going on another shopping trip to Johannesburg not realising she won't be back a few days later. Ndaba holds onto her for a long time and she can see he's fighting back tears.

'Are you really going to leave us? Just like this?'

She doesn't respond and turns and walks away, fighting back her own tears.

She gets on the plane later that day and as it ascends into the air, she feels a deep sense of liberation.

A DIVIDED HOUSE

Nicola is deeply perturbed by the new sleeping arrangements in the Bhunu household and of all the children, she is the most affected by the status quo of her parents' relationship. She adores her father and can't understand why her mother doesn't want to be with him.

'Why don't you sleep with Mummy any more?' Nicola asks Wesley one afternoon while she's sitting on his lap.

'Your mother doesn't love me any more,' he replies. 'That's why I have to have my own room and she has hers.'

Nicola is horrified and runs to Yandisa with tears in her eyes. 'Why don't you love Daddy any more?' she cries. 'It's mean and Jesus says we must love everyone. That is what they teach us at Sunday school. You're mean, Mummy!'

Nicola runs out of the bedroom crying and Yandisa follows her to her room and tries to comfort her but she is inconsolable. She cries until she eventually falls asleep in Yandisa's arms, utterly exhausted. After she has put Nicola to bed, she pauses at the door of Jason's room and tells him her and Wesley are having adult problems but everything is going to be okay.

Jason throws his arms around her and she feels comforted by him. She heads downstairs to confront Wesley, who is watching European League soccer on TV.

'Wesley! What did you say to Nicola about me?'

He ignores her and his eyes remain transfixed to the screen. She reaches for the remote control on the table and switches the TV off.

'Hey! I'm watching that!' he barks at her.

'I'm talking to you. What did you tell the kids about us?'

'Nicola asked me why we don't sleep in the same room any more. I told her the truth, that you don't love me any more.'

'How could you say that?' shouts Yandisa.

Her chest is vibrating with rage whereas Wesley is calm and complacent.

'Children need to be told the truth.'

'Wesley, they're children. They don't understand. You could have made up something to them.'

'Why tell them lies when it's true that you don't love me any more?' He stands up to face her.

'Wesley, it's not right to involve the children in our problems.'

'Well, it's true, isn't it? You don't love me any more.'

'Did you tell them *why* I don't love you any more? Did you tell them about all the other whores?'

'They didn't ask,' he replies flippantly.

His response incenses Yandisa and she's tempted to pick up the thick book on the coffee table and hit him over the head with it but she stops herself and decides to walk away. She's barely out of the living room when he calls out to her, 'So since I'm no longer screwing you, can I bring my girlfriends to the house?'

'Go ahead, Wesley. Your children can see what a bastard you are.'

Yandisa continues upstairs. She refuses to be goaded into a physical confrontation. As she heads to her own bedroom, she walks past Babalwa's room. She can hear the TV is on and she barges into her daughter's room. She shouts at her and reminds Babs about her ghastly report at school for the previous term.

'You can't afford to watch TV and do homework at the same time!'

'I've finished my homework,' replies Babalwa.

'Well, then turn off the TV and study! And you're grounded.'

'Don't come in here and bully me, Yandisa. You can't stand up to Wesley so you'd rather come in here and pick a fight with me.'

Yandisa retaliates by slapping Babalwa across the face.

'Don't you ever speak to me like that! Do you hear me?'

She storms out of the room and leaves Babalwa sobbing quietly. Later, Babalwa looks up and sees Wesley standing at her bedroom door.

'Are you okay?' he asks.

'Actually, I'm not. Why is Yandisa on my case all the time?'

'Your mother is giving us all a hard time,' says Wesley. 'She can't stand me and is on my case about everything.'

'Well, she can't stand me either and sometimes I wonder why she even brought me here!'

'I begged her to bring you here, Babs. I told her that it wasn't right that you carried on living with your grandparents. For years they tried to keep you a secret and she was ashamed of you, Babs.'

Babalwa's eyes fill with tears. Wesley has confirmed what she always suspected.

'Sssh,' whispers Wesley, placing a cajoling arm around her. 'I love you. That's why you're here.'

'Do you really love me?' croaks Babalwa.

'I love you like I love Jason, Nicola and Ethan. You're like a daughter to me.'

Babalwa sobs even harder, burying her head in his chest. Wesley can feel her breasts pressing into him and he feels himself go hard. She smells good too, like wild vanilla. A small voice in his head tells him to push her away, that this is not the way he's supposed to feel about his stepdaughter. But the bigger voice in his head tells him that these feelings are natural.

'Don't cry,' croons Wesley, stroking her back, 'everything is going to be alright.'

She looks up at him from behind a film of tears.

'Do you really mean that?'

'Of course I do.'

Babalwa leans forward and kisses him gently on the lips. Wesley reciprocates, pressing into her and he knows he has crossed a line that can't be uncrossed. At that moment, an alliance is formed between them, fostered in their shared enmity of Yandisa.

391

WHY WOULD YOU STAY?

Xoliswa can't understand why her sister has chosen to return to the toxicity of her marriage. Especially after the family rallied behind her to provide her with all the support she needed, both financial and emotional.

'Why would you stay with him?' she pleads with Yandisa. 'After everything he has done to you. Don't you have a sense of self-worth?'

Yandisa looked her in the eyes, 'Wow, Xolie! You want to talk to *me* about self-worth! Why do you stay with CC? He's just as abusive. He hides you from the rest of the world like a dirty little secret. He uses you to fulfil his pleasure and then throws money at you to keep you quiet. And you want to talk to me about self-worth!'

'Yandisa, that's not the same thing.'

'Yes, it is. You don't think it is but it is. He manipulates you and you fall for it every time. You interfere in my business and ask me why I haven't left Wesley but why haven't you left CC? There are so many single guys out there but you choose to be with a married man.

'Admit it Xolie, you're with him because you're a coward. You're afraid of putting yourself out there. CC is a safe bet because you don't want to get hurt again. Just like me. I stay because I am afraid of starting over and because I have three fucking kids, Xolie! I run a business that barely makes the bottom line any more. That's why I've chosen to stay.'

'I'm not a coward,' says Xoliswa defensively. 'I've put my heart on the line a few times for relationships. You don't know what it's like!'

People who are married with children often assume the dating world is full of opportunities. It isn't. Xoliswa has sampled the various options and reached the conclusion that the single and eligible men are that way for a reason. No one wants them. After Thulani, she had put herself out there. She went on blind dates, she allowed a friend of a friend to introduce her to a fantastic guy. They were always 'fantastic' guys, that was how they were marketed but no one ever tells the truth about them.

There had been Alois Siziba. He wasn't married but had a son from a previous relationship. He often spoke about the mother with great acrimony. He had worked in the same department as Zandile at the City Council years ago and she had sold him to Xolie as a 'sweet, soft-spoken guy'. In other words, boring. Listening to him talk was like watching paint dry but Xoliswa persevered and gave him a chance. She never contemplated having sex with him and his kisses inspired chastity. So for many months they held hands. He was a safe bet. He brought her flowers at work sometimes and took her for lunch. A date was a trip to the movies and if he was feeling adventurous, maybe watching the soccer at Barbourfields Stadium.

Most of the time he wanted her to go to his house and cook for him. He had a lovely three-bedroomed house in the suburbs that he was proud of and time and time again he reminded her how hard he worked to get where he was. He didn't drink which meant she didn't feel comfortable drinking in his presence and while he didn't explicitly tell her *not* to drink, the comments he made when he saw women drinking made it clear how he felt about alcohol.

'*Umfaz' onatha ibeer yisifebe.* A woman who drinks beer is a whore.'

'And wine?' she had asked cheekily.

'*Iwine ngeyamalema*! Wine is for dimwits.'

They started having sex and it was as rigid, as strait-laced and vanilla as he was. He was clear that he didn't want any 'funny business' which meant oral sex was definitely off the table. Once, while watching a movie together, the woman reached for the man's cock and popped it into her mouth like a lollipop and he had been so disgusted, he changed the channel.

'What is this world coming too? Why are people eating each other? It's disgusting.'

Xoliswa had feigned horror but deep down she was thinking that if she married him, she'd never be muffed again. Alois was serious about their relationship and often spoke about marriage. He did propose and he was very surprised when she turned him down. This was followed by rampant verbal abuse.

'How can you say no to marriage?' he said, shocked that she had rejected him. 'Do you have any idea how many women would kill to be married to a man like me?'

'It's just not going to work between us,' she had replied calmly.

'*Hehehe, Xolie, uyazitshela hayikhona*! You are so full of yourself! You think you are in demand but you're not getting any younger. How many men do you think will want you with that bastard child of yours? I'm actually doing you a favour by taking you on.'

Xoliswa was glad to walk away from the relationship but he wasn't done yet and showed up at her office one morning armed with receipts, demanding a refund for all the money he had spent on her. In return, she wrote him an invoice demanding a refund for the lousy sex.

After Alois, she had started dating Ernest Moyo. She met him at Babalwa's school fun day as his son was in Babs' class. Prior to that, she had seen him in Bulawayo business circles and was sure she had met him at a golf day. What she found interesting about him, aside from the fact that he was an eligible divorcee, was that he had full custody of his three kids, ranging in age from five to ten. On their first date he had taken her to his house, a Mediterranean-styled villa with white stonewashed tapioca walls.

'You have a beautiful house,' she had remarked.

'Stick around long enough and it could be yours.'

He took her by the hand and led her into the house and told her he wanted her to meet his children.

They came running when they heard their father beckoning. First was a little girl in a pink frock with smocking at the front, her bushy mane secured in a ponytail.

'Hi Daddy!'

'Hello, angel,' he responded, scooping her up into his arms. 'I want you to meet my friend, Xoliswa.'

'Is she your girlfriend?' asks the little girl, Davina.

They both laugh. Next, Kim who is eight and Delvyn who is ten, come through to meet her. She hits it off with all the children so she knows she's in. His children adore her and she can already see three-year-old Owami fitting in the equation. Their relationship progresses quickly with lots of sleepovers and dates with the children. They go on holiday with the children and she loves the fact that Ernest is a hands-on dad. She finds that an admirable and endearing quality in a man.

Everyone loves Ernest and he sometimes plays golf with Ndaba. On Sundays, Ernest and her go to church together and afterwards they all have Sunday lunch together. Everyone thought the marital bells were ringing loudly until one day Xoliswa stumbled across his Facebook page. There were photos of him in various places, in various poses, with a pretty young woman by the name of Thenjiwe.

Ernest travelled a lot for work and he often left her in his house looking after his kids. She drove all his cars, from the Discovery Land Rover to the sporty two-door Mercedes and even knew the code to his safe. She drove his children to and from school and when Davina had a temperature, she rushed her to the ER. When Delvyn needed a haircut, she took him to the barber at Yandisa's salon. When Kim had a ballet recital and her dad couldn't make it, she stepped in. But as she scoured his profile, there was not one picture of her but plenty of him and his kids and him and Thenjiwe. There was not one photo of any of the holidays they went on together. She then realised that she was nothing but a glorified housekeeper to him. She babysat his children in exchange for sex. She dumped him without a second thought and of course he told her she was over-reacting.

'I want to keep our relationship private!' he told her.

'But you want to keep your other one public? The one you are proud to flaunt?'

'It's not what you think,' he said. 'You're being too rash.'

Breaking up with Ernest had been easy, breaking up with his children had been hard. Many months after the break-up they continued to call her, wanting to see her, telling her how much they missed her. So she was glad when he got a job in Harare and the whole family relocated. He eventually married Thenjiwe and from time to time he would send her messages on Facebook telling her that he missed her and that he had made a mistake. She blocked him.

Then she had tried Munya. Five years younger than her, he had none of the encumbrances of children or an ex-wife. He was mature for his age and said he had no qualms about dating an older woman. He was a go-getter and rapidly climbing the career ladder but for someone who was supposedly single he was always unavailable. He cancelled dates at the last minute. Or his phone would be switched off the whole weekend and he would call her on Monday after some 'hectic' weekend and then want to meet for lunch. However, the sex between them was mind-blowing and it kept Xoliswa going back for more. The memories of the orgasms lingered longer after all the glaring inconsistencies in the relationship. The final straw was when they were supposed to meet for dinner one night and he stood her up.

She had arrived at the restaurant that night a little after 7 pm and Munya was nowhere to be seen. He was obviously running a bit late so she ordered a cappuccino and sipped on it slowly, trying to look nonplussed as she sat alone in the restaurant. A few men were sitting at the bar having drinks and there were two couples gazing into each other's eyes. At another table, a group of young women were having a good time as they all sipped on cocktails. She looked at her watch, it was almost 8 pm and there was still no sign of Munya. She reached for her cellphone and decided to call him but he didn't answer. She tried again but still nothing. She decided to order food and hailed to the waiter to bring her the menu. She ordered lamb chops and chips and polished her plate clean and then ordered a brandy and coke. She tried Munya again but his phone was switched off. She gulped down the brandy and coke, trying to ease her anger. She looked around, feeling like a fool and like she had STOOD UP engraved across her forehead. She beckoned to the waiter and paid her bill. She picked up her handbag and what was left of her dignity and headed back to the hotel. She stopped at a 24-hour bottle store along the way and bought a bottle of Smirnoff Vodka which she took to bed.

That night she decides she's done dating and is going to focus on raising Owami on her own and building the business. She does what most self-help books prescribe, 'dating yourself' and 'loving yourself' and in the midst of it all, Keith reaches out to her a few of times with sms apologies. She asks him about the money he took of hers but he never responds so she blocks him too.

When she meets CC, she's not looking for a man or relationship and is single and happy. But she's tired of masturbating so when CC offers her sex without the commitment and expectation that comes with most relationships, she accepts. Initially, it was just supposed to be a bit of fun. A fling. Every time they had sex, she swore it would be the last time. She tried breaking things off with him a few times, only to wake up in the middle of the night yearning for his touch.

People say the high of illicit sex fades but here they are, two years later, and still at it.

'CC still makes me happy, Yandisa, so that's why I stay. The day he stops making me happy, I'll leave. When was the last time Wesley made you happy?'

Her question lingers in the air and goes unanswered.

SINGLE BUT MARRIED

Living with Thulani and Ntando is almost like Zandile is eaves-dropping on what her sister's life could have been like. They are certainly living large in a duplex cluster in Newlands and Zandile loves the fact that it's so close to her work. Ntando offers her the use of their spare car, a BMW sedan, while Thulani drives a sleek Porsche Cayenne and Ntando a sleek Mercedes convertible. They are both the epitome of success in their chosen careers. Thulani is a chief investment officer with an investment fund while Ntando manages a huge portfolio at one of the big four banks. They earn the kind of salaries that have a lot of zeroes attached as well as huge performance bonuses.

While scaling the corporate ladder, Ntando managed to find the time to have two little boys: Noah and Elijah. From the time she landed in Cape Town, Ntando has been welcoming and conciliatory and has gone out of her way to make her feel at home. Zandile isn't sure whether she's always this nice or if she's just trying to compensate for the awkward bit of history she has with Xoliswa. Thulani acts like the past never happened and makes no mention of her sister. She doesn't see much of him as he works late and often gets home after 8 pm when the boys are already in bed. Ntando also works crazy hours which means Zandile is often at home with the boys and relieves their nanny. Playing with the boys makes her miss her own children. She doesn't call them often because the calls end in tears after they ask her when she's coming home and she has no definitive answer. Ndaba had sent her babies to live with his mother in Sunninghill because he said he wasn't coping on his own. This annoys her no end. How can he not be coping with his own kids? She wonders if it's because he needs a little bit of freedom to mingle. The thought of this makes her insanely jealous. She had never considered that Ndaba would ever cheat on her but here they are living apart thousands of kilometres away from each other for the first time in their marriage.

'Are you going to live like a bachelor in that huge house?' she asks him one evening on the phone.

'I was thinking of getting a roommate,' he replies, 'since my wife abandoned me.'

He laughs but she doesn't find it the least bit funny.

'Only joking! I've decided I'm going to go and live with Mama and the kids. This house is far too big for me now that I'm single but married.'

That does not appease Zandile either. She lets it go because she does not want to fight with him. He tells her that he has put the house on the market for rental as there is interest from NGOs who need long-stay accommodation. And that way the house will generate enough income for maintenance and general upkeep.

'What's going to happen to us, Zandile?'

'I'd like for you and the children to join me here. We could have a good life here, Ndaba. You should see what a good life Ntando and Thulani have here.'

'I told you before, *angizi*. I'm not relocating.'

This is when their conversations become awkward and always lead to her cutting the call short, claiming she has to eat or do one thing or another. Her calls with the members of her family are even more awkward. Her parents berate her for leaving without saying goodbye. Her sudden departure was deliberate because if she had told them she was leaving, they would have definitely tried to talk her out of it. Her father is the only one who is concerned about her welfare and how she is settling in, while her mother, on the other hand, is outraged. Sis Ntombi is even instructed to call her and try talk some sense into her.

'Sisi, do you still want your husband?' Sis Ntombi asks. 'Who do you think will meet his needs while you are traipsing around Cape Town.'

'I am not traipsing around Cape Town. I actually have a job, Auntie.'

'Your job is your husband and kids. It's his job to provide.'

Zandile exhales noisily into the phone, 'I have to go, Auntie. I have a job to do.'

Zandile is tired of being the dutiful daughter and the dutiful wife. Why is she constantly burdened with everyone else's expectations of her? She changes her MTN number to a Vodacom one as she's tired of all the unsolicited advice from her aunts about her life.

She loves her job. It is immensely challenging and she throws herself into it wholeheartedly. She works with a great team of architects and the energy at work is inspiring. There is so much to learn and she's like a sponge, absorbing it all. She's always one of the first to arrive, aside from the cleaning and security staff, and often leaves after 6 pm. On Fridays, most of the team head down to the Slug and Lettuce on Main Road or Foresters Arms on Newlands Avenue and she loves the after-work social life. She's reconnected with some old friends and made new ones. It reminds her of her varsity days except now she actually has the budget to fraternise some of the places. She doesn't earn a lot and her first pay cheque, net of tax, is R16 000 but the fact that she has earned every rand herself, gives her immense satisfaction. She doesn't pay rent and when she tried to contribute to the grocery bill, Ntando dismissed her with the wave of her hand.

'Don't be silly,' she said, 'you're part of the family. You can stay here as long as you want.'

Ntando told her that Thulani's younger sister lived with them for over a year until she found her feet and Thulani's brother stayed with them after he was retrenched. She makes it clear that they have an open-door policy for family. This makes Zandile feel more at ease, especially because of the uncertainty about her future. She is certain about wanting to stay in Cape Town and becoming a professional architect but there is uncertainty about Ndaba and the children joining her. She contemplates what would happen to the children if they got divorced. Who would they end up with? She questions the wisdom of her decision about leaving them and about leaving Bulawayo. She wants a life of her own but she doesn't want her children to be in a broken home.

Being around Thulani and Ntando makes her realise how much she loves being part of a family and how much she loves her husband and children. She loves the rituals of breakfast together and Saturday outings as a family and being around Noah and Elijah makes her miss her children even more. Not a day goes by when she doesn't think of her three musketeers. She doesn't call them all the time because she's worried it might make it worse for them.

Elijah turns one and Thulani and Ntando throw him a huge birthday party. Like most first birthday parties, it's more for the parents and to celebrate surviving the harrowing first year. Noah, who is four, is equally excited and tells everyone that it's his party too. A huge crowd of friends converges at the house for the minion-themed party. Ntando outsourced everything to a party planner who set everything up the day before so all Ntando has to do is show up. Dressed in a yellow organza dress that flows to the ground, she is the perfect host.

Zandile can't help drawing comparisons between Ntando and Xoliswa. While Xoliswa is tall, Ntando is short and petite. So petite that Thulani is prone to swooping her up into his arms and lifting her into the air. She always laughs and throws her head back. She maintains a crop of short hair that is dyed blonde and while she's pretty, she's not stunning like Xoliswa. She is more affable than Xoliswa, who tends to be more aloof and standoffish. She's gregarious and flits around the house like a butterfly, welcoming all their friends.

A spit braai has been organised and the champagne flows. A company has been hired to entertain the children so that the adults can chat to each other and have a few drinks. It is there that Zandile meets Napoleon Bogatsu. He's a single dad with a young son and they soon find a common interest when Napoleon tells her that he's a developer with a fledgling portfolio of retail malls. He's funny and entertaining, keeps Zandile engrossed in his colourful conversation and is quick to fill her glass of champagne. It's a quarter to midnight when he says his goodbyes and asks for her number. She's about to give it to him when she subconsciously fingers her wedding ring.

'I completely respect that,' says Napoleon. 'I was hoping we could discuss business.' He hands her his business card.

Zandile lies in bed that night, her thighs clamped together with longing for Napoleon. She knows it's wrong and that she has no business keeping his number. She tosses and turns all night and wakes up the following morning knowing she needs some kind of resolution to the current conundrum of her marriage.

WHEN A WOMAN IS FED UP

Yandisa is proud to say she has a waist and has effortlessly dropped at least three dress sizes over the past year. Her mother attributes her weight loss to stress. Yandisa doesn't care why she's lost the weight, she just likes her new appearance and she feels a lot lighter on her feet. Wesley and her had decided to start serving food at The Zone in order to attract a new clientele because of the waning clubbing business. The menu is simple and consists of an assortment of braaied meats, *isitshwala*, pork and beef trotters, platters and salads. People arrive at around 3 pm to eat and only leave much later.

'MaiBhunu, you're doing a wonderful job with the food,' says Joe Murape, one of their regular patrons.

'She's a good wife,' says Wesley, joining in the conversation and putting an arm around Yandisa. 'And she bore me three beautiful children.'

Yandisa smiles, 'You helped too!'

'And I enjoyed it,' and gives her a wink.

The men sitting with Joe explode into laughter and their eyes shine with envy. Who wouldn't want a wife like Yandisa? Her tiny waist accentuates her curves and she's wearing a white vest with a myriad of gold chains around her neck which disappear into her cleavage. Her tight-fitting jeans emphasise her bouncy buttocks and curvaceous hips.

'I admire your work ethic,' continues Joe. 'If I worked with my wife, I would kill her!'

Jokes aside, Yandisa thinks of the many times she's contemplated killing Wesley. And the times he almost killed her. Outwardly, they look like a beautiful and successful couple with a happy marriage but if only people knew what happened behind closed doors. She replaced the teeth that Wesley knocked out with two gold crowns and no one is any the wiser what her golden smile is hiding.

She used to hold her head up high and boast about being the woman with the ring on her finger but she knows better now, the ring is a sham. Wesley is her husband in the confines of their home but the minute he drives out the driveway, he belongs to the rest of the world. Everyone else can lay claim to him. He's somebody else's boyfriend, somebody else's boss, somebody else's son. He's public goods. But a year later and they're trying to make things work. They have reconciled and she moved back into his bed. She is his wife again, in every sense of the word and more importantly, the beatings have stopped. He's raised a hand but withdrawn it mid-air and rammed his fist into the wall instead.

When Yandisa closes the kitchen that night at 11 pm, she's relieved to finally be going home. She debates whether to head to church for an all-night vigil as there are ongoing prayers for a turnaround in the country. They are praying for the economy which despite the Government of National Unity being established, is still in intensive care. She goes to find Wesley to say goodbye but she can't see him on the nightclub floor. He must be in his office so she goes upstairs to the second level. She walks past the writhing bodies of two young people groping on the staircase and it reminds of her when she was Babalwa's age. She's going to have a word with the bouncers on her way out as they have no business letting underage children into the nightclub.

She goes to open Wesley's office door but it's locked. That's strange. Has he left the club and not told her? She walks to the end of the corridor and peers out the window and see that his BMW is still there. She realises the door is locked to keep her out.

'Wesley!' she shouts, rapping her knuckles against the door. 'Open the door!'

After a few minutes, the door swings open and Yandisa storms into the office, surprised to see a young woman with bird-like features, perched on the edge of the sofa. She looks ruffled and nervous and there is the whiff of sex in the air. Yandisa knows the smell of pussy. Of freshly eaten pussy. She's sure that if the woman shifts slightly, there'll be come stains on the couch.

'Hi. Is there something I can help you with?' asks Yandisa.

The woman looks at her, 'Who are you?'

Yandisa wants to laugh. This is another one of Wesley's little whores who after they've been screwed, think they own the world. Wesley is sitting at his desk, his hands folded behind his head, observing quietly, a slightly amused expression on his face.

'Don't you come in here and disrespect me! I own half this club which means you're sitting on *my* sofa. I'm married to that man so I guess that makes me his wife. Is that a satisfactory answer for you?'

'Yandisa, don't harass the poor girl,' says Wesley, coming to the woman's rescue. 'She's just looking for a job.'

'What kind of job? We're not hiring at the moment,' says Yandisa in a clipped voice, 'unless you're looking for someone to stroke your balls.'

'Yandisa, stop it,' says Wesley and he then turns to the woman and tells her to leave. She almost gallops out of the room.

Yandisa sees that she was wearing a black shift dress which must have been so easy to bunch around her waist as she fucked her husband. She's a gorgeous young woman. 'Young' being the operative word. She looks like she's probably a few months shy of her 18th birthday. Babalwa's age. Wesley is being a predator, just like Marshall had been with her. Why does history have an uncanny way of repeating itself?

'So you're fucking under-age kids now?'

'Yandisa, you're overreacting again. Nothing happened!'

'No, I'm not overreacting, Wesley. I'm sick and tired of you sticking your dick into everything that walks. I've had it up to here!' and she sweeps the palm of her hand past her neck.

'Yandisa! Keep your voice down, you're causing a scene!'

Yandisa lifts her hands in resignation, 'I don't care who hears, Wesley. I'm tired of this. Tired! How would you feel if I screwed every man in sight?'

'Don't kid yourself, babe. No man wants your tired old pussy. You're done. Just be thankful that I was kind enough to take you in. I can have any woman I want, do you hear me?'

His words sting and she can feel the tingling of humiliation all over. She looks at this man that she calls her husband and wonders why she even tried to make things work. He's no longer beating her physically, he's doing it verbally. The pain of his callous remarks stay with her.

'I can't do this any more, Wesley. I can't.'

Feeling defeated, Yandisa turns around and walks out of his office. Is this what it's going to be like for the rest of her life? Fighting with Wesley and fighting off his girlfriends? The never-ending cycle of abuse?

No. This is not how her story is meant to end. She's tired of being victimised. She needs to be the heroine of her own story.

When Wesley arrives home at midday the next day, he's surprised to find his suitcases and belongings piled in the driveway. Jason's dog is chewing on one of his designer Gianfranco shoes. He storms towards the house but the front door is locked. He tries his key but it won't turn. He goes around to the kitchen and sees MamTembo washing dishes.

'Open the door!' he shouts.

MamTembo is obstinate, 'Mama told us not to open the door.'

Wesley stares at her aghast.

'Do you know who pays your *fucking* salary?'

'Mama said we should keep all the doors locked.'

Wesley briefly walks away and when he comes back, he bricks the window. The glass shatters into the sink but because of the burglar bars MamTembo is not hurt. She runs further into the house screaming. Wesley is undeterred and goes around to the side of the house where their bedroom is. Yandisa is standing on the balcony, pacing like a bull terrier.

'Why are my clothes outside?' yells Wesley.

'I want you to get the fuck out of here,' she replies.

'Are you throwing me out of my own home?'

'You heard me!' screams Yandisa, waving a pistol at him.

At first Wesley thinks it's one of Ethan's toy guns but then Yandisa shoots into the air. It sounds like a crack of thunder and the sound cuts through the midday silence of sprawling suburbia. At that time of day most people are at work and the children are at school so it is mostly domestic workers and gardeners who come out of the nearby houses to see what is happening.

'Are you fucking crazy?!' he screams.

'You have no idea how crazy I can get,' she says, waving the gun at him. 'I'll shoot you and myself if I have to. Leave. Now.'

Wesley doesn't argue with her and picks up his suitcases and quickly loads them into the boot of his BMW. He reverses out of the driveway and almost drives into the Durawall. He skids and speeds away angrily. Yandisa watches him and starts to laugh. MamTembo is standing on the balcony, next to her, shaking with fear.

'Mama, do you think we are safe? Do you think he will come back?'

Yandisa carries on laughing, 'We're safe. I've already asked for the security company to come and guard our gates. Don't worry, MamTembo, he'll never come here again.'

MamTembo's brow is crinkled with worry. She had almost collapsed with fear when she heard the gun go off.

'Mama, where did you get that gun?'

'From a friend,' replies Yandisa, a smile spreading across her face.

A few weeks after she was discharged from hospital, Zandile had taken her to Edna's farm for some fresh air. Edna had divulged that for years Butho had beat her. The revelation surprised Zandile because she never thought Butho was the type of man that would harm anyone.

'Don't be fooled, Zandile. He looks like a good man, like he wouldn't harm a fly. You're just lucky there were people around to help you, Yandisa. We live out here in the wild. Even if I screamed, who would hear me, *emaplazini?'*

Zandile was dumbfounded whereas Yandisa felt comforted hearing that someone else had gone through the very same things she had experienced.

'But why didn't you tell the family?' asks Zandile.

Edna snorts in disgust, 'The family? We lived with his mother and she could hear him punching me in the middle of the night but she didn't do anything. She said that that was what being a woman is all about and that we've have all been there, so it was no big deal. She told me not to antagonise him and if he doesn't come home, don't ask. A good wife never asks.'

Edna pauses to reflect and then continues with her story, 'Sometimes when the beatings got too loud she would knock on the door and only then would he stop. When we moved to the farm I was in trouble and he would beat me until he was exhausted and couldn't beat me any more.'

Zandile is stunned, 'Why didn't you leave?'

'I tried once. I went home but remember my family is not rich like yours and my mother told me to go back to my husband. My uncles wanted to know who would take care of me and my two kids if I came back. I wasn't working so I was entirely dependent on Butho.'

Edna pauses and appears to collect herself, her thoughts vacillating between the past and the present.

'So I went back to him and he beat me up the night I returned. He said I was trying to embarrass him by making our problems public. I ran out of this house naked and he chased me away with a rifle. I thought he was going to kill me.'

Zandile holds her hand to her chest as she tries to imagine the ordeal Edna had gone through.

'I eventually came back to the house once he was asleep and I picked up the rifle and I pulled the trigger. I went crazy!'

As she tells the story, her eyes light up and widen.

'I shot all over the place. I shot him in the leg and he shat himself. He was on the floor, crawling around in fear. "Please don't kill me. Please don't kill me," he repeated over and over again.'

Her voice trails off, reliving the night in her head and then she quickly snaps back to the present.

'Of course I couldn't kill him. He was the father of my children.'

'What happened?' asks Yandisa, literally sitting on the edge of her seat.

'We went to the hospital and we lied and said someone had broken into the farm and tried to steal some of our things. He was discharged after a few days and we came home and lived happily ever after.'

'And he never hit you again?' asks Yandisa.

'Never. That was the last of the beatings. I decided that if I was going to stay in the marriage, it would be on my terms.'

'And he never said a thing to his brothers?' asks Zandile.

'He wouldn't have. He didn't want to lose face in front of the family. I fought for my marriage, Yandisa, because I had no other choice but you have a choice.'

Leaving an abusive marriage is an option that is often never suggested. More often than not it never seems a viable option but Yandisa is starting to think that it is her *only* option.

THE FORGOTTEN WOMAN

Zandile rarely sees much of Thulani and she's only ever in his company with Ntando. Until the week that Ntando goes to Johannesburg for a week on business and for the first time they are alone. Thulani arrives home one evening after the boys have gone to bed and comes downstairs where she is watching *The Office*, a show that her and Ndaba used to watch together after the children had gone to bed. He says he also loves the show and joins her on the couch. He pours himself a whisky and offers her a glass of wine. They have a huge collection in their wine cellar and add to it every time they make a weekend visit out to the winelands.

'How is the job going?' he asks.

'I'm getting the hang of it,' she replies. 'I'm starting to find my mojo.'

'That's great. I'm glad you like it here, Za. You could have a good life here but I hear *malume* is reluctant to move here. That's a shame because with his CV and experience he could get a good job.'

'I keep telling him that and that you and Ntando have a great life here.'

'We do have a good life. Ntando is a sweetheart.'

And then out of the blue, she says, 'Do you think you would have been happy if you'd stayed with Xoliswa?' Maybe the wine is making her more forthright.

'I do think about Xoliswa believe it or not. I think you can be happy with anyone if you put your mind to it.'

Zandile is not sure what to make of his response and takes another swill of her wine.

410

'Are you happy with *malume*, Zandile? Why did you walk out of your marriage?'

'I didn't walk out of my marriage,' replies Zandile defensively, turning to look at him directly.

'Well, that's what everybody in the family is saying. Were you *that* unhappy?'

Who is everybody? she thinks to herself. The Khumalo clan? People have so much to say about things they don't know anything about.

'I'm unhappy about my life and where it's going. I turned thirty and I suddenly wondered if that was all there was.'

Thulani edges closer to her on the couch, narrowing the gap between them.

'It's natural to want to find the meaning of life, Za. I also had those questions and that's why I left Xoliswa. It just didn't make sense any more.'

He puts his glass down and reaches for her hand. He starts stroking it gently and while it might be meant as a friendly gesture, it makes her uncomfortable.

'I know you're probably lonely. How long has it been?'

Zandile quickly pulls her hand away.

'We are both consenting adults, Za. And we're both outsiders in this family. No one needs to know anything.'

Zandile puts her glass down and stares him squarely in the eyes.

'You're out of line, Thulani. I'm going to pretend this conversation never happened.'

The following morning Zandile calls Kirsten and asks if her studio apartment is still available. She says it is, so she moves out of Ntando and Thulani's house that weekend. Ntando is alarmed by her abrupt decision to leave but Zandile tells her it's for the best.

'*Usefun' ukujola*,' says Thulani, once Zandile has left.

That evening when Zandile calls Ndaba to tell him that she's moved into Kirsten's studio, her mother-in-law answers his phone. They exchange all the usual pleasantries and then Selina asks her about her abrupt departure from Ntando and Thulani's house. It seems news travels fast in this family.

'Ntando tells me you left their place, what happened? Did you have a fallout? My niece is troubled by the way you left, Zandile. Especially because they were treating you *so* well.'

'Yes, they were but I wanted a place of my own. They're a family and they need their space.'

'Is that so?' says Selina, her voice thick with sarcasm. 'First you leave your husband in a whirlwind and now you're living on your own. *Usufeba*, Za?'

'Mama *shuwa*?' replies Zandile, shocked at her mother-in-law's insinuation that her leaving was driven by a desire to whore.

'What else are we supposed to think, Zandile? Your husband and kids are here and you're painting the town red and behaving like you are single. Have you forgotten that you are somebody's wife? That you're a mother?'

Zandile hangs up. Her fists are tightly clenched and she holds back the tears that threaten to burst like a dam whose floodgates have been opened after a heavy rainstorm. She decides to call Napoleon. It's a Sunday night and she asks if he wants to meet her for a drink. He agrees and they met at Cubana an hour later.

It's 2 am when Zandile stumbles into her tiny studio apartment with Napoleon in tow. They tumble onto the bed and kiss frenetically, rolling around on the bed. They roll to the floor with a loud thud but are unbothered. Zandile returns Napoleon's kisses with an ardent passion and her body feels like it's on fire. She wants him to kiss her all over so that his wet kisses can extinguish her desire. He kisses her neck and softly nibbles her bare shoulders, making her scream out in unrestrained delight. He removes her gold top and is thrilled to see that she is bra-less. He sucks her one breast while his hand strokes the other, tweaking her nipple. He squeezes her breasts while he kisses her stomach and his tongue dips into her belly button. He pushes up her skirt up and pulls off her G-string roughly and impatiently. He dives between her legs, the sweet smell of her arousal filling his nostrils. Zandile is moaning in ecstasy and is almost immediately gripped by an intense orgasm. She climaxes again when he eases himself into her slick vagina which is warm and receptive.

She wakes up with a splitting headache and Napoleon's thigh entangled in hers. She gently extricates herself and is overcome with guilt as the early morning light illuminates her infidelity. Here she is, naked and in bed with a man who is not her husband. She reaches for her phone. It is 10.10 am. There are missed calls from her husband, from her mother, from her aunt and from her sisters. She goes to shower and washes herself furiously, as if to scrub away the evidence of what transpired a few hours before. Napoleon peeps his head in the shower.

'Can I join you?'

Her first instinct is to reach for the towel to cover herself. He laughs conspiratorially.

'I've seen it already,' he says, with a naughty grin. 'For a woman with three kids you sure as hell have a fine body.'

He grins playfully, ready to devour her again. The lust is evident in his eyes. She feels uneasy and wraps the towel tighter around her body.

'I'm a married woman, Napoleon, what happened between us was a mistake.'

He nods slowly, 'That wasn't what you said last night but you know where to find me when you're unmarried.'

He closes the cubicle door and goes back to the bedroom, a short while later she hears the front door close. She starts to cry and sinks to the floor. When she gets out, she feels relieved in some way and slightly invigorated. She sits on the bed and calls her husband.

'Ah,' he says, 'so now you're available to take my calls.'

'I went to bed early,' she lies, 'and I put my phone on silent.'

'Zandile, I am not happy about you moving into your own place. What does this mean?'

'It means I'm finding my feet. Finding myself. Finding the woman I once was.'

'Well, once you've found everything you're looking for please remember you have a forgotten husband and children who love you. Don't you love us any more?'

Zandile starts to sob, 'I do love you,' choking on her tears and the shame she is feeling from being unfaithful.

'Then come home, Zandile. Your place is here with us.'

'This is my home now, Ndaba. It might not be much but I'm not going anywhere.'

He hangs up and leaves her to drown in her own tears and the sorrow that often goes with a breaking heart.

REUNITED

Ndabenhle's arrival outside Zandile's tiny studio is completely unexpected, just like the sudden changes in the Cape Town weather where it can be winter and summer all in one day. She is shocked to see him standing there and after their last conversation, she assumed their marriage was over.

'What are you doing here?' she asks, unable to mask her surprise.

'Aren't you even going to invite me in?' he replies. 'Or do you have company?'

She ignores his comment and ushers him inside. The door opens into a living room/kitchenette comprised of a fitted stove, fridge and a washing machine. On the other side of the room is a couch and a TV mounted on the wall. At the far end of the room is a double bed with two side tables and a built-in cupboard. There is a door into a tiny bathroom and toilet. Ndaba remarks that it is an efficient use of space but she doesn't want to tell him that she feels slightly claustrophobic and it makes her miss their house in Bulawayo even more.

'Can I get you are drink?' she asks. 'Have you eaten?'

He declines and tells her he had a meal on the plane. He sits on the couch, looking uneasy. They are behaving like strangers to one another, not like a wife and husband with three kids.

She sits down next to him and he turns to face her.

'Is this what you want?' he asks, looking around the room. He's shocked that she left everything she had to live in a closet.

'I want to have my own life, Ndaba. I feel like you've lived your life and lived your dreams and now it's time I live mine.'

'So you want to sleep with other men, Za? Is that it? Am I not

415

enough for you?'

'It's not enough for me to be a wife and a mother. I want a career and I want to feel fulfilled.'

'Do you still love me?' he asks, looking deep in her eyes.

She nods, 'I do. I love you.'

'Zandile, my biggest fear when I married you was that you would grow tired of me. I always wished I'd shared some of my life experiences with you and I never wanted you to feel like you missed out on anything. But I understand I might not be enough for you and that you might want to try other things, other men ...'

She puts her hand over his mouth.

'You're the only man I've ever want to try out.'

Propelled by passion and love and the guilt she feels, she climbs on his lap and straddles him. He gently cups her face in his hands and kisses her deeply and she gasps. They forget about foreplay and within minutes, he slides his throbbing penis inside her. She is wet and juicy and her wetness drives him crazy with desire. He thrusts inside her with short, hard strokes until she cries out, her breath comes in ragged gasps, her body trembling as the waves of an explosive orgasm take over. He holds her firm buttocks and pummels into her harder and harder. He can't get close enough or deep enough to her and she feels him stiffen as he climaxes. They lie on the couch, limp in each other's arms.

'I love you,' she says, looking him in the eyes and kissing him over and over again.

She wants him again and he takes her and they lose count of the number of times they couple. They devour each other over and over again and finally fall asleep in each other's arms.

He is supposed to return to Zimbabwe a few days later but he changes his ticket to leave at the end of the month. He calls his mother to tell her he'll be in Cape Town for a while trying to sort things out with Zandile. Selina tells him she's fine with the kids and has no desire to surrender her babysitting duties just yet. Zandile speaks to them, they sound happy and are more concerned about their father than her which leaves her slightly miffed. Zandile sends her some money for groceries and for the children so she's happy with the arrangement.

They soon settle into a routine and Ndaba gets up every morning and makes her breakfast which she never eats so she takes it to work and has it for lunch. When she gets home in the evenings, he makes sure supper is ready and they have dinner by candlelight. They make love very night, almost like it's some kind of ritual. He tells her it's to make up for the time they spent apart. Their lovemaking reaches levels of intimacy Zandile didn't think were possible and it is during those moments that she knows they were made for each other.

During the day, Ndaba peruses the newspapers looking for job opportunities as him and Zandile had been talking about him and the kids relocating to Cape Town. He applies for a few positions and to his surprise, he is asked to go for a few interviews and quickly lands a job with one of the big banks. He then has to start the arduous process of applying for a work permit and it is at this time that his payout comes through. It gets paid into Zandile's account in South Africa which ensures that he receives his USD package in full. They decide to make the big decision to go house-hunting and as much as they've been enjoying their cosy love nest, the children will be joining them at some point and they need more space. They manage to find a modest three-bedroomed house in Hout Bay that had been repossessed by the bank. It has picturesque seaside views and the mountain view in their backyard and although Zandile has to commute more than thirty minutes to work, they have the best of both worlds.

When the year ends, they fly to Bulawayo for Christmas and collect their children. They arrive in the sleepy town of Bulawayo by midday and Maqhawe and Chandelle pick them up at the airport as they are also home for the Christmas holidays. Zandile and Ndaba are thrilled to meet their curly-haired, blue-eyed niece and nephew, Chanel and Chandler, who they've often spoken to on Skype.

As they drive through town, Ndaba looks at the dreary landscape of Bulawayo. Nothing has changed, or maybe they've just changed too much. Everything has deteriorated and Maqhawe says that things are ridiculously expensive and that they don't regret leaving.

The Khumalo home in Sunninghill towers above most houses in the neighbourhood and has been renovated and refurbished. It has been nine months since Zandile left home but it feels a lot longer. Selina seems to have aged considerably in that time and her skin looks patchy and furrowed like the bark of an acacia tree. She still possesses her acerbic humour and is strong and resilient, the matriarch of the Khumalo family. Zandile greets her mother-in-law and begrudgingly gives her a hug. Their relationship is strained after Zandile's infamous departure. Her reunion with her children is emotional and they have grown so much that they are almost unrecognisable from the photos that she left with. They cry and cling to her. Because Ndaba followed her to South Africa there is a feeling of enmity towards him from the rest of the family. They accuse him of having zero agency and the bottom line is that 'uNdaba udonswa ngamakhala'. He is led by the nose by his wife.

Selina can't understand why Zandile chooses to work when she never needed to when she was in Zimbabwe. Zandile wants to explain to her mother-in-law that it's about her passion for the job and that it gives her a sense of purpose but she knows Selina will obstinately refuse to try and understand. It has become even more important to Zandile that she's known for her own worth and not just as Ndaba's wife, like she has no identity or no interests of her own.

'Zimbabwe has changed, Mama. I lost my job so things are difficult,' says Ndaba, entering the conversation.

'You could have gotten another job if you really wanted to, Ndaba. Nkululeko is still here and things are working out just fine for him and Zodwa.'

'It's about the quality of life, Mama. We have everything we need there. Fuel, running water and the lights are on. You should come and visit so you can see for yourself.'

418

Selina purses her lips tightly together, 'And the violence? I can't sleep at night thinking you might get killed. Zandile, if my son dies there I will never forgive you.'

Ndaba laughs the comment off but Zandile takes the affront very personally. She excuses herself and heads to the kitchen where Nandi is leading the lunch preparations with the help of Edna. She recruits herself into the effort and is joined by Chandelle. By the time lunch is served, the whole family is there and she's genuinely happy to see them all again. Nkululeko and Zodwa arrive late but Zandile is sure their grand entrance is deliberate because Zodwa still deliberately dodges any cooking activities but is very happy to partake in the meal.

Lunch is happy and celebratory and afterwards, once the plates are cleared and the dishes washed, they all gather in the living room. Selina's grandchildren sit around her on the couch, like small vines hanging from a tree. As small and vulnerable as the children are, they represent growth and the extension of the family. In that moment, Zandile feels admiration and newfound respect for Selina. She is the gum that keeps the family together and unifies them and makes sure they all converge together in spite of their differences. Zandile wonders if those bonds will survive her death. Edna will probably step into her shoes and take over that role and Nandi will anchor her.

It would appear from the outside that there are no broken branches in this family tree. That they are a picture of perfection but then she realises that some families just hide the splinters better. Zandile steps forward and kneels before her mother-in-law and apologises for leaving her son and for leaving her grandchildren in the way that she did.

'*Uxolo, Mama,* I could have handled it better.'

'*Hayi, kulungile mntanami,*' replies Selina. 'If you believe what you are doing is for the best, then so be it.'

'Thank you for taking care of my children,' adds Zandile.

'They are our kids and they will always have a home here.'

She visits her own family and the reunion is slightly awkward as her parents are still bitter that she left without saying goodbye. As the week progresses, things start to thaw between them.

Xoliswa comes down from Harare so Zandile gets to spend quality time with both her sisters. XYZ are reunited. They all stay at Yandisa's house because Wesley no longer lives there. There's an air of unbridled freedom and no one feels like they are walking on eggshells. They behave like teenagers and drink too much and stay up too late and even the children think they're crazy. They plan a girls holiday for June that will be just for them. No children and no significant others. They make a pact to do more things together, as sisters.

Before she leaves, Zandile appeals to her father to extend an olive branch to Xoliswa but he is unyielding.

'She's resolute in her sin! Nothing can save her, Zandile.'

Phumla rolls her eyes knowing how hypocritical Abraham is being. It's hard saying goodbye to her parents because she's not sure when she's going see them again. She invites them to visit her and Ndabenhle and the children in Cape Town and Abraham says they will but she knows he doesn't mean it. He couldn't bear to be separated from the flock. But she believes her mother when Phumla says they will visit.

THE OTHER WOMAN

Xoliswa is the first to visit Zandile and Ndabenhle in their new home the following year. She is in Johannesburg for a wedding expo and extends her trip to spend a night in Cape Town. Zandile tries to convince her to stay longer but Xoliswa is dying to get back to her children and CC. 'What does CC want you to be? His second wife?' asks Zandile.

'Does it matter?' replies Xoliswa. 'It is what it is. I am the other woman.'

She flies out of Cape Town the following morning and the sisters' parting is emotional. Xoliswa promises she'll see them soon. Even after all these years, Zandile has still not quite reconciled her sister's relationship with CC and it still bothers her that her sister doesn't want more for herself. To Zandile, anything less than being a wife would feel like she was being short-changed.

She is seated next to a businessman who flirts with her for the duration of the flight to Joburg. He hands her his business card as they land and she hesitates but doesn't throw it away. As she waits for her connecting flight she wonders if she should pursue contacting him but her thoughts are interrupted when CC calls asking her what time she's landing so they can go for dinner. He tells her he misses her and wants to spend time alone with her without the kids.

The beauty of staying in the capital city is that she lives much closer to him but the irony is that she sees less of him than she did when she lived in Bulawayo. Her move to Harare had been precipitated by

421

her pregnancy. She didn't announce it to anyone early on and allowed it to naturally unveil itself. One morning she arrived at church with her bump clearly visibly under her A-line shift dress. After the service she had gone to her parents for lunch and a noisy confrontation ensued.

'What the hell is this?' screams Abraham, pointing at her belly.

'Dad, I'm not a child,' says Xoliswa calmly.

'But you think it's okay to be having children out of wedlock with married men? CC is a married man, Xoliswa!' he barked. 'You want to shame our family, don't you? How do you think this looks?'

'Dad, this is not about you. This is my life and my choices.'

Phumla is sitting at the table holding her head in her hands. She's glad Owami is playing outside and can't hear the confrontation between his mother and his grandfather.

'I want you to leave the church, Xoliswa.'

'*Tata*, please,' intervenes Phumla.

'You stay out of this!' he snaps at her. 'You've always encouraged this relationship and now look what's happened!'

'No, Dad, don't blame Mama for this. I take full responsibility. I wanted to have a second child.'

'And you decided it was okay to have one with another woman's husband?! I preach about Jezebels all the time and now you are one! I want you to leave my church!'

'You're one to preach, Dad! Weren't you married when I was born but now you want to judge me?'

'How dare you talk to me like that!' he shouts furiously.

She has never seen her father this angry but she doesn't care.

'First you kick me out of the business and now you're kicking me out of church,' says Xoliswa.

'Yes, Xolie, it's my church and I want you out. And don't set foot in my house with that bastard child of yours.'

Their parting had been acrimonious and Xoliswa had relocated to Harare and had not been back to her parents' house in two years. She still visited her sisters and her mother would visit her there but she hadn't communicated with her father since that day.

Being in Harare had worked out well for her and she'd set up her new business there, Eventing Africa. CC facilitated her first big break when he ensured she was awarded the tender to do the First Lady's charity dinner to raise money for orphaned children. It had been a huge event and the diplomatic community, important business people and the who's who of Harare had been invited. A lot of money was raised that night and whether the money made it to the orphans was another story but Xoliswa made a name for herself that night and her services were in high demand. In time, she expanded her business to include weddings and she also opened a bridal boutique in Avondale that sold wedding dresses imported from China. Her life was full and frantic and she loved every minute of it.

But between work, kids and travelling, there's hardly any time for stolen moments with CC like they used to have. She doesn't travel much with CC unless it coincides with one of her trips to China to replenish stock for her store. She attends trade shows and expos to keep up with what is happening in the trend-based eventing industry. After Zandile's departure she took on Maria and trusts her implicitly to stay with the children when she travels. Sis Lungile doesn't stay far from her so she often pops in to check on the children. CC often drops by the house to see Owami and Olwethu, more so when she is away. He considers both children his.

That night at dinner, they chat and catch up on what has been happening in each other's lives. Xoliswa tells CC about her latest projects and the two international clients she has secured. One is a wedding for the daughter of a Zimbabwean ambassador who met her Ghanian husband-to-be at Harvard. The other is for a Zimbabwean model who landed herself a rich Nigerian man and has been co-opted into having a Zimbabwean as well as a Nigerian ceremony. She makes CC laugh as she shares anecdotes about some of her clients.

CC was given the tourism and environmental affairs portfolio in the new Government of National Unity, that had been formed after the last highly contested election. He had said that the GNU had been a mistake but nevertheless there did seem to be an air of stability and general optimism about a better future in the country.

'There is some land available to build a new hotel in Victoria Falls. If you were still in construction, you could have applied for it,' says CC.

Xoliswa shakes her head, 'I can't even tell Wandile to pursue it, he's run my father's business to the ground.'

Askaheni Enterprises had been liquidated after going insolvent. Wandile had misappropriated funds and destroyed a family legacy.

'Your father made a huge mistake by giving him that company to run.'

'Well, he's made an even bigger mistake by taking Wandile into the church. Apparently Wandile raped someone in the choir. Can you imagine?'

'What does your dad say about it?' asks CC.

'Apparently they're keeping it quiet because my father said there's no way Wandile would have raped anyone and that this woman is fabricating the story because she is of "loose morals".'

Xoliswa is still mad at her father. Mad that he judged her so harshly and that he protects Wandile at all costs. CC can sense the tension and decides to steer their conversation to less contentious topics.

'How is your mom?'

'She's fine. She called me earlier asking for money and groceries and says that they're really struggling. Vumani sends them some money but it's not enough, she says. They don't want to antagonise their daughter-in-law so they don't ask him for more.'

'Your sisters have never been much help with your parents. Is Zandile doing anything now that she's settled in the Cape? asks CC, as he slices through his kingklip.

'She's trying but it's her husband's family that takes priority. Yandisa is barely making ends meet after parting ways with Wesley and he has cut her off financially.'

'What's the hold-up with their divorce?'

'Wesley won't sign the papers, he says he wants to give things another try. Can you believe him?' says Xoliswa.

CC shakes his head, 'Divorce can be messy.'

'Would you divorce your wife, CC? Would you leave her for me?'

'Would you want me to?' he replies.

The question hangs in the air as Xoliswa considers what her mother once said. That she would forever be the homewrecker. Is that the moniker she wants to follow her for the rest of her life?

'I don't know,' she says. She doesn't want to dwell too much on it. Things are fine with her and CC the way they are. Does she really want to take on the responsibility of being a wife? Of being the main course and not just dessert? Being a mistress does have its perks. Like the freedom of seeing him when she wants to and she doesn't have the hassle of dealing with him 24/7, 365 days a week. She's not sure she wants to change all that.

They decide to skip dessert and are lingering over their Don Pedros when CC motions for the waiter to bring the bill. He tells her he has an early meeting so he wants to get an early night. Xoliswa is slightly disappointed because she'd been hoping he would follow her to her Gunhill home for a bit of lovemaking. They haven't made love for months; this is arguably the downside of being the other woman.

'Kiss my little angel good night,' he says to her and gives her a chaste kiss on the cheek and leaves, followed by one of his aides. She goes home, feeling dejected but quickly reminds herself that this is the life she has chosen for herself. She is the other woman.

The children are fast asleep when she gets home. She showers before climbing into her pyjamas and checks her phone. There's a message from Zandile wanting to know if she got back to Harare safely and a message from CC telling her he loves her very much. There are a few missed calls from Yandisa. It's always missed calls from Yandisa, never messages, and this makes her nervous because she's never sure what to expect. She hopes it's just another money request; *that* she can deal with easily. She's glad that her sister has parted ways with Wesley but she wishes she could also attain financial independence. She's supporting her and her kids, from putting food on their table to keeping the lights on but she knows Yandisa will eventually get there, just like she eventually left Wesley.

She decides she'll call her back in the morning, whatever it is it can wait till then. She climbs into bed and falls asleep almost immediately. It's 2 am when she's woken by the ringing phone and she sees that it's Yandisa calling. She's worried and wonders what has happened and recalls all the nights Yandisa has called her in the middle of the night, crying.

The conversations usually started with her, half asleep, asking Yandisa, 'What did he do this time?'

'It's a long story,' Yandisa would say.

It always was with them.

'Xolie, I swear, this time I've had enough. I'm filing for a divorce.'

Yandisa would wail and say Wesley was being abusive and through her rants, declare that she wanted out of the marriage.

'I'm so done with him, Xolie.'

It was hard to believe her because often she would say that and a week later her profile picture would be of her and Wesley cocooned in a tight embrace.

'What are you going to do?' Xoliswa would ask, knowing she had to tread carefully.

'I'm going to kick him out of the house,' Yandisa would state emphatically. 'This is my house too so why should I be the one to leave? The day I leave this house will be in a coffin.'

Xoliswa doubted that would ever happen. Her sister often said things that never materialised. Until the day she called with bravado in her voice and said she had finally done it. She had kicked him

426

out. Wesley was gone. For a while, Xoliswa was sceptical and kept expecting to get a call from Yandisa telling her that Wesley bought her a beautiful gold chain to say sorry. That they had reconciled. But a month passed and then two and then three. No call ever came and the only calls Yandisa made were ones seeking financial assistance. She remained steadfast in her resolve to start anew so it was a shock to see her calling at this hour.

'Hello,' said Xoliswa. 'Yandisa, are you okay?'

Babalwa was sobbing on the other end. Even before she said it, Xoliswa knew that Yandisa was no more.

THE DEPARTED

Phumla never imagined she would bring a life into the world and would have to bury that same life. Yet she has had to confront that shocking reality, sitting on the mattress, surrounded by mourners who sit in solidarity with her. She still has not quite processed the reason they are all congregated in Yandisa's lounge.

She cannot come to terms with the fact that Yandisa is gone. Sometimes, the front door opens and she expects to see Yandisa bouncing in, full of life and laughter. Yandisa was always a mouthful of apologies. Either for being late or for not showing up when she was supposed to and now she'll always be late.

Phumla is thankful for Xoliswa and Zandile's presence as she is powerless with grief. Xoliswa came home the minute she heard the tragic news and instead of taking care of all the funeral arrangements, like she would have normally done, she sits beside her mother, overcome by her own anguish. Phumla feels anchored with Zandile on one side and Xoliswa on the other.

Vumani has embraced his big brother role and has taken over much of what Xoliswa would have done. He takes care of a lot of the logistics of the funeral while Yothando makes sure the home fires are burning. The circumstances surrounding Yandisa's death meant a police investigation had to be concluded before they were allowed to bury her. The police told Vumani they could not issue a death certificate until a post-mortem had been performed and without a death certificate, they could not get a burial order.

The family spend the day in Burnside and arrive at the Riverside home for the evening vigil. Phumla's sisters, Phatiswa and Phindile, also occupy the space on the mattress. Even her brothers, Songezo and Sonwabile made the journey and while they aren't particularly close, their presence means a lot to Phumla.

Phumla holds her hand to her head. She still can't make sense of the way Yandisa died and there is no doubt in her mind that Wesley, who is being held in a police holding cell waiting to be charged, murdered her daughter. MaNyoni is by her side mourning with her but she cannot bring herself to look at the woman without recrimination. MaNyoni takes Phumla's hands in hers, her tears spilling on her hands and Phumla shouts at her, 'Your son killed my daughter! How can we ever move on from this? I didn't carry my child so that your son could kill her.'

MaNyoni weeps, 'I loved her like my own daughter. I am just as pained as you are.'

Phumla recalls her pregnancy with Yandisa fondly. It had been an easier pregnancy than her first one and she had not been fraught with the anxiety she had experienced when she was pregnant with Xoliswa. There had been no huge expectations or grave talks preceding it as was the case with Xoliswa. Abraham was still very married to Sarah when she fell pregnant and it was something that they never spoke about and something that she rarely admitted to. She had known about Sarah when she met Abraham but she had always told herself she was better than her. That she was a more suitable match for Abraham. She had even convinced herself of that fact until other women came along who thought they were better than *her*. The whole thing filled her with shame, more so now that they were 'church people'.

Yandisa's birth wasn't shrouded in controversy and she was born when Abraham and her had been married for a year. She was their honeymoon baby. She had been a terrible baby, always demanding to be held and constantly crying for attention. She was the baby that kept them awake all night so when Zandile came along a few years later and

429

slept through the night, they were so relieved.

As a toddler, Yandisa threw the most spectacular tantrums and Phumla has vivid memories of shopping at Chitrins and Yandisa demanding a doll. Phumla had said no but Yandisa wouldn't accept it and Phumla had tried cajoling her and then threatening her but Yandisa was unmoved. She threw herself onto the floor and the manager came to see what the commotion was. In the end, to avert any further embarrassment, Phumla gave in to Yandisa's demands. Her and Abraham had always given in and when they did say no, she flouted it in their faces.

Phumla sighs and remembers how Yandisa had always been the difficult child. The other two had been so much easier and Yandisa had always accused her of loving the others more but it wasn't true. She loved them all equally.

A tear rolls down her cheek. How could Wesley have found her daughter so unlovable that he took her life? This it why it is difficult to reconcile her death. People died from long illnesses or in car accidents but her daughter had been murdered. Why Yandisa?

They often say a life is used to repay a life. Is this how she's repaying her own mother for her loss of life? Phumla is no stranger to death and encountered it very early on in life. She was born in February 1948, the year apartheid was enacted into law. She was not birthed in a fancy private hospital and pushed her way into the world in a thatched rondavel whose floor was made of cow dung. There were no nurses to attend to her, only elderly grandmothers from the village who were midwives through experience. She was the last born and had three older siblings: Phatiswa, Xhanti and Phindile.

Her mother haemorrhaged to death as a result of her birth and so the name Phumla was bestowed upon her, because her mother had gone to rest.

Her mother's sister, Vatiswa had strapped her on her back and carried her to work at a nearby farm where she cleaned the Brandt's farmhouse. Phumla grew up on her aunt's back and when she wasn't on her back she was down on the shiny parquet flooring which her Aunt Vatiswa used to shine on all fours until it gleamed. The madam took a liking to Phumla and often played with her before telling Vatiswa to take her, claiming Phumla tired her out. She was a feisty child with thick legs and an infectious laugh and everyone loved her.

She remembers walking kilometres every day to get to school, barefoot and with a threadbare uniform which had been passed down from her older siblings. But there was still laughter and jubilance amongst them. They played *ezilalini* with all the other children from the village and even though she grew up motherless, she always felt loved and protected by her siblings and Aunt Vatiswa. Her father was absent in her memories as he worked in the gold mines in Kimberley and made an annual exodus home at Christmas. When he was around, he was detached from Phumla and as she got older she realised that he blamed her for their mother's death. He considered it her fault. When he remarried a flaming beauty from Gaeleshowe, he stopped coming home.

He had two sons, Songezo and Sonwabile, with his second wife and Phumla often felt that those sons replaced her brother, Xhanti, who was supposed to be the anchor of the family and had died on the mountain during the initiation ceremony.

Death had been a prominent visitor in her life, robbing her of the people she loved. First it had been her mother, then death came for Xhanti and then Vatiswa succumbed to it. She had been sick for many months and her condition started to deteriorate. When she started coughing blood into her apron, Phumla knew the end was near. Her madam had driven her to the hospital 200 kilometres away and Aunt Vatiswa died there and was sent home in a coffin. After her death, it was only Phumla and her two sisters. Soon after the funeral, Phatiswa, who was twenty-two at the time, started a nursing job in Mthatha. Phumla and Phindile moved in with the Brandts and lived in their aunt's former quarters. They continued with their schooling under the auspices of the Brandt family because by this time, their father had stopped supporting them. It had been made clear that they were on their own.

During this time, Phumla and Phindile sometimes cleaned the house and did other chores to earn their keep. Phumla got a glimpse of what family life meant and how the Brandts and their three teenage children sat down and ate dinner with each other. How they held hands and said grace and it wasn't until she lived with them that she saw how birthdays were celebrated. She had never once celebrated hers and she vowed that one day she would have a family and she would raise her daughters differently. They would have all the things that had been denied to her and her sisters.

A piercing scream brings her back to the present, heralding the arrival of another mourner.

'My poor brother!' exclaims Primrose, Wesley's youngest sister, as she walks into the house and pretends to faint. Her older sister, Evelyn, and another relative, receive her at the door. She then walks towards Phumla and throws herself onto the mat. Phumla exhales, and wonders if there will be an end to all the theatrics. Wesley's family is behaving like they have lost a son when it's her daughter's life that has been carelessly extinguished.

Phumla has lost count of the number of Wesley's relatives who have descended on the Riverside home. Some she had met at the wedding while others she is meeting for the first time. They have moved into Yandisa's home with ease. The vigil had started on Sunday evening, the same day the news broke that Yandisa had passed. The matriarchs from the Bhunu side of the family had come in and covered all the pictures and family portraits that hung on the wall. They didn't stop there and covered the mirrors and the television too. The marital bed had been removed and that mattress is the one Phumla is sitting on in the living room.

The other women who could not be accommodated on the mattress have to settle on the reed mats. Sis Ntombi had tried sitting on the mats on the first day but even her generous buttocks couldn't cushion the hard floor. Phumla insisted there was not enough space on the mattress but Sis Lungile had found herself a spot in a corner.

'What happened?' asks Primrose when she eventually calms down and has had some time to gather her wits.

'It's not really clear,' says Evelyn. She takes Primrose aside and talks to her on her own. 'According to Wesley, they were having a fight and Yandisa jumped over the balcony.'

Primrose claps her hands together, 'Why? Why would she do that?'

Evelyn shakes her head, 'I don't understand it either. Apparently Yandisa came home after midnight. Wesley said she was seeing another man and he confronted her about the affair and that's when the fight broke out.'

Primrose shakes her head from side to side, 'I always knew Yandisa was immoral and I know Wesley is many things but he would never kill.'

'I wouldn't put it past him, Prim. Yandisa was a good woman, she really was. I don't know what is going happen to the children.'

Evelyn starts to wail. She had forged a close relationship with Yandisa and her sudden death pains her.

Phumla is aware of the salacious version of her daughter's death that is being peddled around and it is that version that she refutes. She had been with Yandisa at the midnight prayer service the night before and during the service Yandisa had stood up in front of everyone in the church and told them she was tired of living a lie.

'For years I have been hiding my wounds behind big smiles and big sunglasses. For years I have been lying on behalf of Wesley whenever he hurt me. He has slept with half of the women in Bulawayo, yet I still stood by him. But enough is enough so I am leaving him and I ask you, brothers and sisters, to stand by me. Don't judge me. I have been to hell and back in this marriage. Please don't try to talk me out of it or try and pray me out of leaving him. This is God's word to me.'

The church had been dead quiet. Abraham felt so strongly about divorce and had preached against it since the day the church first opened. His go-to verse was always Malachi 2 verse 16, 'I hate divorce, says the Lord, the God of Israel' but he had never gone to the end of the verse which said, 'and I hate a man's covering himself with violence'.

That night he stood up and addressed Yandisa's statement and said to the congregation, 'Divorce is perfectly acceptable on two grounds: sexual immorality and violence, of which my son-in-law is guilty of and shows no repentance. My daughter and her husband were married in this church and many of you were witnesses but I have witnessed his brutality and we can no longer continue to cover his violence. God abhors abuse in the home and would not want for your families to be covered with it. If you find yourself faced with a situation like Yandisa's, remove yourself from it.'

There had been a loud applause from the congregation and Abraham and Phumla stood beside Yandisa. They prayed with her and laid hands over her and after the service, the congregants congratulated her for her bravery and other women shared similar stories.

When Yandisa drove home in the early hours of Sunday morning, it was raining hard and it somehow felt cleansing. She felt liberated by her decision and by the prospect of starting a new life. A life without fear and a life independent of Wesley's mood swings. She wants consistency and predictability.

Mostly, she's tired of fighting. Little did she know that she was driving to the last fight of her life.

THE JUSTICE SYSTEM

Chief Inspector Virima looks at the gruesome pictures of the deceased in the manila folder on his desk. Yandisa Bhunu. Age 34. Height 152 cm. Weight 53 kg. She is just another murder victim who will be a number that forms part of the annual crime statistics. The photos are taken from various angles and the chief inspector has seen so many photos over the years, they no longer affect him. Many of the photos show the victim on the floor, face up, with coagulated blood forming a macabre halo around her head.

The inspector is sipping on his 10 am cup of tea and eating the sandwiches his wife makes him every day. He usually gets jam or butter on his bread but today he appreciates the thick slice of polony. Times are tough, even for a commanding officer like him working for the Bulawayo Metropolitan Criminal Investigation Department.

He carries on perusing the contents of the file and sees photos of the victim before her untimely demise. Such a beautiful woman, he thinks, with an engaging smile that reached her eyes. She was so young, only thirty-four years old at the time of her death. Even in small cities like Bulawayo, big crimes happen.

His cellphone vibrates to life and the name, Advocate Charles, flashes across the screen. He ignores the call; he'll attend to it later. He doesn't want his tea to get cold and he wants to finish his sandwiches. Next, there is a knock on his door. Constable Consetta Ncube walks in. She's wearing her blue shirt with its ZRP lapels and a pristine dark blue form-fitting skirt. Policewomen were required to wear stockings but the prohibitive cost meant that the department had dispensed with the requirements.

435

'Sorry to disturb you chief but that witness is here for questioning.'

'Give me five,' says the chief inspector, wolfing down the rest of his sandwich and washing it down with his black tea. Even milk is a luxury these days.

He makes his way to the interrogation room where the witness is in the company of an attractive woman. Also in attendance is Constable Marima, who had joined the force a year ago and has an inquisitive mind and keen eye. Constable Ncube and Marima are there to merely observe and take notes.

What the chief inspector finds particularly intriguing about this case is the wealth and beauty that surrounded this family especially after seeing pictures of the deceased's home, a double-storey house in Riverside. It is in stark contrast to the way the majority of Zimbabweans are living and a far cry from his modest home in Mahatshula that him and his wife moved into three years ago. While it is a definite upgrade for them from their house in Pumula North, they are battling to finish the construction that still needs to be done. They do what they can to survive and his wife works at the licensing department 'selling licences' to make ends meet. Such is the reality of life.

'Are you Babalwa Bianca Mafu?' he says to the young woman, looking down at his notebook.

She nods and he adds 'Prime Witness' above her name. Her face is pulpy and bruised and he notices from the victim's pictures that her daughter has the same light-coloured complexion as her mother. Her body reveals evidence of the assault she endured the night her mother died. Her features are not her mother's and it makes him wonder about her father.

'And I am her aunt,' says Xoliswa, introducing herself.

She's wearing a black shift dress and flawless make-up and the scent of orange blossom and jasmine wafts around her. The chief inspector finds the smell of her perfume mesmerising.

'Sorry we took a while to present ourselves at the station, Chief Inspector. My niece is deeply traumatised by her mother's death and it is a very hard time for the family.'

Looking at the two women, the chief inspector notices that they both carry their grief with an air of dignity and he enjoys the sound of the woman's lyrical twang in her voice. He wishes she would continue talking.

'I understand,' replies the chief inspector. 'I'm sorry for your loss.'

When the witness starts speaking he can barely understand what she is saying. Her words roll off her tongue into one other and her twang is an octave higher than her aunt's. He has to ask her to repeat many of her answers to his questions as he tries to corroborate what she is saying versus the account that she gave at the time, that reads more like an internal monologue.

She had been dropped at her home by Anesu, her boyfriend. Because it was raining he had driven in, making sure he dropped her close enough to the main entrance. They had both been surprised when they saw Wesley's BMW in the driveway.

Anesu asked her what her stepdad was doing there and she replied that she had no idea.

'Then again you never know with Yandisa and Wesley,' she said.' Maybe they've reconciled again.'

He leaned over to kiss her goodbye and that was when the front door swung open. Wesley charged to the window and started shouting. He hauled the victim out of the car.

'Do you think this is the time to come home?' he barked.

'Wesley, you're hurting me!' squealed Babalwa.

'And you? What gives you the right to drive into my home at this hour and disrespect me? Get the fuck out of here.'

Anesu starts the car and reverses out. After he has gone, Wesley dragged

Babalwa into the house. The house is quiet as the children are all fast asleep. It is way past their bedtime.

'Is this a time to come home?' he says to her.

'What's it to you?' she replies, shrugging his hand away. 'You're not my father. Stop trying to be the fucking father I never had!'

'Who is that punk you were with, Babalwa?'

She doesn't respond and marched upstairs. He followed suit. He hated being ignored and she hated being interrogated. Why was Wesley asking her about her punk boyfriend when he had started having sex with Yandisa again? He said he had loved her. He had lied to her, betrayed her with the one person she loathed the most in this world. It was none of his business.

'Babalwa, I'm talking to you!' he roared.

'Leave me alone,' she replied, walking into her bedroom and slamming the door behind her.

He heard the key turn and knew he had been locked out.

'Open this door!' he screamed.

'Leave me alone Wesley! I said leave me the hell alone!'

She felt the enormity of his rage as he kicked into it. Babalwa had rushed to the other end of the room whose sliding doors opened out onto the balcony. She contemplated jumping over but the fear of falling outweighed the fear of Wesley. She could still hear him screaming as he pummelled the door. Yandisa and her stupidity? Why had she let this monster back into their home?

'What happened next?' prods the chief inspector.

'He broke the door down and came for me. He then beat me up and raped me. I'm glad my mother came home when she did because I don't know if he would have stopped.'

Xoliswa fishes out some tissues from her crocodile leather Hermès bag and hands them to Babalwa. The chief inspector observes how controlled the victim seems to be, even when she is crying. There is no howling like many would do after a tragedy like this. Babalwa dabs at her tears and Constable Marima records everything down in his A5

Marvo notebook. The police department can no longer afford official stationery; another sign of the times.

'Was it the first time he raped you?' asks Virima.

'Inspector, what exactly are you driving at?' interjects Xoliswa.

Babalwa caves and starts crying, 'No, he raped me before.'

Xoliswa's eyes widen. 'Why didn't you say anything, Babs?' unable to hide her shock and treatment at Babalwa's revelation.

'I did. I told Yandisa once and she slapped me across the face and said I was lying. She said I wanted to ruin her marriage. She always chose marriage over me. Always.'

More sobs follow and more notes are made. The inspector continues, seemingly unfazed.

'We get a lot of these cases,' he says, addressing Xoliswa. 'Children are raped every day and the guardians pretend not to see it.'

He looks at Babalwa, 'But that night your mother saw the rape happening and *reacted* to it, correct?'

'Yes, only because she saw it with her own eyes. She tried to pull him off me and that's how the fight happened. At one point, they were fighting near the stairs and Wesley pushed her over the balcony. It was all an accident, I saw it happen. He didn't plan on killing her ...'

Xoliswa holds her hand up to her chest, almost feeling her heart racing. Babalwa's story sounds like something from a Hollywood drama yet it's a scene playing out in their own family. How had they allowed this to happen? Why had Babalwa not reached out to them?

'I *never* wanted to live with Yandisa and Wesley. I hated it there but Gogo forced me. She didn't want me. Nobody wanted me and *all* my life I've been passed around like a ball!'

Her grief is gone and has been replaced by anger.

'That's not true, Babs! We all care about you. *I* care about you!'

'If you care so much, Aunt Xoliswa, where were you when I was getting raped? You weren't there, you were jetting around the world on some or other trip!'

Babalwa's anger gives way to more tears and Xoliswa consoles her. Chief Inspector Virima decides to end the questioning and tells the women they are both free to go.

He returns to his office accompanied by both Constable Ncube and Constable Marima and says to them, without a moment's hesitation, 'I don't believe her statement. Something isn't right.'

A deadly silence follows.

BODY OF EVIDENCE

Chief Inspector Virima visits the crime scene which has been cordoned off from the rest of the house. When he arrives, there are already a few people gathering and his immediate concern is that the crime scene will be tainted as curiosity gets the better of them. He offers cursory condolences to a few people and continues upstairs, unperturbed by the curious glances and whispers he knows he's getting.

He steps gingerly into Babalwa's bedroom, where the confrontation began, and shivers as he walks in. The hairs on his neck stand up and even as a child they often said he had a gift of seeing. He often feels it when he's working on a case like this. There are so many smells in the room. The stale smell of illicit sex. The acrid smell of a rotten, half-eaten hamburger which he later sees in the dustbin. There's a smell of fear hanging over the room and it's almost like he can hear the victim's screams.

The room is messy; there are books strewn across a tiny desk and cosmetics spread across a dressing table. A selection of clothes are in a pile on the bed. He almost trips over some shoes on the floor. There are a few posters on the wall of famous Hollywood actresses and actors which he only recognises because his son has some of them stuck up on the unplastered walls in his room.

A chair has been flung across the room, one of the legs are splintered, and two ornamental silver bedside lamps are lying on the floor. One is broken and he strongly suspects it was a weapon used to hit Yandisa over the head. The lampshade looks like it has been wiped clean like someone has tried to hide the evidence of any fingerprints. The carpet is bloodstained and he follows the stains to the balcony.

As he sees it, Yandisa arrived home and heard screams coming from upstairs. She charged into her daughter's room and saw Wesley on top of his stepdaughter's writhing body, on the bed. She reached for the closest object. A chair. She hit him with it until it splintered and broke. Wesley extricated himself from Babalwa, enraged. He pushes Yandisa into the wall. Blood stains on the window indicate the back of her head hit the pane of glass, without breaking it. At some point in the kerfuffle, Wesley reaches for the lampshade. Or was it Babalwa? He's not sure who hit Yandisa but she had been bludgeoned to death and thrown over the balcony.

'Babalwa *is* lying but I can't prove motive. From what I heard from the domestic worker, she didn't have a good relationship with the mother. Apparently she is rebellious and any attempts at disciplining her, failed. There was constant fighting between mother and daughter and she'd only been living with them for a few years after discovering Yandisa was her biological mother. Prior to that she lived with her grandparents and was told that Yandisa was her sister.'

'So you believe *his* story?' asks Constable Ncube, aghast at how this case seems to be unravelling.

'No, I don't but he's not innocent either. I don't think he wanted to kill the victim but the daughter is lying to protect him. And I need to find out why. Falling from that height wouldn't kill someone, it would only injure them. Broken arms, yes, broken legs, yes, broken neck, yes, but not death. The post-mortem shows that the deceased was concussed prior to her death and was hit over the head with a blunt object. She was already dead when she was thrown over the balcony.

'I don't buy the rape story either. If she was raped why didn't she scream for help? There was a guard on site and he didn't hear any screams coming from the house.'

'But it was raining and there was a thunderstorm that night,' says Constable Marima. 'Also, consider the proximity of the house to the gate. It would have been impossible for the guard to have heard anything anyway.'

It had rained hard that night, pelting against the windows like someone was throwing stones at the glass. The thunder sounded like the crack of a whip cutting through the pitch-black night. There had been a power outage, the lightning flashes like a flickering lightbulb intermittently illuminating Babalwa's bedroom.

'According to the police report, semen was found in her vagina,' adds Constable Ncube.

'But *whose* semen was it? She got home from a date with her boyfriend and they could have had sex. She says they didn't but I don't believe her.'

DNA testing is not offered in Zimbabwe so even if samples were collected from her vagina, there was nothing to link them to Wesley. This remained the biggest stumbling block in reporting rape cases.

'Her bloods reveal high levels of alcohol. This means she was drunk so it casts a bit of doubt on her testimony.'

'But why would she lie about being raped by her stepfather? What would she gain from it?'questions Constable Ncube.

'Look, I believe they had sex and I believe it was consensual,' says Chief Inspector Virima.

'Constable, how can you be so sure it was consensual?' questions Officer Marima.

'There were no signs of forced entry. No lacerations or abrasions to the vagina. As for the facial bruises, she could have been hit by her mother. We have two cases opened against the deceased who was notorious for beating up anyone who came near her husband.'

A heavy silence hangs across the room.

'They weren't expecting her home so soon. We spoke to the guard and Wesley was not allowed access to the house and the domestic worker corroborated this. We have it on file that the deceased had applied for an injunction that prohibited him from entering the premises. The domestic worker says Mr Bhunu arrived at midday that day and dismissed her protest that she was not allowed to enter the house, saying he had full authority to be there.'

'Why didn't she call the wife to verify?' asks Constable Marima.

'Apparently there have been episodes in the past where they had fought and reconciled so she wasn't sure and didn't want to interfere. The guard reports the last person to enter the premises was the daughter who was dropped off at around 9 pm by a man driving a Benz. He says it was dark and raining and he couldn't see who was with the girl.'

Constable Marima looks at his notes and then confers with the chief inspector.

'But Mr Bhunu says he was allowed to spend time with the children and that he had visitation rights on weekends when the wife was at work. The guard on duty says he was not aware of that arrangement.'

The constable scratches his face, 'Not aware or was he bribed?'

The question lingers.

'Let's assume he was allowed to spend time with the kids, why did he hang around?

The chief inspector sees his phone flashing. It's Vumani Mafu. He ignores it.

'So what do we do now?' asks Officer Ncube.

'We've done what we can in the preliminary investigation so we hand over the file to the state prosecutor. The family wants the burial order so they can lay their daughter to rest.'

'Do you think they have a strong case?' asks Constable Ncube. Yandisa used to do her hair at Turning Heads so she has a personal interest in the case. She hadn't been to the salon for a long time as she now wore her hair short and natural because she could no longer afford the treatments. She remembers Yandisa as a cheerful woman who always welcomed customers.

Chief Inspector Virima shrugs, 'The state may go for murder with aggravating circumstances. The rape might be harder to prove. He is looking at ten, maybe twenty, years.'

Constable Ncube looks at Constable Marima and then back at the chief inspector.

The chief inspector's phone vibrates to life again. It's Vumani Mafu. Vumani had paid Virima handsomely to expedite the process of the burial order for the family so he dismisses the officers, telling them there are other pressing cases that need to be attended to. Money is clearly not an issue with the Mafu family and he has a half-finished house project that he needs to complete, so the extra money will come in very useful.

Wesley, through his lawyer, requested bail pending his trial for the alleged murder of his wife and alleged rape of his stepdaughter. He's represented by his long-time friend, Charles, in his capacity as an advocate. JB is in the courtroom too, listening intently, along with Wesley's family, who all have a vested interest in the outcome.

Advocate Charles puts forward a compelling argument that his client did not commit the crime as alleged by the state. According to Wesley, his wife was having an extramarital affair which had led to their separation. He insisted he was still determined to salvage the marriage which is why he had gone to the house on the night in question. He said that after putting the children to sleep, he had waited for his wife to come home but she did not arrive. He tried calling her but her phone was switched off. He claims that, in his frustration, he resorted to drinking and by the time his wife eventually did arrive home, he was inebriated.

He said his stepdaughter arrived home at around 9 pm and he reprimanded her for sneaking out. He said Babalwa often flouted the rules they laid down for her and he was trying to be a good father by disciplining her. He said after the altercation, Babalwa stormed to her room. It was after midnight when his wife finally arrived home and he confronted her about the alleged infidelity which she refuted. During the altercation, his wife ran into her daughter's room and locked the door. She refused to open it which is why he damaged the door. He says the rape allegations are merely a deflection from the real issue at hand because the daughter often covered up for her mother.

'Your honour, my client loves his children. All three of them. These children have lost their mother and now you want them to lose their father too? The accused has lived with Babalwa Mafu for years and in this time there has never been an incident where she says she was harmed by him. My client poses no flight risk and will not interfere with the chief witness or investigations. He is well-invested in businesses in Bulawayo. We hereby ask that the court grant him bail.'

Bail is granted. The magistrate brings down the gavel and the bail hearing is concluded.

EPILOGUE

THE REBIRTH

It is a truth universally acknowledged that a single woman of childbearing age must be in want of a husband. A truth that continues to be supplanted in the minds of many women. A truth that Babalwa embraced that overcast morning in April. The sun was peering out from behind the clouds, undecided as to whether to make an appearance or not. Just like her mother had done years before her, Babalwa emerges from her grandparents' house. Her weave is swept up into a crown on top of her head, a sweeping veil attached. Her smile lights up her face. She's wearing an off-the-shoulder, body-hugging trumpet dress, her lithe figure accentuated. Sis Ntombi adjusts the veil to cover her face and pulls it over her bare shoulders. A bolero is on stand-by in case the weather turns bad. The year is 2010, two years after her mother's death. Babalwa is marrying Anesu Gabe.

'Don't you think you should wait until you've finished your degree?' says Xoliswa when Babs told her she was getting married. She can't understand why Babalwa is in such a hurry to tie the knot.

'A degree won't keep you warm at night, Aunt Xoliswa. Besides, what has a degree ever done for you? Here you are, nearly forty and you're not even married,' says Babalwa.

That quickly silenced Xoliswa, who can't believe how much Babs is like her mother and how she's definitely inherited Yandisa's acerbic tongue.

'Marriage isn't the be-all and end-all,' says Zandile, coming to

449

her older sister's defence.

'Yet here you are, married with three kids, Aunt Zandile. So please can you both allow me to make my own decisions,' says Babalwa.

Anesu had paid lobola a year prior to the actual wedding and him and Babs live together. Her father had been an active participant in the negotiations. Marshall Munyoro appeared in their lives following Yandisa's death and suddenly wanted to do right by his abandoned daughter. He had paid damages and then lobola-d his daughter, as was the custom, so that she could take his last name. It had seemed like a waste because not long after that, Babalwa would discard his last name and take on her husband's. Marshall presided over the lobola negotiations which the Mafu family felt was grossly inappropriate.

'He doesn't deserve a penny of that money,' fumed Xoliswa. 'He denied that he was her father, her whole life.'

'None of you raised me either,' said Babalwa, overhearing her aunt's comments. 'I want to get married and have my own family. A real family; something I never had with any of you. All my life I was the bastard nobody wanted and you passed me around like a stray dog.'

Phumla and Abraham were deeply affronted by Babalwa's sentiments especially considering they had been there for her during her formative years. The absent father had suddenly become the hero of the show. They look on as Marshall sombrely walks Babalwa down the aisle. Down the same stretch of rolling red carpet that her mother had walked down.

The last time the family had all gathered together in church was for Yandisa's funeral. Abraham remembers every detail of the funeral and after two years, the wound has not even slightly healed and the memories always leave him feeling raw. He had opted not to preside over the funeral service. It was one thing to preside over your daughter's wedding but quite another to officiate at her funeral. He chose to be the bereaved father of the deceased. He had failed Yandisa, like all the other women who had been failed and died before her. Phrases like, 'We will never understand God's ways,' or 'It was God's will', made no sense to him.

Was it really God's will that his daughter was bludgeoned to death? He himself had used those words so many times to comfort others but they were very different when they were thrown back at him. The church was full that day, the crowd spilled into the aisles. Abraham had known Yandisa was popular and well-liked and her funeral was affirmation of this. Her former colleagues from the bank came to pay their respects, her employees from the salon and nightclub, customers from the salon and friends from church.

In the crowd Abraham spotted CC. 'Why is *he* here?' he hissed, nudging Phumla.

'Are you forgetting that Xoliswa paid for the casket,' replied Phumla through gritted teeth. While every member of the family had contributed towards the funeral, they knew Xoliswa's contribution was leveraged by CC.

Vumani and Yothando contributed substantially to the funeral costs but they couldn't cover it all. Zandile had bought some groceries, having just bought a house, and with everyone aware that Ndaba was not working, everyone was understanding that was all she could afford to contribute. Sis Ntombi contributed a few dollars and pounds and continuously lamented why Yandisa had not bothered to join a burial society when she was alive. Apparently the salon takings were meagre and Wesley complained that business was slow on his side, so he couldn't afford to contribute much. Nobody even bothered asking Wandile, he was more broke than any of them.

Yandisa had lain in a white, solid wood casket, in her wedding dress, her hands crossed over her chest. That image of her would never leave Abraham for the rest of his days. Abraham turned his attention to the podium where Vumani was calling people up to give testimonies about Yandisa's life. Everyone gave moving tributes about the always happy, always smiling and always laughing, Yandisa.

Xoliswa began her eulogy to her sister. 'Yes, Yandisa could smile through her pain and she could laugh through her tears. She fooled us all with her sunny smile and happy demeanour and she hid so much pain behind that façade of "happily ever after". What saddens me the most is that my sister never really experienced what it meant to be loved. The only real love she experienced was from her children because her husband made her life a living hell,' her eyes resting on Wesley siting in the front row.

Gasps are drawn and people look to one another wondering if they've heard right.

'I'm not going to be polite and diplomatic. My sister's death wasn't polite and her last breath wasn't measured or dignified. She died a violent death and it breaks my heart ...'

Xoliswa's voice falters as she starts to choke on her tears. Vumani stands up to rescue his sister from her own grief but she continues.

'I want to finish, I want to finish,' she insists, tears streaming down her face.

'Yandisa was so many things to us. She was wild, reckless, impetuous, carefree and she had a good heart. Her heart was always in the right place. I pray that she has found the peace she so deeply craved that she never had in her living years.'

Xoliswa dabs at the tears flowing furiously down her face, mascara streaking her cheeks, disregarding the make-up she had flawlessly applied that morning. Members of the congregation are shedding their own tears, disturbed by Xoliswa's powerful words. Then Wesley, not to be outdone by Xoliswa, stands up. Nobody expected him to speak, especially since he was playing the part of the bereaved husband so well but he takes hold of the microphone and addresses the congregation.

'My wife and I had a difficult marriage, just like her sister pointed out. But everyone knows that marriage has its ups and downs. How many of you can say you haven't been through hard times in your marriages? How many of you can say you haven't roughed each other up once or twice over the years? I remember the day I married Yandisa in this church and you were all here to see it. It was the happiest day of my life.'

He pauses to let his words have the desired impact. Abraham realises that his daughter married a psychopath.

'I loved my wife. I loved her with all my heart and I know she loved me too. As hard as that may be to believe, I know she loved me. *I* am the loser here and so are my kids. They don't have a mother and I don't have a wife. I never expected things to end like this and while I know we had our fights, I never imagined I would lose Yandisa this way.'

Wesley looks directly at his in-laws sitting in the front row.

'I hope in time you will find it in your hearts to forgive me. You are angry and I understand that but your forgiveness is all I ask for.'

Wesley steps off the podium, tears streaming down his cheeks. There isn't a dry eye in the congregation. Abraham can hear soft whimpers as Phumla softly cries beside him. He holds her frail hand and she cries harder, slowly wilting like a flower deprived of water.

Abraham clenches his fist. He has preached about forgiveness his whole life but he knows he will never be able to find it in his heart to forgive Wesley for what he did to Yandisa. He remembers the young girl Musawenkosi and how merciful her parents had been towards him when she was killed in that car accident. Is this how he is repaying for her life? His daughter for theirs? Is this how it worked? A life for a life? Even when he falls to his knees, Abraham cannot find the words to pray and in that moment he decides he will give up leadership of the church in favour of Deacon Nyathi.

After the subdued sermon, everyone makes their way to the graveside. A huge tent has been pitched by Doves for the family and close friends. Dark, rolling clouds on the horizon, hint at an impending storm. Sister Ntombi leads the hymnals with *Hamba nhliziyo yami* as Yandisa is lowered into the ground. The emotive singing spurs on a frenzy of crying and the singing continues until Yandisa's body is fully committed to the ground.

Abraham is bent over under the weight of his grief. Phumla sags against him, barely able to stand. Abraham feels his daughter's death so keenly, like a branch of a tree that has been chopped off. He felt some sense of that same loss when Xoliswa moved to Harare. They had been split apart but in that moment standing next to Yandisa's grave, they are united in their pain. Abraham reaches for his daughter's hand and squeezes it reassuringly. Xoliswa looks up at him through a film of tears and sees the pain in his eyes.

'I'm sorry,' he mouths.

Abraham observes Wesley and his attempts to show his grief and he knows there is no remorse behind those fancy Ray Ban sunglasses. Wesley stands at the graveside holding the children's hands. They don't truly understand the enormity of their mother's death and how final it is. They throw flowers onto the grave and Babalwa reads out all the messages of condolence that have been sent to the family.

Abraham is taking comfort in that when they gather again in a year's time to lay Yandisa's tombstone, Wesley will be behind bars. He'll make sure of it.

Two years later and Wesley is very much a free man. The docket in his case mysteriously disappeared and he's living his best life, engaged to Natasha. Yandisa was violently uprooted from the Earth and is now just a memory. They see bits of her in her children, constantly reminding them that she is there with them.

Jason. Nicole and Ethan, and all the other Mafu grandchildren, walk behind Babalwa down the aisle. Owami, Olwethu, Zinhle, Zanele, Zwelihle, the new shoots branching into a new generation. Abraham hopes they will be better. That they will do better.

'I, Babalwa Bianca Munyoro, take you Anesu to be my lawful wedded husband. From the day we met, you have always protected me and provided for me. You have been my shelter through the storms in my life. My refuge in times of trouble. You have laughed with me through the good times and cried with me through the bad. I love you with all that I have and I want to spend the rest of my life loving you and honouring you.'

There is crazy applause from the audience. Abraham looks at Phumla and they both have tears in their eyes.

'I, Anesu Gabriel Gabe, take you Babalwa to be my lawful wedded wife. From the moment I laid eyes on you, I knew that you were mine and every day I want to show you how much I love and cherish you. A lot of people don't see what I see when I look at you. You give me hope, you give me joy, you inspire me to be a better man. I promise to always be there for you, to listen to you, to encourage you as we embark on this journey as man and wife. I love you.'

The wedding vows remind Ndaba of his wedding day and he leans over and kisses his wife and feels closer to Zandile than he ever has.

'And in the eyes of God, they are no longer two but one. Therefore, what God has joined together, let no one separate.' Deacon Nyathi pronounces that the groom may kiss the bride

Xoliswa reflects on the vows CC must have taken with his wife and she feels a pang of guilt. He's seated beside her, his left hand resting on her thigh, his gold wedding band catching the sun. Seemingly unbothered by the irony of the situation as he reaches for her hand and squeezes it.

The church is filled with joyful ululation. The newlyweds walk out underneath a shower of rose petals. In the courtyard, they are showered with hugs and kisses and congratulatory messages. Yandisa would have been so proud of her daughter and is surely looking down on her from heaven with tears in her eyes.

The land on the church property that had been earmarked for a school, Abraham and Phumla instead decide to use to build a shelter for abused women. They call it Yandisa Uthando Shelter for Abused Women. It's not enough to tell women to leave, they need a place of refuge that they can go to when they *do* leave.

While the church is there to save souls, it is also there to save lives.

ACKNOWLEDGEMENTS

I started writing this book in my twenties when I was in my first year of varsity. In my mid-twenties I submitted it to Weaver Press, which responded with my first noteworthy two-page rejection letter. I was ready to give up writing but my late cousin, Nqobile, convinced me to reread the rejection letter and see the positives as opposed to focusing on the negatives. And so I began the arduous process of rewriting the manuscript and afterwards I shelved it. In my early thirties I approached another publisher who suggested I rewrite it with one sister instead of three, which I duly did. Sadly, the publisher died and the book never saw the light of day. I revisited the manuscript after my 40th birthday and reworked what might have been the tenth draft. When I submitted it to Pan Macmillan, I wasn't quite convinced but they were sold.

Thank you once again to my publisher, Andrea Nattrass, for taking me on together with the editorial team of Jane Bowman and Sibongile Machika. It was a pleasure to work with Jane on this project and I appreciate her meticulous editorial skills. A profound thanks to the marketing, publicity and sales teams who work tirelessly behind the scenes to ensure this book lands in your hands.

A Family Affair is about sisterhood. I am a big sister but even big sisters need sisters. I want to acknowledge the women who are my big sisters and have played an integral role in my life.

To Clara, for accommodating me in your studio every morning so I could write. A big chunk of this book was written under your auspices. But beyond this, thank you for always having your door and heart open for my son and me.

To Cynthia, I truly appreciate your unwavering support. You held me down as I transitioned to full-time writing and your words of encouragement kept me going even when I began to have doubts as to the path I was taking.

To Michelle and Nicole, you make loving thy neighbors an absolute pleasure. Thank you for the memories and may we continue to create more.

To Aileen, for always being thoughtful. To Sindisiwe, for your generous spirit. I am truly blessed to have you both in my life.

To Tash, for finally reading me after years of knowing me! I am glad I converted you.

And finally, to the readers who keep reading me. Thank you for buying into what was a dream but is now a reality. For the most part, writing is a lonely but pleasurable process and I always look forward to engaging with you.

A bigger thank you to those of you who have organised yourselves into bookclubs that make this engagement possible and intimate. I want to recognise the members of the following bookclubs for the robust discussions and raucous laughter: Afrokulcha, Bafati Bebumbene, Black Women Read, Between the Covers, The Fat Cats, Literary Alliance, The Book Club with No Name, The Book Revue, The Bookwormers GP, The Dainty Literates, The Interesting Bookclub, Reading Between the Covers, The Womanist Bookclub, Yerhu Book Club.

Long live bookclubbing!

Yours writefully.